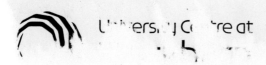

University Centre at

Empire in British Girls' Literature and Culture

Critical Approaches to Children's Literature

Series Editors: **Kerry Mallan** and **Clare Bradford**

Critical Approaches to Children's Literature is an innovative series concerned with the best contemporary scholarship and criticism on children's and young adult literature, film, and media texts. The series addresses new and developing areas of children's literature research as well as bringing contemporary perspectives to historical texts. The series has a distinctive take on scholarship, delivering quality works of criticism written in an accessible style for a range of readers, both academic and professional. The series is invaluable for undergraduate students in children's literature as well as advanced students and established scholars.

Published titles include:

Margaret Mackey
NARRATIVE PLEASURES IN YOUNG ADULT NOVELS,
FILMS AND VIDEO GAMES
Critical Approaches to Children's Literature

Michelle J. Smith
EMPIRE IN BRITISH GIRLS' LITERATURE AND CULTURE
Imperial Girls, 1880–1915

Forthcoming titles:

Clare Bradford, Kerry Mallan, John Stephens and Robyn McCallum
NEW WORLD ORDERS IN CONTEMPORARY CHILDREN'S LITERATURE

Elizabeth Bullen
CLASS IN CONTEMPORARY CHILDREN'S LITERATURE

Pamela Knights
READING BALLET AND PERFORMANCE NARRATIVES FOR CHILDREN

Kate McInally
DESIRING GIRLS IN YOUNG ADULT FICTION

Susan Napier
MIYAZAKI HAYAO AND THE USES OF ENCHANTMENT

Andrew O'Malley
CHILDREN'S LITERATURE, POPULAR CULTURE AND *ROBINSON CRUSOE*

Critical Approaches to Children's Literature
Series Standing Order ISBN 978–0–230–22786–6 (hardback)
978–0–230–22787–3 (paperback)
(*outside North America only*)

You can receive future titles in this series as they are published by placing a standing order. Please contact your bookseller or, in case of difficulty, write to us at the address below with your name and address, the title of the series and one of the ISBNs quoted above.

Customer Services Department, Macmillan Distribution Ltd, Houndmills, Basingstoke, Hampshire RG21 6XS, England

Empire in British Girls' Literature and Culture

Imperial Girls, 1880–1915

Michelle J. Smith
Research Fellow in Literary Studies, University of Melbourne, Australia

First published 2011 by
PALGRAVE MACMILLAN

Palgrave Macmillan in the UK is an imprint of Macmillan Publishers Limited, registered in England, company number 785998, of Houndmills, Basingstoke, Hampshire RG21 6XS.

Palgrave Macmillan in the US is a division of St Martin's Press LLC, 175 Fifth Avenue, New York, NY 10010.

Palgrave Macmillan is the global academic imprint of the above companies and has companies and representatives throughout the world.

Palgrave® and Macmillan® are registered trademarks in the United States, the United Kingdom, Europe and other countries.

ISBN: 978–0–230–27286–6 hardback

This book is printed on paper suitable for recycling and made from fully managed and sustained forest sources. Logging, pulping and manufacturing processes are expected to conform to the environmental regulations of the country of origin.

A catalogue record for this book is available from the British Library.

Library of Congress Cataloging-in-Publication Data

Smith, Michelle J., 1979–
    Empire in British girls' literature and culture : imperial girls, 1880–1915 / Michelle J. Smith.
        p. cm.
    Includes bibliographical references and index.
    ISBN 978–0–230–27286–6 (alk. paper)
        1. Children's literature, English—History and criticism. 2. Imperialism in literature. 3. Popular literature—England—History and criticism. 4. Girls—Books and reading—England—History. 5. Great Britain—Colonies—In literature. I. Title.

PR990.S59 2011
820.9'92827—dc22   2011012462

10 9 8 7 6 5 4 3 2 1
20 19 18 17 16 15 14 13 12 11

Printed and bound in Great Britain by
CPI Antony Rowe, Chippenham and Eastbourne

For Julie Ann Smith (1945–2010), whose love and encouragement created this book.

Contents

Figures

Series Preface

The *Critical Approaches to Children's Literature* series was initiated in 2008 by Kerry Mallan and Clare Bradford. The aim of the series is to identify and publish the best contemporary scholarship and criticism on children's and young adult literature, film, and media texts. The series is open to theoretically informed scholarship covering a wide range of critical perspectives on historical and contemporary texts from diverse national and cultural settings. Critical Approaches aims to make a significant contribution to the expanding field of children's literature research by publishing quality books that promote informed discussion and debate about the production and reception of children's literature and its criticism.

Kerry Mallan and Clare Bradford

Acknowledgements

I had a strange fixation with reading the acknowledgements pages of books I consulted during my doctoral research. For one, acknowledgements pages were an insight into how scholarly work was done, a record of just how many people contributed to any monograph. And, voyeuristically, they provided a peephole into the lives of scholars who seemed like celebrities who could not be imagined doing mundane things outside the ivory tower like scrubbing mould from the shower tiles. When I began this research, I could not imagine how I would ever amass enough people to thank on such a page in the future. Surely enough, the process of three years of doctoral research and almost three years since has seen my network of scholarly friends and colleagues expand.

Dr Clara Tuite has consistently gone beyond the formal requirements of a PhD supervisor, providing critique (encased within a diplomatic velvet glove), support, and encouragement. Not to mention an inordinate number of references and pep talks. Also at the University of Melbourne, Professor Stephanie Trigg and Professor Ken Gelder provided valuable comments during my candidature. My thesis examiners, Professor Sally Mitchell and Professor Mavis Reimer, have also fostered my continued development as a scholar, and this monograph has been improved as a result of their reports. Dr Terri Doughty kindly provided me with her essay on Bessie Marchant in advance of its publication. Dr Kristine Moruzi has been an ideal friend and colleague during my PhD candidature and throughout the postdoctoral journey. Her ongoing encouragement and pointed questioning of chapter drafts have not only kept me thinking positively in spite of academe's trials but also improved my scholarship.

In the time since my graduation, I have been swept up in the warm embrace of the children's literature team at Deakin University, Melbourne. Dr Liz Parsons, a tornado of support, drew me into a world of opportunity and collegiality that could not possibly exist elsewhere. If the sheer magnitude of Liz's scholarly assistance can be reduced to a cake, then Professor Clare Bradford is the royal icing on top. I am indebted to both Liz and Clare for offering me teaching roles and extremely valuable opportunities to engage in collaborative work. Both Clare Bradford and Professor Kerry Mallan at Queensland University of

Technology, as series editors, were instrumental in bringing this monograph to fruition. I am also grateful for the chances I have had to work with and for other fine scholars including Professor Barbara Creed, Professor Jeanette Hoorn, and Dr Elizabeth Bullen.

With gratitude, I must also acknowledge the editors and publishers of publications in which earlier versions and segments of some of these chapters have previously appeared: Chapter 2 in *Childhood in Edwardian Fiction: Worlds Enough and Time*, edited by Adrienne E. Gavin and Andrew F. Humphries (Palgrave Macmillan); Chapter 3 in *The Lion and the Unicorn*; Chapter 4 on E. Nesbit in *ELT: English Literature in Transition, 1880–1920* with thanks to Robert Langenfeld; and Chapter 5 in *Limina*, with thanks to the Editorial Collective; and Chapter 6 in *Victorian Settler Narratives: Emigrants, Cosmopolitans and Returnees in Nineteenth-Century Literature*, edited by Tamara S. Wagner, by kind permission of Pickering & Chatto.

As I learned in reading acknowledgments pages, long-suffering family members should be mentioned in closing. It is important to place these people at the end, as a well-structured sentence should emphasise its most vital element just before the full stop. My mother and father, Julie and Brian Smith, have given everything to help me through school and university, sacrificing all the while so that I was never denied any opportunity. This book would not exist without them and all that they have taught me. The final shot at compensating attention-deprived family members must be directed at the academic author's partner, who has suffered the laptop intruding on all attempts at watching television and materialising on supposed holidays. Thank you, Chris, for your love, for feigning interest in Victorian girlhood, and for enduring the constant presence of academic work at home. I couldn't do this without you. And I wouldn't want to either.

Introduction: Imperial Girls in British Literature and Culture

Empire in British Girls' Literature and Culture aims to reveal a nuanced portrait of 'imperial girls' in British print culture by viewing familiar texts through the lens of empire and devoting substantial attention to girls' genres largely neglected in existing scholarship. Peter Hunt and Karen Sands observe that 'the importance of the Empire to British children's literature ... is taken as a truism by children's literature historians' (1999, p. 40). The omnipresence of empire in British culture, they argue, has inspired a critical neglect of children's books as 'agents of the empire-builders' such that 'the extent and nature value of that affect ... has not yet been examined, precisely because it is so apparently obvious' (Hunt and Sands, 1999, p. 40). Furthermore, postcolonial studies have largely examined those marginalised by imperialism, the colonised, rather than the centre, 'the imperialist coloniser' (Hunt and Sands, 1999, p. 41). This book interrogates the 'obvious' and fixates on the 'centre' in its address of what Hunt and Sands describe as the 'invisibility' of the colonial and postcolonial in British children's texts. It examines how girls were shaped by, and were imagined as shaping, the British Empire in a range of print culture in the late nineteenth and early twentieth century. It also situates these girls' texts in the context of discourses of the period about femininity, education, race, and reading as located in contemporary magazine and newspaper articles and books.[1]

While both the gender and age of the girl may superficially seem to remove her from any significant contribution to empire, as Sheila Rowbotham notes, 'it was impossible to ignore the Empire in tales for girls' (1989, p. 219). This study identifies various relationships constructed in girls' texts between girlhood and imperialism that operate both within real and imagined scenarios, at home in Britain and beyond its civilised bounds. In a range of late Victorian and Edwardian print culture for girls, a new figure of juvenile femininity emerges. She is both strong and independent, and these qualities enable her to be of benefit or use to the nation. Juvenile readers were an expanding segment of the publishing market in the late Victorian period owing to improving literacy as a result of education reforms, developments in technology that made printed material more affordable and the effects of the economies of scale involved in publishing for a larger audience. The profuse output of children's fiction and periodicals in this period intersected with cultural contestations of mid-Victorian gender norms, with challenges to femininity most commonly exemplified by the figure of the New Woman of the *fin de siècle*. The period is also the high point of the so-called New Imperialism, in which the acquisition of further territory for Britain and the growth of existing colonial settlements were supported at home by a web of rhetoric that combined the ideologies of imperialism, national degeneration, racial superiority, and patriotism. As Daphne M. Kutzer notes, British imperialism was in its ascendancy during the time of the so-called Golden Age of children's literature, from 1860 to 1930 (2000, p. 7). *Empire in British Girls' Literature and Culture* identifies an interrelationship between three categories of culture from 1880 to 1915 – gender, empire, and print culture – with specific focus on texts for girl readers.

Rowbotham, in 'Imperial Responsibilities and England's Daughters' in *Good Girls Make Good Wives* (1989), has already shown us that fiction for girls reveals attitudes toward empire and the way it contributed to society. She nevertheless concurs with the critical consensus that girls' fiction 'is generally less overtly imperialist in tone, as girls were largely excluded from active participation in the great colonial adventure until well into the twentieth century, if then' (1989, p. 187). While the girls' novels Rowbotham examines are not anti-imperialist by her account, she argues that many mirror the negative realities of empire by emphasising its drawbacks for females, rather than its opportunities for excitement and adventure as in boys' stories (1989, p. 188). Especially after the mid-1870s, Rowbotham contends that authors for boys were able to 'gloss over' the risks for men in the empire, but writers for women and girls could not ignore 'the drawbacks': 'It was hardly realistic to show the majority of women as facing anything other than the fate of Evelyn Everett Green's Dorothy Ewing waiting for news of her brother on an expedition to Tibet or Mrs George de Horne Vaizey's Norah Bertrand waiting for her lover's return from making his fortune in India' (1989, p. 189). Rowbotham identifies a trend in this period for heroines to have family or friends involved in imperial service, which may subsequently draw girls in to missionary work, for instance (1989, p. 200). Though Rowbotham's work is among the few substantive accounts of empire in girls' literature, along with J.S. Bratton's chapter in *Imperialism and Juvenile Femininity* (1989), it neglects a body of texts that do not fixate on its drawbacks, on stagnantly waiting for male relatives to return home or dutifully accompanying men with higher callings, but that often independently place girls in situations of risk and scenarios of adventure in the Empire. While the domestic, maternal contribution was an important element of girls' imperial role – women were central to the family and the family unit was formulated as the root of England's 'moral pre-eminence on which her worldly success was founded' (Rowbotham, 1989, p. 196) – it is but one of several ways in which an imperial role was formulated for girls in late Victorian and Edwardian print culture.

There were important functions allocated to girls within the British imperial project that are promoted and, at times, celebrated in a variety of texts for girls. The parts in the British Empire identified for girls drew upon the ideas of a woman's aptitude for 'civilising' indigenous inhabitants of colonial locations and 'raising up' the working classes at home, a racialised notion of motherhood (in terms of her responsibility for building healthy future citizens through her children) and the potential need for her to survive without male assistance either in a rugged colonial location or in the event of war at home. As Catherine Driscoll theorises, girlhood is 'articulated in relation to future role – who or what the girl will be or do as woman' (2002, p. 108). Tasks such as mothering are presented in late Victorian girls' print culture as part of the work of preparing readers for one of the most important functions they will undertake as women. Yet girls are credited with the capacity for a broad range of action *as* girls, rather than only in respect to their future role. In the texts considered in the following chapters, girls participate in dangerous and heroic activities, such as conducting rescues, foiling robberies, nursing on battlefields, intervening in scenes of dire poverty on London streets, and independently maintaining colonial properties. The movement of girls into these arenas of action and adventure owes much to imperial justification. In both fiction and non-fiction examples, girls who move beyond the domestic out of necessity or for the benefit of empire are not subject to critique but, conversely, are celebrated. This study explores the implications of this relative freedom and identifies the tension between critique and celebration in these representations of unconventional femininity.

Empire in British Girls' Literature and Culture traverses a range of print culture, examining the creation and negotiation of expectations for girls in the imperial project within them and analysing generic variations and specificities that establish the complexity of representations of imperialism in girls' texts. In this way, I adopt Clare Bradford's formulation of children's texts as both reflectors and producers of culture. As she writes, 'children's books do not merely mirror what exists; rather, they formulate and produce concepts and ideologies, always within the context of adult views about what children should know and value' (2001, p. 5). Juvenile periodicals, which became increasingly prevalent and popular in the late Victorian era, were a crucial site for the presentation of adult views on all aspects of boyhood or girlhood. In the *Girl's Own Paper* diverse forms of content, including non-fiction, fiction, reader correspondence, and advertisements, merge prescriptive advice with idealised examples of girlhood. These adult formulations are also supported and refined through the contributions of essays and letters from girl readers. The pervasiveness of imperialism is manifest in the *Girl's Own Paper*'s identification of girls' capacity for the maintenance of the Empire through improving Britain's weakest citizens at home and 'civilising' natives in the colonies.

At the turn of the century, several fictional genres were produced especially for the attention of girl readers. Girls' school stories, best exemplified by L.T. Meade's novels, were transformed and popularised in the early twentieth century by Angela Brazil, substantially later than boys' school stories, such as Thomas Hughes's *Tom Brown's Schooldays* (1857). Adventure novels set in rugged colonial locations featuring girl protagonists, most notably those of Bessie Marchant, whose tales of 'plucky' heroines commanded an almost exclusively female readership, were also published at the turn of the twentieth century. In E. Nesbit's Psammead Trilogy (1902, 1904, 1906), the fantasy genre enables a girl protagonist to act not only as an idealised maternal leader of her siblings, but also as an explorer in space and time. Domestic fiction, such as Frances Hodgson Burnett's *A Little Princess* (1905) and *The Secret Garden* (1911), returns girls from the reaches of empire to England, allowing them to display their abilities to improve others at home. *The Handbook for Girl Guides*, produced for the newly formed offshoot of the Boy Scouts in 1912, draws together stories of inspiration and adventure, conduct advice, instruction in nursing and physical fitness, and directions for games and activities for girls. It overtly seeks to direct the behaviour and thoughts of girls in light of the perceived needs of the Empire. Finally, the robinsonade, the most popular manifestation of children's adventure fiction in the nineteenth century, overwhelmingly featured boy protagonists. It warrants specialised attention because, intriguingly, girl Crusoes emerge in late Victorian periodicals and group castaway novels prior to the popularity of Marchant's girls' adventures. Girl Crusoes become central to their narratives to the point where lone girls and groups of girls are cast adrift to survive on uncivilised shores. The genre provides a fitting conclusion to this narrative of girlhood and empire in its eventual critique of imperial masculinity, several examples of which were produced within the context of the beginning of imperial decline.

While it was a pervasive aspect of British culture, the mere presence of imperial sentiment in print culture for girls does not necessarily mean that girl readers internalised these views, or that the colonial lives depicted in texts were a reality for more than a small proportion of actual girls.[2] Indeed as studies of boys' literature and culture, such as Troy Boone's *Youth of Darkest England* (2005), suggest, readers may have filtered out imperialistic propaganda. What is being examined here is the cultural ideal of girlhood as it intersected with empire in fictional representations and non-fiction discourses of mothering, physical activity, education, and employment. This is an important area of enquiry because imperialism has not yet been fully mapped onto juvenile femininity, and the capacity to show how imperial motivations were integral to the development of girls' culture has not yet been exploited.

The relationship of boys' literature to empire has attracted significant critical attention, manifested in works such as Joseph Bristow's *Empire Boys: Adventures in a Man's World* (1991) and Martin Green's *Dreams of Adventure, Deeds of Empire* (1979) and edited collections such as Jeffrey Richards' *Imperialism and Juvenile Literature* (1989). Among scholars of children's literature, there have been several explanations offered for the privileging of boys' texts more generally. Jacqueline Rose, for instance, argues that boys' literature has more of a tradition and established genres, such as the adventure story and public-school tale, while girls' literature is more of a 'miscellany' (1984, p. 84). *Empire in British Girls' Literature and Culture* aims to demonstrate, however, that adventure and school stories featuring girl protagonists were similarly established and popular for girl readers, albeit some decades after the equivalent genres for boys. While Green champions the boys' adventure novel for expressing 'the energizing myth of English imperialism' (1979, p. 3), it has also tended to obscure the same genre for girls. Green identifies a transformation in mid-nineteenth-century culture's conception of children, but one in which girls' fiction is eliminated from view: 'Children's literature became boys' literature; it focused its attention on the Empire and the Frontier; and the virtues it taught were dash, pluck, and lion-heartedness, not obedience, duty, and piety' (1979, p. 220). Contrary to Green's suggestion that boys' literature enveloped children's literature, the following chapters show how imperial literature for girls emerges, whether in the genre of girls' adventures or inherent in domestic and school settings.

In these texts informed by empire, girls redefine the bounds of accept-able femininity. Claudia Nelson has problematised the idea of strict gender divisions in Victorian childhood, arguing that effeminacy was idealised in children's culture: 'The closer men could approximate the Angel [in the House], the better for humankind' (1991, p. 5). However, at the *fin de siècle* feminine traits were not idealised for boys, given that organisations such as the Boy Scouts, which sought to produce strong young men, intended to counter the 'softening' influence of mothers. Moreover, the idealised girl was not modelled on the domestic Angel, but was an amalgam borne of traditional expectations and new oppor-tunities in education and employment. While Nelson considers the work of women in slums or on battlefields as integral to the functions of the Angel (whom she argues is the only model of womanliness in the period), the texts I examine, although they do include girls 'civilising' and nursing, celebrate a new figure of juvenile femininity and advocate strength and independence where it may be of benefit or use to the nation.

Sally Mitchell's *The New Girl: Girls' Culture in England 1880–1915*, the definitive text on girlhood of this era, not only identifies the 'provi-sional free space' of girlhood – poised between childhood and adult-hood – but suggests that both working-class and middle-class girls 'occupied a separate culture' (1995, p. 3). My own argument is in accord with Mitchell's definition of the girl as neither child nor adult and the suggestion that girls' culture is unique. In this account of girlhood, I aim to expand that definition in relation to empire. Within this con-text, the space of girlhood allows for behaviour and activity that may have transgressed what was acceptable for women, or even for girls, with the justification of imperial benefit removed. Two of the key com-ponents Mitchell flags as necessary for the 'new girl's' creation are work outside the home and the elevation of the age of marriage, which cre-ated a period of independence between the parental and the marital home. In Claudia Nelson and Lynne Vallone's edited collection on girls' culture, Mitchell identifies the uniqueness of the girl, and her ability to break with convention, as compared with an adult: 'The ascription of immaturity and liminality gives her permission to behave in ways that might not be appropriate for a woman' (1996, p. 245). Not only does the transitional nature of girlhood expand the bounds of acceptable feminine behaviour, but so too does the need to contribute to the health of the Empire.

In his influential study of childhood, Philippe Ariés suggests that until the eighteenth century, adolescence was confused with childhood (1962, p. 25). The category of girlhood in the late nineteenth century emerges as a distinct period of development separate from that of early childhood, which tended to encompass both sexes. Kimberley Reynolds observes that the purpose of separate literature for girls and boys was to encourage the passage into adulthood with traits applicable to the respective child's sex: 'Through address, expectation, and content which provides an analogue for cultural organization, boys are encouraged to become masculine and girls feminine' (1990, p. 43). The creation of print culture specifically for girls helped to address the concern – although it never could alleviate it – about girls reading material that may have compromised the feminine ideal (1990, p. 97). Reynolds therefore views girls' fiction of late Victorian and Edwardian England as having a 'strongly conservative drive' (1990, p. xix), through its insistence upon feminine ideals that were subject to challenge in reality. The texts considered in the following chapters exercise caution about what constitutes acceptable femininity, but this is offset by the recognition that the 'modern' or 'new' girl was necessarily different to her predecessors. These manifestations of print culture praise her capability and usefulness to national and imperial needs.

The 'girl' reader of this period was not equated with childhood or even adolescence, but could be aged anywhere from ten years old to her mid-twenties.[3] The fictional girl protagonists considered in *Empire in British Girls' Literature and Culture* are aged primarily from 11 to 18 years old, while members of the Girl Guides were aged from 11 to 16. The readership of the *Girl's Own Paper*, however, which can be reasonably assumed from the entrants to its prize competitions, includes 'girls' aged in their early twenties (tapering off at the age of 24, the ideal age at which girls should be married, according to the magazine's advice). Because of its expanse and variable span, girlhood has been regarded as a less clearly defined developmental period than boyhood.[4] In contrast to the space of boyhood, domestic responsibilities (or 'conditioning as embryonic little mother and homemakers', as Mary Cadogan and Patricia Craig put it (1976, p. 73)), were likely to impinge on play for girls. Moreover, the ideal adult woman could be regarded as childlike,[5] or as Patricia Meyer

Spacks suggests, irrespective of age, 'a woman remains an adolescent until she marries' (1981, p. 194). The intrusion of domestic tasks and instruction into the childhood of girls and the prolonged infantilisation of women until marriage help to explain the protracted nature of girlhood and how readers of the age of 12 and 22 found common points of reading interest in periodicals such as the *Girl's Own Paper*.

Situating the girl in the empire

Philippa Levine gestures toward increasing critical attention on the subject of gender and empire in her introduction to an edited collection on the topic: 'While the Empire may still seem a very stuffy and masculine environment...that apparent stuffiness and masculinity are themselves now under scrutiny from a gendered perspective' (2004, p. 12). Though the process of recovering women from the edges of imperial history has begun, the next step in interrogating empire from a gendered perspective is to consider how it was imagined that girls could be drawn into its work. The British imperial project did not simply entail mustering military forces and facilitating emigration to existing colonies. To bolster support it entailed fostering patriotism, dedication to the Empire, and improving the physical and moral well-being of its citizens by stemming perceived degeneration. In response to the number of British men who were unfit to fight in the Second Boer War (1899–1902), the physical strength of individuals became an imperial concern, and mothers, particularly in the working classes, were blamed for domestic ineptitude and failing to raise healthy children.

Anna Davin's influential article 'Imperialism and Motherhood' (1978) identifies the connections between fears of degeneration after the Second Boer War and notes the perception of mothers as essential to the development of the 'imperial race'. Davin suggests that raising children became a duty of national significance once children were regarded as a national asset, and one in which the state could intervene. If mothers were deemed responsible for national strength and were perceived as failing in this task, then ensuring that the next generation of mothers was competent was of critical importance for the nation's future. Learning to mother, which also extended to encompass nursing or 'civilising' functions, is a preoccupation in both fiction and non-fiction texts for late Victorian girls. The focus of the rhetoric concerned with empire-building, however, was, as Davin explains, on male children: 'Mothers thus became responsible to the nation above all for the production and rearing of healthy sons; in spite of "the elevation of motherhood" the production of healthy future mothers was much less commonly demanded' (1978, p. 26). Concern about the development of boys rests upon their physical well-being or survival in infancy, responsibility for which is assigned to mothers, whereas texts for girls not only seek to inculcate this responsibility, but direct girls' interests, bodies, and behaviours.

The need to maintain the superiority of the British race, and 'improve' the areas in which it was feared to be deteriorating, necessarily involved considerations of class and opened up another area for the direction of imperial girlhood. If working-class girls in England's cities were thought 'uncivilised' then they could not be expected to fulfil their future function as responsible mothers. While girls could be constructed as civilisers in imperial locations, they could also channel their improving abilities toward the working classes at home. Angelique Richardson describes the fears that fuelled eugenic campaigns for racial improvement:

> To imagine parts of London as outside civilization was to play with the startling idea that the imperial headquarters housed, in its midst, unsurveyed outposts of empire, or territory not yet won. It was also to express a yet more shocking idea; that somehow Britain, home to an imperial race, with an empire to rule, had managed to breed its own savages, and house them, inadequately, in the very heart of civilization. (2003, p. 26)

Race and class were frequently conflated, most obviously in the middle-class desire to 'raise' each group from a 'primitive' state. There is an earlier precedent for such views in Matthew Arnold's *Culture and Anarchy* (1869), which equates the working classes with savages for their mutual lack of culture. As Robert J.C. Young observes, this equation of the 'white race' with civilisation and, in turn, of civilisation with culture, not only functioned to elevate it above others, but also supported the perception of culture as 'the defining feature of the upper and middle-classes' (1995, p. 95). This exclusion of the working classes from 'culture' did not preclude the perceived need to incorporate them in the imperial project, however, if only superficially. In his examination of the relationship between working-class children and the British Empire, Troy Boone describes 'social imperialism' as an 'incorporative fantasy' (p. 2005, p. 5). This prevalent illusion of working-class inclusion in the imperial project suggests that the 'higher self' – an ideal that is integral to pedagogical texts – is synonymous with self-identification as a loyal citizen of the English nation and the British Empire (Boone,

2005, p. 5). The idea of a unified conception of 'Englishness' that could be sent to the colonies, he suggests, could work to unify England, as well as settlers and natives in the colonies, in addition to enforcing a middle-class worldview. The girls' texts considered here gesture toward the ways primarily middle-class readers could aid in elevating the living conditions of less fortunate girls and, by association, their morality and contribution to the nation's 'common good'.

The work of girls within the Empire and at home for imperial benefit, even within fiction, is nevertheless fraught with anxiety about maintaining appropriate femininity. Julia Bush suggests that women's imperialist associations largely sidestepped any challenge to gender distinctions but harnessed the different contribution that women could make to empire-building. As the focus shifted from conquest to the viability of colonisation, the necessity of female abilities became relevant: 'The established links between female imperialism, maternal caring, and the transmission of moral and cultural values appeared to suggest a field of womanly duty' (Bush, 2000, p. 128). Furthermore, conceptions of racial motherhood invested maternity with power to make or break the physical strength of a nation. Jane Mackay and Pat Thane note the ways social and natural sciences considered the nature of sex difference and advanced the idea of the female role as the 'guardian' and 'conduit' of the race (1986, p. 199). If the maternal role was infused with the responsibility for racial survival, it was essential to preserve femininity untainted by masculine behaviours that might compromise her ability to do so. The girls discussed in *Empire in British Girls' Literature and Culture* do not simply adapt masculine behaviours or become 'tomboys', but are, at the same time as being brave, adventurous, and bold, careful to maintain their femininity.

In her analysis of late nineteenth-century writing, Deirdre David identifies a dominant ideal that prescribed greater sacrificial cultural labour for women than men for the moral good of the nation and the Empire (1995, p. 112). In almost all writing on empire, the purpose of British women's suffering was, David suggests, both useful and sensible: 'to produce moral transformation in the uncivilized peoples who engage in barbarous rituals such as suttee' (1995, p. 94). The following chapters examine particular texts that espouse ideas of racial motherhood, such as *The Handbook for Girl Guides*, and moral transformation of both 'heathens' abroad and the degenerate classes at home, including the *Girl's Own Paper* and Frances Hodgson Burnett's *A Little Princess*. Nevertheless, while the maintenance of womanliness is a preoccupation across the range of late Victorian and Edwardian girls' texts that are examined, the bounds of acceptable action expand when girls are transported to imperial locations or when engaging in preparations to assist in national defence.

With an inherent assumption of racial superiority, popular texts included representations of British people as 'civilising' both people and places of the Empire. Rita Kranidis notes that the colonies 'are represented as being in an infantile state of development, a place whose identity has not yet been determined, a kind of "nowhere" and "nothing" in reference to class systems and cultural formations' (1999, p. 69). As women held the primary responsibility for raising children out of immaturity, a field of expertise in developing colonies presents itself, in addition to that of 'civilising' native peoples. The civilising function can also be viewed as a way in which women could gain subjecthood. Rosemary Marangoly George identifies the way in which British women could define themselves against the racial 'Other', particularly Indian women, and also promote the idea that the imperial project required the skills of women to succeed. What enabled this, George suggests, was the creation of homes in the colonies, with home being the 'unit of civilization' on which the imperial project depended (1993–4, p. 107). Comparing the running of the home with the running of the Empire and associating indigenous peoples with children informed the idea that 'Managing a home and managing the Empire were ultimately part of the same project' (George, 1993–4, p. 112).

Yet how was domestic ideology to be reconciled with more active imperial duties and with women's own aspirations, for employment among other things? J.S. Bratton suggests that the biological and spiritual aspects of ideal femininity were contradictory, as proper passivity led to weakness, which was a detrimental and dangerous attribute in a colony. She notes that even writings that commented on the mental and physical unfitness of some women leaving for the colonies 'stressed the prime importance of refinement, of home-centred feminine culture' (1989, p. 197). The middle-class girl had to learn to be wife and mother to pioneer and soldier and was 'therefore the depository of the "home values" and guarantor of "higher" feelings and motives for the men's conquests' (Bratton, 1989, p. 196). Women are constructed as the nation's very moral fibre, and any perceived moral decline could be associated with potential imperial decline. There is a similar focus in girls' fiction on domestic skills, caring for siblings, and nursing the sick, but this is mediated by the view that in times of imperial crisis such as war or colonial settlement the norms that apply at home in peacetime may be transgressed if necessity or survival demands it. The moral function of the girl is still upheld. To distinguish these girls' texts from Bratton's description of women as the motivator for male imperial conquest, girls in Marchant's fiction, girls' robinsonades, and *The Handbook for Girl Guides* are representatives and upholders of empire in their own right. There is almost universal admiration for and promotion of active, physically strong girls in girls' print culture of the period, which is accommodated within – rather than opposing – womanliness. To further complicate these representations, imperial girls in print culture also defy a common perception about women. Levine argues that women in the period of empire were 'like children, a group apart from men and a group to be defined and managed by men' (2004, p. 6), but despite being both female and often a 'child', the imperial girl in British print culture often eludes definition and control by men.

Developments that radically reworked the education system contributed toward an increasing number of literate girl readers. These pedagogical changes also show the infiltration of imperial imperatives into the upbringing of girls. The formal education of girls and developing pedagogical approaches became critically linked with empire due to concerns about physical deterioration after the Second Boer War, the quest for 'national efficiency', and the manifestation of these in the convening of the 1904 Inter-Departmental Committee on Deterioration. These events produced a crucial dilemma in respect to girls: would formal education produce better mothers, or would it detract from their nurturing abilities? Carol Dyhouse sets out the conflicting views about the effect of increased education for girls on motherhood: 'around the turn of the century the conservative arguments for confining women to their "traditional role" as housewives and mothers was being rephrased in terms or social Darwinistic assumptions about evolution and racial progress' (1976, p. 47). Domestic skills were consequently integral to girls' formal education, with grants made to schools for the teaching of domestic subjects especially after the 1904 Committee. Rowbotham notes that from the mid-1870s women's movement beyond the domestic sphere enabled greater fulfilment and increased feminine capacity, yet traditional domesticity still lay at the core of the 'good' girl. Even advocates for intellectual education drew upon its potential to improve girls' domestic skills for the benefit of husbands and children. Or, as Ellen Jordan terms it, the 'bluestocking syllogism' legitimated education in the broader cultural realm without endangering the femininity of girl students (1991, p. 450).

Cultivating a healthy mind also necessitated the training of a healthy body in which to house it. In girls' print culture, physical strength is encouraged for health and to enable girls to conduct arduous tasks within the Empire. Sport provided girls with newfound corporeal freedoms, and physical education in schools counteracted concerns about the deleterious effects of excessive academic work for developing girls and their ability to bear healthy children and counteracted wider, national fears about physical deterioration. As early as the mid–nineteenth century, political theorist Herbert Spencer, in his essay 'Physical Education' (1859), argued that healthy mothers were a critical element in combating the degeneration of the race, advocating the improvement of physical exercise within girls' schools.[6] While, as Kathleen McCrone notes, a greater variety of exercises were introduced in response to anxiety about national deterioration, 'real physical education' and games involving competition were not common until the 1880s. Both McCrone and Paul Atkinson emphasise the socialising and controlling function of games and drills, which made them acceptable pursuits within girls' schools. As I identify more broadly throughout the following chapters, imperial imperatives similarly contributed to a range of new freedoms for girls.

Historicising the girl reader

Richard Altick's foundational history of nineteenth-century readers, *The English Common Reader*, points to the effects of cheaper publications and an increasingly literate populace on Victorian culture at large:

> Above all, the democratizing of reading led to a far-reaching revolution in English culture. No longer were books and periodicals written chiefly for the comfortable few; more and more, as the century progressed, it was the ill-educated mass audience with pennies in its pocket that called the tune to which writers and editors dance. (1957, p. 5)

This revolution likewise filtered through to the burgeoning juvenile publishing market, with a proliferation of widely-read periodicals for boys or girls making their debut in the late Victorian period, reaching a greater readership than those that had been distributed through Sunday schools in the first half of the century. Mary Cadogan and Patricia Craig wrote the first comprehensive overview of girls' fiction and periodical reading from 1839 to 1975. They note that in the last two decades of the nineteenth century, 'stories of school life and robust adventure in outposts of empire were taking over from hearth and home' (1976, p. 45). The emergence of girls' genres that eagerly broke out of the domestic realm and the reinforcement of stereotypes inspired a particular need to define what constituted ideal reading material even if simultaneously, as Mitchell points out, the divide between adult recommendation and books enjoyed by girls continued to expand (1995, p. 4).

The increasing availability and range of printed material published for young people – including relatively affordable publications that were accessible to lower-middle-class and working-class children – ensured that what children, especially girls, read was a popular middle-class and religious concern. Guides to channelling girls' reading, most commonly middle-class girls' reading, toward texts that were savoury, well-written, and potentially self-improving were published in book form or featured as articles within periodicals.[7] Charlotte Yonge, well-known for her morally directed, High Church works as an author and as editor of *The Monthly Packet* (1851–99), in which she was supremely concerned with directing Anglican girls' reading,[8] wrote *What Books to Lend and What to Give* in 1887. Its very title alludes to the perceived influence of books on developing and otherwise unoccupied minds, and the need to provide 'good' lest 'evil' be easily found. Yonge draws particular notice to the idle girl or woman who spares too much time for reading:

> The corresponding class of girls and young women are for the most part indiscriminate devourers of fiction, and, like the women before mentioned, need to have their appetite rightly directed. But there is more hope of them than of their elders, and their ideal is capable of being raised by high-minded tales, which may refine their notions. (1887, p. 10)

Not only are girls regarded as impressionable and indiscriminate in their reading tastes, but they are also ripe for 'shaping' with the right books, unlike women who are already formed and who may have aged beyond the point of 'raising'.

Edward G. Salmon's 'What Girls Read', published in *The Nineteenth Century* just one year before Yonge's guide, acknowledges the prolific nature and quality of the authors of girls' literature. He suggests that it has a place to occupy between childhood and womanhood (where novels may require 'discreet judgment'): the end of girls' literature is that 'whilst it advances beyond the nursery, it stops short of the full blaze of the drawing-room' (1886, p. 523). This statement fashions a unique position for the girl, as Mitchell describes, as an occupant of a space that is neither childhood nor adulthood, even though girls could be required to perform adult domestic tasks. Salmon is, nevertheless, particularly troubled by the influence of inappropriate fiction (or 'trash') on those who reside in the 'houses of the poor':[9] 'high-flown conceits and pretensions of the poorer girls of the period, their dislike of manual work and love of freedom, spring largely from notions imbibed in the course of a perusal of their penny fictions' (1886, p. 523). Reading is credited with the power to lure girls away from their appropriate realm of activity, disrupting their place within an ordered society. Extrapolating from Salmon's concern about working-class girls being led to desire a life devoid of labour (and indeed working-class reading was seen to require the greatest degree of supervision), so too might middle-class girls be distracted from the wifely and motherly duties upon which the nation's future seemed to rest.

Girls' literature, Salmon notes, is intended to 'build up' women, as boys' literature is meant to 'build up' men. Therefore, while he does not disapprove of girls reading boys' books and periodicals (he suggests that girls who do so seek 'lively movement'), he is careful to distinguish the different purposes of books for each sex: 'If in choosing the books that boys shall read it is necessary to remember that we are choosing mental food for the future chiefs of a great race, it is equally important not to forget in choosing books for girls that we are choosing mental food for the future wives and mothers of that race' (1886, p. 526). The effect of reading on girls for both Yonge and Salmon elicits tangible effects. Indeed, Salmon even makes the point that the influence of girls' books is just as 'real' as that of 'burglar and bushranging fiction' among boys (1886, p. 523). With the growing availability of girls' periodicals, the evolving girls' school stories, and girls' adventure fiction, the late Victorian period generated a range of texts that served as 'mental food' for girls that invoked the idea of racial motherhood and direct participation in the Empire.

A central category throughout this analysis is the late Victorian and Edwardian 'new girl'. She was a cultural figure more than a reality, and she was shaped by challenges to Victorian conceptions of ideal femininity. Gender norms were destabilised by both the decadent and the dandy and their subversion of masculinity and, similarly, by the figure of the New Woman. The juvenile equivalent of the emancipated woman, which Gillian Avery terms the 'modern girl', was also disliked for her challenges to convention displayed by bicycle riding, participating in mixed bathing, and having 'forthright and independent views on topics which the old-fashioned girl would never have tackled' (1975, p. 202). Most damning of all, she was seen as a 'hoyden' wanting to escape from the home, and therefore she posed a threat to the glorified mother of the imperial race. Sally Ledger notes the way in which eugenist thought impacted upon discourse on the New Woman: 'The feeling was, amongst supporters of the establishment, that Britain's women urgently needed to raise up a strong British "race" in order to sustain the nation's (supposed) supremacy, and the New Woman was construed (or constructed) as a threat to this national need' (1997, p. 18). Yet New Woman writers themselves at times appropriated the ideology of racial motherhood, in the same manner in which feminists used 'civilising' discourse to justify women's place in imperial locations.[10] The imperial girls in the texts I examine represent an amalgam of the 'new girl', with her desire for education, physical capabilities and independence, and conventional femininity that acknowledges maternal and domestic responsibilities. In this way, the imperial girl in late Victorian and Edwardian print culture is construed not as a threat to the nation, but as an essential element of its success.

Imperialism became a media preoccupation, as Paula Krebs suggests, not only in response to the Second Boer War, but also prior to it because of the 'scramble for Africa' in the last two decades of the nineteenth century (1999, p. 29). The impact of empire and the repercussions of critical events such as the war upon boys' publications have been noted in several studies. For example, Steve Attridge comments upon the reaction to the war in boys' novels, comics, and papers, which included war statistics and storylines about battles and encouraged boys to fight 'as' the nation and for the boy reader to conceive of himself as an element of empire (2003, p. 56). Joseph Bristow more broadly considers how imperialism made the boy into 'an aggrandized subject – British born and bred – with the future of the world lying on his shoulders' (1991, p. 19). Like Attridge, Bristow argues that a boy's reading, with a focus on adventure fiction, could imbue him with the sense that he was integral to the imperial project and shared in both its glory and racial supremacy: 'Everywhere the nation's young hero encountered texts and illustrations that made him the subject of his reading' (1991, p. 41). If the young boy hero found himself immortalised in texts 'everywhere', what of the young girl reader? While fictional heroines of empire were neither as prevalent nor as obviously engaged in imperial tasks, I suggest that within the cultural context of racial degeneration, fostered by the inherent belief in British racial superiority, girls were similarly depicted as vital to its success.

Rashna B. Singh's comprehensive study of children's literature and empire is built upon the importance of the typology of character, suggesting that 'Character was how the British triumphed' (2004, p. 34).

The British character (something that formal schooling and organisations such as the Girl Guides aimed to refine and improve in the individual) was associated with superior racial qualities that stood in stark contrast with the negative traits of those who ought to be colonised (the lazy, dishonest, chaotic, degenerate, effeminate, and childlike) (Singh, 2004, p. 31). The superior British characteristics that Singh identifies (courage, strength, virility, and exertion, among others) are bound most tightly to the figure of the British male. If we accept Singh's view, the late Victorian girl reader was unlikely to have a clear sense of obligation to her country and her importance to the Empire. For instance, Singh concludes that while the *Boy's Own Paper* repeatedly refers to British triumphs abroad, '[n]o such wealth of reference may be found in the equivalent girls' periodical ... Even in 1900, whole issues go by with no reference to the colonies whatsoever' (2004, p. 56). I argue that the promotion of 'service of mankind' and 'duties' that Singh identifies in the *Girl's Own Paper* as unrelated to adventure or to the Empire are, in fact, essential aspects of girls' contribution to the imperial project. While there are few overt celebrations of Britons at war in the magazine during this time, there is significant and clear engagement with empire in articles on lady travellers, missionaries, colonial settlers,[11] and war nurses. Moreover, the advice columns, correspondence pages, and non-fiction articles are almost invariably grounded in ideology that promotes an ideal girl who could raise healthy children and improve the lower classes at home (inescapable aspects of the desire for racial strength), potentially civilise 'natives' in imperial locations such as India, and be physically and mentally equipped to live in a rough colonial environment while gracefully bringing the domesticity of home to it.

Chapter 1, 'Shaping the 'Useful' Girl: The *Girl's Own Paper*, 1880–1907', examines the *Girl's Own Paper*, its creation of a girl readership, and the relationship it creates between the idealised girl and empire. I commence with this magazine because its large readership renders it the most important example of girls' print culture of the era. It considers an emerging girls' culture during the term of Charles Peters' editorship (1880–1907) and focuses on the construction of the girl as both a newly emerging market for periodicals and a potential purchaser of consumer goods. An analysis of the content contributed by girl readers themselves suggests that the periodical enabled prescriptive advice on acceptable behaviour. As Driscoll's genealogy of girlhood proposes, girls' magazines functioned as guidance manuals but emphasised self-surveillance and self-production, especially in content such as the 'problem' pages. They are also another site where education or socialisation could be conducted within the home. This chapter demonstrates that an ideal English girl subjectivity was created in the magazine, which its readers should strive to mimic through self-improvement. This 'ideal girl' is important to the nation, and she is superior to the native girls in the colonies because of her education (not above the white colonial girls who were also subscribers to the *Girl's Own Paper*, however). She is therefore encouraged to 'improve' the downtrodden girls overseas and the working-class girls at home. She could both transmit cultural values at home and 'civilise' people and places outside of England. The girl is in formation not only as a readership category in the late Victorian period, but also as a consumer identity. Advertisements in the *Girl's Own Paper* build upon social Darwinist views espoused in its non-fiction articles to promote both a 'civilising function' that girls could enact in the colonies and an improvement of the physical strength of its current and future citizens.

Chapter 2, 'Developing Pedagogy and Hybridised Femininity in the Girls' School Story', turns to the changing conditions in girls' education, particularly the developing pedagogy of public secondary schools and also broader social concerns regarding motherhood and national degeneration as they intersect with empire, and relates these to girls' schools as represented in the early school stories (1906–14) of Angela Brazil. These novels register transitions in academic curricula and physical education built upon ideas of preparation for motherhood and being 'of use' to the nation. Examining texts intended for teachers of the period, this chapter focuses on the connection of the training of girls with racial strength. It suggests that the construction of women as purveyors of moral values within the home (and within the Empire at large) was an inherent foundation of developing curricula. Like the Girl Guide scheme, drawing out the best in the individual's character is a focus, but the individual's development is also closely tied to benefits that may contribute toward the 'common weal'.

Mirroring the historical importance of formal education in cultural transmission as it became more prevalent, Shirley Foster and Judy Simmons suggest that the school-story form created by Brazil is the first to 'replace' the family as the primary mode of influence on the girl (1995, p. 18). This chapter proposes that in Brazil's school settings a 'modern' femininity is melded with traditionally acceptable qualities to produce a hybrid model of juvenile femininity that is positively celebrated. It also identifies where pedagogical aims for girls intersect with imperial ideology that promotes physically strong citizens, seeks to combat degeneration, and stresses the importance of individual

development and actions to the nation – in order to consider the formation of an idealised female subjectivity and the 'taming' of unruly or
colonial girls. Within the confines of the school setting (or the women-
only 'world of girls' that Rosemary Auchmuty identifies in *The World
of Girls* (1992)), there are sets of regulations and procedures that mimic
or have similar functions to those which girls may have in the nation,
broadly speaking.

The genre of boys' adventure fiction was popular with both sexes.
While it emerged at the turn of the century, much later than the equivalent boys' novels and serials, there was a genre of adventure fiction
featuring girl protagonists who are positively depicted for their bravery.
In Chapter 3, 'Adventurous Girls of the British Empire: The Novels of
Bessie Marchant', I examine how fictional girls of the Empire who do
not reside in the 'mother country' negotiate acceptable behaviour in
survival situations in the works of the most prominent and popular
author of girls' adventure fiction, Bessie Marchant. Her adventure stories for girls, authored from 1900, place brave heroines in distant cor-
ners of the Empire. The question of what happened to 'Britishness' once
citizens relocated was a pertinent one, given that more than five-and-a-
half million Britons settled overseas in the Victorian era, predominantly
in the United States of America, Canada, Australia, and New Zealand
(Archibald, 2002, pp. 1–2). In contrast to Diana Archibald's suggestion
that women in the colonies who maintained British cultural practices
functioned as 'angels in the bush' (2002, p. 91), I argue that the heroines
of Marchant's novels are sufficiently adventurous to complicate such
an interpretation. Indeed, my aim is to suggest that her girl protagonists are depicted as more active and less restrained by expectations
of feminine behaviour when they must adapt to life in less 'civilised'
lands for the benefit of expanding and strengthening the Empire. This
examination will, in turn, answer how conflicts between the contradictory ideals of 'proper' femininity and physical strength were resolved
away from the comforts of Britain. The 'civilising' function as it relates
to indigenous inhabitants is noticeably absent in Marchant's novels,
which largely elide any native presence. Nursing, which Davin counts
among the acceptable 'surrogate' vocations for motherhood along with
teaching or emigration to the colonies (1978, p. 51), is one way in which
Marchant's heroines bring civility to colonial locations.

Chapter 4, 'Fantastic and Domestic Girls and the Idolisation of
"Improving" Others', draws together two different genres of children's
literature to contrast novels in which girls are able to apply their mothering skills in countries far removed from England (interacting with

native peoples) and within their family or city (improving the working classes at home). It focuses first upon E. Nesbit's trilogy of fantasy novels *Five Children and It* (1902), *The Phoenix and the Carpet* (1904), and *The Story of the Amulet* (1906). Nesbit is frequently associated with a diminution in the level of didacticism inherent in children's fiction. She is also credited with injecting feminism into her novels through her active heroines. For instance, Alison Lurie suggests, 'Her books are full of girls who are as brave and adventurous as their brothers' (1990, p. 105). Nesbit's trilogy uniquely enables the children within it to function as the first British travellers to imaginary and historical places. This chapter proposes that the girl protagonist, Anthea, enacts functions that support the imperial project: civilising 'native' inhabitants and mothering her brothers away from parental help. Moreover, her leadership decisions and moral focus are depicted positively, whereas Nesbit critiques and parodies the arrogance of her brothers when they rehearse the part of boys' adventure heroes or real-world British conquerors.

The second section of Chapter 4 examines the implications of the imperial project in domestic settings in two works by Frances Hodgson Burnett: *A Little Princess* (1906) and *The Secret Garden* (1911). In these two novels, the inherent nature of imperialism in late Victorian and Edwardian culture is evidenced by their presentation of the idea that English children are most appropriately raised within England, with strong adult guidance and a culture of self-discipline, and that, for girls in particular, cultivating the ability to care for and 'improve' others is a crucial indicator of satisfactory development. In *A Little Princess*, this takes the form of pointing out the need for middle-class intervention in the lot of the poor, who may tend toward savagery without work or purpose. The connection between outdoor exercise and improved character (exhibited in the motto *mens sana in corpore sano*, which is discussed in pedagogical texts in Chapter 2) is strongly forged in *The Secret Garden*, and in both novels improvements in character are evinced once the protagonists are removed from the environment of India.

Chapter 5, 'Be(ing) Prepared: Girl Guides, Colonial Life, and National Strength', seeks to bridge a gap in the feminist critique of gender and empire with regard to the founding of the Girl Guides organisation in 1909. Unlike the representations in previous chapters that reflect and construct the British ideal of girlhood through periodical and fictional forms, this chapter focuses on the popular Girl Guides organisation to examine how girls were explicitly directed toward assisting the nation through maternity and nursing. Michael Mitterauer, in his *History of Youth*, suggests that many of the thresholds that marked the passing of youth were applicable only to males: 'Male and female youth were so different that until the end of the nineteenth century the concepts relating to the age-group were entirely gender-specific. Only then did a sexually inclusive collective concept of youth emerge. But even so, the turning points of the biography of youth continued to be very different for the two sexes' (1992, p. 87). Yet despite such acknowledgement of a gendered gulf in the nineteenth century, previous studies of the Boy Scouts, which, like studies of boys' fiction, have been more prolific, have only briefly considered the Guides and view the organisation as merely derivative. In contrast, this chapter contends that the aims and activities of the Girl Guides were unique and notes that its origins, and printed material such as the first handbook, *The Handbook for Girl Guides; or, How Girls Can Help Build Up the Empire* (1912), were predicated upon a firm belief in the active role women, and girls specifically, could play in the British imperial project. Subsequent published editions of the handbook modify these imperial elements, making the 1912 edition a crucial source in which to examine the manifestation of empire and gender. This chapter argues that, although tempered by an emphasis on raising children in order to prevent the 'deterioration' of the British race, *The Handbook for Girl Guides* permits increased non-domestic activity for Edwardian girls, which is justified by the need to prepare for home defence in case of foreign attack and for life in the colonies.

The final chapter, 'Microcosms of Girlhood: Reworking the Robinsonade for Girls', turns to an enduring manifestation of the adventure genre and takes account of how it registers transformations in late Victorian girlhood that were encouraged by imperial concerns. The island setting of the castaway narrative functions as a microcosm in which the 'new girl' can display her competence removed from the restrictions of culture. The girl castaway effectively demonstrates her capacities for settling land and self-preservation in the face of uncultivated environments and threats posed by indigenous inhabitants. While these 'girl Crusoes' display appropriate femininity, they are able to not only move beyond the domestic because their survival is contingent upon their ability to do so but also take pleasure in the exploration of uncultivated environments. These girl Crusoes actively seek adventure, often have the capacity to defend themselves physically, and, as a result, constitute the core of these texts rather than inhabiting their periphery as did the girls and women of earlier children's robinsonades. This chapter positions the girl Crusoe as the ultimate symbol of imperial femininity, representing girls who can function as capable settlers even in the absence of a pre-existing British colony.

Empire in British Girls' Literature and Culture examines the diverse ways in which the late Victorian and Edwardian girl was constructed in print culture as contributing to the imperial project, both at home – through mothering and through improving the poor – and in the world at large, in the capacity of colonists, nurses, explorers, castaways, or 'civilisers'. In particular, this study focuses upon the agency that girls were permitted with imperial justification, projecting the perceived need for future women who not only could endure the hardships of Britain's imperial responsibility through male absence, but could hold their own in the Empire just as capably. In other instances, girls' texts go so far as to critique masculine approaches to settlement and colonial rule, elevating feminine abilities in ways that also critique the imperial project at the same time as accepting its founding doctrines, such as that of racial superiority. At the core of this study is the desire to understand how the proliferation of imperial discourse in this period identified parts for every female citizen in upholding the Empire on which it was said that the sun never set.

1
Shaping the 'Useful' Girl: The *Girl's Own Paper*, 1880–1907

> Kisses, it is said, are not accompanied by so loud a report as cannon-balls, but they echo a great deal longer through the universe.
>
> James Mason (1881) 'A Girl's Influence',
> The *Girl's Own Paper*, p. 425

I begin this examination of girlhood and empire with a girls' magazine as a case study, for, as Margaret Beetham suggests, magazines explicitly interact with the culture which produces them and which they produce. Rather than simply functioning as purveyors of ideology, magazines are places 'where meanings are contested and made' (Beetham, 1996, p. 5). The late nineteenth century is a particularly rich period in which to examine magazines for young women and how definitions of femininity were 'made' and negotiated within them. Bolstered by increasing literacy, the juvenile publishing market flourished in the late nineteenth century. While books were part of this efflorescence of children's print culture, periodicals, which were more affordable, had wider distributions and greater readerships.

The *Girl's Own Paper* (GOP) was, along with the *Boy's Own Paper* (BOP), the first magazine to capture a massive juvenile audience. Kirsten Drotner identifies the 1860s as the decade in which the possibility of the adolescent female audience was discovered (1988, p. 119). Through the following decades of the nineteenth century, numerous magazines for girls were published, including the evangelical periodical *The Monthly Packet* (1851–99), *The English Girls' Journal and Ladies' Magazine* (1863–5), *The Young Englishwoman* (1864–9, continued 1870–7 as *Beeton's Young Englishwoman* and 1878–91 as *Sylvia's Home Journal*), *Aunt Judy's Magazine* (1866–85), and *Every Girl's Magazine* (1878–88). Girls were often assumed to be part of the audience of women's magazines; however, the *GOP* pioneered a new style of magazine squarely aimed at young girls. Along with L.T. Meade's *Atalanta* (1887–93), the *Girl's Realm* (1898–1915), and *The Young Woman* (1892–1915), the *GOP* participated in the 're-working of the concept of the "girl"' in the periodical press in the 1880s and 1890s (Beetham, 1996, p. 137).

In addition to providing insight into the shifting formulation of the 'girl' in late Victorian print culture, a girls' magazine is a vital element in this study of girlhood and empire because as Hilary Fraser, Stephanie Green, and Judith Johnston show, the question of empire, like the woman question, 'was contested, formulated, and framed within the pages of the periodical press' (2003, p. 121). While the *GOP* has received the greatest scholarly attention of all Victorian girls' periodicals, perhaps because of its popularity (see Mackay and Thane, 1986; Mitchell, 1995; and Skelding, 2001), scant attention has been directed to its part in producing and contesting girls' participation in empire in existing histories. Conversely, Christopher Banham points out that the British Empire 'has become the single most developed theme of study in the historiography of Victorian boys' periodicals' (2007, p. 151). Both Terri Doughty's (2011) and Fraser, Green, and Johnston's examination of stories in the *GOP* as examples of 'gendered pro-emigration propaganda' (2003, p. 140) suggest the magazine's potential for reading the part formulated for middle-class girls within the Empire. Furthermore, its popularity and recognition by adults as a favourable magazine for girls allows for identification of how imperial concerns became entwined in the construction of an ideal girl in what Kimberley Reynolds describes as an 'ultimately conservative' magazine (1990, p. 150).

In this chapter, I examine the paper and its picture of emerging girls' culture through its construction of the girl reader, its production of the ideal girl through reader contributions and correspondence, and its creation of the girl consumer in advertisements, in the volumes produced during the term of Charles Peters' editorship, from 1880 to 1907. After Peters' death, former contributing writer Flora Klickmann assumed the role of editor. She discontinued the more affordable weekly parts and reversed the trend toward ostensibly differentiated publications for girls by changing the title to *The Girl's Own Paper and Women's Magazine*. In this twenty-seven year period, I consider the ways in which the *GOP*'s formation of the girl as a reader and a consumer implicate her in the maintenance of empire both within England and in its colonies. I chart how imperial sentiment interacted with the developing girls' culture presented in the paper and how it sometimes espoused progressive views when they might contribute to the formation of an idealised girl who would be useful to those around her and to the nation.

The imperial duties identified for girls in the *GOP* partially originate from its religious affiliation. The magazine was first published in January 1880 by the largest evangelical publisher of the time, the Religious Tract Society (RTS), which was founded in 1799 to create tracts that were to be distributed to countries in the British imperial world, Europe, the United States of America, and regions where missionaries worked, such as China. Banham suggests that the RTS 'supported empire' because the greater the British presence overseas, the greater its scope for missionary work (2007, p. 154). In 1879, after several decades of progress toward popular non-tract publications with a broader readership, the RTS had begun a similar publication for boys, the *Boy's Own Paper*. Both magazines were initially envisaged as a preferable alternative for the working-class, lower-middle-class, or middle-class evangelical boy or girl to read in place of the popular penny dreadfuls and romances (Doughty, 2004, p. 7).

As articles in the *GOP* suggest, the RTS imbued reading with the potential either to lead developing minds astray or, as it hoped with its own publishing ventures, to shape morally upright and productive girls and boys. The RTS had a spiritual mission that is borne out in its focus on leading girls to live productive, moral lives and its investment of middle-class girls with the capacity to improve the lives of wayward girls at home and non-Christians outside of Britain. The RTS's decision to incorporate material, such as fiction, that was less didactic – and thus held greater appeal for the young people who would be buying the magazines – into both of its juvenile periodicals contributed to their great popularity and profitability. Due to the *BOP*'s and the *GOP*'s tone, style, price (only one penny weekly), and content (which minimised overtly religious or morally prescriptive articles in comparison with the tracts), both papers were extremely appealing to their target audience and became the best-selling periodicals for girls and boys. The *GOP* was more successful, having doubled the readership (260,000) of the *BOP* after its first year, and becoming the more consistently profitable in both sales and advertising revenue. In 1888, after slight declines in circulation after their spectacular debuts, the average print-run figures were 153,000 for the *BOP* and 189,000 for the *GOP* (McAleer, 1992, p. 217; Reed, 1997, p. 86).

The *GOP* and the *BOP* were not published under the RTS imprint, but rather, as the title page of each edition shows, issued from the Leisure Hour Office (with *The Leisure Hour* being a 'family journal' that ran from 1852 to 1905). Aileen Fyfe suggests that this tactic would have enabled evangelical readers to potentially recognise these as RTS publications from the publication address, but not the working-class audience who may have identified an RTS publication as patronising from the middle class (2004, p. 180). An answer to a correspondent from 1881 hints at the purported broad class focus of the *GOP*: '[it] is intended for all classes, and we try to supply something that may be suitable to every reader in each number' (p. 400). The aim to speak to girls of different classes sometimes resulted in contradictory views on a particular subject by different authors being printed in the same volume of the paper, seemingly expressing variant expectations for girls of the working and middle classes.[1] The *GOP* does not subscribe to an overarching view on a number of contested issues for girls, such as physical education, for example. Skelding describes the magazine's traversal of divergent notions of femininity as 'steer[ing] an uneasy course between two extremes' (2001, p. 36). It is this very diversity of opinion in the paper – inherent in the periodical form itself, which Beetham notes 'refuses... a single authorial voice' (1996, p. 12) – that contributes to the *GOP*'s richness and energy on contested issues of femininity, work, education, and sport.

With editorial avoidance of sensational fiction and its focus on practical duty, contemporary critics, such as author Charlotte Yonge, regarded the *GOP* as a harmless choice for girls. In *What Books to Lend and What to Give*, Yonge remarks of the *GOP*: 'Hardly equal to the Boy's [Own Paper], but very much appreciated by girls in their teens, whose want it seems to satisfy in a sensible, innocent way' (1887, p. 109). Edward G. Salmon in his article 'What Girls Read' is critical of magazines for girls that have 'lapsed into the penny dreadful, composed of impossible love stories, of jealousies, murders, and suicides' (1886, p. 520). The *GOP*, however, is one of the two girls' magazines that Salmon regards as advantageous for 'young ladies in their teens' (1886, p. 520), particularly because of the charity that the *GOP*'s prize competitions encouraged. The paper is, therefore, firmly ensconced in dominant ideologies about gender, posing little challenge to adult perceptions of appropriate femininity. Yet although Salmon praises the *GOP* (and excludes it from his pronouncement that there is hardly a magazine read by girls 'which it would not be a moral benefit to have swept off the face of the earth' (1886, p. 523)), he does suggest that it is not purchased sufficiently by the very people of whose reading choices he does not approve – the working classes. In its attribution to girls of a role in 'elevating' the working classes, the *GOP* implies a middle-class readership, in spite of the existence of working-class readers and contributors, such as the authors of articles published as part of the series 'My Daily Round: A Competition for Girls Who Work With Their Hands' (1896).

While fictional serials comprised a significant part of the *GOP*,[2] in this chapter I concentrate on non-fiction articles of advice and instruction on education, self-improvement, health, and the Empire, as well as contributions of girls themselves, such as prize competitions and correspondence columns. The girl subjectivity in formation is more clearly expressed in the non-fiction pages than in the often didactic serials, which often belaboured the points that were crystallised in the non-fiction articles. Non-fiction articles directly address, debate, and offer opinions on girls' employment, education, travel, and physical recreation, revealing conflicting views by different authors across the volumes.

First, I define the *GOP*'s readership by setting out what the term 'girl' encompassed, and then consider how the periodical enabled prescriptive advice on acceptable behaviour through the publication of readers' contributions, and how the formation of this readership occurred in tandem with the construction of girls as a consumer group. Having established the readership of the *GOP*, I argue that the magazine creates an ideal English girl subjectivity, which its readers should strive to mimic through self-improvement. This ideal girl was considered important to the nation itself, superior to the native girls in the colonies because of her education, and therefore encouraged to improve the downtrodden girls overseas and the equivalent girl at home – the working-class girl. With consideration of the contradictory views of femininity presented, I suggest that emphasis was placed upon creating girls who were domestically competent, but also educated and capable of other paid work, or colonial emigration. In this way, the *GOP* prefigures the centrality of preparedness for calamity to idealised British femininity that later becomes evident in girls' adventure fiction and the Girl Guides organisation.

Reading and the formation of the ideal girl subject

The periodical played a unique role in the lives of its readers, through its direct mode of address, its creation of a community of readers, and its contemporary subject matter. For newly forming readerships, consumer groups, and categories, such as girls and 'girlhood', magazines attempt to corral readers into acceptable models of behaviour. Kathryn Shevelow, for instance, identifies the ways in which the eighteenth-century popular periodical for women contributed to the production of a new ideology of ideal femininity, while trying to 'exert influence as a purveyor of values' (1989, p. 3). While girl readers and contributors played a part in negotiating and producing such values, it is crucial to account for the overt socialising function of print culture for young people and the restricted possibilities for reader resistance because of the authority of adult editors and authors. The *GOP*'s non-fiction articles advised girls about appropriate behaviour in almost every facet of current and future life: how to manage a household once married, how to entertain guests, how to cook, how to clean, how to conduct home nursing and infant care, what to wear, what kinds of paid employment and education were acceptable, how to develop skills through hobbies (via the publication of musical scores and clothing patterns, for example), and also what to read.

The *GOP* had an improving function, attempting to shape girls who would be useful in the years between the end of their education and the beginning of work or motherhood, or in their leisure hours. The 'Answers to Correspondents' column often included girls' praise for the publication, and it enabled dialogue on the moral and social focus of the paper. An answer to 'English Girl' in 1883 conveys the editor's gratification at the correspondent's expressed feeling of mental and physical improvement from reading the *GOP*. 'English Girl' writes that the paper is 'influencing its readers to lead nobler and purer lives', which is then confirmed in the editorial response as 'exactly our principal aim' (p. 6). Girl readers were encouraged to study and cultivate their skills at home, rather than becoming engrossed in trivial pastimes that did not improve character, knowledge, health, or usefulness. In addition to 'classes' that improved girls' skills in art and writing composition (in which work was critiqued), there was a *Girl's Own* Cookery Class (composed of girls who had educated themselves in cookery with aid of its columns) and a *Girl's Own* Shorthand Class. Here, however, I am concerned not only with 'private' improving activities, but with the advice on public behaviour, careers, emigration, and service to the nation in the periodical intended 'for sensible girls' (*GOP Annual* Advertisement, 1904, p. 6).

In the 1880s and 1890s, the assumption that women's magazines also addressed girl readers was transformed as girls were targeted as a discrete readership (Beetham, 1992, p. 137). What constituted a 'girl' reader is more complex than female childhood. In terms of age and geography, the *GOP*'s readership can be estimated from the age statistics included in the results of its numerous art and craft competitions and the locations provided for overseas letter writers in the correspondence column. The 'A Hundred Famous Cities' competition held in 1891 attracted 887 entrants, who were primarily aged between 13 and 23 (the youngest and oldest entrants were 11 and 38, respectively)[3] (p. 206). The declining number of readers who entered competitions after the age of twenty-four correlates with the advice given by the paper that recommends twenty-five or twenty-six onwards as the ideal age for a girl to marry after gaining worldly experience and serving her parents ('Answers', 1892, p. 623). A reader fourteen years of age, who enquires as to whether it is proper for her to be married, is informed in no uncertain terms that she is far too young to be mistress of a house, a wife, and a guide to her children: 'A child scarcely out of the nursery, in a short frock and a pinafore!' ('Answers', 1891, p. 176). Similar exchanges, in which girls have written to ask of the appropriateness of an activity for their age or circumstances, are included regularly in the correspondence column, making these pages a distillation of the paper's purposes and values. The need of readers to seek confirmation with the editors about the appropriateness of particular activities for girls of certain ages confirms the uncertain and unstable nature of the division between girlhood and adulthood. The letters from readers also show these ideals being contested through ignorance of the advice contained in the *GOP*'s previous numbers, and indeed sometimes girls are instructed to consult earlier volumes for answers to their queries.

The increased age for first marriage for women in the late nineteenth century meant that the 'girl' readership took in a substantial proportion of young women in their late teens and early twenties. Marriage was not necessarily a disincentive for every reader to continue her interest in the paper, however. The *GOP* doctor, Dr Gordon Stables, known as 'Medicus' in his regular health columns, remarked that after twenty years of writing for the paper he knew that its circulation was immense 'because first and foremost I get letters from every quarter of the world about it, not only from lassics in their teens, but from ladies grown up, who have bairnies of their own' (1905, pp. 11–12). The magazine's readership was mostly adolescent girls but also included many young women who were expecting to marry and some who were newly wed. In addition to a small readership of older women who were likely mothers of girl readers (as reflected in the competition statistics), the paper was also read by boys, as occasional published letters suggest, but perhaps not in as great numbers as girls who were purported to have read boys' periodicals and novels.

The international readership of the *GOP*, composed largely of girls of British parentage but also of girls seeking to learn English, was a significant one. In the early 1880s, monthly parts of the *GOP* could be forwarded for twopence to Canada, the United States, or 'any of the continental countries' ('Answers', 1883, p. 192). While the *GOP* largely circulated within Britain, the lists of competition prize-winners show a substantial readership of international girls, particularly in the colonies. In 1884, a prize competition for which girls were asked to write essays on '100 Famous Women' attracted almost 5000 entries from girls in countries including Greece, Portugal, Paraguay, Malta, Cape Verde Islands, Cape Colony, China, Antigua, India, Natal, Canada, Jamaica, the Colonies of Australia, New Zealand, and Tasmania (p. 569). This diversity of locations was replicated in dozens more competitions. Precisely what proportion of the readership was located outside England is unclear (international correspondents may have had a greater chance of having their letters responded to or of winning competition prizes),[4] but what is certain is that it was important for the *GOP* to cultivate a vision of shared girls' culture that could spread across the world via the British colonies.

The interactive formation of girls' identity

In the previous section, I described the constitution of the *GOP*'s readership, setting out to define to whom the *Girl's Own Paper*, with its titular reference to ownership, belonged. The address to this category of 'girls' as readers is an essential element of the magazine's creation of an international community of girls, in the same way as Beetham proposes occurs in women's magazines: 'The woman's magazine, by addressing the reader "as woman", always creates the potential for an imagined community of women, or for women as an imagined community' (1996, p. 209). Beetham's statement alerts us to both the *GOP*'s elision of difference in its formulation of 'our girls' as a neat community of readers and the mythology inherent in its picture of British girls' culture. While I have already noted the magazine's overt attempts at instilling values and correct patterns of behaviour in girl readers, Fraser, Johnstone, and Green, like Beetham, stress that the periodical press is not 'an oppressive organ of a dominant ideology' but 'a crucial site of ideological struggle' (2003, p. 37). The model of the interactive reader, who helps to produce meaning, is preferred to allow for some reader resistance. In particular, Fraser et al. view the reader contributions to a journal's economy as a form of resistance (2003, p. 75). Girls sought visible entry to the community of *GOP* readers through its correspondence column and essay competitions but, while girls were clearly engaged with their production as students, mothers, workers, and emigrants, these contributions largely function prescriptively, bolstering the *GOP*'s construction of the ideal, self-sacrificial girl.

Shevelow suggests that periodicals created and projected an audience identity that was shaped by reader correspondence: 'the appearance of reader participation was one of the most important components of the periodical's attempts to collect and define a new audience, to project an image of a community of readers mutually engaged in the production of the text' (1989, p. 38). She argues that engaging the readership in the publication established continuity between the lives of readers and the print medium, encouraging them to consult the popular periodical for instruction on their private lives. Indeed, the regular publication of the *GOP* meant that it could take girls through the issues they would face and teach them the skills in which they would need to be competent, from pre-puberty to marriage and beyond. Girls' engagement with the *GOP* also extended beyond its pages and into the world. In 1881, a competition seeking submissions of needlework and paintings resulted in a 'Girl's Own Exhibition', and appeals were occasionally made to readers for donations to initiate and maintain charitable ventures, one of which was 'The Girl's Own Home'. The home was established from readers' funds to aid London's 'working girls' and is marketed as 'a home of your own for them' (1881, p. 59), showing the paper's complex class interactions, in which the middle-class reader is privileged above the working-class reader.

In addition to the weekly puzzle competitions, there were regular prize competitions which enabled girl readers to publish written and photographic works. Substantial essays authored by girls beginning in 1880 on 'The Life of Some Famous English Woman Born in the Eighteenth Century' and continuing with 'My Daily Round' ('A Competition for All Girls Who Work with Their Hands') (1896) and 'My Room', to select two of many examples, were usually published across a few editions of the paper. The third prize essay in 'My Daily Round' is written by a downtrodden girl whose mother has died and who is left to care for her siblings and sew shirts from home, while nursing her invalid sister. Her day comprises paid work from home, domestic tasks to care for her siblings, and nursing for her sister, but she claims to be satisfied that she is doing good, rather than expressing a wish for leisure time: 'at 27 (my age then) I did not feel equal to the responsibilities of father, mother, husband, & wife together with the duties of nurse, but still after nearly a year's trial I am proud of my home hospital & pleased to think I am useful to others…' (1896, p. 117).

The winning essays embody the conceptions of self-sacrifice, concern for the poor, and domestic capability that the paper espouses in its own non-fiction articles. In her analysis of the *Athenian Mercury*, Shevelow suggests that self-representations contributed by women readers could function prescriptively (1989, p. 61). The creation of public discourse out of the private lives of women constructed a desirable model of femininity (Shevelow, 1989, p. 190). Indeed, the published tales written by girls about their own lives, as selected by the *GOP* editors, were public examples of how girls should ideally live: that is, by avoiding idleness and non-productive or non-improving time. For instance, 'Carnation', the winner of the 1897 competition for 'Stay at Home Girls', tells of reading to elderly women at a workhouse, meetings with the Girls' Friendly Society, preparing meals for her siblings, taking communion, and studying to be a Sunday school teacher. The diverse essays contributed by middle-class girls to the 'Competition for Professional Girls' followed the *GOP*'s prescriptive advice about leisure (a subject that was not a focus of the essays in 'My Daily Round'). Agnes Eugenie Smith, a nurse who won the first prize in the competition, in addition to the long, sacrificial hours her work requires, writes about the alternate afternoons of leisure the hospital allows:

> I do not for one moment hold that we should, as it were step outside the world altogether – should give up our music and singing, our bicycling and our visiting – by no means! A girl will find in her time off duty that a run on her 'bike', or an hour at the piano, and even a pleasant chat over a cosy cup of afternoon tea will all help to invigorate her, and so she will be more fitted for her evening's work, than if e.g. she had gone to her *bed*. ('Competition for Professional Girls', 1897, p. 412)

Shevelow's argument that early periodicals provided their readers with images of themselves can be applied to the newly emerging identity of the British girl reader and the *GOP*. Shevelow maintains that the printing of readers' letters, poetry, and essays 'concretised a reading public on the page' (1989, p. 48), and indeed the *GOP* achieved this for the late Victorian and Edwardian girl reader. Girls wrote to the 'Answers to Correspondents' column about miscellaneous issues, with a focus on advice on employment, artistic work, education, and health. The column proved so popular that it was often necessary to extend its span of pages in order to keep up with reader demand for answers. The eagerness of girls to correspond with the *GOP* is potentially puzzling when one considers the sometimes blunt tone of replies regarding girls' prospects. For instance, a girl under the pseudonym 'Free Flowing' is advised to consider being a domestic help in place of a governess: 'You are not sufficiently well qualified to take a situation as a governess. Your writing is too bad, and your grammar incorrect' ('Answers', 1891, p. 16). The ideals of usefulness espoused in the non-fiction articles are also reinforced in the editor's answers to girls who are advised against novel-reading, daydreaming, and early engagements (18 and under); they are given assistance in learning how to obtain passage to the colonies and are criticised for careless spelling and handwriting. In the face of the often harsh editorial responses, becoming a part of the visible readership community through letter-writing was nevertheless important for the *GOP* reader. Girls sought to translate their reading to active contribution not only through letters, but also submitted essays, artwork, photographs, crafts, and performed acts of charity, aware that their participation would be read through the prescriptive advice the *GOP* gave about ideal behaviour, essay composition, and so on.

Advertising, empire, and the girl consumer

The late Victorian era is a critical one for the development of the printed advertisement, not only because of a rapidly expanding periodical market but also because of the formation of the girl consumer as a largely discrete entity. Beetham suggests that magazines, as commodities that advertise other commodities, are 'deeply involved in capitalist production and consumption as well as circulating in the cultural economy of collective meanings and constructing an identity for the individual reader as gendered and sexual being (1996, p. 2). The gendered identities constructed for late Victorian and Edwardian girls in *GOP* advertisements, as future wives and mothers, are inextricably entangled with imperial concerns, primarily through the assertion of the superiority of British commodities and fixation on products' capacity to ensure physical strength, but also through the representation of the British civilising function, in soap ads particularly.

In the pages of the widely circulating *GOP*, targeted at girls who were still forming their purchasing tastes, and also to be viewed by their mothers, advertisements were placed in their own supplement, which was included in the monthly parts in addition to indexes and coloured plates. Those magazines bound into annuals from their weekly or monthly parts have had their covers and advertising supplements removed. My consideration of advertisements is restricted to those numbers that I could source unbound – rarities, given their comparative fragility – or on microfilm, which are concentrated in the period from 1899 to 1905. The advertisements that are available nevertheless indicate the way in which commodity culture became ingrained in the construction of the late Victorian and Edwardian ideal girl and girls' culture. Given the amount of leisure time that the middle-class adolescent girl had, particularly as she delayed marriage longer than her predecessors, the girl occupied a period in which she could buy goods but did not necessarily have to conduct paid work. The purchasing of suitable objects, as Rachel Bowlby suggests, also enables the construction of self as 'social subject' (1985, p. 28). In the largest periodical for the newly forming category of girl reader, her identity was being built not only as a reader, but also as a consumer.

Thomas Richards connects the excess of commodities displayed at the 1851 Crystal Palace exhibition with the belief that English economic productivity served the interests of empire and was a blueprint for the world (1990, p. 120). English commodities, even when taken into the colonial world, asserted their superior 'Englishness' against the foreign: 'For in the hands of the 1890's advertisers the commodity was represented as the bulwark of Empire – as both a stabilizing influence and a major weapon in England's struggle against a bewildering variety of enemies' (Richards, 1990, p. 142). The alliance between the commodity and the state that Richards identifies is also present in *GOP* advertisements. This connection between consumer goods and empire is illustrated by an early-twentieth-century advertisement for Bovril (Figure 1.1).

The large heading reads 'How the British Empire spells Bovril', with the pictorial representations of British territory inserted in jigsaw style into the product name (1904, pp. 2–3). The explanatory text further spells out this connection of consumer goods and the Empire: 'And illustrates the close association of this Imperial British Nourishment with the whole of King Edward's Dominions at Home and Beyond the Seas'. Another advertisement, for Quaker Oats, depicts the commodity as resulting from connections between the countries that compose the British Empire, with the Oats presented as 'The Empire's Breakfast', produced by Britain's subjects elsewhere:

> From British soil by British folk,
> These oats are shipped in British oak
> To England where they soon provoke
> *The Smile that won't come off*
> Because these Quaker Oats are grown
> In countries that are Britain's own … (1903, p. 7)

HOW the BRITISH EMPIRE spells BOVRIL

NOTE.

The shapes are correct, but the sizes are not in proportion.

Each number indicates a separate part of the Empire.

And illustrates the close association of this Imperial British Nourishment with the whole of King Edward's Dominions at Home and Beyond the Seas. How many parts can you name?

Figure 1.1 Bovril advertisement, the *Girl's Own Paper*, Christmas advertisement sheet, 1904, p. 2–3.

The countries of the Empire are clearly identified as 'British', and the benefits of imperial domination flow through to English families at their breakfast tables who enjoy the consumer spoils. The positive resonances of empire are also shown as benefiting colonised peoples who are depicted in advertisements in the *GOP*. The Christmas advertisement supplement in 1902 includes a full-page advertisement for Sunlight Soap, which shows a black baby with a black doll (Figure 1.2). Anne McClintock's perceptive study of the relationship between soap advertising and empire notes a shift in imperialist culture at the end of the nineteenth century in which 'scientific racism' was superseded by 'commodity racism' which 'converted the imperial progress narrative into mass-produced consumer spectacles' (1994, p. 133). Soap became intrinsically related to the civilising mission in advertisements, providing a connection between gendered domestic work and racial improvement. The delicate lace clothing the child wears is impeccably white, rehearsing one of the four 'fetishes' of soap advertising that McClintock identifies, and the heading of the advertisement reinforces the contrast between the child's dark skin and the purity of clean clothing: 'So Clean and White' (1902, p. 4). This ad evokes the civilising function developed elsewhere in the *GOP*, in which British girls and women were encouraged to improve conditions in British colonies for their native inhabitants. It also crudely supports the tenor of non-fiction articles published throughout the decades of the *GOP* that highlighted white women's civilising capabilities, with its suggestion that contact with British women or goods could give them a veneer of acceptable whiteness, even if their ultimate difference was acknowledged as unchangeable.

A small proportion of the *GOP*'s readership was aged in their twenties and thirties, and indeed the 1908 transition to becoming a 'women's

Figure 1.2   Sunlight Soap advertisement, the *Girl's Own Paper*, October advertisement supplement, 1902, p. 4.

magazine' as well as a girls' publication was surely built upon a pre-existing adult readership. Patterns of consumption, however, Richards suggests, were first formed at adolescence, when biology became a reason to desire commodities (1990, pp. 243–4). Medical discourse invaded advertising to produce pills that promised to cure sometimes all or a range of ailments (such as Carter's Little Liver Pills, Eno's 'Fruit Salt', Owbridge's Lung Tonic, Bile Beans for Biliousness), solutions for the menstruating girl who wanted to remain active (Southall's Sanitary Towels, Hartmann's Hygienic Towellettes, Beecham's Pills ('specially suited for the ailments peculiar to Females of all ages')), and skin treatments that promised to improve the complexion (Dr Mackenzie's arsenical soap, Rowland's Kalydor – for the removal of freckles, tans, and cure of skin redness and roughness). Such was their prevalence, particularly in the religious press, that Lori Anne Loeb proposes that in 1880 patent medicine advertisements comprised one-quarter of all periodical advertisements (1994, p. 105). Building stronger girls is the focus of many ads that proffer potions and pills that promise to cure frail bodies and feeble or nervous constitutions, connecting with the magazine's editorial presentation of physical strength as essential to cultivating ideal femininity. While the precise forms of physicality that were acceptable were contested, these advertisements supported the *GOP*'s own text in seeking to rid girls of physical weakness that could impair their ability to be productive centres of their homes.

Some advertisements were presented in article format with no illustration, lending them greater authority and scope for drawing on medical authorities. An advertorial for Mother Seigel's Curative Syrup includes the testimonial of Miss Sarah Harriett Austin. The ad contends, 'plenty of women are more courageous than some big men, but then their nerves are alright' (1900, p. 2), which stands in contrast with the tale of Austin, who suffered from rapid loss of flesh such that her clothing hung from her (she was 'as thin as a shadow'). She lay on the couch all day and 'became extremely nervous and could not bear the least noise, or anyone to speak to me' (1900, p. 2). In this advertisement, 'an eminent medical authority' says that the root of acute nervousness is imperfect digestion and 'impurities in the food supply' (1900, p. 2). Many other advertisements featured in the *GOP* cited medical authorities, from the *Lancet* to the *GOP*'s own doctor, to support the efficacy of products that were not even medicinal in nature, such as toffee and jellies.

Loeb argues that concerns about deviancy and disease enabled many advertisements to connect private consumption to nationalistically infused public goals such as community health and sanitation: 'This prevalent marketing strategy eschews the self-interest of buyers and sellers for a commercial brand of altruism that pushes the consumer to consider realities beyond the walled garden' (1994, p. 152). The clearest publicly directed goal of *GOP* advertisements was ensuring the health of children, who were the future custodians of the nation and the Empire. In addition to foods such as custard powder, oats, and relish, many advertisements proclaimed products that promised to aid girls in maintaining the health of those in their care, or for whom they would care in womanhood. They also draw on the idea of encouraging strength in the nation's children through better nutrition. An advertisement for Van Houten's Cocoa illustrates a nursery scene in which a mother delivers warm cocoa to her three children, who are seated at a table. The text, which promotes the cocoa's encouragement of 'health, strength and good digestion', clearly invests child-rearing with implications for the nation: 'The nursery is the training ground of the future generation. Whether the manhood and womanhood of the next decade will be physically and mentally healthy and vigorous depends largely upon the manner in which the children are fed' (1904, p. 3). The girls of the period were ascribed responsibility for the purchasing decisions that would determine whether Britain's future children were adequately nourished. This example is not as pointedly connected with defence of the Empire as an exemplary Eno's Fruit Salt advertisement from 1889 in which the consumption of the product is credited, via a testimonial taken from *Mess Stories*, with the winning of Kandahar during the Afghan War (Hindley and Hindley, 1972, pp. 98–9). Nevertheless, by playing upon the concerns developed in *GOP* articles that connected health with national strength, these advertisements entangled girls' purchasing power as consumers with the fate of nation and, by extension, its empire. The focus shifts from 'ensuring male potency in the arena of war' (1994, p. 149), as McClintock suggests of Eno's marketing, to equipping future mothers with the consumer goods that would ensure their own strength and capacity to raise healthy children, in whom the future of the Empire is invested.

Situating the British girl internationally

At the same time as producing an idealised vision of British girlhood, the *GOP* sought to create an international community of girl readers, particularly among its imperial outposts. One editor suggests that all readers are embraced as 'our girls' whether they are 'British or foreign, old or young, correspondents or only readers' ('Answers', 1884, p. 383). Nevertheless, while the definition of 'Britishness' encompassed girls of British parentage in imperial locations, 'foreign' girls were clearly not the implied readers of the paper. By the beginning of the twentieth century, the quantity of letters received from girls who wished to correspond with others from overseas (which included girls writing from 'Buda-pesth' and Shanghai, China) was so plentiful that they were removed from the correspondence column and inserted into the advertisements page of the monthly parts and weekly numbers. In this 'Girl's Own Column' girls could also buy from and sell to each other, advertise that they were seeking a work situation, and exchange items such as 'pictorial post-cards'.

The non-fiction articles thoroughly detail the magazine's outlook upon the community of girls worldwide and the relationship of British girls to this community. 'The Girls of the World' series (1885–6) by Emma Brewer foregrounds the future of England with emphasis on the treatment and education of its girls. It also draws together thematic foci regarding femininity and empire: proficient mothering, 'civilising' at home and abroad, and 'usefulness' (which could culminate in work overseas). The first article in the series presents statistics of greater male infant mortality. While the survival rate of girls is used overtly to counteract perceptions of girls as 'delicate, fragile flowers' (Brewer, 1885, p. 95), the mortality rate of boys also implicitly raises concerns about mothering and national strength. The third article suggests that English girls are superior to boys in the areas of reading, spelling, and imagination. This serves to champion their suitability to establish schools in places such as India to combat ignorance, idleness, and superstition among native girls. Lack of education nevertheless connotes savagery not only for those in India, but also for the poor at home in England, who are labelled 'criminal': 'They have often had no training but in vice, and not unfrequently they are more uncivilised than the savage' (1886, p. 269). Brewer identifies a place for girls to 'civilise' not only indigenous peoples but also the working classes at home. The article on 'occupations' explicitly connects idleness with unhappiness and disease. It encourages girls to be useful to others (contributing to the wealth of the country), but also interprets the occupations open to women as signs of a nation's degree of civility (1886, p. 346). The individual is flawed if she is idle, yet, at a national level, swathes of idle people are symptomatic of deterioration. One avenue identified for the direction of women's and girls' work is in the colonies, such as Australia where there are '1,342,680 women and girls, nearly two-thirds of whom are cheerfully and resolutely setting to work with hands and brains to do their part in the elevation of women by means of steady persistent work' (1886, p. 349). Girls' and women's labour is vital not only for combating idleness, and its bedfellow national deterioration, but also for their own advancement, a combination that I shall discuss below with regard to feminist appropriations of civilising discourse.

While the *GOP* published articles that condemned girls who were too independent or who mimicked masculine traits, these restrictions coexisted with the prevalent belief that the better conditions for women and girls in England signified its superiority. In the third chapter in Brewer's series, she writes, 'Perhaps there is no surer test of the real condition of a country than the position of its women and girls, and there is no denying that in these days it is a noble and important one in most of the civilised countries of the world' (1885, p. 198). Women are allocated a valued and vital role in the development of the nation by governing the home and influencing their fathers, brothers, and husbands:

> If we keep these homes of ours pure, refined, and virtuous, we wage war against decay, and occupy the proud place of helping to build up the country, and strengthen the hands of the State. [...] Wherever the homes of the land fall below this standard, statistics prove that the strength, life, and progress of that country is sapped, notwithstanding its armies, its laws, and its institutions. (1885, p. 198)

Therefore, every girl's education is vitally important, regardless of class, as all have the 'power' to form their children into strong, moral citizens. The poor are nevertheless specifically important in terms of improving hygiene (for disease prevention) and curtailing general depravity. For instance, Brewer claims that where domestic and social traits have been improved through the education of working-class girls and women 'there is less crime, less drunkenness, less scandal, less improvidence' (1885, p. 198). Education of the working classes promises to elevate them from these moral ills and halt the 'decay' that Brewer blames for stymieing national progress.

In Chapter 2, I discuss the relationship of formal education to preparing girls for imparting the right morals to their families, a role that Meg Gomersall describes as that of a 'moral missionary' (1997, p. 79). In a cultural climate in which formal education increasingly involved domestic instruction, in the *GOP*, girls' education is praised for its potential to make England's women better wives and mothers, and also more useful citizens in their own right. Not only did the magazine include articles on girls' life at colleges, but it also criticised attitudes that rendered women ineligible to be admitted to examinations because of the belief that it would 'unsex' them and render them poor mothers and wives, such as in 'Education for Women at Oxford' (1884, p. 695). As Laura Morgan Green contends, domestic ideology was also used by feminists to advocate for the involvement of women in the public sphere, and in turn the moral and religious responsibilities that accompanied it supported the contention that women's societal involvement benefited the nation (2001, p. 6). Arguments for women's further education, therefore, often suggested that it would increase capacity for 'womanly' duties, rather than situating education in opposition to the domestic. The *GOP* shared the view that education was not necessarily a threat to the work of wife and mother. Women's advancement is supported in Norma Lorimer's 'The Strides of Women', in which she praises the women of Queen Victoria's reign for being pioneers of women rights, and the queen herself for enabling change: 'Women are now no longer dubbed "bluestockings", or regarded as unwomanly if they go in for a college education, or adopt a profession which at once places them on the place of equality, intellectual and practical, with men' (1898, p. 570).

The New Woman, feminists, and educated women such as the 'Girton Girl' were, however, often the subject of ridicule in the wider periodical press.[5] In championing the cause of female education, the *GOP*, however, marks intelligent, stimulated women as a sign of civilisation. While domestic work is clearly not to be neglected or avoided, the *GOP* maintains that it is not a woman's destiny merely to sit and darn: 'Why was she endowed with mental faculties, if they were not be used?' (Lee, 1892, p. 285). This is not to suggest that the *GOP* promotes intellectual pursuits for their own sake. Rather, intellectual training can help a woman become a better companion to her husband, a better sister to her brothers, and a better mother to her children. Moreover, intellectual pursuits need not be opposed with womanliness, but may assist her in being a better trainer of the future generations.

The *GOP* not only conceived of an ideal British girl subjectivity, but also compared her with girls of the world, who were often depicted as less fortunate or less emancipated than their British counterparts. From 1883 to 1884, there were features on French, Belgian, Swedish, Mongolian, Russian, Italian, Greek, and German girls. 'A Dutch Girl' champions the English girl's progressive freedoms as superior to the conditions in which girls live overseas, even within Western nations. The Dutch girl is described as looking up to the English girl because the

English girl can take up employment yet not lose her womanly manners, whereas the Dutch girl may lose her caste position if she works: 'So it is no wonder that the girls look on England as the land of promise, where woman, though not *un*womanly, can be independent and still considered' (Stratenus, 1884, p. 797).

The *GOP* situated British girls in the colonies as equal addressees who were integral to its readership, encouraging their participation in its competitions and seeking to direct their conduct: 'How varied are the surroundings amid which THE GIRL'S OWN PAPER is perused by its multitudes of readers! While numbers are reading it around English fire-sides, others are enjoying it at the height of an Australian summer, and others again in a burning tropical clime' ('A Zenana Missionary', 1885, p. 492). Native girls in countries such as India are, however, more often constructed as the subject of concern for British girls, rather than being included in the worldwide readership community. The preceding observation about the *GOP*'s readers introduces an article on the life of girls in India, in which girls are separated into two categories: English girls living in India and native Indian girls. As the author, 'a Zenana Missionary', conducts a tour through Bombay, we are led to the house of an English family and are informed that many of the ladies in dwellings such as this do not do anything to help 'the poor native women'. We are also encouraged to sympathise for English girls born in India whose parents have not been able to return them to their homeland: 'Did it ever occur to you that there could be English girls who have never seen snow in the winter, nor primroses in the spring, and who have no idea of the autumnal glory of our woods?' (1885, p. 492). This passage casts doubt upon whether girls born of English parentage in India can be entirely civilised because of the environment in which they have been raised, much like Mary Lennox in Frances Hodgson Burnett's *The Secret Garden*, but they are nevertheless classified as 'English'.

There is hope for these girls, in the English-speaking schools in the cities; a hope which is contrasted with the 'darker picture' of the life of the native Hindu girl who was formerly subject to female infanticide and is still compelled to marry at an early age (as young as five or six) (Figure 1.3). Additionally, the form of womanhood depicted – one of near imprisonment in the zenanas without physical exercise – is condemned and sensationally rendered. Inderpal Grewal suggests that the zenana took on the symbolic function of the harem, which was similarly seen as problematic and evil, and the Indian woman was figured as passive and exploited (1996, p. 51). In this *GOP* article, the suggestion that dolls have been put into palanquins 'to amuse a child-bride'

THE FORMER METHOD OF LETTING GIRL INFANTS "CEASE TO LIVE."

Figure 1.3   Illustration of the practice of female infanticide. A Zenana Missionary, 'Girl Life in India', The *Girl's Own Paper*, 6, 1885, 492.

reinforces the disdain and alarm at the treatment of the Indian girl, who is figured as lacking the important training period of girlhood before being pushed into womanhood. The missionary orphanages and schools for native girls are therefore praised for their improving potential: 'from these many lightbearers go forth to dark homes around; but such girls can hardly be counted by hundreds, while there are millions of heathens' (1885, p. 494). The emphasis on the amount of work yet to be done to enlighten the 'millions' of non-Christians in India about English customs serves as a call to substantial numbers of British *GOP* readers.

Social Darwinism could encompass ideas of white racial superiority that justified conquering and colonisation as well as fears about racial deterioration and its potential to threaten global domination. By playing upon social Darwinist discourse, feminists used the Indian woman as a figure by which to justify the British civilising mission and a way in which to advance arguments for English women's emancipation. Antoinette Burton notes that colonial concerns, specifically the perception of the 'trapped' Indian woman in the zenana that this article reproduces, enabled the professionalisation of female doctors in the Victorian period (1996, p. 369). She argues that as the civilising mission became entangled with the idea of professional work for women, empire 'gave the very category of women's work new and permissible scope, national and imperial prestige, and a secular, world-civilizing status as well' (1996, p. 390). The feminist cause and the expanding realm of women's work was linked with the maintenance of the British Empire, just as lobbying for physical education for schoolgirls was connected with social Darwinist concerns about racial strength.

The missionary who authored this article took a copy of the paper into a zenana in order to teach a 'bibi' (Indian wife or consort) the pattern of a jacket for a child. The use of the paper to improve the Indian woman's care of her child and domestic capabilities is illustrative of the *GOP*'s aim to encourage a widespread 'elevation' of native women in British territory through the work of its girls: 'Now, dear girls, I have not been telling you all this simply to entertain you; I want to interest you for a higher purpose, that you may do what you can for the poor Indian girls who are without your advantages' (1885, p. 494). The stark comparison between the English girl and her 'imprisoned' Indian counterpart is an example of the feminist rhetoric that constructed Indian women as helpless colonial subjects. Early feminists used the Victorian ideals that endowed women with a moral superiority (and the potential to 'improve' or 'civilise') in order to support their efforts to enable women to move beyond the private sphere and affirm an emancipated role in the realm of the British Empire (Burton, 1992, p. 138). Burton argues that by twisting the ideology of racial superiority, which suggested that the strength of the nation would dwindle if mothers were occupied outside the home, liberal feminists used 'racial responsibility' as a strategy to justify their work as 'imperial citizens' (Burton, 1992, p. 138).[6] Rather than being perceived as a threat to social order, the woman working to 'civilise' in the name of her country and her empire became a racial saviour and an idealised example of womanhood.

Into the twentieth century, the supposed suffering of the Indian girl, who is deprived of an education and forced into marriage and hard work at an age when English girls were still playing with toys, remained a subject of concern. Girls are again implored to help these 'miserable' sisters in the 1901 article 'Child-Wives': 'If the girls of England only realised the needs of their Eastern sisters, they would do their utmost to share with them the good things they themselves enjoy, the best of all being the knowledge of God and His Son …. There is not one amongst us who cannot do something. Have we done it?' (Dibdin, 1901, p. 805). While author Emily Dibdin encourages religious charity, she also portrays the Indian woman, or in this case, girl, as inferior to Western women in order to prove the unique place of British women as civilisers. Other articles and responses to correspondents provide advice as to how English girls can aid India's less fortunate girls and women through educational, spiritual, and medical missionary work. A striking example is found in the series 'Medical Women for India', in which physician Frances E. Hoggan discusses women who teach girls in the zenanas, noting the brevity of Indian girls' formal education (1884, pp. 281–3). These vignettes of Indian girls consistently invoke negative comparisons when considered alongside the vision of the educated, useful, and independent English 'new girl', whom the *GOP* alternately praised and criticised.

The 'new girl' and the physical ideal

Terri Doughty argues that the *GOP*'s editor, Charles Peters, contained the 'new girl', who walked a precarious tightrope between childhood and marriage, 'by providing content that fed into the development of an idealized girl culture while still seeming to direct girl readers away from the more 'dangerous' aspects of that culture' (2004, p. 9). The 'self-culture' the *GOP* encouraged, she suggests, was not progressive but intended to prevent idleness and prepare her for her role as wife and mother (Doughty, 2004, p. 57). Indeed, combating idleness in the adolescent years is a prime fixation of the *GOP*. If girls are lazy in youth, then it is feared that their character in later life will be fixed: 'And yet if the girl is mother to the woman – that is to say, if the woman will be what the girl now is, this time, which is essentially one for settling habits, cannot be anything less than the most important in life. If the girl spends it in thoughtless idleness and discontented trifling, the result will be seen in the character of the woman' (Author of 'How to be Happy Though Married', 1886, pp. 769–70). Throughout the paper, girlhood is conceived of as a brief opportunity in which to inculcate desirable qualities.

While 'doing one's duty' as a girl in preparation for womanhood is often presented as a prelude to marriage, there is strong acceptance of single women who work with the right motivations and without 'roughness'. This tendency may have stemmed from the surplus of women of marriageable age and the encouragement of emigration to find husbands or conduct work in the colonies; or more significantly because of the delayed marriage age for women in the late Victorian period which meant some women could live outside the family home before finding a husband. An article on 'Girls Then and Now' by Lily Watson suggests that 'today's girl' is more independent than the early Victorian girl: 'Such a phenomenon as the "Bachelor Girl", with a latchkey and chambers of her own, was unknown. The Professional Girl was a rarity. The Political Girl was nowhere to be found at all. The Revolting Daughter was (though here and there she might exist) by no means a conspicuous feature of society' (1903, p. 420). Famous figures who are praised for their actions as single women with a 'rightly lived' life include Florence Nightingale, Christina Rossetti, Miss Ingelow, Frances Mary Buss, Miss Mary Kingsley, and Ellen Watson.

Different articles by different authors in different years give contradictory views on the subject of the 'new girl', and on other contentious subjects such as work outside the home, independence, and exercise. Hilary Skelding notes the shifting notions of radical and domestic femininity inherent in the *GOP* and suggests that this reflected the uncertainty of women's place in the late nineteenth century (2001, p. 36). As the *GOP*'s readership spanned the working and middle classes, the ideals it encouraged also varied depending on which classes of girl were considered. The middle-class girl, for instance, was encouraged to help working-class girls improve their character, whereas the working-class girl would be warned against improper or mannish behaviour. The columns of Medicus (Dr Gordon Stables) regularly deviate from medical subjects and present conservative viewpoints on contemporary girlhood that are sometimes antifeminist. In the instance of the 'new girl', two years after the article that praised her national importance, Medicus argues that girls in their teens have become lazy, directionless, and boyish. The 'new girl' he situates as 'a second edition of the new woman. Just an imbecile offshoot' (1904, p. 107). He is particularly concerned about what he terms the 'tom-girl' in her late teens and early twenties who renders herself unmarriageable because she believes she can care for herself (living a 'half-he' life) and ignoring knowledge of housework (1904, p. 107). She is contradictorily portrayed as active as a 'tom-girl', yet also idle in reading 'trashy love-serials of the every-day magazines' (1904, p. 107). This contradiction embodies the two greatest social fears connected with imperial maintenance: namely that girls and women would neglect mothering and domestic tasks if they undertook 'masculine' pursuits, and that inefficiency and laziness in individual citizens would make for a weak nation.

Fear for the health of the nation emerges in this column, as Stables suggests that the aristocracy are weak and depend upon the recruitment of healthy members of the middle classes. The 'new girl' is seemingly a threat to maintaining a strong middle class, not only because she will not care for her husband and children effectively, but also because she damages herself physically and mentally with her idleness: 'Her spine gets bent forward like a raspberry cane, and her head refuses after a time to poise well...She gets stout about the waist, loses her figure and never grows, or if she does grow, it is to lankiness and scragginess. The mind suffers; it becomes languid and lax' (1904, p. 108). Within such conservative ideology that seeks to bolster racial strength, exercise for girls is promoted as essential for ensuring their own physical health and also that of the children they will bear in future. Girlhood is the critical time in which to form the woman physically, morally, and intellectually. If, like Medicus' metaphor of the raspberry cane, a girl begins to take an undesirable form in her juvenile years, it will be impossible to correct the 'deformity' of character or body in adulthood when both will already be set.

In the *GOP*'s first decades, physical education was recognised as important for girls for forming a healthy body, with emphasis upon fostering a strong base of citizens rather than girls' independence or equality with boys. Intellectual and physical education were critically interrelated, with a balance between the two pursuits advocated in the *GOP* and pedagogical texts of the period. As I discuss in Chapter 2, by the 1890s physical education was incorporated into the curricula of most schools for middle-class girls, and the inception of Swedish gymnastics saw girls of the lower classes gain access to some form of institutionalised exercise. Increasing anxiety about the health of the nation saw opposition to active lifestyles for girls and women, within the parameters of feminine behaviour, decline. Madame (Martina Bergman) Österberg was appointed by the London School Board as the first Swedish women's gymnastics teacher in 1878 and founded her own Physical Training College in 1885. Österberg lobbied for a national system of gymnastics in schools by connecting the playing of games with stimulating brave deeds and noble thoughts – ideas that became integrated in British nationalism (Hargreaves, 1994, p. 75). As Jennifer Hargreaves argues, Österberg promoted the social Darwinist view that the nation could be improved only through strengthening its future mothers physically and morally: 'Justifications for female exercise idealized the woman's body and her ability to bear healthy children' (1994, p. 77). As feminist reformers had played on these concerns to support their arguments for women's emancipation, so too did the reformers of physical education.

The beliefs of headmistresses who promoted physical education in girls' schools, such as Österberg and Frances Buss of the North London Collegiate School, which held that mental activity and physical exercise were complementary, are evident in the *GOP*'s depictions of sport. The paper suggests that sport improves the nervous dispositions girls once commonly claimed to suffer from, and sport strengthens their characters and physical forms, under the rubric of a sound mind in a sound body.[7] One article praises the 'disappearance of all false notions as to the charm of the anaemic complexion, wasp-like waist, and tendency to swoon on the slightest provocation' (Watson, 1902, p. 61) that is achieved by moderate athleticism. Yet the encouragement of physical activity in order to complement the intellect or assist in mothering is tempered, as in Sir Benjamin Ward Richardson's 'On Recreation for Girls', by instruction to avoid competitiveness, steer clear of roughness, and ensure that recreational games do not impinge upon domestic duties: 'One of the great dangers at the present time is that women, in their anxiety to compete in various recreative exercises, are given to forget the fact that, *nolens volens*, they are born to do what men can never do; that if the race is to progress they must some day become mothers, that they must undertake special maternal duties ...' (1894, p. 546). Excessive cultivation of competition and strength may create an incompatible opposition with the traits of mothering, making a girl vulgar and unsuitable for training children.

The development of organised sports in boys' public schools initially imbued physical activity with masculine associations such as endurance and aggression. Therefore, while the *GOP* encouraged girls' participation in team games and solitary exercise, inevitable qualifications were added. In 'Man-Games That Murder Beauty', Stables laments the loss of womanly elegance in girls who 'go in for these hoydenish man-games and tom-boy exercises' (1907, p. 503). If girls participate in exercises that he deems appropriate only for boys, such as hockey, running and jumping, golf, and cricket (after the age of 15), then they will lose their beauty and potentially gain 'square jaws and flabby mock-turtle cheeks' (the result of cycling excessively) (1907, p. 503). Indeed, cycling was the sport upon which debates about girls' exercise concentrated, and it was the most frequently discussed and illustrated, with a competition to find the prettiest photograph of a girl riding a bicycle conducted in 1896. In 'The Dress for Bicycling', Dora De Blaquiére promotes cycling as an emancipator of women, and a healthy pursuit if girls do not strain themselves (1895, p. 12).

Stables' columns encouraged self-discipline, such as regulating the time of rising in the morning, conducting light exercises, eating slowly, employing the mind and body, caring for the teeth, and so on (1892, p. 427). More than a decade earlier, he suggested that it is crucial that this advice be instilled in girls rather than women, because 'evil habits' are compared with weeds: easy to pull out when small, but not when they have been permitted to take root (1884, pp. 218–19). Girls must learn something good each day in order to cultivate acceptable 'mental and moral habits' in adult life. Stables' advice often deviated from health and into the general behaviour and outlook of girls such as loosening their tight corsets, not wearing too much frippery, and avoiding idleness. In a column devoted to the subject, he suggests that work is the lot of all beings, and its avoidance threatens the health of the individual and society. The metaphor he uses, recalling broader fears of racial degeneration, is one of disease: 'Idleness, indeed, is a kind of a moral cancer that eats away all nervous power, and ends by totally destroying both health and happiness' (1884, p. 622). In this equation of physical well-being with moral health, idleness took on the characteristics of a supreme sin. This 'sin', which the Girl Guides organisation would later rally against, also attracts disdain in the *GOP*. In the following section, the countries of the British Empire are presented as requiring the 'civilising influence' of British girls, and within this conception it is unthinkable that girls should sit at home in boredom. As James Mason remarks in the article 'About Industry and Idleness', 'Beyond ourselves and beyond our homes lies the great world calling upon us incessantly to lend our aid so long as sickness and poverty and ignorance endure' (1881, pp. 707–8).

Living and working in the Empire

In an article from 1906 on 'Empire Day', the British relationship with the Empire is constructed as one in which its 'children' (Australia, Canada, New Zealand, India, Burma, the West Indies, Egypt, and South Africa) need its consideration for their advancement. In return for fulfilling its obligations to the colonies, England can expect support in the event of war. Using the example of the struggle in South Africa and the assistance given by soldiers from Canada, Australia, and New Zealand, the article suggests: 'Keep in tough [sic] with your colonies, and you will never want for succourers' (1906, p. 491). Once again, a unique part for English girls as moral guides is located in the imperial project:

> Girls of England, your influence is beyond anything that you can conceive of. You can do so much to enlarge the thoughts and ideas of those around you. Your brothers, and later on your lovers, will look

to you for the high inspiration of their lives... they look to you to
help them with your strong faith, with your large-heartedness, with
your high ideals. (1906, p. 491)

Yet there is not only a general suggestion that girls will influence their
children when they become mothers for the good of the nation, but
a plea for readers to influence British colonies: 'It is for you – the girl-
readers of the "G.O.P." – to help us to draw that loving arm of Britannia
more closely round her daughter [the Colonies]. Girls of Britain, do
not fail us!' (p. 491). Girls' place in the imperial project may extend
beyond raising healthy children to working to civilise or populate the
colonies.

Rosemary Marangoly George, building upon the work of Gayatri
Chakravorty Spivak in 'Three Women's Texts and a Critique of
Imperialism' (1985), which constructs the white female subject as
dependent upon imperialism, also argues that the 'modern female subject' in England was established through the colonial occupation of
India. As I discussed earlier, this 'full individual' self, as George terms
the attainment of an emancipated female subject, was achieved through
defining the English woman against the racial Other. However, she
argues that this was largely achieved through the English home in the
colonies because they enabled encounters with the comparatively 'inferior' colonial subject. The domestic, when tied to the goals of empire,
George suggests, was prescribed as the most fulfilling location for the
modern female subject (1993–4, p. 97). In addition to depictions of life
in the colonies in serial fiction, such as several Australian stories by
Ethel Turner, and the frequent provision of advice of in the correspondence column on how to emigrate, girl and women writers contributed
their own accounts of setting up a life or homes in Africa ('Letter from
Zululand' (1903)), and on a farm in a harsh region of Canada ('A Sketch
of Farm Life in Manitoba' (1902)). Preparation for domestic life in an
'uncivilised' country is encouraged.

While not set in a British colony, a serial article by Julia Couron
describes the challenges of raising a child and maintaining a home in
Texas. Couron admires the natural environment, is distrustful of the
native 'Indians', and encourages girls to train themselves for the possibility that they too may have to leave England's comforts. She questions
why girls of all classes should not be made to practice the household
work necessary in an almost uncivilised country 'where they can obtain
no help, and must perforce work for themselves, or live in a state of perpetual untidiness and dirt' (1884, p. 776). She raises the possibility of

husbands needing to travel abroad in the event of financial difficulty, a situation that may befall any wife. Such a journey would prove impossible, however, if the woman knows nothing of managing her household and children, so she must be taught as a daughter, then she will easily 'fit the shoulder to the burthen' (1884, p. 776). Girlhood is again constructed as a unique period during which to equip oneself with the life skills that a woman will require. This perception of girlhood as a preparatory period prefigures the founding principle of the Girl Guides and a broader sense of national preparedness in the event of war, which I shall discuss with regard to nursing in Chapter 5.

The acceptance of girls' capacity to travel and endure hardship was important to champion if the *GOP* was to encourage colonial settlement and travel for employment opportunities such as nursing and missionary work. The *GOP* notes that more girls and women are travelling overseas, and this freedom to travel brings with it a new vision of womanhood:

> Our grandmothers. Why the very name brings back the thought of slim domestic girls in country gardens, busy with their *potpourri*, or their lavender bags, and content with their quiet reading of the *Vicar of Wakefield*, or the numberless stories of Miss Edgeworth, beginning with her *Purple Jar*. The very thought of crossing the channel was repugnant to the minds of our mothers' mothers.... whereas now we shake hands calmly with our nearest relations and receive their good wishes that we may not be too cold in Siberia nor roasted to death in Rangoon, with as much *sangfroid* as though we were going to the nearest town to do some shopping. (Wignall, 1898, pp. 582–3)

In this vision of the Empire, the world shrinks for the English girl, as travel to one of Britain's distant 'possessions' becomes as likely and accepted as local travel.

These accounts of female adventurers promote women's survival capacity in rough conditions, and their unique skills that could aid men. The adventures of female explorers were documented in Edward Whymper's 'Famous Lady Travellers' series of 1884–5, which included women who journeyed to Arabia, Fiji, and Hawaii. The first, a historical account of the Peruvian-born Madame Godin – who outlasted all the members in her expedition in the jungle – shows her to be as brave as any man (particularly braver than the native 'Indians' who desert the party). She cut the shoes from her dead brother's feet and travelled along through the jungle surviving on water and wild fruits (Whymper,

1884, p. 107). The second tale, of Lady Baker, emphasises the voluntary nature of her expedition to accompany her husband in 1862 to explore the sources of the Nile: 'It was a deliberate plunge into a region which was known to be full of dangers, and peopled by races exhibiting the worst characteristics of mankind' (1885, p. 353). Previously she had spent four years in equatorial Africa, where the Arabs she met were said to exclaim that there was no other woman in the world as tough. On the Nile expedition, despite suffering from a fever, Baker's feminine negotiating skills enabled her to prevent a mutiny, as she encouraged a compromise between her husband (the leader of the expedition) and a prisoner whom he had taken (1885, p. 354).

The established colonies were understood as prime locations for young British women to emigrate to, if they were in search of a husband, were in search of employment, or had been orphaned. An article on 'Miss Rye's Girls' Homes' documents the travel of a group of orphaned and ill-cared-for London girls who are to be taken to a 'great new land', Canada. To the girls, who may never have visited the British countryside, this journey is positioned as an adventure and an opportunity to counter the weakening effects of city life and factory work: 'Several had been taken from their little playmates in the alleys and dirty streets, and had never known what it is to see green fields and a sky unclouded by smoke' (1884, p. 488). The girls are appreciative of the lack of pollution and quietness, which means that unlike in England, '[t]here are no fevers, no agues, very little rheumatism, and even the stock of colds there is much less' (1884, p. 490). For the poorest of England's girls, the healthful opportunity to make a new life in a colony is considered preferable to life in England without sufficient parental guidance, yet it also aids in solving the problem of degeneration at home by removing those who populated the lowest societal rung.

Particularly in the aftermath of the Second Boer War, the paper encouraged girls to aid in the colonies and presented accounts of colonial girls. One article in the former category was a plea to educated English girls to teach girls in African schools to persist with tasks rather than shirking them, and to conduct domestic and nursing training (Johnson, 1900, p. 196). 'The Emigration of Girls to South Africa' also called for trained and capable women to aid in colonisation of 'our South African possessions'. This work was considered vital in tandem with the work of men despite the way in which people sometimes ignore 'the very important part women must necessarily take in the scheme of civilisation' ('The Emigration of Girls', 1902, p. 59). Single women are, in fact, very valuable for the Empire, as in the colonies there is 'unlimited scope' for women's work, particularly in South Africa, where the Boer women are labelled ignorant: 'Here is the opportunity for English women to show what they are made of, to show how they apply the spirit of Imperialism to themselves, to show they understand what "Empire" means. For surely it will be women's work to influence women' ('The Emigration of Girls', 1902, p. 59). For women living dull, purposeless lives, helping in 'this scheme of civilization' is presented as an exciting opportunity and one which promises a potential husband given the limited number of women in the Transvaal.

A serial diary of a nurse's voyage to aid the army in South Africa not only highlights the rugged terrain and difficulty of the work, but also creates a sense of adventure. The heroine stays in a mud hut, hears the beat of the sentry's tread outside during the night, and must cross fallen bridges. The anonymous writer conducts exhausting work tidying beds, washing patients, and setting the makeshift hospital at Dewetsdorp in order, while making do on field rations, yet she remarks: 'It's real nursing here, real war, and really interesting' ('Log of Voyage', 1900, p. 743). There is also the account of a young woman who relocated to South Africa to live on a farm in 1894, in part to improve her weak chest through the purportedly better climate. Colonial life is represented as challenging and potentially dangerous: 'I felt a wee bit nervous for they had no locks on any of the doors, only latches, nor any fastenings on the window, and there were any number of Kaffirs, snakes, and horrid crawley things about' (R.M.W., 1896, p. 571). The setting induces loneliness and is remotely located, away from churches, doctors, and the mail, all the markers of England. Despite the avowedly difficult conditions, 'Girl Volunteers for South Africa' suggests that over 3000 girls volunteered for 100 positions with the Board of Education teaching the Boer children. The living conditions are not glamourised (tents in camps with a shortage of water) and the life girls will endure is presented as far removed from the refinement presented in other articles on maintaining domestic order (1902, p. 243). To a limited extent, the *GOP* draws on adventure mythology in its presentation of work in the Empire, a method that is more fully realised in Bessie Marchant's novels and the first Girl Guide handbook.

Aiding the middle-class girl to work, and improving the working-class girl

The *GOP* did not promote a rebellious, individualistic girl subjectivity, but within its intent to encourage busy lives, which fulfilled a sense

of national duty, independent occupations for girls were regularly promoted. A series on 'New Employment for Girls' suggests that girls could
attempt work as a nurse, a midwife, a governess, or a foreign missionary,
as well as less typical occupations such as surgeon, dentist, chemist,
bank treasurer, and mandolin and zither playing. Nursing is promoted
in the 'Work for All' series on suitable employments for girls as not only
a useful competency for wives and mothers, but also a useful 'calling'
(1883, pp. 119–20). The approval of nursing as a suitable occupation
stems from its combination of caring for others and also the ability
to 'improve' them. For instance, girls are advised that British women
nurses and doctors are vital in India, where women will not seek treatment from male doctors. India presents not only an opportunity for
women's employment where it may not exist in Britain, and a chance
for improved medical care for the Indian women, but also an opportunity for these women to 'improve the tone of the female portion of the
British community in India'. Specifically, 'a careful study of the climate,
with reference to the laws of health, etc., may enable them to teach
their countrywomen how to enjoy the glories of the "Golden Indies"
with less cost of health and physical and moral energy' ('Work for All',
1883, p. 119).

Work itself was vital to the existence of the category of girlhood.
Sally Mitchell observes that work was a central component in the creation of a distinct period between childhood and adulthood (1994, p.
256).Within the framework of encouraging girls toward work that was
thought beneficial to England, women's work is presented as just as
skilled and valuable as that of men. Not all kinds of work are viewed
in this way, however. Work performed by the poor, unskilled, and relatively uneducated girl was seen as tragic. Gareth Stedman Jones's *Outcast
London* considers the implications of irregular and casualised work on
those who occupied the poorest rung of society. A labour surplus and
jobs that were paid from day to day and even hourly induced low living
standards and poverty, but moralisers instead blamed drunkenesss for
the lot of the working poor (Stedman Jones, 1971, p. 93). Not only was
there concern about 'semi-mendicant' or 'semi-criminal children' on
the streets (improved somewhat by compulsory school attendance after
the 1870 Education Act), but it was feared that the city of London was
a magnet for the idle, degenerate, and criminal 'residuum' of society,
who threatened to contaminate the classes above them (Stedman Jones,
1971, pp. 13, 85, 289). As such, Stedman Jones suggests that areas of
working-class housing were avoided by all but those who resided there,
including by most authorities: 'The poor districts became an immense

terra incognita periodically mapped out by intrepid missionaries and explorers who catered to an insatiable middle-class demand for travellers' tales' (1971, p. 14). The *GOP* depicts several such 'travellers' tales' in the guise of stories about working-class girls engaged in unskilled work.

Articles such as 'The Flower Girls of London' document the lives of sick and starving girls who live on the streets. They draw on the application of the 'civilising' function at home in England to figure girls of the lower working classes as the subject of pity and in need of aid just as much as girls located in non-Christian countries. In a later part of the serial (which ran from 1891 to 1892), the shady nature of some of the sellers is linked with the dirty, sickness-inducing conditions of their homes: 'In a girl's bringing up, the home is always a very important influence for good or for evil, and if some of those we have visited – pictures of wretchedness, want, and depravity – could be laid open to public gaze, there would be scarcely a dry eye among the beholders, that any of England's women and girls should be so lodged' ('Flower Girls', 1892, p. 283). The work of missionaries bound for 'heathens' overseas is contrasted with the situation of some of England's own girls who are 'untamed savage[s]': 'Will they find anywhere on the face of the earth vice more hideous, lives more miserable and wretched, than we can show them here?' ('Flower Girls', 1892, p. 283). Stedman Jones points out that, in an oversupplied labour market, the factory work most commonly performed by unmarried girls, such as making jam, confectionery, mineral water, hemp, jute, matches, and paper bags, was subject to fluctuation with the seasons and earnings were not only low, but irregular (1971, p. 85).

An article on girls employed in match manufacture in the East End of London attempts to reveal the lives of girls who require middle-class benevolent intervention to *GOP* readers and reinforces the idea that home influences rather than menial work itself produced bad characters and reckless natures. Author Lloyd Lester pities the debauched leisure activities the girls choose, such as penny shows, waxworks, drinking, and music halls, but he praises the effects of work conducted by 'Miss Nash' to improve the factory girls: 'There is more love for domestic virtues, and thrift in money matters' (p. 1895, 149). In this article, and the periodical generally, young women working with England's poor are constructed as undertaking a 'civilising' mission of as much national import as those who travel to the far reaches of the Empire to aid native women.

The same volume also includes Lester's 'The Cinderellas of the National Household: Jute Girls in the East End', which reinforces the belief that the home life of the girls is to blame for 'the low stand-ard of habit and custom, the objectionable behaviour those who most truly love the girls are bound to deprecate so sorrowfully' (1896, p. 649). Lower-working-class parents who do not restrain their children are blamed for their uncontrolled foolish and rough behaviour. In contrast, the girls who work hard to fulfil their 'duty' to the nation are praised as worthy members of the state: such a girl is 'one of its most practical sup-porters, in fact, contributing loyally her individual quota of industry to the common-weal which must be benefited thereby' (1896, p. 649). The working girl is as necessary to the nation as a statesman or ruler. The girls in the jute factory, who are approximately 14 years of age, are said by the owner of the factory to be improving in character due to benevo-lent efforts to develop their education (1896, p. 651). Some girls, nev-ertheless, still present problems in the evening when they take to the streets uncontrolled and drunk: '[I]f they would only study to become homemakers and teach the little ones to love home, however shabby or humble it might be, then we should find no formidable obstacles in the path of the poor little Cinderella towards better things' (1896, p. 651). Organisations that seek to awaken the love of domestic pursuits, such as the Factory Girl's Mission, aim to give factory girls the self-control to engage in acceptable recreational pursuits at home rather than on the streets.

Work in the home: Service to the nation

Hilary Skelding argues that unlike the way the *BOP* constructed its read-ership the *GOP* did not construct girlhood as a period distinct from the nursery and womanhood; girls were seemingly expected to move from infancy to adulthood with no period of transition (2001, p. 40). She contrasts the view of girls as 'mothers and wives in training' with the *BOP*'s treatment of boys 'as boys' and its inclusion of entertaining rather than didactic content. I suggest, however, that the sense of girls as 'mothers and wives in training' *was* the transitional period that the *GOP* constructed for girls. As Skelding suggests, there is less content in the *GOP* with a pure focus of entertainment (as reflected in the signifi-cantly lower proportion of fiction), yet the understanding of girlhood as a time to improve the self, rather than to engage in leisure for lei-sure's sake, does not mean that readers were figured as either adults or infants. As the construction of the ideal English girl highlighted tasks such as strengthening the nation through motherhood, assisting in improving girls around the world, and helping to build the population in British colonies, the period of girlhood was regarded as time in which girls should improve themselves to approximate this vision of capable femininity.

Articles on the care of children that praised the work of mothers and the benefits for the nation of their work were frequently included for the purposes of training the 'future mothers' of our race' (Lamb, 1881, p. 474). Caring for others, particularly children, is marked as the duty of most girls. Nevertheless, the *GOP*, reinforcing the perceived importance of this work for the nation and the Empire, takes the position that women's work in the home is just as valuable as men's work in the public sphere. Caring effectively for her children is not presented as a woman's only vocation, but it can be a great service to her country when performed assiduously:

> The work of the Prime Minister or chief servant of England is no doubt very great, but it may be that the best mother of England, whoever she is, serves her country even more...When people grow up and get fixed habits, clergymen can do comparatively little to reform them, but a mother can harden in goodness the pliable character of her child. (Hardy, 1885, p. 797)

Girls are warned against becoming slovenly mothers in a purported non-fiction article written by a mother named Amy Irvine, who as a young woman kept an untidy house and was faced with a sick baby who eventually died. This tale equates poor domestic skills with serious consequences, but there is the possibility of reform, as Irvine tells that she now has other children to love: 'but if you came into my little home, I think you would never believe it was once dirty and untidy – in spite of the children's boots – and sometimes they do make a mess. Fred is so proud of them, and just now Mrs. Grieves has come in and said he's been declaring that he's got the best wife of anyone in the yard, and the happiest home' (Irvine, 1896, p. 343). The contrast is stark between the couplings of untidiness and deceased children and careful order and loving praise. The condemnation of idleness is consequently a recurring subject in articles related to health, particularly, as I have shown in the columns of Medicus.

There are representations of deified domesticity in the *GOP* akin to the Angel in the House, such as in 'Higher Thoughts on Housekeeping'. Alice King compares the talented girl housekeeper with a glow worm who will 'shed around her a soft brightness which shines on others, and does not make herself shine' (1884, p. 235). Yet the work involved in keeping a household is regarded as not only important to the well-being of society through improvement in health, but also as difficult and requiring intellectual power. Directing energy toward the useful, rather than ornamental tasks such as needlework and music, is favoured, because every girl must be competent in housework in order for her education to be complete (King, 1884, p. 236). In some instances, despite the coexisting articles on adventurous women negotiating untamed lands, housework is deemed to be the eventual lot and 'natural sphere' of all girls, regardless of whether they take employment beforehand. In an article on 'London's Future Housewives and their Teachers' the unavoidability of this work is made clear: 'Has it ever struck any of my readers that, whatever the boys may do in the way of work, sooner or later that of girls is certain? They are going to be the wives or housekeepers of these or other boys' (1899, p. 737).

While proper attention to mothering is strenuously encouraged, the *GOP* does concede that a significant proportion of women will always remain single and that they should not be despised or regarded as 'superfluous' (Caulfeild, 1885, p. 262). However, attention to the proper care of children – that is, creating tomorrow's citizens – is substantial. The same article that concedes that not all girls can marry also addresses the 'training' of the young, especially boys. Boys are figured as leaving their mothers' shaping hands at earlier age, and both 'upper classes' and the 'so-called "working-classes"' are implored to take 'special care...as to their training when very young' (1885, p. 263). Women are constructed as moral guardians, and as such S.F.A. Caulfeild suggests that poor mothers of boys are the cause of men who become degraded wife-beaters and drunkards: 'The blame, in most cases, lies at the door of the incompetent mother!' (1885, p. 263). Girls therefore inherited responsibility not only for their own behaviour but also for that of men with whom they would interact, taking on the totality of the burden of the nation's character.

Conclusion

While firmly grounded in work, home, and motherhood, the *GOP* is a site where several important intersections between gender and imperialism coexist. Through its dialogue with readers, representations of the 'ideal' girl, instructive articles, and its advertisements, the *GOP* documents a newly forming subjectivity of the 'girl reader'. While this marked girlhood as a unique period, it is evident that girlhood was a category in formation, as it could not always be neatly demarcated from childhood or adulthood. The importance of education, both physical and intellectual, for the ideal English girl was negotiated with expectations of refined femininity; both of these motivations, however, show the influences of imperial concerns upon the paper's writers and editorial direction. Indeed, articles on the 'civilising' work that girls could aid with in the colonies, particularly India, were representative of the relationship between feminist lobbying to find a place for women's education and work outside the home with imperial concepts such as British racial superiority.

2
Developing Pedagogy and Hybridised Femininity in the Girls' School Story

> Girls! Girls everywhere! Girls in the passages, girls in the hall, racing upstairs and scurrying downstairs, diving into dormitories and running into classrooms, overflowing on to the landing and hustling along the corridor – everywhere, girls! There were tall and short, and fat and thin, and all degrees from pretty to plain; girls with fair hair and girls with dark hair, blue-eyed, brown-eyed, and grey-eyed girls; demure girls, romping girls, clever girls, stupid girls – but never a silent girl (1914, p. 9).
>
> Angela Brazil, *The School by the Sea*

The rise of the girl reader inspired the creation of genres of fiction specifically marketed for her consumption. The girls' school story appeared in the 1880s, substantially later than the mid-Victorian boys' genre, and, as it became a publishing phenomenon in the twentieth century, developed to reflect modern femininity. Beginning with eighteenth-century fiction with a school setting, such as Sarah Fielding's *The Governess; or, Little Female Academy* (1749), and through to the influential *Tom Brown's Schooldays* (1857) – which marked the beginning of the truly popular boys' school stories, and later featured in periodicals such as the *Boy's Own Paper* – the school story assumed many different forms before girls' school novels proliferated.

Transformations in girls' education had a substantial impact on what and how girls read and their participation in the world beyond the home. This chapter relates the changing conditions in girls' education in Britain, particularly the developing pedagogy of public secondary schools, to social concerns about motherhood and national degenera-tion. The examination of curricula interrogates texts intended for teach-ers of the period and argues that the construction of British women as purveyors of moral values within the home (and within the Empire at large) was forcefully and importantly conducted within the increasing number of girls' schools. Engaging with the continued use of the doc-trine of 'separate spheres' to justify 'differently directed' curricula, as described by Ruskin, it foregrounds the ways that domestic tasks were elevated to a level of national importance.

Sally Mitchell suggests that '[s]choolgirl tales also support the period's high imperialism' (1995, p. 89), but she does not pursue analysis of the genre, and the femininity depicted within it, in imperial terms. This chapter seeks to complement Mitchell's work, as well as Mavis Reimer's studies of the girls' school story, by formulating how the genre inher-ently supported imperialism and mirrored pedagogic texts that imbued girls' schooling with import for the strength of the nation. Mitchell reminds us that these stories do not aspire to reflect reality and are bet-ter understood as depictions of fantasy (1995, p. 99). Written after the late Victorian social and cultural shifts that placed more girls in schools for a longer duration and thereby created a literate girl readership and girls' culture, Brazil's stories are a site in which a new vision of fictional juvenile femininity is unproblematically realised and embraced. These novels certainly do not record the lived reality of most girls of high school age, and the construction of modern femininity as essential to imperial maintenance is an integral element of the fantasy generated by the girls' school story.

I propose that Angela Brazil's early school stories, eleven novels writ-ten from 1906 to the end-point of this study in 1915, register transi-tions in academic curricula and physical education that were built upon ideas of preparation for motherhood and being 'of use' to the nation. They were not oppressively didactic, had an informal tone, and were extremely popular with readers, as shown by her prodigious output of forty-six girls' school novels. The novels present a 'modern' girlhood that is melded with traditionally acceptable qualities to produce a hybrid model of juvenile femininity that was not only acceptable but which could be celebrated, as in the quotation which introduces this chapter that revels in the chaos and movement of the schoolgirl. As Sheila Fletcher remarks, Brazil evokes 'an exciting sense of the changes that were overtaking girls' schools; and team games, along with the gymnasium, laboratory, and the tentative discussion of careers, appear as emblems of that brave new world which was rising from its Victorian foundations' (1984, p. 78). Indeed, Brazil's novels present a very different world of girls in comparison with the books that the author herself recalls reading in childhood: 'pretty and pathetic little books of the type of *Jessica's First Prayer*' in which the heroine usually died in the final chapter (1925, p. 166).

While her books champion a 'world of girls', the idealised female subjectivity presented within them necessitates the curtailment of some freedoms. In Brazil's novels, unruly or colonial girls must be tamed within the enclosed system of order of the school. The need for the individual girl to conform in this way serves as a contrast with the later chapters in this study in which English girl settlers in imperial locations must become wilder in order to preserve themselves and their family members. While both Brazil's novels and pedagogical texts of the period focus on drawing out the best in the individual's character, each girl's development is also closely tied to benefits that may contribute toward the 'common weal', which serves as a metaphor for contribution to nation, and by extension, empire.

As I discussed in the previous chapter, the *Girl's Own Paper* figures girls as purveyors of moral values at home, and more broadly in the Empire. The shaping of the girl was most importantly conducted within the increasing number of girls' schools of the late Victorian period. Changes enacted by the Education Department, combined with broader societal shifts that saw middle-class women enter into public employment, made appropriate educational content for girls of critical concern. The main expansion of colleges for women and girls' public schools occurred after 1870; there was an increase in the number of high schools for girls; an examination system enabling comparison of educational standards was introduced; and women were gradually admitted to university. The Schools Inquiry Commission, known as the Taunton Commission (1864–8), examined the state of endowed secondary schools and proprietary schools and revealed serious shortcomings, notably the very small number of girls' high schools in the system. In her 1907 book on English girls' high schools, the headmistress of Manchester High School, Sara Burstall, quotes from the Schools Inquiry Commission (1867) upon the faults in girls' education prior to eventual reforms such as the Endowed Schools Act (1869): 'Want of thoroughness and foundation; slovenliness and showy superficiality; inattention to rudiments; undue time given to accomplishments, and these not taught intelligently or in any scientific manner; want of organisation' (1907, p. 6).

The Education Act of 1870 (applicable to England and Wales) was a significant move toward a national public education system, although the burden of tuition costs, and lost incomes from child workers, may have rendered formal education prohibitive for some families, and it did not extend to secondary schooling. In areas that were covered by a School Board, every child was entitled to attend school, and additionally a process of certification was adopted for head teachers.[1] Subsequent Acts of 1876 and 1880 made school attendance compulsory for all children and established minimum leaving ages (raised from 10 to 11 in 1893, and to 12 in 1899) (Horn, 1989, p. 22). It was not until the 1902 Act that public secondary education was similarly accessible. The cumulative effect of these educational reforms meant that Brazil's school stories were published at a time when almost all children had some formal school education, and its duration was extended for many of them. These advancements inadvertently created a theme of almost universal relevance for British children's literature for an increased number of literate boys and girls, even if the kinds of schools and classes of children most frequently depicted did not resonate with the realities of working-class readers.

Separate spheres, 'Differently directed' curricula

The Schools Inquiry Commission noted that girls' schools were especially problematic prior to reform, citing a focus on frivolous accomplishments that were not related to pedagogic principles and lack of serious ideological investment in girls' academic potential. Girls' rights to a substantial education along the lines of the curricula of boys' schools was a battle that had to be fought. Advocates for girls' education often marshalled social Darwinist views of education's potential to aid in the combat of racial degeneration. In support of the belief that girls, like boys, required a thorough education, Burstall suggests that girls need not require a substantially different curriculum: 'After all a girl is a human being, with a right to complete development, to a share in the spiritual inheritance of the race, to the opportunities of making the best of her faculties, of pursuing more advanced studies if she has the ability' (1907, p. 13). Burstall's use of the term 'race' imbues the responsibility of motherhood with supreme importance for the benefit of national strength. An equivalent education could be advocated on national grounds if curricula are explicitly linked with the natural place of women in the home: 'We see clearly now that the normal work of woman is to be the maker of a home, to be a wife, and above all a mother. Does a liberal education fit her for this? The answer is surely yes, if it makes her a better woman, abler and stronger in body, in intellect, and in character' (1907, p. 13). Support for a 'liberal education' is predicated on its capacity to prepare the girl for work in the home and for forming the character of her children. (Burstall does concede that some girls may need to work or might remain unmarried, however.) The question was how to ensure that improvements in these areas were appropriately directed for girls. That is, how far should what she calls 'technical instruction' be extended, if the intention behind its inclusion in the curriculum was for improvement in domestic skills?

The conception of separate male and female spheres in Victorian England has been problematised in recent scholarship, such as Leonore Davidoff and Catherine Hall's *Family Fortunes: Men and Women of the English Middle Class, 1780–1850*, for its middle-class orientation and impossibly neat construction of the public-private divide, even though 'public was not really public and private not really private' (2002, p. 33). Nevertheless, the ideology of separate spheres informed debate about girls' education, which was mired in the belief that once girls and boys became women and men they would not be able to use knowledge gained through education for the same purpose. One popular manifestation of separate spheres ideology was John Ruskin's 'Of Queens' Gardens' in *Sesame and Lilies*, which provided an influential view of the domestic sphere as a sacred place in which women could exert their 'true queenly power' (1865, p. 122). Ruskin contends that a girl should receive a similar education, with the same degree of seriousness, as a boy but that it must be 'differently directed', as her command of knowledge need not be progressive but 'general and accomplished for daily and helpful use' (1865, pp. 160–1). Ruskin's view of girls learning similar material to boys but for a different purpose is evident in Burstall's approach over forty years later, in which she promotes the incorporation of scientific subjects into the curriculum for girls as useful preparation for domestic duties and childcare: 'these life sciences [nature study, botany, and zoology] are as important in the woman's characteristic activity for the young of the race as are physics and chemistry for men's industries' (1907, pp. 110–11). Yet there is a focus on moral training 'in the virtues of accuracy, neatness and order' for later life, and a need to ensure that girls do not have free influence on one another within school as do boys: 'The question is not the same for girls, whose work in the world is not to go out and rule, or in ordinary cases to deal in a practical way with large numbers of various kinds of other girls and women' (1907, p. 175).

Education for the home does not require the same instruction as education for public life. Nevertheless, it is formulated as nationally important: 'The teaching of cookery and the domestic arts to girls of every class is advocated on national grounds, as is the teaching of military drill and marksmanship to boys' (Burstall, 1907, p. 194). Burstall suggests that curriculum differences reflect biological difference, and she echoes Ruskin in her suggestion that the 'natural duty' of men is for national defence in the event of war, whereas women are duty-bound to perform housework, the skills for which must be learnt at school. The aim of practical instruction in domestic skills, such as sewing, knitting, cookery, and hygiene, was to encourage better care and standards in the home, in part to combat infant and child mortality. The moral responsibility of household management was also significant in itself, imbuing the formulation of curricula in girls' schools with importance for the physical and moral strength of the nation.

Education was understood as a process of developing the child to his or her full potential, with the overarching ethos that this process would benefit society as a whole. By comparing the development of each child with representations of the advancement of the nation, education was intimately related to empire. Dorothea Beale, head of Cheltenham Ladies' College (1858–1906), and founder of St Hilda's teachers' training college, suggests that encouraging each child to develop his or her full potential is important for the 'common good':

> The most civilised nations are devoting their best energies to the work of education, realising that upon this depends their very existence – that it is not by starving the individual life, and merging it in the general, but by developing each to perfection, that the common good will be secured. (1892, p. 3)

The refinement of educational practice is assumed as vital to ensure that England remains grouped with the 'most civilised nations' and marks out its superiority in comparison with those whose children remain 'undeveloped'. The notion of full development and application of the self is privileged above simply subordinating individual advancement to national needs. At work here is a discourse of distinguishing the self, which is underwritten by a form of utilitarianism entwined with conceptions of national strength. The distinguishing of the self within the constraints of a set of ideals – such as physical and moral strength – that supports the imperial project contributes to the 'common good' rather than the individual alone. For the working classes, there is an implication that the 'civility' of the nation may be dragged down by 'undeveloped' individuals. A national system of schooling therefore needs to cultivate the physical and moral strength of children of all classes, even if there were variations in methodologies for each. (For instance, in physical education, military-style drill for the working classes was favoured as compared with organised team sports for the middle-classes.)

Curricula for boys and girls also varied substantially in practical training, reflecting the ongoing prevalence of the belief that the purpose of education for each sex – and the way in which each could work to civilise the nation and possibly the Empire – was different. A number of Board of Education curriculum requirements and financial inducements encouraged focus upon domestic capabilities in girls' schools. For instance, domestic economy was made a compulsory subject for girls in state elementary schools by the Education Department code of 1878, and several grants were made payable to schools for adopting particular subjects (from 1874 for domestic economy, cookery from 1882, and laundry work in 1889) (Gomersall, 1997, p. 108). In 1900 a special grant was made available to schools for the teaching of 'Household Management', which incorporated cooking, laundry, and 'housewifery' (Dyhouse, 1977, p. 48). In her paper 'Home Arts' in *Public Schools for Girls*, Margaret A. Gilliland comments on this movement to incorporate domestic education into the school curriculum which enables girls to become 'builders of homes and makers of men' (1911, p. 155): 'The old "blue-stocking" type, who prided herself on not knowing how to sew and mend, and who thought cooking menial, and beneath her, no longer appeals to anyone [...] But at the same time we no longer share the conception of a woman's whole duty held by our grandmothers' (1911, p. 152). The blue-stocking figure is invoked to caution against excessive emphasis on education to the neglect of domesticity. A process of negotiation is evident, in which mid-Victorian conceptions of women's domestic duty are modified to incorporate ideas of feminine freedom while still upholding the value of domestic work for the nation.

Arguments for the importance of girls' education flagged not only schooling's potential to create better mothers through practical domestic instruction, but also the prospect that increasing intellectual pursuits would better equip girls to become moral and academic guides for their children and companions to their husbands. Dorothea Beale, in her introduction to *Work and Play in Girls' Schools by Three Headmistresses*, draws less of a distinction between the education of boys and girls than Burstall, by suggesting that teaching should aim to develop 'to the highest excellence the intellectual powers common to both [sexes]' (1898, p. 7). Beale argues that the intellectual education of girls will prepare them for, rather than detract from, domesticity: 'Surely women trained in good schools and colleges have as wives and mothers shared the labours and entered more fully as companions into the lives of husbands and children' (1898, p. 5). Intended as a practical manual for secondary school teachers, *Work and Play* details a course of instruction spanning academic disciplines including the humanities, mathematics, science, and 'aesthetics' (music, art) in addition to separate sections on 'The Moral Side of Education' and 'Cultivation of the Body'. The intellectual instruction of the girl is inseparable from the moral responsibility she will take up in the home and her ability to propagate physical health in her children.

The age at which schooling commenced for girls was considered important to instil the right morals, particularly for children of the working classes, whose faults of 'heredity' may require pre-emptive counteraction. School authorities attempted to lengthen the duration of schooling for girls with methods such as reduced fees for early admission and different rates for the duration of a girl's education if she entered school earlier (Pederson, 1987, p. 189). Lucy H.M. Soulsby, in 'The Moral Side of Education', discusses the aim to transform ill-bred children as early as possible through school instruction:

> Though we teachers do not, as a rule, get children at the early stage when most can be done with them, yet in the schoolroom days we find their brains still plastic enough for us to work cheerfully and hopefully, in the teeth of the many hereditary evils which would crush our efforts, were it not that we believe education to be able to cope on fairly equal terms with heredity. (1898, p. 385)

Soulsby suggests that the preschool years are most productive for teaching children, emphasising the perception that training the rising generation of girls to be intelligent, capable mothers could only be effective before their characters were irreversibly formed. Yet she also flags the perceived potential of teaching to raise the current generation of working-class children to a level of intelligence and health above that of their families. Within this ideology, which implicates degeneration as a hereditary ailment that could worsen with each generation, education becomes a vital strategy to halt the cumulative deleterious effects of physical and, by association, moral degeneration. Matthew Arnold's *Culture and Anarchy* (1869) marks an important transition in thought on race, in this respect, with a shift to a cultural consideration of racial identity that consequently ascribes a particular importance to the provision of education. Arnold marks off culture's ability to transform society by connecting it with civilisation (that which can serve as a dividing line between one race and 'savage' races that lack civilisation).

Robert J.C. Young suggests that culture additionally created a distinction between the English upper and middle classes and the working classes: 'As the defining feature of whiteness, civilization merged with its quasi-synonym "cultivation", and thus the scale of difference which separated the white from the other races was quickly extended so that culture became the defining feature of the upper and middle classes' (1995, p. 95). Class difference was therefore also subject to racialisation, through which the 'inferior' classes could be situated as abnormal racial degenerates. Anne McClintock notes that in the second half of the nineteenth century a dialectic emerged between the domestication of the colonies and the 'racialising' of the metropolis that could be used as a form of social domination:

> In the metropolis, the idea of racial deviance was evoked to police the 'degenerate' classes – the militant working class, the Irish, Jews, feminists, gays and lesbians, prostitutes, criminals, alcoholics and the insane – who were collectively figured as racial deviants, atavistic throwbacks to a primitive moment in human prehistory, surviving ominously in the heart of the modern, imperial metropolis. (1995, p. 43)

In his conception of culture as the 'pursuit of perfection', however, Arnold suggests that it seeks to do away with classes by making all men 'live in an atmosphere of sweetness and light' (1869, p. 70). For Arnold, members of any class may have the humane instinct to 'extricate' their 'best self', but it depends upon whether this instinct meets with 'what is fitted to help and elicit it' (1869, p. 109). Education is constructed not only as the road to culture (with the motivation of attaining perfection), but also as a possible aid in strengthening the English 'race'. Late Victorian pedagogical texts also elicit this desire to draw out the best in each child and, additionally, to make every girl, irrespective of class, physically strong, for the benefit of the nation.

Healthy minds in healthy bodies

Physical education is an integral component of Ruskin's conception of the private sphere as a queenly preserve. He suggests that physical training is a vital prerequisite to enable a woman's mind to be filled with the knowledge that will assist her in aiding 'the work of men' (1865, p. 154). The scientific theories of Herbert Spencer connected the neglect of physical exercise with the project seeking to counter perceived national degeneration and later warned against excessive focus on intellectual education impairing reproductive health, such as in his *Principles of Biology* (1867), giving conservatively motivated support to the aim of cultivating girls' bodies. Similar attempts to intertwine the development of intellectual strength with a healthy body pervaded newly developing theories of physical education. Doubts lingered over the threat of overexertion and potential for indecorous behaviour, but the necessity of physical education is repeated in instructive manuals for teachers of the period. Jane Frances Dove, in her 'Cultivation of the Body', argues that the unproductive regime of school life (as contrasted with 'useful' work that may keep the body active, such as gardening or building a house) renders games a necessity:

> I think I do not speak too strongly when I say that games, *i.e.*, active games in the open air, are essential to a healthy existence, and that most of the qualities, if not all, that conduce to the supremacy of our country in so many quarters of the globe, are fostered, if not solely developed, by the means of games. (1898, p. 398)

The relationship of sport to the strength of the British Empire echoes Beale's notion of individual development fuelling the advancement of society. Dove suggests that games for girls – with the obvious exception of football – have a 'higher function', which fosters not only a good temper, self-reliance, determination, and courage, but also 'learning to sink individual preferences in the effort of loyally working with others for the common good' (1898, p. 400). Even the family unit must be subordinated to the needs of the community and the nation: 'The woman who indulges in family selfishness is a bad citizen. To be a good citizen, it is essential that she should have wide interests, a sense of discipline and organisation, *esprit de corps*, a power of corporate action' (1898, p. 401). This stipulation complicates any interpretation of the girl's future role as purely a maternal and spousal support role: the girl herself must contribute to the nation.

The cultivation of a healthy body took on a special significance for girls' schools not only for the purpose of educating and strengthening future mothers but also in monitoring the health of girls themselves. Mothers were often deemed lacking in their ability to adequately nourish their children; and the group environment of the school, with the benefit of a gym mistress, was suited to keeping a check on weight, height, general health (particularly in identifying defects such as stoops or 'crooked backs') and for conducting group exercises to encourage physical strength.[2] In her introduction to *Work and Play*, Beale expresses dismay at the permanent detrimental effects of poor health in childhood:

> We are shocked when we hear of mothers ignorant of physiology, feeding infants on bread and tea, and giving soothing syrups; we recognise the danger of too many sweets, and of cigars for growing boys – these have parallels in their mental dietary...It is wonderful how much unwholesome food can be disposed of by a vigorous child – there is a fit of sickness and it is gone; but we see in the adult bodily framework, the stunted skeleton, the decaying teeth, etc., the effect of starvation during years of growth. To deprive the child of the mental food and exercise necessary for this development of his growth is a fatal error, the consequences of which are irreparable. (1898, p. 17)

Sufficient physical health through adequate nutrition and exercise is coupled with the development of the intellect; and both abilities are presented as irreversibly stunted or damaged if not sufficiently overseen in childhood, or as potentially detrimental to the body or mind if over-exerted. Intellectual balance meant restricting academic work periods depending upon the age of the child. *Work and Play in Girls' Schools'* sample timetable prescribes that girls up until the age of 11 or 12 should study only for three hours per day, 14 year olds for up to four hours, and for those aged up to 16 six hours is 'the utmost a girl of any age ought to attempt' (1898, p. 412) unless she wishes to risk becoming 'anaemic and weak-backed' (1898, p. 414). Time spent outside intellectual pursuits was used for practical instruction in skills that would develop her abilities to perform domestic tasks and playing games or other exercise.

One widely adopted system of physical training was Swedish gymnastics, popularised by Madame Bergman Österberg, who was appointed to the London School Board in 1881 as an expert in physical training. Gymnastics functioned like military drill in boys' schools by promoting health and obedience conducive to wider social order, with a focus on strict control of pupils by the instructor. A minority of high schools, including those run by Frances Mary Buss, used the 'German' (sometimes referred to as 'English') system of gymnastics, which involved dancing and musical accompaniment. *Public Schools for Girls* prefers the German system, with the suggestions[3] that it involves 'less strain on the high nerve centres' (so as not to overload the brain after complex mental work) and cultivates grace and rhythm via music (the Swedish system is regarded as 'not sufficiently feminine') (Burstall, 1911, p. 214). The amount of time devoted to exercise varies according to age, with younger children generally having more frequent, daily lessons. Concerns about overexertion lingered, particularly for older girls. While Burstall concedes that physical education needs more attention in some schools, she is concerned about the danger of making a 'fetish of exercise' (1911, p. 214) causing overstrain or vanity. She nevertheless makes a special case for the physical education on racial strength grounds:

> Important as are bodily vigour and active strength – kinetic energy – in the men of a country who may have to endure the supreme test of physical fitness in war, the vitality and *passive strength* – potential energy – of its women are even more important, since Nature has ordained women to be the mothers of the race. Thus on every ground, intellectual, individual and national, the high schools have been from the beginning obliged to secure healthy physical conditions for their girls, and to plan for the maximum of physical efficiency. (Burstall, 1911, p. 90) [my emphasis]

The justification Burstall provides for organised exercise employs a contradictory term: passive strength. While the power and agility of men is actively cultivated for the imminent possibility of war, the bodily strength of girls and women is reserved in abeyance until its 'potential' is realised in motherhood. The inclusion of exercise in the school curriculum, and the resultant strength gained for girls, is not equated with the reasons for physical training for boys, and thus avoids masculine associations and the transgression of 'passive' femininity. Physical education for girls is constructed as meshing with gender norms by assisting in their ability to bear strong children and for ensuring their own healthy maturation, which may be impeded by an unbalanced emphasis on intellectual education.

This brief overview of several pedagogical texts of the late Victorian and Edwardian period shows how the grounds of national and imperial benefit not only influenced the developing curricula of British girls' schools, but were used to advocate for improvements in girls' education. In my consideration of Angela Brazil's school stories below, these associations are rendered in fictional terms, with the fantasy of girls' education extending on these precepts to celebrate protagonists who meld traditional femininity with modern girlhood.

Regulating the modern girl in a miniature world

The title of L.T. Meade's most famous school story, *A World of Girls* (1886), provides an apt phrase for describing the idea of an enclosed system of order that is prevalent throughout Angela Brazil's stories, quite clearly set out in *The Leader of the Lower School* (1913): 'A large school is a state in miniature. Quite apart from the rule of the mistresses, it has its own particular institution and its own system of self-government. In their special domain its officers are of quite as much importance as Members of Parliament' (p. 44). The girls' school was a female preserve with almost exclusively female teaching staff, and school stories provided an ongoing enclosed 'world' for the girl reader in which heroines who could be admired or emulated were located. Gill Frith suggests this segregation allowed a display of less restrictive behaviour for girls, outside of the accepted markers of the 'feminine': 'In a world of girls, to be female is *normal*, and not a *problem*. To be assertive, physically active, daring, ambitious, is not a source of tension. In the absence of boys, girls "break bounds", have adventures, transgress rules, catch spies' (1985, p. 121). The potential to break these bounds is built upon the elaborate regulation of the girls' schools presented, in which the freedoms of the modern girl are safely bounded.

Mavis Reimer argues that, like women of the middle-classes who worked outside the home, 'schoolgirls threatened the stability of domestic ideology when they moved into the public sphere of school' (1999, p. 47). In Angela Brazil's novels, the extent to which girls are located in the public sphere is controlled by the situation of most schools in the country or in isolated locations. *The Nicest Girl in the School* (1906) is set in a girls' school that is housed in a former Franciscan monastery. The contrast between the historical and contemporary purposes of the building emphasises the cultural significance of the schoolgirl figure:

> ...it now seemed a strange irony of fate that feminine petticoats should reign supreme within the very walls where the grey brothers had lived in such seclusion. The old refectory where they had dined, and the cloister where they had been wont to meditate, were now given up to a lively, laughing crew of girls, whose twentieth-century costumes among the quaint surroundings made a curious blend of ancient and modern. (p. 32)

The schoolgirl comes to represent modernity, with her feminine freedom contrasted with an austere vision of masculinity. The monastery is described as 'a little self-contained kingdom, shut off from the rest of the world' (p. 33), and with tennis courts, playing fields, an art studio, music practice rooms, a laboratory, a gymnasium, a home farm, a fruit and vegetable garden, and a sanatorium, there is little reason for the boarders to ever move outside the school bounds.

The School by the Sea (1914) is set in an isolated former convent at the end of a narrow peninsula, which is similarly described as a 'kingdom by the sea' (p. 21). The location again enables the creation of a separate world of girls, but also makes for an even stronger contrast between an older, quiet vision of femininity and the active one which the girls' school creates:

> No pale-faced novices these, with downcast eyes and cheeks sunken with fasting; no timid glances, no soft ethereal footfalls or gliding garments – the old order had changed indeed, and yielded place to a rosy, racy, healthy, hearty, well-grown set of twentieth-century schoolgirls, overflowing with vigorous young life and abounding spirits, mentally and physically fit, and about as different from their medieval forerunners as a hockey stick from a spindle. (pp. 10–11)

The hockey stick is a signifier of physical activity and a marker of difference for the modern girl and is contrasted with the domestic via the image of a spindle, a symbol of laborious and outmoded women's work. The building in which women were once cloistered and silent dates from the fourteenth century, but the necessity of providing a different education for contemporary girls is foregrounded for reasons of health and individual development: 'Inside the ancient walls everything was strictly modern and hygienic, with the latest patterns of desks, the most sanitary wall papers, and each up-to-date appliance that educational authorities might suggest or devise' (p. 26). This blending of historical restriction with contemporary opportunity for girls provides an apt metaphor for their education more generally, the limits of which are subject to negotiation between old and new visions of femininity.

This tension is effectively embodied by Gwen Gascoyne, the heroine of *The Youngest Girl in the Fifth* (1913), who often wishes that she were a boy. Gwen is not a boarder at her school, unlike most Brazil protagonists, and a greater burden is placed upon her own self-development outside her school, Rodenhurst. Gwen's life with her father, siblings, and friend Dick Chambers is uniquely important to the narrative. Her interactions with Dick enable contrasts between the 'modern' girl and Victorian femininity, with Gwen envious of the way Dick can run for a bus without skirts hampering his movement. While Dick remarks that girls are ordinarily afraid of crisis situations and incapable of action, Gwen explains that 'modern girls' are active and demonstrates this when she rescues a boy who fell when climbing: 'They used to do the shrieking business in old fashioned novels. It's gone out of fashion since hockey came in' (p. 81). The frightened, passive girl is relegated to the pages of fiction, distanced from the real modern girl, but simultaneously the reader is of course presented with fictional modern girls in the story she is reading.

Hockey, which was eventually adopted widely in schools for the middle classes, represents active girlhood and a shift to include such team games in the realm of acceptable physical activity. The team sport was supported by a belief that it prepared students for working with others in employment in later life (McCrone, 1984, p. 127), a justification that took longer to apply to girls than boys. As in the views of Burstall that I discussed earlier, the influence of groups of girls on one another was not considered as beneficial as it might be for boys. By the time of Brazil's school stories, it had been more than a decade since hockey had infiltrated most schools – the symbolic final acceptance of which is evident in 1891 when Dorothea Beale of Cheltenham Ladies' College relented and adopted hockey at the school despite her earlier fears of compromising womanliness (Fletcher, 1984, p. 34). Organised team sports in girls' school stories are associated with alteration in the ideal girl from one who is weak to one who is strong and capable of physical exertion. Gwen demonstrates the determined qualities that will later bring success on her and the school in the sporting arena when she rescues schoolteacher Miss Roberts, who breaks her leg in an avalanche, with calm capability as a result of her having taken a St John's Ambulance course. While individual achievement is championed, such as on the sporting field, it is usually located within a girl's broader efforts to contribute to the school community, which functions as a replica of the world at large.

Becoming a 'unit' within the community

Angela Brazil's own school experiences lead her to reminisce that there was 'no common ground upon which we [girl pupils] could meet, no mutual object to be gained' (1926, p. 150). Her vision of a school system in which social responsibility was central is rendered fictionally throughout her school stories: 'If we had had prefects, and had ever been taught the elements of citizenship and social service, and that our school was a world in miniature where we might help one another, it would, I think, have brought in a totally different element' (1926, p. 150). In *A Pair of Schoolgirls: A Story of School Days* (1912), day school Avondale College introduces a scheme that more than half of the girls choose to join based upon the model of the Girl Guides: a Guild of First Aid and Field Ambulance. Like the Guides, the purpose of the Guild is 'character training, as developed through work for others. Every member of the Guild was pledged to Chivalry, Patriotism, Self-reliance, and Helpfulness; and her aim was to acquire knowledge to make her of service, not only to herself, but to the community' (p. 156).

One student's mother demonstrates the real fears that I note in Chapter 5 about masculine traits being imparted on girls who participated in Guiding: 'You see, she thought it was something like the Boy Scouts, and she said she couldn't have me careering about the country on Saturday afternoons – she didn't approve of it for girls' (p. 156). The differentiation of Guiding, or in this case, Guild activities, from those intended for boys is predicated upon a caring or altruistic component. Miss Tempest emphasises these aspects of the Guild, coupling them with feminine capacity for improving the working classes or the uncivilised: 'There is nobody who cannot make some little corner of the world better by her presence, and be of use to her poorer neighbours' (p. 157). Membership of the Guild involves pledging to sew one item per year for a charity basket to be sent to the Ragged School Mission – a genteel act of benevolence that may have eased the minds of mothers – but the real focus of activity is upon the ambulance classes, in which legs are placed in hockey-stick splints and jaws are bandaged shut. The training culminates in a camp drill and practice in fieldwork day, with boys from the local orphanage brought in to act as injured soldiers to lend an air of authenticity to the proceedings:

> The officers and patrol leaders at once took command, and began to instruct each group of ambulance workers in the particular duties they were expected to perform. One detachment started to build a fire (there is a science in the building of fires in the open), a second ran up the Red Cross flag and arranged a temporary hospital with supplies from the transport wagon, while a third went out to render first aid to the wounded. (p. 162)

The fieldwork practice runs with the precision of a military operation, with patrols of girls each assigned to a particular task, including camp cookery, nursing, and signalling. While there is a comical aspect to the descriptions of the girls' urgent responses to imaginary danger, a realistic consideration of such work as a future employment possibility is also delivered:[4] 'Alison, who had helped put up a tent, and given imaginary chloroform under the directions of a supposed army surgeon, was immensely proud of herself, and half-inclined to regard the work of the Red Cross Sisterhood as her vocation in life' (p. 164). The combination of adventure and excitement (Alison calls the training 'ripping') with a more traditional caring vocation is an example of the modern form of girlhood celebrated in Brazil's novels that amalgamates new and old visions of femininity.

The fieldwork drill practice also encourages individual capability and skills that can work for the benefit of all. Miss Cavendish, the Girton-educated principal in *The New Girl at St. Chad's*, compares the discipline in her school to an army, with each girl required to preserve its rules for the good of the whole. However, she also likens each individual to a different flower requiring specialised cultivation: 'You cannot successfully grow roses and carnations with the same treatment' (p. 55). The heroine, Honor Fitzgerald, a stereotypical 'wild', 'hot-headed', and 'idle' Irish girl, is thoughtless regarding her sick mother (who regards her as 'the direct opposite of her ideal of girlhood' (p. 26)) and unable to submit to discipline from a string of governesses. Despite some initial incidents at the school prompted by her selfishness, Honor comes to feel that she is a 'unit' in a larger community and recognises the importance of fitting in with 'universal custom' and the notion of *esprit de corps* (p. 58). This thread throughout many of Brazil's pre-war novels differentiates them from other girls' school stories of the period, with Gillian Avery suggesting that *esprit de corps* and zeal for games only came to 'dominate the girls' stories between the wars as they had dominated the boys' stories rather earlier' (1975, p. 207). The school and the individuals within it in this novel are presented as a small-scale version of the nation and its citizens:

> A large public school is indeed a vast democracy, and members are estimated only by the value they prove themselves to be to the commonweal: their private possessions and affairs matter little to the general community, but their examination successes, cricket scores, or tennis championships are of vital importance. (Brazil, 1912, pp. 186–7)

Honor's transformation from a selfish, idle girl is rapid, with the narrative confined to one thirteen-week school term. She becomes 'so much more thoughtful, sympathetic, and considerate, with such higher ideals and noble aspirations, that she scarcely seemed the same' (p. 287). Her brief time at St. Chad's most significantly leads Honor to show a concern for others in her immediate family, particularly her sick mother, and for the 'commonweal', evoked by the reference to 'higher ideals and noble aspirations'.

Girls of empire in Brazil's school stories

Miss Drummond, the principal in *A Forth Form Friendship* (1912), views herself as conversant with the latest in pedagogical methods, and she demonstrates the fusion of old and new modes of femininity in practical terms:

> We can very well emulate our great-grandmothers in this respect ... and thus make a happy combination of ancient and modern. Because you are studying French and algebra is no reason at all why you should not also know how to fry an omelet or boil a potato. A cultivated brain ought surely to be able to grasp domestic economy better than an untrained one, and an educated woman who is really helpful is worth more than an ignorant one. (p. 46)

Contrary to suggestions that academic study for girls would negatively impact upon the acquisition of domestic skills, she argues that one form of knowledge may complement the other. Nevertheless, the purpose of this domestic training is, for the headmistress, not as restrictive for girls as the coupling of complex mathematics and cookery might suggest (i.e. that academic learning may be pursued only as an accomplishment rather than as a vocation).[5]

The school principal connects the imperatives of empire with the domestic skills acquired at a specially constructed training cottage, and she also poses the possibility that these abilities may be more useful in 'some emergency' than any other subject taught at school: 'I think, also, that a great future for many of our English girls lies in the Colonies, where domestic help is often at a premium, and the most delicately nurtured lady must sometimes set to work, and be her own cook and laundress' (p. 46). A crucial point to note is the acceptance that a colonial environment, by necessity, warrants behaviour and activities that may be outside the scope of a 'delicately nurtured lady' in England. In Chapter 3, I discuss the expanded spectrum of acceptable and, indeed, praiseworthy skills and actions of the girl heroines in Bessie Marchant's adventure novels set in colonial locations and rugged countries outside of the Empire. Further, as I shall argue in Chapter 5, the idea that girls should train or prepare for tasks they may need to perform in the less 'civilised' environments of colonies (especially in light of the need for more English settler women) is one of the foundation points of the Girl Guides organisation.

The imperial girl in England is nevertheless fodder for transformation in Brazil's novels. The initial alienation of a number of heroines stems from their ignorance of the school codes of behaviour, and this lack of knowledge sometimes issues from their relationship to empire. Brazil's schoolgirl heroine must prove herself to her classmates, providing a contrast between acceptable feminine behaviour in the colonies and 'at home' in England. Brazil's first story set almost entirely in a girls' school, *The Fortunes of Philippa: A School Story* (1906), is fundamentally concerned with imperialism. Its plot mirrors the life of Brazil's mother, as she notes in *My Own Schooldays* (1925). Angelica Brazil (née McKinnel), born to a Scottish father (who owned the first line of steamships to travel between Liverpool and Rio de Janeiro) and a Spanish mother, was raised for a decade in Rio de Janeiro and then schooled in England. The novel begins with the eponymous Philippa Seaton resident in San Carlos, South America, where she has lived for ten years. Like many of Brazil's heroines, Philippa has suffered the loss of her mother. She has been raised by her father (the British Consul and a plantation owner), Juanita ('a mulatto nurse'), and Tasso ('the black bearer'), and she lives vicariously through reading books. Her father has kept her restricted in the Government house, not wishing for her to associate with the local children, and wants her to return to England to 'learn English ways' (p. 8). He is fearful that Philippa has not learnt music, French, dance, or sewing, accomplishments that she would have acquired under the influence of an English mother:

> I believe I have kept you here too long already. You're ten years old now, growing a tall girl, and not learning half the things you ought to. I feel there's something wrong about you, but I don't know quite how to set it right. After all, I suppose a man can't expect to bring up a girl entirely by himself. (p. 7)

Philippa's father detects a problematic difference between his daughter, whom he attempts to protect from contaminating imperial influences, and the way in which English girls ought to behave. And to a girl who has known no life outside the tropics, England is a strange and almost frightening place. The plantation servants warn her that the climate will be cold enough to freeze off her fingers, that there will be vastly different foods from the salads and sauces of Argentina (such as beef and plum-pudding), and that it will require a perilous sea journey to reach (p. 11). Philippa is initially strongly aligned with the local servants Juanita and Tasso, and her first dispute with her uncle's family in England concerns the plan to modify her ways before she attends school, particularly her use of Spanish. Philippa is emphatic that she will return to her Brazilian home and continue to speak Spanish as 'Juanita and Tasso can't speak anything else' (p. 29). Her cousin Lucy displays a bigoted attitude to Philippa's friendship with Tasso, stating that she likes 'white people'. The first-person narration of this novel, however, which is unique for Brazil, enables a more critical view of beliefs in racial inferiority than her earlier *A Terrible Tomboy* (1904), which includes overt racism regarding idle, slatternly, and savage 'Spanish-looking' gypsies and African Americans. This is achieved through Philippa's sympathetic association with Tasso, who is 'devoted', saves her from death by drowning, and tirelessly entertains her with stories and songs. However, the protagonist's admiration of her faithful servant friends is obviously grounded in a racial hierarchy, with the 'white race' deemed superior and others infantilised and subordinated. For example, Philippa suggests that Tasso is entertaining and patient with children such as herself because black servants 'have much of the child in their nature' (Brazil, 1906, p. 13).

Despite Philippa's initial resolve, after two years in England she forgets her 'foreign ways', including the Spanish language, and is then considered by her Aunt Agatha as ready to be schooled. It is necessary to first eliminate the worst and most obvious markers of Philippa's 'foreignness', which is distinguished from simply being 'colonial', before she can be polished in the subtleties of suitable behaviour for an English schoolgirl. Philippa is sent to a small school called the Hollies, which accommodates only forty girls. The school amalgamates contemporary models of femininity (signified by sport, maths, and chemistry) with traditional restrictions and domestic accomplishments (darning, deportment, and learning how to receive visitors):

We learnt mathematics at The Hollies, but we curtsied to our teachers as we left the room; we had chemistry classes in a well-fitted laboratory, but we were taught the most exquisite darning and the finest of open hem-stitch; we played cricket, hockey, and all modern games, but we used backboards and were made to walk round the school-room balancing books upon our heads; we had the best of professors for languages and literature, and we were taught to receive visitors graciously, to dispense afternoon tea, arrange flowers, and to write and answer invitations correctly. (p. 54)

After a year at the school, at the age of 13 and now in the Third Form, Philippa's aunt believes her to be 'greatly improved', and her past in San Carlos seems unreal to her (p. 142). *The Fortunes of Philippa* does not present Philippa's transition from uncultivated imperial to English as seamlessly enabled by her schooling, however. Fears about the deleterious effects of intellectual exertion upon developing girls are played out when Philippa begins to sit crookedly because of an aching back, lolling on her desk from exhaustion, and fidgeting from nervousness. Lack of access to the outside world, Philippa claims, 'is apt to have a rather depressing influence upon some dispositions' (p. 148). Because of the isolation of the boarding school, Philippa's problems become all-consuming; she begins to neglect her personal appearance and the tidiness of her room, and finally a stressful incident leads to Philippa fainting. The doctor determines it is 'a decided case of nervous breakdown, due to overwork' (p. 162), and Philippa travels with her aunt to Brighton to recover. Philippa's breakdown is the catalyst for change in the Hollies' timetable, serving as a demonstration of the feared ill consequences of mental and physical overexertion upon girls in schools: academic work hours are relaxed, and walks up and down the high road are replaced by 'daily rambles' over the hills or among the woods. The teacher responsible for the strenuous regulation, Miss Percy, leaves the school and is replaced by a new teacher, with an interest in natural history, who promises a less regimented curriculum.

In a familiar plot device for Brazil novels, Philippa's father is reported to have gone down with the ship *Ignacia* bound for London. Eventually it is revealed that he survived the disaster, has sold the plantations, and will return permanently to England. The novel closes after Philippa has left school, conducting the housework for her father (to take the place of her deceased mother), and aspiring to work to improve the local village so as not to be 'aimless' (p. 206). She is still in contact with the servants in South America, and loyal servant Tasso has followed her father to England. Yet while some contact with the imperial world remains, the transformation of Philippa through her schooling into an acceptably British girl is made clear: 'my father says that the little foreign plant which he sent over so long ago to harden in our gray northern clime has taken root, and changed from a tropical blossom into an English rose' (p. 208). The transformation from an exotic flower into a quintessentially English one, at its simplest level, represents the cultural assimilation of Philippa to a more refined and less 'wild' or uncultivated version of juvenile femininity. Her change from blossom to a more sophisticated rose also marks a maturation process of 'blooming' that Amy King, in her study of the botanical vernacular and female protagonists in the English novel, suggests functioned in the mid–nineteenth century as 'a culturally pervasive shorthand for young female subjectivity' (2003, p. 194). Through her transformation from blossom to rose, Philippa has acquired an acceptable *English* subjectivity.

The protagonist of *The Leader of the Lower School* (1913), Gipsy Latimer, is similar to the earlier Philippa in that her foreign ways clash with the regulation of British girls' schools. Gipsy is, however, far more extensively travelled around the Empire, having attended schools in New Zealand, Australia, and South Africa, as well as America. She even identifies herself as 'American and British and Colonial and Spanish all mixed up' (p. 14). At fourteen years of age, she has attended more than seven schools, has no mother, and is compelled to attend a boarding school when her father, who is a mining engineer, decides to return to South Africa. From the outset a distinction is made between the English and the colonial girl:

> She had grown up a thorough little Colonial, self-dependent and resourceful, able to catch her own horse and saddle it, to ride barebacked on occasion, and to be prepared for the hundred and one accidents and emergencies of bush life. She had taken a hand at camp cookery, helped to head cattle, understood the making of 'billy' tea, and could find her own way where a town-bred girl would have been hopelessly lost. The roving life had fostered her naturally enterprising disposition; she loved change and variety and adventure, and in fact was as thorough-hearted a young gipsy as any black-eyed Romany who sells brooms in the wake of a caravan. (p. 21)

The reason for the adoption of the name 'Gipsy' in place of her more genteel birth name, 'Azalea', is made apparent in the description of her desire for adventure and travel. It also hints at an uncivilised streak in her character, as well as her mother's Spanish heritage. She is particularly constructed as 'Other' during a bazaar conducted by the girls during which she wears a 'half-Spanish' costume: 'Her rich dark hair was allowed to hang loose ... She wore sequin ornaments and a quantity of Oriental bangles, which enhanced, and gave her the appearance of a true Romany' (p. 137). While the descriptions of her competence in colonial tasks is not condemnatory given the context of the extreme environments in the reaches of the Empire, her education is flagged as markedly different from English girls' because it is designed for less restricted, colonial girls: 'At her various schools she had of course learnt to submit to some kind of discipline, but her classmates were Colonials, accustomed to far more freedom than is accorded to English girls, and the rules were not nearly so strict as in similar establishments at home' (p. 21). She has 'independent Colonial notions' which stand in contrast with 'more sober' English mores (p. 30), particularly those of the headmistress, Miss Poppleton, at Briarcroft Hall, a private school near the Lake District in Cumberland. Gipsy is warned that she must learn 'English ways' and 'English speech', but unlike Philippa, she is sent directly to school without any behaviour modification and her wild colonial ways are deemed 'ripping' by the other girls (p. 41).

Her non-English ways allow her to influence the school positively, yet she is sometimes the object of fun because of her undisciplined behaviour and inability to be obedient, a clear marker that she must curtail her behaviour in a genre in which the inevitable resolution involves acceptance, popularity, and success. Gipsy's first major impact upon her peers occurs when she decides that the distribution of money in the school guilds (needlework, photography, drama, music, and athletics), primarily to those in the sixth form, constitutes 'tyranny' based upon her experience of fairness in other countries. She organises a vote for the junior school to separate its funds from the senior school, and she leads a patriotic chant to stir up support: 'Rule Britannia! Britannia rules the waves! Juniors never, never, never, will be slaves!' (p. 67). Following the successful separation of the junior school students from the seniors, Gipsy founds a school magazine, for which she contributes a serial, 'The Girl Pioneer of Wild Cat Creek' (p. 106). Her popularity nevertheless begins to grate upon some of the girls, and once her father fails to pay her fees and she is faced with the possibility of being sent to live with her relatives in New Zealand, a metaphor of imperial conquest is invoked as she is teased as an 'American turkey' which is 'losing its top-knot', or as having been 'tamed by the British lion!' (p. 118).

The physical differences between the colonial girl and the English girl are significant in this novel. Teacher Miss Yorke is 'Colonial born', can ride a horse – she could have even 'sat a kangaroo' – and mirrors the physical abilities of Gipsy, who astonishes her classmates by riding an unbroken colt, despite its wild bucking. Gipsy attributes her adventurous attitude to colonial life and is not afraid to hike in the local area without permission because the terrain in Cumberland is 'civilized' in comparison with the U.S. Rockies and parts of New Zealand. When driven to seek out her father, after being falsely accused of repeatedly leaving the school boundaries, Gipsy attempts to return to Cape Town herself, and she resolves to work onboard a 'South African liner' as a stewardess, declaring that there is no shame in work for an American or colonial girl and emphasising that her transformation to English girl is still incomplete (p. 212). Gipsy is rescued from her ill-conceived plan, and soon after a letter is discovered from her father noting that her school expenses will be paid and that he is about to set out prospecting for minerals in an 'unexplored district at the sources of one of the tributaries of the Zambesi' (p. 224). The novel concludes with his return to England and declaration that, after finding gold on his expedition, he has no further need to travel the world. Gipsy's schooling has finally quelled her desire to roam, and she is ecstatic at the prospect of remaining in England and moving into the senior school.

A similar conception of differences between the colonial girl and the English girl is borne out in *The School by the Sea* (1914). The students are visited by a woman named Miss Barlow, who had been connected with the Girl Guides in Australia, and who talks with them about her colonial experiences. The traits of colonial girls are again deemed to be admirable in the colonial context, but colonial education is deemed lacking for a proper English girl:

> They are more resourceful, and very bright in suggesting fresh ideas, but they are not so willing to submit to discipline. They are more ready to copy a corps of roughriders than a Roman cohort. No doubt it is owing to the way they are brought up [...] It is training that makes them helpful and energetic, but perhaps a little too independent to accord entirely with the standards we keep at home. Our girls are more sheltered and guarded, and it is only natural that they should have a different style from those who must hold their own. (p. 182)

The education of the two heroines discussed here corrects them by removing any trace of imperial or colonial femininity, which is no longer necessary in a land in which they do not need to 'hold their own'. This does not mean, however, that as a corpus of texts Brazil's novels delicately separate English girls from empire. Rather, in the novels which feature English protagonists, the concerns of national strength and imperial maintenance permeate the hybrid model of traditional and modern femininity in both academic and physical pursuits.

3
Adventurous Girls of the British Empire: The Novels of Bessie Marchant

Historically, the genre of adventure fiction most readily recalls books for boys and male heroes rather than girl readers and female protagonists. These include enduringly well-known works such as H. Rider Haggard's *King Solomon's Mines* (1885) and *She* (1887), the early to mid-Victorian boys' stories of Frederick Marryat, W.H.G. Kingston, and R.M. Ballantyne, and the late Victorian G.A. Henty's tales (his more than 100 adventure stories sold in excess of 25 million copies).[1] The novel of adventure at the conclusion of the nineteenth century recounted tales of male exploration on land or sea, and quests or conquests in real or imagined lands removed from the gentility of civilised England. These generic features were aligned with masculine traits of activity and strength, and while girls could and did indeed read boys' adventure books, examples with female protagonists were uncommon in the Victorian period. Joseph Bristow argues that between 1870 and 1900, 'narratives celebrating empire and techniques in teaching reading and writing gradually converged... [B]oth inside and outside the classroom, there was more and more emphasis on heroic adventure, and this involved a number of shifts in attitude towards juvenile publishing and curriculum design' (1991, pp. 20–1). The works Bristow refers to were, of course, written by male authors about masculine adventurers.

The novels of Bessie Marchant – sometimes called 'the girls' Henty'[2] – began to be published as the nineteenth century drew to a close. Her girl heroines act independently in isolated areas in Australia, New Zealand, Canada, India, South America, India, South Africa, Siberia, and Central America. From 1894 until her death in 1941, Marchant wrote more than 130 novels, many of which celebrated the capacity of British or colonial girls to rise to any challenge set before them in rugged environments. Her short adventure stories were also regularly published in girls' magazines and annuals, such as *The Girl's Realm*. As J.S. Bratton argues, Marchant is one of the few writers of the period who could produce a narrative in which girls confronted with story flashpoints involving violence did not faint (1989, p. 201). She presents girl protagonists who display physical strength, exert independence, and, in some cases, challenge British race and class ideology, yet are considered 'worthy' representations of femininity. The emergent popularity of a girls' adventure genre, decades after the publication of equivalent books for boys, speaks not only about the development of literary genres for the girl reader, but also about the place constructed for girls within the Empire in response to British imperial anxieties. Terri Doughty, for instance, considers Marchant's novels in the context of female emigration and the promotion of settlement (2011).

Marchant's novels function as rehearsals of colonial life in which men may be absent. They regulate appropriate moments in which work that would ordinarily be a marker of unfeminine traits is not only acceptable, but in fact admirable. Mirroring a historical cultural climate of 'readiness' for war and preparation for life in the colonies, Marchant's girl heroines engage in adventure only out of necessity. Adventurous acts are performed to ensure survival in rough environments, save lives, and prevent crime. The task of empire is depicted as inherently arduous, and outdoor work is often inescapable for girls. That is, however, until the frequent plot resolution of marriage contains the necessity of most forms of adventure and sometimes removes the heroine's independent rule over property. The heroine's domestic responsibility cannot be abrogated when threats, such as those posed by a rugged colonial or imperial environment, dissipate.[3] However, it is important to note that Marchant's novels are not preoccupied with maintaining British identity in foreign lands. First, they do not, in most instances, present the heroines engaging in any meaningful contact with indigenous inhabitants. The minor attention devoted to indigenous peoples limits opportunities to mark out racial and cultural differences through the performance of a 'civilising' function. Similarly, the fact that several of Marchant's heroines remain unmarried indicates a lack of anxiety about containing threats of miscegenation.

Marchant's novels were well received at the time of publication, and her reputation for creating adventurous heroines was not sufficiently subversive to prevent the Religious Tract Society from publishing some of them (albeit not her girls' adventures). Bratton suggests that, unlike

Henty, whose works were regarded as educational for boys of the British Empire, 'the respected girls' writers where [sic] those who deliberately set out to provide usefully instructive books which could be read instead of the "cheap romances" to which Marchant's books approached' (1989, p. 206). While her works are not instructive, short quotations from reviews for a number of her novels included at the front of her books, and also on an advertising flyer from Blackie and Sons that I found inserted in one of them, point to her novels being regarded as offering admirable characterisations of girlhood (Figure 3.1). A reviewer from *Outlook* praises the heroines of *Sisters of Silver Creek: A Story of Western Canada* as 'excellent types of normal, healthy-minded girls', and brave Margaret Alford of *A Girl of the Fortunate Isles* is considered 'a heroine worthy to take her stand beside any girl heroine of Miss Alcott's or Mrs. Molesworth's' by *Ladies' Field*. The latter assessment, in particular, situates Marchant's work alongside acceptable domestic fiction with a strong focus on morality and development of character.

According to some critics, Marchant's fiction reflects or even presages significant historical shifts in what constituted acceptable British juvenile femininity.[4] Mary Cadogan and Patricia Craig view her work as foreshadowing actual cultural transformation (1976, p. 57). Somewhat contradictorily, Cadogan and Craig also argue that Marchant was unable to break with tradition in a revolutionary manner by virtue of the fact that her stories were written for girls, yet they also regard her heroines as inspiring real-world change: 'Inspired by the example of Bessie Marchant's heroines, girls were beginning to question the truth of Charles Kingsley's " ... Men Must Work and Women Must Weep ... ": no longer content to be simply backers-up of male empire builders, girls were seeking new worlds of their own to conquer' (1976, p. 59).

Donald Hettinga ascribes less cultural significance to Marchant's novels. He suggests that they are 'safe, uplifting adventures' with exotic settings that are 'not at all far from home' (1996, p. 169) and serve merely as a contrast to British life through the eyes of 'the only slightly modern British woman' (1996, p. 168). While he acknowledges that societal reasons are sometimes to blame for instances of frailty displayed by Marchant's heroines, Hettinga argues that in other cases such frailty is caused by their own self-pity and self-indulgence. For instance, when confronted with an emergency, several heroines 'wonder to themselves why they are women when the task before them seems so obviously to cry out for a man' (1996, p. 169). However, Marchant's heroines do maintain strong attributes consistently throughout her novels for so long as necessity requires that they do so, and the tasks that seem to

Messrs. BLACKIE & SON'S PUBLICATIONS

Charming Stories for Girls

BESSIE MARCHANT

Extra crown 8vo, cloth extra
Beautifully illustrated

A Countess from Canada. Illustrated
by CYRUS CUNEO. 5*s*.

Daughters of the Dominion: A
Story of the Canadian Frontier. 5*s*.
"A vigorous and most acceptable story of Colonial life."
—**Morning Post**.

Sisters of Silver Creek: A Story of
Western Canada. 5*s*.
"The three heroines are of the kind that will at once
win sympathy."—**Glasgow Herald**.

Greta's Domain: A Tale of Chiloe. 3*s*. 6*d*.

Three Girls in Mexico: A Story of Life
in the Interior. 3*s*. 6*d*.

A Courageous Girl: A Story of Uruguay.
3*s*. 6*d*.
"Its novelty and variety can hardly fail to please."
—**Spectator**.

Figure 3.1 Front of loose advertisement sheet for Bessie Marchant's novels,
Blackie and Son's, undated.

'cry out for a man' are approached with vigour, and sometimes even relish.

Hettinga proposes that Marchant wanted readers to value the qualities of self-reliance and independence in women, but that she did not feel 'secure enough' about their values to create consistently strong characters. This chapter will nevertheless foreground the variety of outcomes for her heroines. Marchant's stories enable a range of hitherto unidentified possibilities for their girl heroines, yet some scholars have not sought to identify these nuances. Bernard Porter, for instance, states that he 'looked through' (2004, p. 388) a handful of Marchant's stories in his study of imperialism. And although Richard Phillips does conduct a reading of *Daughters of the Dominion*, he overlooks other Marchant texts, arguing that *Daughters* is representative '[s]ince there is relatively little variation between [her novels]' (1997, p. 100). The novels considered in this chapter depict physically and mentally strong protagonists with various degrees of independence, from those who use their own property to become self-sufficient to those who take up employment to support themselves or accept a proposal of marriage.

Marchant's heroines are presented in a positive light for their adaptability in times of calamity or necessity, such as through the death, illness, or absence of adults, even if doing so necessitates rough work. In the novels, mothers can be seen as the keepers of English ways and English femininity and their death[5] or absence from the narrative enables the emergence of new ways without conflict with the old. Calamity befalls the girl protagonists frequently such that acts of physicality and resourceful capability are performed out of necessity rather than to challenge gender norms. While many heroines already show an independent or tomboyish streak, they are also usually hard-working, intent on self-improvement, and selfless. These girls are physically strong, rarely falling ill or becoming weak in tropical climates, unlike some minor female characters who turn pale and droop 'like wilted flowers' (Marchant, 1900, p. 40). The outdoor work or dangerous journeys the heroines undertake are presented as inescapable because of location or situation, and therefore they do not function as challenges to female domestic responsibilities. Significantly, the difficult ventures are not willingly chosen, and they are undertaken not at the expense of household and familial duties but often to ensure that the family unit and household remains intact.

Doughty argues that Marchant equates frontier life with freedom (2011). Nevertheless, though courage and strength in times of necessity are celebrated qualities in girls, women who take up rough work with no need to do so are criticised. The women in *Jenny's Adventure; or, On the Trail for Klondyke* (1909) who set out to work a gold claim dressed in men's clothing with picks and shovels may die of 'over exertion' on the trail according to the opinion of a local shopkeeper. The town doctor observes that even though some of them may survive, 'it doesn't seem to me to be a woman's work' (p. 120). The concerns about these gold-prospecting women stand in contrast to the survival of girls through a long period stranded in the wild with a broken leg (*No Ordinary Girl* (1907)), confinement to an area where smallpox sufferers are sent to die (*The Girl Captives* (1900)), and riding a horse across a rugged mountain range at night in a storm to prevent a murder (*A Courageous Girl* (1909)). The isolation of colonial and exotic locations, coupled with sickness and misadventure, often leaves the heroine alone with no choice but to take on tasks to ensure her survival and the survival of others, as well as the maintenance of property or livestock.

Civilising through nursing

Two strands of activity celebrated when practiced by girls within the adventure context are the maintenance of settlements in the colonies and nursing the sick and injured. The desire to maintain the expanse of the British Empire and protect the mother country itself from attack, in addition to anxieties about national degeneration, led to fears about being unprepared for conflict. This created a cultural climate that encouraged preparation for catastrophe, which was, as I shall consider in Chapter 5, exemplified in relation to youth by the Scouting and Guiding movements initiated in 1908 and 1909 respectively. The Guide motto, 'Be Prepared', reflects the desire to train girls to take on tasks outside the domestic in times of crisis. The foci of the Girl Guides' activities were nursing and first-aid training (although colonial situations were sometimes discussed), directed in spirit toward military casualties and work in the battlefield and based upon the work of the Voluntary Aid Detachment (VAD) nursing reserve scheme. Between 1906 and 1914, the VAD, the vast majority of whom were women, conducted open-air exercises but also trained in domestic skills such as food preparation and laundry work.

In the early part of the twentieth century, nursing became an important occupation in both domestic and military senses. The work of nursing fell within the bounds of acceptable femininity for its association with caregiving, despite the way in which it enabled female travel, mobility, and outdoor work. The foundations for its acceptability as a public occupation were laid some forty years earlier through Florence Nightingale's popularisation of nursing as a responsibility for all women. Her influential *Notes on Nursing: What It Is and What It Is Not* (1860) was intended as a guide for 'every woman' in England who has to tend to the health of others, particularly children, thereby leading to the assertion that 'every woman is a nurse' (p. 1). Intriguingly, in order to truly be able to care for others, women were called upon to demonstrate strength. Mary Poovey's analysis of the social construction of Nightingale as 'housewifely' is instructive here. Poovey assigns two faces to the mythic figure of Nightingale: the self-denying caretaker and the tough-minded, persevering administrator. She argues that the two versions of Nightingale 'consolidated two narratives about patriotic service that were culturally available at mid-century – a domestic narrative [female] of maternal nurturing and self-sacrifice and a military narrative [male] of individual assertion and will' (1988, p. 169). In several of Marchant's protagonists, we shall see this consolidation operate in their acts of bravery and strength, which both complement, and are justified by, the performance of the domestic tasks in inherent in nursing.

Aside from its applications in the family home, nursing was a public occupation that could be conducted in the far reaches of the Empire. Nightingale's image of the ideal professional nurse, Kristine Swenson suggests, conformed to an image of middle-class domesticity and was built upon the idea of gender complementarity: 'Because disease arose from filth, it must be fought not with (male) medicines, but with (female) cleanliness' (2005, p. 33). The prevention of disease, performed primarily through domestic tasks – hygiene as 'the handmaid of civilization' – was integral to the nurse's function. The association of nursing with the domestic, even when conducted overseas, situated it not as a challenge to appropriate spheres of work for men and women, but as a task ideally suited to women accustomed to household tasks and instructing servants. Professional nursing, especially as constructed by Nightingale, played upon Victorian gender norms, yet the possibility of working overseas did offer the potential for adventure and distinction, as Anne Summers observes: 'The archetypally feminine functions of caring, mothering, serving and housekeeping were given a setting of high drama, and elevated into the means by which women could achieve unequivocal public honour' (1988, p. 6).

Nursing also serves to partially contain fears about disease and the deleterious effects of harsh climates when English bodies are located outside England. In *The Girl Captives*, the Indian environment is presented as physically taxing, encouraging cholera and smallpox outbreaks, and its searing sun induces blindness. An epidemic of malarial fever, in fact, serves as a crucial factor in enabling the hostile Kajids to mount an attack on the town in which the heroine resides. When the fever begins to claim victims, the post shuts down and in the confusion the Kajids enact their plan to kidnap wealthy residents and hold them to ransom. Chrissie, the protagonist, the children of the upper-class Boyd family (Gwen, Jessie, baby Wyn), and their aunt Juliet are taken captive. During their imprisonment, Gwen falls ill and Chrissie must nurse her without a fire or medication and little food. When they are banished outside the city walls – where jackals and hyenas roam – the other girls panic in the frightening conditions, but Chrissie sets about meeting obvious practical needs such as drawing water. She further demonstrates bravery when she refuses to leave Juliet and Wyn after they contract smallpox and are taken to the 'court-of-the-doomed' and left for dead, despite the risk to her own life. Chrissie also transfers her nursing skills to a native woman whose husband has fallen ill, showing her how to massage his limbs and make a shelter for him within their home. She demonstrates the way in which proper attention to domestic hygiene can serve as a preventative for potentially fatal disease or stem its effect. The centrality of nursing to the maintenance of empire is evinced here through its minimisation of the risk of death for colonists, and the depiction of disease itself as posing a military risk. Chrissie's display of both domestic capability and physical strength is reminiscent of Nightingale's conception of nursing as a non-threatening occupation for women that permits individual assertion.

The performance of extraordinarily brave acts by Marchant's heroines is the most commonly emphasised aspect of her fiction in brief surveys of her works. In *Jenny's Adventure*, for instance, the 13-year-old heroine, Jenny Burton, must care for her younger brother while her father prospects in a rugged area in Canada. Eventually the children are determined to join their father and they set out from Juneau with an American couple, the Perrys, along the rough trail to Dawson City. Not only are Jenny's parents removed from her life through death and distance, but Mr. Perry also falls ill along the trail and Mrs. Perry proves worthless in situations requiring a strong constitution. Isolated from help, Jenny chops firewood, but the situation becomes dire when her brother falls ill and rain sets in. Despite the impossibility of such a disease in Canada, his condition is pronounced to be malarial fever by a passing doctor and Jenny must also nurse him until the doctor can return with provisions. The Perrys selfishly abandon the children, leaving Jenny to care for her brother alone in the wild. While she is a 'town-bred girl' whose domestic capability has previously been foregrounded, Jenny soon adjusts to her environment, even fending off a wolf with a stick.

The eponymous heroine of *The Adventures of Phyllis: A Story of the Argentine* (1910) demonstrates a similar degree of bravery and shows the need for English girls to be capable of performing new, physical tasks when living far from the comforts of home. Phyllis Talbot has had no previous nursing experience, but she calls on first-aid lessons when she discovers a delirious elderly man, in need of nursing care, in an isolated area. She responds admirably to the situation, ignoring the abject presence of dead rats and her patient's bloodied and sore-encrusted head: '[S]he was strong and vigorous; moreover, she had the faculty of rising to the occasion, and, tired though she was with her long journey, the determination not to be beaten by circumstances was strong upon her' (p. 40). Phyllis's immediate competence owes something to her first-aid lessons and supports the idea of the spirit of national preparation for catastrophe discussed earlier.

Nursing also proves to be a path to independence for Phyllis. It allows her to work and live away from her family, and also to remain unmarried at the novel's conclusion as a strong girl caring for 'weak things' rather than being taken care of herself by a husband like other Marchant heroines. Phyllis's family is resident in Buenos Aires, and after some ill-fated investments by her father, the three daughters and two brothers must adjust to life without money and servants. Phyllis is adamant that she would rather 'be a scullery maid' than live with her soon-to-be-married eldest sister, so she assumes a position as a nursery governess on Mendoza with an English family, the Maurices. She is hard-working and, unlike Hettinga's description of Marchant's heroines as bemoaning the performance of tasks which seem to call for men, she actually wishes that she was male so that she could be independent: 'Why did she have to suffer so keenly when all she wanted was a chance to work? The bread of idleness which she was now eating was surely bitter enough; if only she had been a boy, and able to take her life in her own hands, like Horace and Fred [her brothers], how much happier she would have been!' (p. 15). The options for an occupation for Phyllis are limited, but nursing permits her to remain unmarried and satisfied by the pleasures of her work. The Maurice family has an invalid child, Freda, who provides the possibility of long-term employment for Phyllis, and her independence along with it: '[W]hen Freda said with a ripple of pleased laughter: "Oh, I should love to have you carry me in your arms, because you look so nice and strong," Phyllis straightaway decided that the care of weak things was her vocation, and lifting the small invalid in her arms, carried her out to the sunshine' (p. 270).

Nell, the heroine of *Daughters of the Dominion: A Story of the Canadian Frontier* (1909), also has aspirations to be a nurse and, in a show of her desire to be proficient in the domestic sphere, laments that she cannot keep house properly because of poverty. As an orphan, Nell lacks guidance from a parental figure. However, she displays both the expected norms of a cultivated British girl and the strength necessary for life in the Empire. As Phillips observes, Nell is 'not a girl in boys' shoes, but a girl assuming the assertive and strong role demanded by the adventure story in which she finds herself' (1997, p. 102). Her assertive qualities are nevertheless balanced by her desire to care for others. When a starving young man named Dick Brunson passes the shack, she catches him 'in her strong young arms' to prevent him falling; yet she also loves to nurse 'sick things' including family members and animals (Marchant, 1909, p. 20). Nell is marked as less genteel than a British girl, notably when she has difficulty sewing, but she works to become proficient in delicate tasks as well as arduous ones:

> Nell's hands and arms, roughened and strengthened by much wood-sawing and chopping, digging, and similar tasks, felt the awkwardness of what our great-grandmothers called sewing white seam. But sewing is a distinctly feminine accomplishment; and as Nell yearned to excel in all womanly occupations, she persevered with needles and cotton until she became an adept at the gentle art. (p. 147)

When the family property is sold, Nell, like Phyllis, wants to make her own living: she is determined not to be the family's servant and sets out to seek employment. After her first job nursing a sick woman on a homestead, she finds temporary work as a telegraph operator that leads to an offer of a permanent position in a mining town devoid of women. Her real vocation, however, is one that draws on traditional feminine skills: she cooks and sells food to the miners. With a lack of women settlers, many miners lose their health and even die without female care, particularly because of inadequate hygiene during food preparation and storage: 'A good many of the poor fellows come out from England, and have been used to proper cooked food all their lives; but when they get up at the mines, and have to get along on hard tack and reesty bacon...why it ain't long before they go wrong themselves' (p. 173). After Nell sustains an injury when attempting to foil a robbery, she can no longer work as a telegraph operator and considers channelling her desire to help the sick into a medical career. The town doctor, however, dissuades her from a profession because 'there is always a crying need for bright capable women in what are mistakenly called the humbler walks of life' (p. 257). Despite her swift acquisition of the skills of telegraph operation and fearless nature in foiling a robbery, Nell embraces marriage, and she combines this with nurturing pursuits such as caring for children and cooking food for the miners – a task that retains a therapeutic strand from her initial desire to nurse, given the prevalence of illness induced by poor food hygiene, but which remains within the 'humbler walks of life'.

Indigenous peoples: Conspicuous in their absence

In the previous section, I suggested that Marchant's heroines can bring civility to imperial locations through nursing. By drawing on both domestic/maternal and military narratives, her heroines display elements of the mythologised wartime nurse. The acceptability of the caring aspects of nursing allows the heroines to perform heroic tasks and undertake dangerous adventures without compromising their representation as admirable protagonists. I now turn to the absence of a more conventional feminine civilising function in Marchant's novels: bringing British ways to native inhabitants of its colonies. Marchant's heroines rarely interact significantly with any indigenous inhabitants; indeed in most of her adventures, they do not engage with them at all.

In her study of empire in children's fiction, Daphne M. Kutzer discusses the moral agency of the Victorian woman and its significance in imperial locations: 'Bringing civilization to the "savages" meant upholding the moral virtues epitomised by English womanhood, and thus, English womanhood often functioned as a convenient symbol for the virtues of civilization' (2000, p. 5). Rather than assuming the role of moral guides through the upholding of virtuous behaviour or direct intervention in the practices of indigenous inhabitants, Marchant's physically strong protagonists conduct strenuous labour to maintain property and tend to sick and injured bodies. Nevertheless, while these girls primarily assume a different imperial task than that which may have been idealised for British women, their minimal interaction with native inhabitants does provide further opportunity for the demonstration of bravery.

Two of Marchant's early adventure stories, both from 1900, are set in India. *The Girl Captives: A Story of the Indian Frontier* is a typical girls' adventure, while the other novel, *In the Toils of the Tribesmen: A Story of the Indian Frontier*, exhibits a greater religious influence than is typical of girls' adventures. It concerns a missionary family toiling against the superstitious and 'ignorant' ways (such as the practice of suttee) of the natives, attempting to bring the 'civilising influences of the Christian religion' (*Toils*, p. 2).[6] While the narrative concerns the actions of men rather than focusing on a girl adventurer, the eldest daughter, Coralie Blake, does attempt to exact influence on an Indian girl named Amrita, particularly regarding cleanliness. Amrita eventually takes up rule as a Ranee, and after Coralie receives her education in England (she identifies herself as an 'English girl'), she makes the decision to return to India, concerned that Amrita is still a 'heathen' and that the people still sit in 'darkness'. Amrita is transformed through the impact of Coralie's ideals and because of a bout of severe sickness. Her men now fight for the English, and her concern for her own people increases: 'Vain, to a certain extent, she always might be, and fond of fine dress, but half her selfishness was gone, and it was for her people, and their real welfare, that most of her thought and care were spent. The British Government expressed itself well pleased at the rare fidelity of this tribe' (p. 345). *In the Toils of the Tribesmen* is unique among Marchant's works for the interest the heroine demonstrates in transforming the native people to British ways, perhaps reflecting the importance of India as the 'jewel in the Crown' of the Empire. In Marchant's succeeding novels, attempts to civilise the native inhabitants are not part of the heroine's purview. The anxieties about the maintenance of empire in the first decade of the twentieth century may serve as an explanation for why these novels focus on nursing (with its relationship to preparedness for war) and maintenance of British homes in imperial locations rather than transformation of indigenous peoples.

The Girl Captives fits the mould of Marchant's girls' adventures to a greater degree, although it does engage significantly with the native people and is fascinated with the bringing together of races, and the maintenance of order between them. It begins with an exoticised visual spectacle of a marketplace complete with tigers, elephants, Patialan pilgrims cutting themselves with knives, 'solemn-toned Hindoos', 'hill Kajids', Chinese, Jews, Turks, Germans, Swedes, American tourists, and the 'familiar British soldier, good-natured and obliging' (p. 10). The heroine, fourteen-year-old Chrissie Felton, is closely aligned with her father, a captain stationed at Rampoostan.

In *Orientalism*, Edward W. Said identifies the omnipresence of particular views of the Orient in the nineteenth century that worked to justify Western intervention. The Orient was figured as separate, with 'its eccentricity, its backwardness, its silent indifference, its feminine penetrability, its supine malleability' (2003, p. 206) opposed with Western progress and rationality, which were in turn aligned with the masculine. In *The Girl Captives*, Marchant places emphasis on the native Kajids as 'Other', rather than identifying any transformative potential through civilising. The Kajids reside in the hills, and they are cruel, opportunistic, and lacking in compassion, rendering them antithetical to the English missionaries who figure in the novel. The feminisation of the Orient is elemental in constructing its inferiority, and similarly the Kajid's ruler, 'the Great Nom', is feminised in a demonstration of their weakness as a people. He is dressed in yellow petticoats and mocked on account of the way in which his 'drapery' buries the mule he rides upon. He also speaks formally, yet with comic mistakes, undermining his pretensions to 'royalty', a label which can only be rightfully attributed to the British monarchy in imperialist discourse. Despite his amusing appearance, the Great Nom's treatment of his own people is heartless in the face of a disease outbreak: all sufferers are condemned to die in a courtyard in which scattered fragments of human bone are picked clean by crows. His cruelty particularly contrasts with the selfless decision by Chrissie to nurse her friends despite risk to her own health and, with the prevalence of nursing in Marchant's girls' adventures generally, serving as a sign of British refinement and civility above the almost animalistic abandonment of the sick practiced by the Kajid ruler.

Contrary to Sally Mitchell's suggestion[7] that in Marchant's early books 'girls listened and watched while men acted' (1995, p. 137), Chrissie is very active, particularly when juxtaposed with her mother, who is constantly ill and remains cosseted in her room. Chrissie attempts to learn to fire a gun when there is fear of attack from the Kajids, purportedly so that she can at least shoot herself. With her mother's incapacity and the likely absence of her father and other English military men in the event of attack, Chrissie's use of the gun is not unfeminine; it fits within the scope of ordinarily rough or 'masculine' activities that are acceptable when necessity or survival demands it. Moreover, while it is not overtly stated, Chrissie's desire to be capable of killing herself speaks about fears of maintaining individual sexual purity and, uniquely for Marchant's novels, about the purity of the English among barbaric natives. She provides shooting lessons to two other girls, but can no longer bear to do so after the accidental death of a chicken: 'It was almost ludicrous to see how Chrissie grieved for that poor chicken, and the shuddering horror with which she viewed the mutilated corpse of her victim' (p. 75). The other girls call her cowardly and ask how she would kill a Kajid, and

Chrissie concedes that she could not do so if her victim were to scream. After that she refuses to touch a gun again. Her bravery and willingness to teach herself how to use a weapon are balanced by her demonstration of an inability to intentionally kill and her exaggerated emotional response to the death of a chicken, serving as a reinforcement of the notion that she has not drifted into masculine ways. This is particularly relevant because of the lack of imminent danger during which such temporary drifting might be justified. This incident also identifies the enemy with an animal that is generally regarded as dispensable, as if grieving over the death of a Kajid would be a similarly ludicrous response to that of grieving for the chicken. This view of the Kajid further demonstrates the way in which girls do not 'civilise' in Marchant's novels: the Kajids are not pitied nor viewed as requiring a 'lift' in their morals from British culture and Christianity, but are expendable obstacles in the path of British rule.

In *The Girl Captives,* adults maintain established imperial ideals. Older girls are afforded more freedom to act than a child, but they also have the capacity to think and act in ways that may need to be curtailed in adulthood. In the opening chapter, at the market, Chrissie takes delight in holding an Indian baby, despite the protestations of her escort, Private Ford. When the baby takes ill, his parents approach the Felton home to ask for help. Chrissie takes the baby in, calls for a doctor, and ensures that the baby is cared for. She seeks to shock Ford, 'who was a staunch upholder of class distinctions, and looked upon coloured people as not merely inferior to his own race, but in point of intelligence and capacity as ranking even lower than a horse' (p. 23). It is also telling that Captain Felton thinks his wife would not have assisted the child because of 'national prejudice, and all that sort of thing' (p. 37).

The indigenous peoples of Canada, Australia, South Africa, and South America are not entirely absent from the narratives of Marchant's other novels. However, they are bit players, in the background, rather than fully developed characters whom the heroines might seek to 'improve'.[8] *Sisters of Silver Creek: A Story of Western Canada* (1908) is set in the Pheasant Hills near an 'Indian' reservation. One of the three sisters, Pattie, is petrified of the Native Americans to the point of having nightmares about them, but her sister Kitty remarks that her fear is irrational: 'I don't expect there is an Indian in the Reservation who knows how to scalp anything, unless he is an educated red man and has read Fenimore Cooper's stories (p. 117). The indigenous people are not even credited with knowledge of their own history and cultural practices (only written history by a non-native writer could provide them with this), and they are also equated with beggars, particularly when one man refuses an offer of food after approaching the sisters' home:

> This was a stolid-looking Indian, clad in civilized garments, but with his hair hanging in a wild matted mass, stuck through with quills, an iron skewer or two, and some rusty screws and nails, which he evidently regarded as a valuable treasure-trove. He demanded 'ter-backer' with a professional whine which would not have disgraced individuals of his class in London or Paris. (p. 139)

The portrait of the 'Indian' suggests that colonisation has brought with it a veneer of civility, in the form of his tailored clothing, but that his nature remains 'wild' and 'primitive', as evidenced by his lack of grooming and his self-adornment with valueless objects. That settler Canadians should seek to civilise or improve this lazy 'Indian' is an option not discussed. The comparison of his manner with beggars 'of his class' in cities elsewhere tellingly conflates conceptions of race with those of class. As a white English woman with a private-school education and little lived experience of racial difference – Marchant never travelled abroad[9] but read *The Geographical Magazine* and researched at the Bodleian Library, Oxford (Major, 1991, p. 33) – she may have used this association of the 'Indian' with beggars or those of the lowest classes as the only vocabulary of difference available to her. Likening him to a beggar in a large 'civilised' city spreads the lower-class tropes of laziness, lack of cultivation, and a neglect of hygiene coupled with the threat of contagion to the category of race.

The convergence of race and class is a subject considered by Anne McClintock in her study of empire, *Imperial Leather* (1995). She argues that these categories, as well as gender, cannot be considered as operating in isolation from each other; for instance, racial rhetoric was invoked to construct distinctions between what we would today consider as 'classes' (1995, p. 54). That is, in order to uphold the superiority of the 'universal standard' – the white male child – those within England who strayed from the ideal had to be categorised as deviations from the normal type, or as belonging to degenerate classes. As McClintock suggests:

> [T]he iconography of *domestic degeneracy* was widely used to mediate the manifold contradictions in imperial hierarchy – not only with respect to the Irish but also to the other 'white negroes': Jews, prostitutes, the working-class, domestic workers and so on, where

skin color as a marker of power was imprecise and inadequate. (1995, p. 53)

Just as 'races' were constructed as having inherent traits that justified the rule of one (who was intelligent, strong, and hard-working) over another (who was stupid, weak, and lazy), so too could the English poor be considered as possessing 'biological flaws' which McClintock notes were considered a threat to the wealth and health of the 'imperial race'.

When other races do figure at all in Marchant's novels, they are often categorised as inferior to the 'English'. *The Heroine of the Ranch* (1914), set in Tierra del Fuego with a heroine named Kate M'Auslane, portrays the native servants as lazy – they neglect the care of the M'Auslane family home when Kate's mother dies and there is no one to oversee them. Kate's uncle Sandy drives the natives to do the housework, noting that laziness is an inborn feature of their race: 'A lazy set they are! But, poor things, what can you expect of people who are descended from generations of loungers?' (p. 213). The presentation of laziness as a long-standing racial character flaw rather than something easily corrected also reinforces the neglect of civilising actions by the heroines.

A counterpoint to the previous examples of the treatment of race, and a rare instance of the civilising function in Marchant's stories, is evident in *The Black Cockatoo: A Story of Western Australia* (1910), a shorter novel with a simpler vocabulary, perhaps aimed at a younger readership. Unlike the girls' adventures, *The Black Cockatoo* depicts a family of five children of mixed age and sex, primarily focusing on two of the youngest. The Payntter children are not permitted to play with the indigenous children who 'squat' on their property, the Woola Run. The indigenous Australians are deemed lazy (they are considered not sufficiently knowledgeable in domestic matters to be hired as servants and too idle to seek to learn the skills), superstitious (afraid that hearing the noise of a 'Joono' or type of ghost will result in death), and uncivilised (they live in 'shelters' considered too ramshackle to be afforded the term 'hut'). Nine-year-old Tom is aggravated by their presence because they purportedly steal sheep from the property, and he devises a strategy to scare them from the land that entails playing a French horn to mimic the supposed sound of the Joonos. True to their depiction as highly superstitious and ignorant, the indigenous people flee the camp 'in wild confusion' upon hearing the noise.

Tom and his sister Ellie (aged eleven) become lost in the bush after the prank, and the rest of the narrative relates to the family's search for the two children and their survival away from home. Indigenous Australians are positioned as both threat and saviour in the harsh outback environment: while a tracker named Biboo is enlisted to help find the children, there is also rumour of a party of 'cannibal natives' collecting prisoners for a 'war feast'. Tom and Ellie struggle to find food and water. They decide that the only thing they can do to aid in their survival is pray. The arrival of Yarra, an unaccompanied indigenous girl, saves the children from certain death. Yarra is marked as uncivilised and unfeminine, clad in a dirty man's work shirt, but the three roasted frogs she provides Tom and Ellie stave off starvation, and she locates water holes that the two children were unable to find. The children's rescue is primarily attributed to 'Providence', however, rather than the usefulness and wisdom of native survival skills. Yarra is not shown to impart her knowledge of the natural environment to the children; she merely supplies them with food and water to survive so long as they remain in danger. The transfer of knowledge from one culture to another takes place only from the 'civilised' to the 'uncivilised', with the indigenous girl shown as benefiting from her first religious instruction: 'It was they who taught Yarra to give thanks also for an escape as great as theirs, and the black girl was quick to respond to the teaching she received' (p. 282). Nevertheless, without the intervention of Yarra, the children would surely have perished. This inescapably situates the indigenous girl as something of a saviour, even if her knowledge and survival abilities are not valued once danger has passed in a land where British colonisation seeks to 'civilise' both the land and its native inhabitants.

A girl's own piece of the empire

As I have suggested, nursing could enable a life for the heroine without reliance on her own family or a husband, although sometimes only temporarily. The ownership or management of land functions similarly in several novels. In an article that considers three Marchant novels with similar plots, Bratton argues that the heroines have power which is enacted through 'domination' of their environment:

> The settings are exotic in order to provide the ground for physical adventures, but they are more than that; they are one of the most important elements in the ideological pattern. In each of these three novels, a girl owns a sizeable chunk of the world – in two out of three she is sole possessor, in her own right and name. (1989, p. 204)

In the works that Bratton refers to, the heroines' fathers are elderly
and incapacitated, and each heroine possesses the family estate legally
and conducts all the work and management of the household. Bratton
argues that the solution to the narrative problem posed by the bringing
together of domestic and imperialistic values is for the 'nest' to become
an empire in the absence of a capable male head of the household:

> [H]ome duties become the paradigm of her conquest of the wider
> world. Thrift and forethought are scaled up from the kitchen to the
> gold-mine and the camel-farm; motherly rule through personal devo-
> tion is transferred from the brood of children to the tribe of retain-
> ers. The sacred ties of the hearth become, by extension which had
> after all been made before, those of the feudal domain, but without
> the displacement which that had previously entailed on to a male
> head of the house. (1989, p. 205)

Like the heroines who pursue occupations such as nursing or cooking
for miners, those who manage land do not usurp the part of men, but
instead work toward self-sufficiency or the maintenance of family property in their absence. Bratton argues that the heroines' feudal rule 'more
than fulfil[s] the lord's role in the romantic vision of that system, tending and standing for their people at home and abroad' (1989, p. 204). In
other words, the English girl can represent the superior racial qualities
and values of her home country. One way she can do this is by bringing
humane treatment to those employed on her property.

The imposition of British ways on an estate is demonstrated in *No
Ordinary Girl: A Story of Central America*. Orphan Daisy Kennard, who
has been raised by her aunt and uncle in Quebec, is a successful student
who wishes to become a teacher in Panama City. She is sent to spend
six months in the hills with a new pupil, an orphaned heiress named
Senorita Juanita del Maestrante, who is later revealed as Daisy's long-
lost twin sister, 'Nita'. Juanita is adept at shooting and stalking wild
sheep, and she is presented as the energetic leader of the 600 natives
who live in huts on the plantation. The natives were initially treated
as slaves: they were physically abused and could be sold at will. The
next son in line inherited the estate and married an English wife, who
encouraged more civil treatment of the native people: '[she] so coaxed
and persuaded her husband, that in consequence of her pleading the
slaves became merely servants, with no property, it is true, but free to
go or come as they chose, no longer to be beaten to death at the pleasure of their master' (1907, p. 152). The transformation from slave to

employee is an initiative brought into practice by a British woman, a sign of compassion and of her moral superiority that is demonstrated in other novels through the performance of nursing.

Despite Juanita's being in charge, there is still a male figure at the plantation. Juanita's mother's second husband, Captain Lander, is present, but he takes little interest in the estate's management. When he is on his deathbed, however, Marchant creates another scenario in which girls must survive without male assistance. (The native men, of course, might as well be entirely absent, although they are useful for assistance in physical tasks.) The additional determination and strength required of girls in remote locations is foregrounded in Marchant's description of the situation:

> It would have been a trying experience to face if it had come to her in the haunts of civilization [...] but up here in the heart of the wilderness, walled in by rugged mountain ranges, the tragedy that was looming grew all the more solemn and terrible by reason of the solitude and isolation of the scene. (pp. 131–2)

Daisy is left to care for Lander while Juanita travels to seek help. When Juanita is feared dead, Lander appoints Daisy the mistress of the plantation. As a relative newcomer to Panama, and with what she imagines as no connection to the estate, Daisy displays reluctance to exercise control on the property, blushing with embarrassment when she must tell the servants that she, 'a stranger', has become an authority over them.

Daisy's hesitancy to rule, combined with the lack of a civilising function that I have already identified, differentiates these works from those that Ross G. Forman discusses in his essay on the children's adventure tale in Latin America, which includes an analysis of Marchant's 1918 novel *Lois in Charge; or, A Girl of Grit*. Within what Forman calls the 'extracolonial' location of Brazil (that is, outside its actual colonies, but in countries deemed suited to mass immigration and trade), he suggests that the focus is on settlement and religious and ideological conversion, aims that were more familiar within formal colonies such as Australia and India. The marriage plot that resolves many Marchant novels can therefore be seen in some instances as containing the threat of interracial relationships. Yet with several unmarried heroines and the almost total absence of indigenous peoples, the focus on the maintenance of a 'British identity' in a foreign culture and inflecting local surroundings with 'a British ethos' (2000, p. 456) that Forman notes is not detectable across the range of Marchant's novels.

Forman suggests that girls' texts set in Brazil depict not only the progression from girl to woman, but also – in a parallel of the transformation of 'unformed' to 'formed' land – the creation of a 'miniature England' beyond the Empire. This domestication includes the limited geographical scope in the girls' novels in comparison with the cross-country travels of the male novels (girl protagonists remain resident in Brazil in their 'mini-Empires' and marry, whereas male protagonists return to Britain) and, second, the taming and domesticating of the land through farming. Forman argues that farms function as microcosms of Britain, incorporating Brazil (located outside the British territories) into the middle-class home:

> Through the resulting emphasis on hearth and home, the girls' novels seek to doubly domesticate Brazil, first by making Brazil (and, by extension, the extracolonial in general) into a central space for the consolidation of heterosexual romance between Britons, and second, by linking this discussion of domestic virtue to the domestication of the frontier in the British-occupied settlements described. (2000, p. 471)

The woman becomes not only the head of the household but also caretaker of land (a plantation) and has an expanded range of functions 'because the role of the family expands to encompass control over a mostly self-contained, local economic system' (Forman, 2000, p. 480). Because opportunities for women in England after the war were limited, Forman suggests these post–World War I novels support the social drive to encourage women to seek homes and husbands in the colonies, whereas in the mother country the heroine's pluck would 'interfere.' However, contrary to Forman, in the three pre-war novels I examine that depict heroines who become caretakers of land (in Canada and Uruguay) there is less focus upon the creation of a 'miniature England' than that which he observes in Brazilian settings. Instead, Marchant enables her heroines, within the bounds of acceptability, to lead independent lives.

In two Marchant novels, property enables each heroine to derive her own income. In *Sisters of Silver Creek*, one of the eponymous sisters, Sue Walsh, attains self-sufficiency once she begins to cultivate land. After their mother's death, Sue moves to Silver Creek in Canada with her sisters and is forced to gain competence in a variety of tasks for which she has never been trained. In addition to tending animals, she seeks to create her own income by making blackberry jam, with her success leading to further expansion of cultivated areas. Sue's strength in the wild is at odds with her sister Pattie's desire to nurture children and Kitty's wish to care for others. Reflecting on the way in which she has been forced to adapt, Sue makes an observation that touches upon the shifting bounds of expected behaviour when English people relocate to the colonies: 'I fancy numbers of people have to do in Canada what they would never have dreamed of doing in England' (1908, p. 73). After several years, Sue is both a business manager and a landholder but still fears she may remain unmarried since she has 'worn considerably with the passing of the busy years' and is called 'old maid Sue' (p. 365) – yet marriage comes to her eventually, courtesy of a man who has been living in Jamaica with whom she has been corresponding for some years. While it is not suggested that Sue will give up her jam business, her independent command of property is curtailed by her marriage and her work is not presented as ultimately satisfying on its own.

In contrast, the eponymous heroine of *Greta's Domain: A Tale of Chiloé* (1911) remains truly autonomous, does not marry,[10] and has her own property. While travelling by steamer, Greta's mother and her siblings become ill with suspected smallpox, and they are compelled to disembark in Chile. Greta must nurse her mother and siblings while the family remains in poverty until they collect their inheritance of a property from an uncle in England. The ship's captain places the family in a vacant house, and he promises to collect them on his return. When fragments of the crashed vessel are found, hopes for receipt of the inheritance seem dashed. Greta's mother shirks her responsibilities, leaving most of the work to her daughter. However, Greta willingly establishes her own 'domain': 'the queer old house over-looking the bay Greta felt to be her very own. ... It is my domain, and I just love to plan it all out, as if I were going to stay here all my life...' (p. 201). The inheritance does not eventuate, and Greta has already decided that she does not wish to return home despite being 'proud' of being an English girl. She intends to apply to remain at the property and will weave household objects to sell to become self-sufficient and remain independent. Conveniently, in what Hettinga would call another of Marchant's 'outrageous coincidences' (1996, p. 169), the family discovers a chest of stolen jewels in the house and uses half of the $1000 reward to purchase the dwelling and the land on which it sits to enable Greta's domain to truly become her own.

A Courageous Girl: A Story of Uruguay (1909) also places an English girl in control of an allotment of land in South America, but this tale is unique for the way in which it presents a girl taking charge while her father is still alive. Anne Beauchamp, a fourteen-year-old English girl, is the daughter of a sheep farmer in Uruguay. After three years of study at a private school in Hampstead, Anne returns to Uruguay improved in domestic work, but finds that her father, Victor, has a gambling problem and has been forced to sell the estancia house. Anne's former nurse, an Italian woman named Risla, now herds the sheep, and when her father is absent both Risla and Anne must supervise the Basque shepherds. Anne's 'rule' is initially resented by the men, 'but there was an air of authority about her which they could not resist [...] dragged thereto by the dogged determination of this girl who so lately had been in the schoolroom' (p. 69). While her father had been eager for her to learn more about domestic work, her tomboy experience with the shepherds proves useful when she must organise the shearing and lasso the sheep, which she does 'as well or better than any man on the place' (p. 97). Robert Laidlaw, the new owner of the estancia, believes that a woman who attempts 'men's labour' cannot retain 'her gentle womanliness' (p. 91) and does not think Anne should step into her father's role. Yet Laidlaw concedes that she handles the men better than himself or her father. When the burden of her father's trouble weighs upon her, Laidlaw suggests that she should allow him to deliver her from hardship as her husband. Anne's sense of family duty and the need to be 'true to the highest aims in life,' however, overcomes any desires for herself, and she resolves to stay with her father.

When Risla and her father go missing, Anne takes up more 'man's work' as a manager. Management of property is not represented as conflicting with idealised feminine qualities. The differentiation of acceptable and unacceptable tasks pertains to the justification behind the actions and whether such tasks are performed by choice to challenge gender norms or in order to support domestic goals of maintaining the family home or protecting family welfare. Upon her father's eventual death, with her familial responsibility fulfilled, she accepts Laidlaw's marriage proposal. He promises to relieve her from drudgery, and she is happy to 'stay at home and do pleasant work,' the novel closing with her sighing with content upon Laidlaw's arm (p. 287). Despite her wild adventures, including regularly riding cross-saddle and once carrying a revolver on a dangerous journey, Anne embraces the prospect of relative ease presented by domesticity. Her brave deeds and resilience throughout the narrative are tied to familial need, and once this justification disappears, she settles for a quiet life with a husband.

Marchant's girl heroines do not fixate on romance and rarely display interest in relationships with men while they are engaged in survival or averting catastrophe. However, many of the novels conclude with a sudden marriage proposal, as in the examples of *Sisters of Silver Creek* and *A*

Courageous Girl. Deborah Gorham proposes that in late Victorian fiction with an independent modern girl protagonist, the plot resolution involves recognition that such behaviour is confined to girlhood: 'in the end, the heroine is always made to realise superior value of femininity and of a life dedicated to domesticity' (1982, p. 108). This observation does not strictly hold in Marchant's pre-war adventure novels, however, as a few heroines remain unmarried and, among those who do marry, some are afforded a level of continued independence within the marriage plot. For example, in *The Loyalty of Hester Hope: A Story of British Columbia* (1914), a strong sense of Hester's continued enjoyment of hard work on her own land in rural Canada is conveyed at its conclusion, irrespective of her marriage.

The example of Hester shows that the heroine's engagement or marriage does not necessarily mark a capitulation to domesticity. However, *The Adventures of Phyllis* touches upon part of the problem that marriage can reconcile for other independent heroines in Marchant's novels. Phyllis initially refuses a marriage proposal, but when she realises that she would have to return to her family home, she considers that marriage will afford her a residence of her own. However, the words of her suitor – 'Phyllis, give me the right to take care of you' (1910, p. 338) – seem contrary to her expressed desire for and attempts to take her life into her own hands in the previous 200 pages. While her actions as a girl are not considered inappropriate or to be regretted, there is an implication that, with a husband to call on in times of crisis, extraordinary feats of courage and physical endeavour are no longer necessary.

Indeed, as this chapter has argued, it is the necessity of adventurous actions or rough work in extraordinary circumstances in imperial locations that makes them acceptable for these fictional girls to perform. In the early twentieth century, encouragement of the growth of colonial settlements was supported in Britain by a web of rhetoric that combined the ideologies of imperialism, national degeneration, racial superiority, and patriotism. Marchant's fiction taps into this spirit of preparation for potential emigration to a colony, or for war, with her depictions of strong and capable heroines. Furthermore, it presents several outcomes for adventurous heroines that include possibilities beyond the generic marriage plot and its curtailment of 'tomboyish' activities. While we gain an overall sense that Marchant's heroines will settle either in marriage or in maintaining property at the conclusion of each narrative, she does not necessarily limit the acceptability of rough work, independence, and self-sufficiency to the period of girlhood.

4
Fantastic and Domestic Girls and the Idolisation of 'Improving' Others

The protagonists of E. Nesbit's trilogy of fantasy novels, which comprises *Five Children and It* (1902), *The Phoenix and the Carpet* (1904), and *The Story of the Amulet* (1906),[1] act as the first British travellers to historical places and imaginary realms, including a tropical island inhabited by 'primitives'. Though Nesbit's stories were not exclusively intended for girl readers, their girl protagonists nevertheless support the imperial project through civilising 'native' inhabitants and mothering their brothers away from parental help. British colonialism was grounded in the logic of the parent-child relationship, with the phrase 'mother country' used to refer to the imperial centre, marking Britain's colonies as children in need of development and instruction. Within the language of a parental influence, colonial rule, however, has been largely conceptualised in masculine terms.[2] In the first half of this chapter, I consider how Nesbit's trilogy reconfigures the imperial parent-child/ruler-colony metaphor through the girl protagonist, Anthea, whose maternal capabilities aid not only in exploration, but also in negotiating with and placating indigenous peoples. More pointedly, I propose that Nesbit inserts mothering into the imperial parent-child metaphor.

From what some would regard as the 'safety'[3] of fantasised locations of displacement and distance, Nesbit's Psammead novels examine changing Edwardian conceptions of gender and nation. They also show a complex relationship to empire, not only recasting the parent-child dynamic in female terms, but also allowing for substantial criticism of imperialism and contemporary industrialised cities. Kimberley Reynolds includes Nesbit's novels among those of Mrs Ewing and Frances Hodgson Burnett for their incorporation of appropriate models of femininity into boys' adventure stories, generating a new generic form for children's literature. She suggests that they 'replace the ethos of confidence, mastery and independence based on masculine superiority with one based on class. In them sex roles are unambiguous, and accordingly the adventures have been domesticated...the emphasis is on celebrating family life rather than on conquering foreign lands and exotic peoples' (1990, p. 94). To distinguish my own argument from Reynolds', this chapter emphasises Nesbit's girl protagonist's interactions with other nations and exotic people and their implicit criticism of masculine imperial encounters. Significantly, Nesbit reconfigures the category of the heroic to situate maternal relations within it, promoting a unique vision of feminine heroism rather than mimicry of male actions coded as heroic. The leadership role accorded to the heroine, Anthea, because of her maternal instincts is nevertheless ideologically problematic because it is primarily demonstrated through what could be characterised as postcolonial infantilisation of indigenous peoples.

Frances Hodgson Burnett's two most famous novels stand in relatively contemporaneous contrast with Nesbit's trilogy for their presentation of realistic plots in which girls who have been raised in India must adjust to English domestic life without parental guidance. The shift to England does not, of course, extinguish the importance of empire in their narratives. As David Cannadine explains, 'home' was also bound up in empire: 'Britain was very much a part of the empire, just as the rest of the empire was very much part of Britain' (2001, p. xvii). *A Little Princess* was published in 1905,[4] and *The Secret Garden* was serialised in *The American Magazine* from 1910 and published as a novel in 1911. The second half of this chapter problematises British identity within the Empire by suggesting that the implicit arguments of these novels are that English children are most appropriately raised within England, with strong adult guidance and a culture of self-discipline. Moreover, for girls, cultivating their ability to care for and 'improve' others (a domestic, classed version of 'civilising' the racial Other), particularly the working classes and poor who threatened to compromise the superiority of the Empire's centre through weakness and depravity, is a crucial indicator of satisfactory development.

Society, rather than the individual,[5] is Nesbit's major concern. The Psammead trilogy's narratives purposely maintain that the children are not extraordinary of intelligence, appearance, or morality. The premise Nesbit constructs is that they are fallible and subject to ethical dilemmas just like her implied reader. She writes, 'in fact, they were rather like you' (1904, p. 13). The way in which the trilogy criticises English city life is ultimately demonstrated by a utopian society in which the care of children is of supreme importance and is symbolic of socialist ideals to protect the powerless and disenfranchised. Nesbit and her husband, Hubert Bland, were among the founding members of the Fabian Society, the aim of which, she wrote in a letter to friend Ada Breakall, was to 'improve the social system' (Moore, 1933, p. 64). Her collection of political poems, *Ballads and Lyrics of Socialism: 1883–1908*, includes 'Two Voices' (1886), in which she contrasts the 'fair' world of nature with the 'dark'-faced city occupied by the 'lonely' and 'unhelped'. As does *The Story of the Amulet*, Nesbit's poem condemns the way in which workers are exploited (they are left 'hungry and sad' with 'starving children' (pp. 24–8)).

The Psammead books depict the adventures of a family group of children, including three boys and two girls (Anthea, Robert, Cyril, Jane, and a baby who is referred to as 'the Lamb'), in which they are impelled by three magical items or beings. The magical device in the first book is Nesbit's own creation, the Psammead (a 'sand fairy'), a creature that is able to grant wishes. The second book dispenses with the Psammead. The children are bought a new nursery carpet, which not only proves to be a magic transportation device once owned by royalty, but also contains an egg from which they are able to hatch a living specimen of the mythical phoenix. The Psammead reappears in the third novel (when it has been captured and is offered for sale in a pet shop), but does not grant wishes because the children promised at the conclusion of *Five Children and It* not to make any future demands upon it. Instead, the Psammead directs them toward an ancient amulet for sale in a shop, which proves to have to the power to transport the children in time and, unlike the titular device in fellow Fabian Society member H.G. Wells' *The Time Machine* (1895), also in place.

This capacity for time and space travel enables the children to visit ancient Egypt, Babylon, Tyre, Atlantis, and ancient Britain. Nesbit also injects fantastic elements into the novels' reality. This mode of fantasy, dubbed the 'intrusion fantasy' after the rupture caused to normality, must, according to Farah Mendlesohn's theory of fantasy, encompass a return to normality in which the intrusion must be 'negotiated with or defeated, sent back to whence it came, or controlled' (2008, p. 115). In some respects, this logic of return is pervasive in the Psammead novels because of their initial appearance in serial form in *The Strand* magazine as self-contained chapter-length episodes that begin and conclude in the realist landscape. The stories both allow fantasy to 'intrude' into reality and give scope for the child protagonists to interact with the world of the past, present, and future independent of adult supervision.

In Nesbit's novels, the absence of any meaningful regular adult presence means that the children must be self-regulating for almost the entire narrative.[6] In contrast with Victorian and Edwardian children's fiction that included a moral guide figure who directed juvenile protagonists to make correct decisions, the Psammead does not act as the children's guide. This leaves the children uniquely situated without adult instruction and allows them unmediated interaction as representatives of a mythically extended empire across time and space. As the eldest child, and in the absence of the children's mother, Anthea often takes on a maternal role with her siblings, guiding them toward morally right actions including not taking money from strangers and adopting good manners. The combination of Anthea's altruism and flashes of bravery in the most dangerous of situations construct her as the leader of the children's adventures.[7]

While Nesbit herself is notable for her unconventional femininity – she wore her hair short, she cycled, she smoked, and she wore 'aesthetic gowns' (Avery, 2005, viii) – her protagonist Anthea's femininity is rather more traditionally rendered. In the first novel, readers are informed almost immediately that Anthea intends 'to be a good housekeeper some day' (1902, p. 15). Prior to her departure in *The Story of the Amulet*, the children's mother reminds Anthea that as the eldest girl she must try 'to make the others happy' (1906, p. 4). As Amelia A. Rutledge argues, Nesbit is at her most conservative in books in which the children work in a group: 'In her stories of the "Five Children," the female characters, especially Anthea, the elder of the two girls are the nurturing exemplars of empathy' (1999, p. 229). While Anthea does indeed serve as a moral guide and mother-substitute to her siblings, in contrast with Rutledge's construction of a binary of 'male active agency and aggression in opposition to female passivity and altruism' (1999, p. 229), the combination of Anthea's altruistic ways and moments of heroism in the most dangerous of situations position her at the helm of the children's adventures. Moreover, in interactions with other people, particularly the indigenous inhabitants of places they visit, Anthea's techniques are more successful than her brothers' more impulsive and aggressive tendencies, which Nesbit criticises through parody of the masculine adventure genre. The children's group dynamics offer a modified view of imperial encounters and colonial settlement as 'fatherly', instead often foregrounding the superiority of maternal approaches in these situations.

Caring for others as the motivating force for Anthea's bravery also arguably constitutes a shift in the parameters of heroism. Rather than masculinising a female hero in a logic that suggests girls can be heroic

if they approximate male behaviours, Nesbit offers an alternative heroism grounded in capacities traditionally associated with women. The
novels link exciting adventures with maternal impulses. For example,
after Robert accidentally wishes in anger that 'everybody' would want
his baby brother, Anthea must be powerfully protective when a band
of idle, ragged gypsies wants to take possession of him. She bravely
clutches the baby despite the demands of several women. One of these
women has excessively reproduced – she has nineteen children of her
own – and is racially threatening, with her face 'the hue of mahogany,
and her hair jet-black, in greasy curls' (1902, p. 72). A further example
of Anthea's mothering qualities is her interaction with an elderly man
who lives in the same building as the children, who proves to be an
expert on ancient history and who assists in the children's adventures
with the amulet. Upon visiting his home, she observes that he has failed
to eat his dinner, and she reminds him, as her mother reminds her own
father, to eat regular meals, because he does not have a woman to take
care of him (1906, p. 42). This mothering continues when she takes
responsibility for bringing him breakfast in the mornings. Through
Nesbit's focus on women's capacity for nurturing in these adventures,
she elevates the status of women and collective, supportive behaviours,
in direct contradiction of the phallocentric logic of male heroes on an
individualist quest in which they are rewarded for violence and aggression, in what amounts to a compelling feminist alternative.[8]

Readers are given descriptions of events and places via comparisons
with boys' adventure books and magazines including Charles Kingsley's
Westward Ho! (1855), H. Rider Haggard's *Allan Quartermain* (1887), and
Boys of England. These popular cultural forms provide the protagonists
with their knowledge of the world outside England and give them
prompts for how to interact with the unknown. When the children
arrive in ancient Egypt in *The Story of the Amulet*, Cyril delivers a mes-
sage inspired by an article he had read in the *Daily Telegraph*: ' "we come
from the world where the sun never sets. And peace with honour is
what we want. We are the great Anglo-Saxon or conquering race. Not
that we want to conquer *you*," he added hastily' (1906, p. 61). In *The
Phoenix and the Carpet*, when the children wish to aid their mother in
gathering items for a bazaar, they wish for the carpet to transport them
to somewhere people 'will give us heaps of Indian things' (1904, p. 91).
When they arrive, the children recognise the place as India instantly
because of architectural features such as domed roofs and because of a
man riding an elephant, but also because of the signs of imperial rule:
'two English soldiers went along the road, talking like in Mr Kipling's

books – so after that no one could have any doubt as to where they were' (1904, p. 91). The presence of a presumably dark-skinned man riding an elephant does not serve in this instance to confirm the children's location. Rather, this sign of a colonising presence resonates with the images that they have in their minds from the works of an English novelist in order to deduce the nation, and it suggests the normalisation of colonial rule in their real-world Britain home.

Robert takes inspiration from British explorers and imperial traders when, at the conclusion of *Five Children and It*, he remarks upon the method he will use as an adult to be able to buy his mother diamonds as gifts: 'I shall make so much money exploring in Africa I shan't know what to do with it' (1902, p. 224). He has perhaps conflated the two pursuits, in that exploration in itself is unlikely to bring riches, but there is a general association between wealth for England and contact with the nations it sought to conquer or colonise. The premise that imperial wealth is there to be claimed by British men, as found in boys' adventure fiction, also extends to the explorer or coloniser being justified in taking goods if survival depends upon it. In the same novel, when trapped on a church tower after an ill-fated wish for wings, and finding a well-stocked larder, Robert's brother Cyril remarks, 'if the country you're in won't *sell* provisions, you *take* them. In wars I mean. I'm quite certain you do' (1902, p. 99). While Robert compares his idea with those of generals such as Napoleon and the Duke of Marlborough and argues that it is justified by 'necessity', Anthea injects a moral view of the situation and suggests that the act is wrong. She insists that the children 'club' their money and leave it to compensate the owner, inviting the child reader to criticise Robert's approach. Here Nesbit also satirises Robert's flawed application of military logic. To justify the proposed theft of food, Robert misquotes Elizabethan poet Sir Philip Sidney as having said, 'My necessity is greater than his' (1902, p. 99). Sidney, however, is famous for selflessly offering his water bottle to a wounded soldier when he had incurred a fatal injury at the Battle of Zutphen in 1586 with the words 'Thy necessity is yet greater than mine'. Humour in the trilogy is almost exclusively reserved for instances when the boys attempt to take command and is also borne out, as I shall discuss later, through parody.

Anthea herself is later compared with a general in her unflurried actions and 'far-seeing promptitude' in her preparations for the arrival of hordes of 'Red Indians', thus bringing together the virtues of both a maternal moral guide and an active, mentally strong leader. This episode is typical of her acts of bravery in protecting the Lamb, as she breaks open the family missionary box and a jug with savings in it in order to have the housekeeper take him away from the house. Immediately after he is safe, Anthea begins to cry: 'Jane did not understand at all how a person could be so brave and like a general, and then suddenly give way and go flat like an air-balloon when you prick it' (1902, p. 208). The comparison with a pricked balloon also resembles the instantaneous return to normality in the narrative when magic ceases to operate. With the return to normality there is a degree of social regulation, with Anthea losing her bravado and demonstrating a typical sign of feminine weakness through her tears. During a period of danger, Anthea's 'general-like' bravado in order to protect her siblings (as a mother would protect her child) is justified, yet when the threat passes, she returns to a more conventional femininity. The conflation of her general-like courage with her tears also serves to emphasise Anthea's heroic characterisation as a girl rather than as a surrogate boy.

In a similarly telling episode, an unintended, careless wish by Cyril – who is in the midst of reading *The Last of the Mohicans* – leads to the presence of the 'Red Indians' in England. Anthea not only ensures the baby is taken to safety, but takes a leadership role in this intimidating conflict with members of another race by making a white truce flag. Her peaceful attempt at a solution results in a pow-wow with Chief Golden Eagle:

> 'And I,' said Anthea, with sudden inspiration, 'am the Black Panther – chief of the – the – the Mazawattee tribe. My brothers – I don't mean – yes, I do – the tribe – I mean the Mazawattees – are in ambush below the brow of yonder hill.' (1902, p. 215)

Anthea lacks sufficient knowledge of Native American customs – perhaps never having read the same adventure stories as her frustrated brother Cyril – and, in her speech, refers to their clothing as 'wigwams' and to eating 'juicy fresh-caught moccasins' (1902, p. 216). Tales of Native Americans in circulation at the time read by children included James Fenimore Cooper's *Leatherstocking Tales* (1823–41), which included *The Last of the Mohicans* (1826), Henry Wadsworth Longfellow's 'Song of Hiawatha' (1855), American author Edward S. Ellis' boys' dime novels, and innumerable stories in English boys' periodicals featuring adventure fiction, such *Boys of the Empire* (first published in 1888). Despite their fearsome appearance (they have 'dark, cruel faces'), the 'Indians' are defeated in part because of the children's propensity for play and imagination. The wigs the children make in order to mimic the appearance of the Indians serve as substitutes for having their heads scalped: 'The poor untutored savages had indeed scalped the children. But they had only, so to speak, scalped them of the black calico ring-lets!' (1902, p. 219). The 'victory' scored because of the children's abil-ity to outwit the adult 'savages' not only infantilises them, but situates them as intellectually inferior as a race, below the capability of English children. Jacqueline Rose suggests that Rousseau's conception of child-hood innocence had important political repercussions that connected the immaturity of childhood with the immaturity of particular nations or peoples:

> Childhood is seen as the place where an older form of culture is preserved (nature or oral tradition), but the effect of this in turn is that this same form of culture is *infantilised*. At this level, children's fiction has a set of long-established links with the colonialism which identified the new world with the infantile state of man. Along the lines of what is almost a semantic slippage, the child is assumed to have some special relation to a world which – in our eyes at least – was only born when we found it. (Rose, 1984, p. 50)

In these kinds of constructions of childhood as the location of primi-tivism, the development of the child to adulthood is figured as an evolution. Jo-Ann Wallace, in her theorisation of children's literature and postcolonialism, suggests, 'The child as primitive must learn to control his body as well as his spirit; he is in need of physical, moral, and intellectual discipline or training' (1994, p. 174). While I am argu-ing that Nesbit's novels do infantilise native peoples, I follow Clare Bradford's caution against reading children as a colonised group spoken for by adults in the same way as Said describes the Oriental as spoken for by the Orientalist. As Bradford argues, the conflation of children with colonised peoples ignores the question of race and the fact that children develop into adults, whereas 'Orientals never transmute into Orientalists' (2007, p. 7). While Nesbit favourably contrasts past civili-sations with contemporary England, the Psammead books do ascribe a childlike lack of development or immaturity to several groups of 'native' people that the children interact with. This results not in an equation of childhood with non-white Others, however, but in the elevation of the British children above them. Anthea is integral to the reconfiguration of the parent-child dynamic in imperial encounters in maternal terms, particularly in *The Story of the Amulet*. Her capacity to placate infanti-lised native peoples, which is firmly established by her ability to care for and guide her siblings, is what enables the children to maintain British superiority over the 'natives' they encounter.

The first place to which the children travel via the power of the magic amulet is ancient Egypt. The ancient Egyptians live in archaic wood, twig, and clay dwellings which have low doors that are compared with those of dog-kennels, enabling undeveloped civilisations to be denied humanity. They are also denied the status of adults. Like other peoples the children visit, the ancient Egyptians are also infantilised. Anthea's distinct mothering traits prove to be successful in dealing with the overzealous natives. She gives the group one of Jane's lacy collars in order to pacify them, but speaks in the manner in which she would speak to an infant in order to situate herself as a superior: 'She spoke in the tone of authority which she had always found successful when she had not time to coax her baby brother to do as he was told. The tone was just as successful now' (1906, p. 62). While her tone is authoritative, it replicates the relationship between a mother and child. To reinforce this reconfiguration of imperial encounters in maternal terms, the masculine method of conquering civilisations and attempting to dominate through force or intimidation is not effective. This is demonstrated when Cyril attempts to compel a girl to give him information as to the location of the tribe's sacred place (where the other half of the amulet may be located) by looking at her 'nastily'. After this method fails, Anthea presents the girl with a ring she had previously admired and is rewarded with the information.

In the instance of outright conflict with adults in other lands, Anthea's strategies do not prove useful, however, and function to mark out limits to the actions of girls and women in imperial locations. Girls must be excluded from this preserve of masculine activity that mimics male imperial conquest, but Nesbit, at the same time as demarcating this realm, is nevertheless critical of it. When there is a fight in the Egyptian village, Robert loads his toy cap gun and Cyril tightens his belt, while Jane attempts not to cry and Anthea sets some flowers in a pot of water – a totally useless response to the situation. While the boys do not actively participate in the fighting, the 'weapon' Robert carries enables them to successfully dupe the Egyptians. He informs the people that his pistol will speak back to tell them that the children should guard their secret item; the loud noise of the cap going off does indeed convince the local people of Robert's claim. Yet his impulsiveness is detrimental to the children's quest, such as when he is excited by an evening with the king and queen of Babylon, asks outright for the amulet's other half, and the children are jailed below a moat underneath the river Euphrates. While the gun assists the children's quest, it is ultimately the cause of much greater harm, criticising the boys' more aggressive approach that more closely approximates actual imperial encounters. When Jane explains to Julius Caesar (after the 'learned gentleman' who has accompanied them on their journey wishes to see him) about the existence of guns, Robert shows him his toy one and explains the mechanics of the real weapon. After his conversation with Jane and Robert in which they talk up the achievements of Britain, Caesar resolves that he will indeed seek to invade it and that he will seek to manufacture guns (1906, p. 194).

One way in which the narrative makes explicit its criticism of aggressive and arrogant imperial behaviour demonstrated by the boys is through parody, which operates on several levels in Nesbit's trilogy. Jenny Bourne Taylor suggests that the children themselves 'repeatedly enact parodies of the colonial encounter, in a way that satirizes their Anglo-Saxon arrogance, and in which imperial conquest merges into ethnographic exploration' (Taylor, 1998, p. 110). As she notes, there is also a sense that the children are recapitulating stories previously published. Satire is almost always reserved for the boys in the group: Anthea does not display arrogance about her Englishness or attempt to mimic the actions of adventure-novel protagonists. On their first journey to Egypt, Robert remarks, 'what a lot we could teach them if we stayed here' (1906, p. 64), in a reversal of the usual practice of adults socialising children. While Cyril adds that they might be able to learn something themselves, after first-hand views of the way to build huts, hunt, make boats, and fish, Cyril's attitude toward these achievements is reminiscent of an adult contemplating the efforts of a child: ' "It is really wonderful," said Cyril patronizingly, "when you consider that it's all eight thousand years ago" ' (1906, pp. 65–6). Nesbit's criticism of contemporary society and her comparatively favourable assessment of past and future civilisations also lend a parodic note to Cyril's assessment, which rehearses a wider British attitude to the inferiority of native peoples that in turn justified the process of colonisation.

The one instance of colonisation in the trilogy is feminised by Nesbit and occurs in *The Phoenix and the Carpet* when the children travel with their cook to a tropical island complete with groves of palm trees and a profusion of flowers. The female cook takes on elements of a male coloniser in relation to the land and its native people, but she primarily enacts a feminine 'civilising' function and upholds 'superior' British morals. The inhabitants of the island, who reside in huts, are regarded as savages. In a demonstration of the wider way in which the children function as representatives of British imperialism, Robert proposes to the group that they should pose as missionaries to avoid any potential violence. Yet the inhabitants prove not to speak coherently, and the children run into the sea for safety on the premise that 'savages' must despise water because they are 'always dirty'. The 'savages', interpreting the cook's white cap (a marker of servitude in England) as the 'crown' of a prophecy, would like to make her their queen. This desire culminates in a ceremony in which drums are beaten, 'strange' songs sung, and frenetic dances performed until the point of exhaustion, reinforcing their depiction as primitive. Flattered by the opportunity to become a member of royalty, the cook decides to remain on the island, and upon Anthea's return she is dressed in a white robe and is being fanned with peacock feathers by 'copper-coloured boys' (1906, p. 82). The cook has already begun to teach them to understand English, and she intends to bring order – and with it civility – to the island by cleaning her hut and teaching the natives how to prepare more sophisticated food.

While the cook has attained a regal position amongst her 'court' of natives and is worshipped by them, it is not considered that she would take one of the 'copper-coloured savages' to be her husband, for obvious imperial reasons including miscegenation. It is convenient, then, that a fair-skinned burglar whom the children have previously befriended is brought to the island, is attractive to the cook, and is willing to propose to her. The final barrier to their union proves to be the lack of order with regard to marriage and religion among the island's native people: 'I don't believe these here savages would know how to keep a registering office, even if I was to show them' (1906, p. 221). As a British woman functioning as the upholder of morality, the cook delivers the ultimatum that if a genuine clergyman cannot be sourced then she will not be married. When the carpet is able to transport Reverend Septimus Blenkinsop from the children's homeland to enable the ceremony to proceed, not only is order brought to the island through the arrival of a suitable (white) English man to form a married union, but organised religion brings a degree of civility to it. The final civilising steps are the introduction of clothing that covers the body and the transformation of the island's vegetation with English plants. The newly married couple request for the children to bring them radish and parsley seed, broccoli, and mixed kale, which the burglar plants with a handmade wooden spade, and the cook learns to weave in order to manufacture a shirt and trousers 'of the most radiant whiteness' (1906, p. 224). Nesbit's novel concludes with the depiction of the cook and the burglar in glowing white clothing amidst the dark-skinned natives. The lowly Irish cook and the criminal, disempowered within Britain's social order, are empowered through imperialism. There is a degree of ideological progression in this challenge to class distinctions enabled by imperial conquest, but it is necessary for the non-white Other to be subordinated to enable this empowerment.

As these alternately parodic and supportive representations of British colonialism suggest, in the trilogy there is a coexistence of seemingly divergent ideologies. What could be considered a straightforward narrative of imperial superiority in some instances is also complicated by a socialist analysis of the faults of industrial society and neglect of its citizens, as Anita Moss (1991) and Suzanne Rahn (2006) have shown. *The Story of the Amulet* enables a citizen of one of the places the children visit – and one which can be perceived to have extremely negative connotations[9] – to be transported to, and make judgements upon, contemporary England. The queen of Babylon visits modern London, embarking on a cab tour that passes the grandest buildings, such as Buckingham Palace and Westminster Abbey. She is not impressed by the sight of the city and is, in fact, shocked by how 'neglected' what she identifies as 'slaves' seem to be and asks why their 'masters' do not look after them better. The slaves are, in fact, ordinary city workers, but the children do not understand the queen's criticism of free workers and are unable to explain 'the wage-system of modern England' (1906, p. 149). The obvious criticism of capitalism delivered here, as Rahn notes, is that the working man in contemporary society, for all of his freedom, may be in a worse position than a Babylonian slave (2006, p. 194).

The ancient queen's visit to London both idealises and expresses nostalgia for pre-industrial societies. As Eitan Bar-Yosef argues: 'Nesbit's fantasy of reverse colonization suggests that these foreign and ancient civilizations embody social ideals that the British Empire has lost' (2003, p. 15). His notion of a 'reverse colonization fantasy' touches upon the fear of foreign and ancient civilizations being superior by virtue of embodying qualities lost by the British Empire and also the fear of 'going native'. Rose's discussion of the adventure story as colonial fantasy which draws together the child and the primitive as child is instructive here. She suggests that childhood is imbued with the ability to transcend the imperfections of civilised society. In Nesbit's novels, the child mediates the contradiction of seeing modern society as degenerate while 'still wishing to preserve its superiority over an otherwise idealised primitive state' (Rose, 1984, p. 53). Framing the criticism of contemporary cities, which are representative of British progress and civilisation, is an implicit acceptance of Britain as a colonising force, which is buttressed by the presentation of Nesbit's child protagonists as often more resourceful and intelligent than non-white inhabitants of other lands and times.

In *The Story of the Amulet*, the forgotten people of 'civilised' England are embodied in the figure of an orphaned, dirty, shabbily dressed girl named Imogen (or 'The Little Black Girl') whom the children find. At only eight years old, she is due to be sent to a workhouse because there is no one to care for her. The Psammead delivers a criticism of contemporary England in his response: ' "You don't suppose anyone would want a child like that in *your* times – in *your* towns?" said the Psammead in irritated tones. "You've got your country into such a mess that there's no room for half your children – and no one wants them" ' (1906, p. 186). The place where the children find a home for her is in Britain's distant past, in which people live in huts surrounded by mud fences. Imogen is revealed to be the lost daughter of the queen of ancient Britain, and the civilised treatment of children in ancient times is contrasted with neglect in modern life. For instance, the children of the past are lavished with attention: 'You would have thought, to see them, that a child was something to make a fuss about, not a bit of rubbish to be hustled about the streets and hidden away in the Workhouse' (1906, p. 191). Children are, of course, esteemed with importance in imperial discourse that wishes to champion the future of the British Empire and its people, but for Nesbit they also hold the promise of a utopian future. The condition of children in each of the time periods depicted in *The Story of the Amulet* speaks of the respective society's relative merits. In industrialised Britain, the reader confronts dirty, unwanted children in the streets, whereas in the future the care of children is a supreme priority for all.

In the utopian future the children visit to learn the present location of the second half of the amulet, Nesbit's criticism of Edwardian society is most fully realised. The future city of London has a profusion of beautiful gardens, and even the museum pigeons are bright and clean. It is superior to the present London not only aesthetically, but socially, largely as a result of a maternal emphasis on childcare taking precedence. Men as well as women take responsibility for the care of babies, and an almost obsessive focus upon the health and safety of children is the norm: the interior of houses have padded walls to prevent injury, and, similarly, there are no fireplaces for children to burn themselves upon. Every resident enrols in a 'Duties of Citizenship Course' that teaches the ideals of a socialist society, and small children are taught a rhyme for similar effect: 'I must not litter the beautiful street/With bits of paper or things to eat;/I must not pick the public flowers/They are not *mine*, but they are *ours*' (1906, p. 238). With the aid of the amulet, the children transport a mother from the future to their own time, and we are left in no doubt that the sight of grey skies, men fighting in the street, and people hurrying to get to their homes situates the present England, with its lesser focus on community, as inferior.

The neglect of children – those with the potential to realise a future utopia – in the present signals Nesbit's view that not only is contemporary industrialised London less ideal than a future with a maternal emphasis, but it has deteriorated in this aspect from the past. In supposedly more primitive civilisations, such as that of ancient Britain, there are no 'unwanted' children such as Imogen, who is unable to find a loving home in the present. Implicit in this criticism of contemporary Britain, as I have argued, is Nesbit's parody of the British masculine imperial encounter and her rendering of a favourable preliminary sketch of what female-led imperial encounters might resemble. Her fantasy trilogy can then be read as a more complex text that attempts to envision different possibilities for configuring nation and gender in other places and times, rather than as a simple reflector of British imperial ideology. Nevertheless, while the magical adventures depicted in the trilogy challenge ideas of both nationalism and gender norms in carving out a feminine model of heroism, there is ultimately a tendency for Anthea's leadership to dissipate outside the transgressive space of the fantastic. Similarly, beyond rare examples of independent lady travellers, whose reluctant welcome into the male preserve of the Royal Geographical Society showed the lingering association of heroism and adventure with masculinity,[10] such female-led imperial encounters were impossible constructs in reality.

Frances Hodgson Burnett's *The Secret Garden* and *A Little Princess*: The empire at home

The garden at the heart of *The Secret Garden* (1911) is a figurative symbol not only of the rebirth of the indulged 'cripple' Colin Craven, but also of the bounds of gender and place of empire at home. Thoughts of gender and gardens necessarily recall Ruskin's 'Of Queen's Gardens'.[11] As I discussed in Chapter 2 in relation to education, Ruskin celebrates women's queenly preserve in the home which, as its title suggests, extends into the private domestic garden. More than gesturing toward a female association with nurturing and growth, Ruskin also likens the garden to the nation: 'The whole country is but a little garden, not more than enough for your children to run on the lawns of' (1865, p. 173). György Tóth argues that gardening was incorporated into the philosophy of social reform and improving the living conditions of the urban poor such that 'Late Victorians thus cultivated their Empire by tending their gardens' (2003, p. 120). Using the example of the kindergarten, or children's garden – which was influenced by the concept of the idyllic British countryside as a both symbolic and real place for a child to grow within – Tóth suggests that the garden was assumed as an actual and metaphoric answer to British problems (2003, p. 141). As a specific example, socialist activist Margaret McMillan, who was influenced by the founder of the kindergarten, Friedrich Froebel, established a 'city garden' for sick and impoverished children in South London in 1911. Jerry Phillips suggests that gardens were viewed as a form of social therapy for rescuing culture and stemming national decline: 'Thus, the urban garden was not only called upon to take the slum out of the working-class child, it was also set the task of building fit bodies and keeping the bulldog spirit in place' (1993, p. 178). The restorative power attributed to nature for the sick and neglected children of England in these historical examples is a useful context in which to approach Hodgson Burnett's heroine Mary Lennox, who is initially weak in both body and spirit after being raised as an imperial girl in India.

Until the age of nine, Mary is primarily cared for by an Ayah, who must keep her out of her mother's sight. When a cholera outbreak kills her Ayah and her mother and father, Mary lacks empathy to the degree that she is more distressed about being forgotten about in the panic of death and evacuation than about the loss of her family. She is sent 'home' – a problematic term to use for a girl who does not even know where England is – to Misselthwaite Manor, the Yorkshire estate of her uncle, Archibald Craven. The two greatest contrasts that Mary confronts upon her arrival are those of environment and racial difference. First, Mary dislikes the moors where the manor is situated initially, but she comes to find that the fresh winds improve her health and character: 'In India she had always felt hot and too languid to care much about anything' (p. 48). Unlike in Nesbit's trilogy, in which there is a general association of disease and ill health with England's cities that can be countered in warmer climates, Hodgson Burnett connects humid climates with illness, death, and the development of negative character traits. Second, the servants who attend to Mary, notably Martha, are afforded more respect, and are depicted as possessing opinions and desires, unlike the Indian servants to whom she had grown accustomed:

> The native servants she had been used to in India were not in the least like this. They were obsequious and servile and did not presume

to talk to their masters as if they were their equals. They made salaams and called them 'protector of the poor' and names of that sort. Indian servants were commanded to do things, not asked. It was not the custom to say 'Please' and 'Thank you', and Mary had always slapped her Ayah in the face when she was angry. (p. 25)

The relationship of children as subordinate to adults is reversed in the colonial environment, in which racial difference trumps age difference. Martha had believed that as Mary was from India that she would be 'a black', to the extreme insult of Mary, who remarks that 'natives' 'are not people', but 'servants who must salaam to you' (p. 27). The coldness between Mary and her Ayah, however, is not necessarily indicative of relationships between British children and their Indian caregivers.[12] After her experience with subordinate Indian servants, Mary's expectations of Martha are wildly divergent from the reality of English hired help. Martha differs from Mary's Ayah not only because she is an English woman, but also because of her lack of education and, intriguingly, her class. She is 'an untrained Yorkshire rustic' who has not been taught to be subservient like a lady's maid, and she carries expectations that children should wait upon themselves based upon her own experience with her brothers and sisters in a poor family.

It is from this 'rustic' knowledge that improvements in Mary's character and health are enabled. The English environment itself is conducive to good health, particularly signified by an increased appetite, according to the folk wisdom that Martha communicates to Mary: 'It'll do you good and give you some stomach for your meat' (p. 33). The alteration in Mary's physical well-being is associated with an improvement in her character. The connection between outdoor exercise and improved character is drawn on several occasions when Mary's improved strength and disposition are noted:

> Just as it had given her an appetite, and fighting with the wind had stirred her blood, so the same things had stirred her mind. In India she had always been too hot and languid and weak to care much about anything but in this place she was beginning to care and to want to do new things. Already she felt less 'contrary', though she did not know why. (p. 68)

It is also integral to Colin's transformation and reinvigoration through the natural world that he demonstrate prowess in physical pursuits in addition to improving his character and making himself a useful member of society. After the 'magic' works upon him, Colin intends to be an athlete prior to a life of making scientific discoveries.

Mary's development of strength is precipitated when impoverished Mrs Sowerby (the mother of Martha and Dickon, who becomes a friend to Mary) buys her a skipping rope. Through the combination of fresh air and exercise, there is soon an emphasis on Mary's flushed red cheeks, and on the natural world, through descriptions of the sun shining and wind blowing. After a month at the manor spending time outdoors, Mary has gained weight, and her complexion has also improved. Ben Weatherstaff perceives that her skin has become 'not quite so yeller' (p. 91), marking a physical sign of not only an improvement in health but perhaps also the loss of some of her undesirable character traits that were attributed to her time spent in India. When she is angered later at the thought of losing the garden, becoming contrary once more, she is again 'imperious and Indian' (p. 101).

Singh's examination of the novel's symbiosis between climate and character similarly suggests that transformation in the novel is 'wrought essentially by the outdoors, by nature, by wholesome activity, and by wholesome people like Dickon' (2004, p. 122), particularly because of the very 'Englishness' of the outdoors. Several writers in the late nineteenth century explicitly linked climate with racial characteristics. Charles Pearson, in his best-selling *National Life and Character: A Forecast* (1893), suggested that the 'higher' white races could not labour in the same climates as non-whites; J.W. Fortescue, in 'The Influence of Climate on Race' in *Nineteenth Century*, focused on the likely effects of climate on race in British colonies. Fortescue proposed that an English man cannot remain 'the same creature' if removed from 'eternal leaden skies, fogs and other damp' and located in the climate of New Zealand, for example (1893, p. 864). He argues that cold climates with harsh winters compel human industriousness, in the sheer pursuit of survival, and that comfortable climates induce changes in racial characteristics such that, for example, 'with each succeeding generation the national character in New Zealand will diverge further from its English prototype' (1893, p. 865). At its most racist extent, Fortescue's article proposes that the climates of excessively warm colonised lands are seen as 'working against the white man and for his coloured rival' (1893, p. 866). In *The Secret Garden*, the production of the idealised English child requires not only that he or she be raised in England's climate but that the health-giving benefits of its natural environment be *combined* with the virtues of its civilisation. The Indian climate induces languidness and with its lack of civilisation is detrimental to character and strength, as in the case of Mary. However, so too does English civility, when removed from outdoor exertion and interaction with the natural environment, induce serious character flaws in Colin. Like Nesbit's biting portrait of London in *The Story of the Amulet*, the potential deleterious effects of the domestic complicates the idea that civilisation is automatically produced by the sophisticated dwellings of the town or city in comparison with the untamed, natural environments of most colonial locations. As Elizabeth Lennox Keyser proposes in her influential reading of the novel, Mary's 'savagery' or 'ability to set aside the civilized veneer which has thinly disguised everyone else's hostility toward Colin' (1983, p. 7) is what enables transformation of the household.

Ben Weatherstaff, the estate gardener, with his knowledge of the development and nurturing of plants, is the first person to confront Mary with an assessment of her character and appearance as 'sour'. He discusses with Mary the delicate process of cultivating flowers from seed, including the gradual cycle by which leaves emerge from the ground and develop. She is, however, unfamiliar with his description of the slow movement of nature in England after her experience in a different climate: ' "Everything is hot, and wet, and green after the rains in India," said Mary. "And I think things grow up in the night" ' (Hodgson Burnett, 1911, p. 64). Mary's own development is comparable with that of Indian vegetation that grows rapidly of its own accord without being tended into the right, contained shape. This association recalls Medicus' botanical metaphor in the *Girl's Own Paper* in which girls taking the physically degenerate shape of a raspberry cane indicates undesirable qualities being fixed in place during childhood development. It is not until Mary returns to England and is cultivated by adults that her character and her health improve. In contrast, Dickon is representative of the strength-giving properties of the English outdoors and its consequent effect on character, with his natural affinity with all kinds of animals and his connection with plants. Indeed, his aptitude for the natural world has an almost magical association, with Colin referring to him as an 'animal charmer' (p. 199) and Martha noting her mother's observation that 'he just whispers things out o' th' ground' (p. 83).

In both of Burnett's novels (*The Secret Garden* and *A Little Princess*), pandering to children by allowing them to rule, rather than be subjected to adult guidance, is exposed as detrimental to character formation. With a deceased mother and a disinterested father who defers parental responsibility, Colin is weak and ill-tempered because he has been permitted to wallow in anxiety about the onset of an illness from which he does not suffer. Colin is repeatedly compared with a rajah, such as when Mary recalls a boy rajah in India who was covered in jewels and comments to Colin that '[h]e spoke to his people just as you spoke to Martha' (p. 144). Phillips argues that Colin recalls an Oriental despotism that has its roots in India, but which is accommodated by the British class structure that places him in a ruling position over servants such as Martha (1993, p. 181). The text works, he suggests, to remove those aspects of the East – typified by the description as a rajah – considered unsuitable for elite social performance in an English setting (1993, p. 182). While, if we read his negative traits as Indian, the improvement in Colin's character can be seen as de-Orientalising him, Hodgson Burnett's depiction of Colin as a rajah primarily exposes the harmful effects of allowing children who have not yet been shaped by adults to rule themselves, let alone rule others. Colin had 'lived on a sort of desert island all his life and as he had been the king of it he had made his own manners and had had no one to compare himself with' (1911, p. 233). His description as a self-made king on a 'desert island' creates an association between children and 'savages' (such as those in Nesbit's *The Phoenix and the Carpet*) who require outside intervention in order to instil order and discipline. In contrast with Nesbit's narratives, in which children are elevated above 'savages' in a demonstration of British racial superiority that justifies imperialism and colonialism, Hodgson Burnett equates the lack of development of both children and indigenous peoples in a way that supports imperialism through rehearsing the parent-child metaphor.

Raising up or improving others is one avenue to measure female success in the cultural historical context of fears of national degeneration and its impact upon imperial strength. Lissa Paul's study of *The Secret Garden* nevertheless expresses frustration with the usurping of Mary's tale by Colin's in its later stages. Paul argues that Mary's self-discovery necessitates her learning how to follow rather than lead and encompasses a loss of self: 'Mary's female identity quest more or less fizzles out: she goes through all the difficult parts, then Colin gets all the rewards promised in a male quest' (1990, p. 162). Claudia Nelson makes a similar point when she suggests that by the twentieth century, 'the romance of masculine power colors even woman-authored adventure stories', which is demonstrated in *The Secret Garden* 'not only by underscoring the moral virtue of physical strength but also by suggesting that this quality is unique to maleness' (1991, p. 141). Both of these arguments posit that Mary's quest is somehow unfulfilled and that she is disempowered. I suggest, however, that Mary succeeds in attaining as much power as she can within a framework of regulation. By assisting

Colin to full strength, she uses an autonomous but altruistic form of femininity to raise him to his 'rightful' position.

Mary plays a supportive and nurturing role by discovering and bringing life to the garden that eventually enables Colin to rule. In this way, Mary's function resembles that of a mother whose imperial responsibility it is to raise healthy children and to aid her husband. Complicating Phillips' argument about his despotism, there are more frequent comparisons between Colin and a rajah as he is shaken out of his self-indulgent pity and acquires strength and determination. He has been born into a family with an estate, just as a rajah has been born into a ruling house. When Colin rejects his nurse in favour of venturing into the fresh air, he does so with such an air about him that Mary is reminded of the native Indian prince 'with his diamonds and emeralds and pearls stuck all over him and the great rubies on the small dark hand he had waved to command his servants to approach with salaams and receive his orders' (1911, p. 193). Mary's support and guidance allows Colin to flourish and eventually to develop sufficient strength of body and character to indicate that he will be able to become the ruler of Misselthwaite as an adult. His transformation into a little rajah is further demonstrated when he asks Mary to tell him what phrase is used in India when people wish to dismiss others from their presence, and he adopts a wave of his hand and says, 'You have my permission to go' to Mr Roach (p. 208). *The Secret Garden's* conclusion brings Colin to pre-eminence, as he assumes his rightful place as household head. In an overarching sense, and also because of the shift in narrative focus to Colin, the novel expresses the idea that assisting others to succeed is the reward of the female quest, even if it is underappreciated. Yet it is not Hodgson Burnett who fails to celebrate female selflessness in assisting the triumphs of others as achievement. Rather, any such perception lies with the privileging of masculine rule and strength that allows Colin's coming to power to overshadow the work of Mary, who enables it.

A Little Princess: Being the Whole Story of Sara Crewe Now Told for the First Time (1905) had its genesis in Hodgson Burnett's novel *Sara Crewe; or, What Happened at Miss Minchin's*. The story, first serialised in *St. Nicholas* from December 1887 until February 1888, was modified for English and New York productions of a stage play, then expanded as a novel at the subsequent request of her publisher. As in *The Secret Garden*, *A Little Princess* depicts English soil as the best place upon which to raise English children. In contrast with Bessie Marchant's adventures, in which the moral and physical strength of independent, adventurous colonial girl heroines is celebrated, Hodgson Burnett's female protagonists have weak characters after spending their early lives in India being indulged rather than adequately guided by their parents. As Roderick McGillis argues in his study of the novel, time spent in the colonies in which children are not being 'cultivated' appropriately at home jeopardises the health of the nation by weakening its future adult citizens (1996, p. 13).

Sara Crewe is introduced at the age of seven years old as an 'odd-looking little girl' who is disoriented by her imperial experience. She feels as if she 'had lived a long, long time' during her seven years in India, and her travel across the world to England presents a stark contrast in climate and environment: 'Principally, she was thinking of what a queer thing it was that at one time one was in India in the blazing sun, and then in the middle of the ocean, and then driving in a strange vehicle through strange streets where the day was as dark as the night' (p. 2). The Indian climate is regarded as 'very bad' for children and is avoided by sending them 'as soon as possible' to school in England. Sara's father, Captain Crewe, reassures her that she can return to India to look after him (something that she desires) once her education is complete. The Indian climate, then, is particularly deleterious for the juvenile body and, inextricably, the character that is in development, which is later shown to flourish on English soil. India is, nevertheless, also a hazardous place for English adults – in these instances connected with the shock and stress of failed investment in a diamond mine – with Captain Crewe perishing there and his partner, Mr Carrisford, almost succumbing to brain fever. And, of course, in *The Secret Garden* Mary's parents die as the result of a cholera outbreak, further equating the Indian environment with the physical decline of British visitors.

At Miss Minchin's Select Seminary, Sara enjoys greater privileges than most of the pupils as a parlour boarder, with her own bedroom and sitting room, a pony and carriage for transportation, and a maid to replace her Ayah. Sara is associated with wealth, and wealth, in turn, is associated with imperial privilege. The shop assistants who observe her father buying presents for her remark that 'the odd little girl .... must be at least some foreign princess – perhaps the little daughter of an Indian rajah' (p. 9). While Sara has been pampered in India and upon her arrival at Miss Minchin's at her father's request, she does wish to aid those in trouble, particularly other school pupils: ' "If Sara had been a boy and lived a few centuries ago," her father used to say, "she would have gone about the country with her sword drawn, rescuing and defending every one in distress" ' (p. 27). She is driven to care for those who are weaker than herself, particularly in her maternal protection of Lottie, a younger child whose mother has also died. Unlike Mary, who was raised in India until she was nine, the younger Sara, sent to England 'as soon as possible', has not developed weakened physical characteristics or selfish personality traits.

By the time of her eleventh birthday, Sara's father becomes ill and soon dies of a uniquely debilitating combination of 'jungle fever and business troubles' (p. 90), leaving Sara with no one to fund her board and education. When her wealth is stripped and she needs to earn her own keep, Sara's leisure time is ended. Greedy and heartless headmistress Miss Minchin informs her that she will have no time to play with dolls (signalling a premature end to childhood for the poor) and that she must not only work, but also 'improve' herself and make herself 'useful'. The need to be useful, as in the *Girl's Own Paper*, is entwined with discourse on the strength and character of the nation, with the idle constructed not only as failing to contribute to society but as weakening it through degeneracy. For someone without wealth such as Sara, only her labour for Miss Minchin prevents her from becoming a beggar. The removal of wealth also prompts Sara to consider whether it alters her class position. Can she still be a 'princess' if she does not lead a life of leisure? She contrasts her own situation several years before in which the native Indians were her 'servants and her slaves' with her likely future: teaching, and being compelled to wear plain and ugly clothing that would 'make her look somehow like a servant' (p. 166). While she is treated no better than the scullery maid, Becky, with whom she shares a room, Sara is dedicated to maintaining her education by reading each night. She contemplates whether she could ever become 'like' Becky in the sense that Becky's speech, with its dropped 'h's, reveals her limited education and is a permanent indicator of her class.

The idea of being a princess, as referred to in the novel's title, is related to a middle-class appropriation of the aristocratic principle of *noblesse oblige*, in which the middle classes may assume the role of 'missionaries' at home by educating and raising up the lower classes. Sara imagines that if she were an actual princess she could 'scatter largess to the populace' (p. 64). As she is only playing at being a princess, she declares: 'I can invent little things to do for people... I'll pretend that to do things people like is scattering largess. I've scattered largess' (p. 64). McGillis does note the way in which females are championed as sacrificial nurturers, but nevertheless he considers *A Little Princess* to be a female reworking of the Crusoe story in that Sara constructs a 'civilized living space in a modern urban wasteland represented by Miss Minchin and her single-minded business practices and by the poverty visible in the London streets' (1996, p. 13). In contrast with McGillis' reading, I would suggest that Sara is credited not so much with constructing a civilised space for herself – it is Ram Dass who physically transforms her bare room – but rather with the inspiration of change in and nurturance of others, particularly the poor and downtrodden, contributing to the civility of the city. Rather than championing her survival capacity, which is difficult to maintain in contrast with the children who are forced to eke out an existence on the street, the emphasis is on the middle-class girl's capacity, within her limited political and social power, to improve the working classes.

While England is marked as a healthier place for children to develop than India, the impact of poverty upon its 'stock' is a preoccupation in *A Little Princess*. Deprived of adequate sustenance at the seminary, Sara finds a fourpenny piece, and she buys six buns, but, despite her hunger, consumes only one herself after noticing a child ('one of populace') hungrier than herself on the street: 'The little ravening London savage was still snatching and devouring when she turned away. She was too ravenous to give any thanks, even if she had been taught politeness – which she had not. She was only a poor little wild animal' (1905, p. 193). This association between the poor of England and animals recalls the practice of equating native 'savages' with animals, which suggests that even English citizens can be 'reduced' to a primitive level if society allows them to remain uneducated and without the necessities of survival. Troy Boone notes that from the 1890s onward, degeneration theory about the urban poor superseded the 'demoralization theory' postulated earlier in the century (2005, p. 89). While the latter theory blamed individual character for poverty and required moral training and 'self-help' to correct, degeneration theory suggested that environmental forces were the culprit. This shift, therefore, transfers responsibility for the alleviation of urban poverty from the poor themselves to other members of society capable of raising them from it.

In *A Little Princess*, responsibility is attributed to the middle class to ensure that those on the lowest societal rung do not descend into savagery. For example, after witnessing Sara's kind deed the bread-shop proprietor, Mrs Brown, agrees to give buns to the girl from the street (who is named Anne) whenever she would like them. Mrs Brown takes this obligation one step further by transforming Anne into a clean, well-dressed, useful girl by providing her with work: 'She looked shy, but she had a nice face, now that she was no longer a savage, and the wild look had gone from her eyes' (1905, p. 300). There is another example of *noblesse oblige* with regard to Sara herself. As her clothes have become shabby and too small, a family of children she has been admiring for their togetherness watches her while she completes her errands, believing her to be a beggar. One of the children, with little understanding of the true cost of living, eventually presents Sara with a sixpence, in the belief that it will assist her for life and raise her from poverty. The children observe, however, that she does not display subservience by curtseying as most 'beggars' would. Even in poverty, Sara is imbued with dignity.

When Sara is deprived of all comfort and compelled to work by Miss Minchin, she is also isolated because of her new status as an employee rather than a pupil of the school. She befriends a rat, is friendly with the sparrows, and derives what pleasure she can from teaching the young pupils at the school. Singh suggests that Sara's stoicism and selfless acts under duress are exemplary of British racial qualities: 'In Sara, Burnett projects all the qualities the British held most dear in their self-concept. Her courage and resilience, her determination and diligence, her grace under fire make her a shining example of the attributes they considered the endowment of race' (2004, p. 131). These superior qualities of the British race were also necessarily invoked when justifying imperial conquests or in military propaganda. It is fitting, then, that Sara likens her situation to that of a battlefield and her stoicism to that of a soldier: ' "Soldiers don't complain," she would say between her small, shut teeth. "I am not going to do it; I will pretend this is part of a war" ' (Hodgson Burnett, 1905, p. 114). Sara, like *The Secret Garden*'s Mary, is initially presented to the reader as a motherless girl who must relate with an authoritative father. Just as her father bravely served his country, so too does Sara strive to rise to any challenge set before her.

One the narrative shifts to England, the first imperial presence is detected when Mr Carrisford takes up lodgings next door to the school; the signs of his arrival are 'Oriental ornaments' and a Buddha in a shrine. After sighting these objects, Becky believes that he is 'an' eathen' who worships idols. She articulates a civilising impulse when she observes that 'Somebody outghter send him a trac'. You can get a trac' for a penny' (p. 156). Yet perhaps because of her class position, she does not consider instilling Christian ways in heathens herself. Ram Dass, Mr Carrisford's Indian servant, first appears when he emerges through a skylight, possibly, Sara imagines, because he had come to see the sun, a rare sight in England: 'but it was not the head or body of a little girl or a housemaid; it was the picturesque white-swathed form and dark-faced, gleaming-eyed, white-turbaned head of a native Indian – "a Lascar" ' (p. 162). This initial description of Ram Dass – in which he must first be differentiated from a girl or housemaid and read through a feminine aesthetic category as 'picturesque' – serves to both Orientalise and feminise him. This effeminacy foreshadows his association with the domestic through his skilled transformation of Sara's living quarters using delicate and visually pleasing objects and furnishings. Race is subordinated to class when Ram Dass views Sara's sparsely furnished room and still remains subservient: 'She had seen that his quick native eyes had taken in at a glance all the bare shabbiness of the room, but he spoke to her as if he were speaking to the little daughter of a rajah, and pretended that he observed nothing' (p. 165). Nevertheless, his refusal to acknowledge the neglectful state of Sara's room also demonstrates a form of tact and social propriety associated with Englishness. As an Indian servant, Ram Dass exhibits greater concern for this English child and her surroundings than the English woman who is charged with raising children, Miss Minchin. His exemplary manners and kind deeds (as 'an'eathen') expose her failings all the more.

Ram Dass acts as a magical agent by transforming Sara's sparsely furnished lodgings into a luxury abode without his presence being detected. He wishes to make her dreams and visions 'real things'. Indeed, Sara attributes the appearance of lavish goods, such as bedding and clothing, which Ram Dass places in her room, to 'the Magic', using the same term that is applied to transformation in *The Secret Garden*. The description of his ability to move silently, as if his feet were made of velvet, fits with the air of 'Oriental' mystery. When Ram Dass discusses his intentions to help Sara, he suggests that it will resemble a story from the *Arabian Nights*: 'Only an Oriental could have planned it. It does not belong to London fogs' (p. 204). The reference to 'London fogs' distances 'magic' and hope from the English city, instead connecting it with neglect and the failure of the wealthy or comfortably situated to intervene significantly to 'improve' the poor. Ram Dass's transformation of the situation of an ostensibly penniless girl sets off a chain of charitable events in which people seek to help members of 'the populace'.

While England is championed in both of Hodgson Burnett's novels as a superior environment to India in which to raise healthy children with selfless characters, *A Little Princess* – although not as overtly as Nesbit's fantasy trilogy – critiques contemporary politics and social conditions that could produce 'forgotten' citizens. At an individual level, the heartlessness of some city residents is exposed, exemplified in its worst instance by Miss Minchin. More broadly, the failure of the middle class to act in assisting those drifting toward savagery is denounced. The overt socialism at work in Nesbit's novels deploys a vision of a utopian future to expose the failings of contemporary city life. Hodgson

Burnett's novels touch upon similar social concerns, including those of national strength and urban poverty, and in some small ways she too draws on socialist thought, such as through her championing of the redeeming power of the garden for sick children. Foremost in the works of both authors, however, is a demonstration of the way in which girls may act as moral guides in the absence of maternal figures, raising up those who are in poverty or facilitating the development and success of others.

5
Be(ing) Prepared: Girl Guides, Colonial Life, and National Strength

> The adaptation to girls of what is essentially a boy's book is a difficult task, and this adaptation is very well done; but a patchwork is never as satisfactory as an original work' (1932, p. 94).
>
> Rose Kerr, official Guide historian and former Guides' International Commissioner

Most British youth groups with a nationalistic or imperial focus in the late Victorian and Edwardian period were created for boys, such as the enduring and internationally popular Boy Scouts. As I have argued in the previous chapters, however, there was a place imagined for girls within the imperial project. Girls' involvement in the maintenance of the Empire was configured as equally important, if not more so, than that of the boys who were trained for front-line military defence. However, despite the uniqueness of the Girl Guides' 'character training' for girls, the Guide movement has, until recently, been critically ignored or briefly considered only as a mere derivative of the Scouts (Springhall, 1977, p. 130). Tammy M. Proctor's history *Scouting for Girls: A Century of Girl Guides and Girl Scouts* (2009) has rightfully begun the process of treating the subject of girls in Scouting as an important area of inquiry in its own right and reassessing Guiding's 'underrated impact on the modern world' (p. xx). Despite such critical re-evaluation of the cultural importance of the girls' movement, little attention has been paid to Guiding's founding handbook, which has been regarded as 'essentially a rewritten version of *Scouting for Boys*' (Rosenthal, 1984, p. 11). This kind of dismissal ignores significant changes which were made to the scheme and its original handbook, *The Handbook for Girl Guides; or, How Girls Can Help Build the Empire*,[1] in order to make the movement suitable for Edwardian girls. In this study of British girlhood and empire, the alteration or replacement of sections of *Scouting for Boys* to create *The Handbook for Girl Guides* helps to reveal how girls' contribution to the Empire had to substantially differ from boys' and how this contribution was formulated in an instructional manual read by both women leaders and girls themselves.[2]

With a gesture toward the characteristics of late Victorian children's literature, Elleke Boehmer suggests that *Scouting for Boys*' conjunction of colonial disorder and play invites a reading of the text *as* children's literature (2004, p. xxx). While there is necessarily instructional and didactic content in *The Handbook for Girl Guides*, I adopt a similar approach in my reading of it as a literary text – with its adventure stories, poems, songs, role plays, and accounts of the bravery of real girls and famous women – that demonstrates the ideological construction of the part which girls were being prepared to play in aiding the Empire. The seven elements of training are connected by the pursuit of cultivating national strength and preparation for war or colonial life: 'Girl Guides' Pursuits', 'Finding the Injured' (including 'woodcraft' and tracking), 'Tending the Injured', 'Frontier Life', 'Home Life' (including housekeeping, care of children, and preserving health), 'Patriotism', and 'Hints to Instructors.' The original handbook documents a unique period in the movement and in girls' culture that was superseded in 1918 by a substantially revised handbook that omitted much of the imperial sentiment of its predecessor.

Lieutenant General Robert Baden-Powell collated *Scouting for Boys* from a variety of sources, including extracts from adventure novels, newspaper cuttings, and travel writing (Boehmer, 2004, p. xi.). The views of Samuel Smiles, who was the author of *Self Help* (1859), and imagery derived from Rudyard Kipling's *The Jungle Books* (1894–5) and *Kim* (1901), as well as the public school code, 'muscular Christianity' as represented in the writing of Charles Kingsley (which entwines athleticism, religious belief, and the ability to control one's surroundings), popular imperialism, and social Darwinism were immediate and easily detectable influences.[3] *Scouting for Boys* was initially sold in six illustrated fortnightly parts from 15 January 1908 for 4d [pence], before it was collected in a single edition in May of the same year for 2s [shillings]. Primarily intended for use by pre-existing boys' groups such as the Boys' Brigade, *Scouting for Boys* was nevertheless still affordable (even if not 'cheap') for middle-class and working-class boys and girls, who in some instances may have pooled their money to buy it. This is borne out by the fact that contrary to Baden-Powell's original plan, thousands of children began working from the text themselves without adult instruction: a number of girls formed their own 'Girl Scout' patrols in England, in Scotland, and even as far away as New Zealand (Kerr, 1932, p. 59).

There are conflicting historical perspectives as to whether or not Baden-Powell tolerated these unofficial female members. Allen Warren suggests Baden-Powell was anxious about letting girls into the Scouting scheme for fear of compromising its aim to encourage 'manliness' (1990, p. 101). Official 'historian' and former International Guide Commissioner Rose Kerr portrays Baden-Powell as having 'hardened his heart' against girls participating in Scouting activities because it may have subjected the scheme to ridicule, but when he saw a troop of 'Girl Scouts' arrive at the Crystal Palace rally 'his heart melted within him' (1932, p. 12). In contrast, biographer Tim Jeal cites Baden-Powell in the first Boy Scout pamphlet in 1907 to suggest that he felt, initially at least, that Scouting could be the basis for valuable training for girls (1989, p. 469). Baden-Powell was nevertheless forced to confront the issue of girls within his movement at the Crystal Palace rally of Boy Scouts – the first large Scout rally – held in September 1909. A group of uninvited girls who had formed their own Scout patrols attended the rally, some wearing Scout hats and carrying staves. However small, the contingent was sufficient to impact upon Baden-Powell, for one month later, in October 1909, the Boy Scout Headquarters Gazette noted that all applications from potential girl members should be forwarded to headquarters. According to the official history of the Girl Guides written by Kerr, 'new arrangements' were being made (1932, p. 28). These 'new arrangements' meant that girls could no longer become Scouts. Six thousand girls had already registered as Scouts, and by the time Baden-Powell's sister, Agnes, assumed control, they numbered 8000.

The Scout name, however, was not deemed suitable. The new organisation feared attracting unfavourable public opinion about girls participating in the same scheme, arguing that this had the potential to upset the boys and derail the intent to 'toughen' them – or instil manliness – away from the supposed softening influence of their mothers. The new name, which was taken from the famous Gurkha regiment of Guides in India, was not, however, welcomed universally by the former 'Girl Scouts'. Moreover, the name change also extended to the patrols within the organisation: the Guide handbook suggests patrol names such as 'Violets', 'Fuchsias', and 'Bluebells' (Baden-Powell and Baden-Powell,

1912, p. 25). The official history of the Guides notes the thoughts of one of the Girl Scouts of the 1st Mayfair Troop who perceived a symbolic alteration in the level of adventure and excitement with the shift from animal names to those of flowers: 'When Guides first started, we refused to join them, for having been Peewits and Kangaroos, we thought it was a great come down to become White Roses and Lilies-of-the-Valley!' (Kerr, 1932, p. 35).

The decision to use a different nomenclature for the female branch of the Scouts is significant in itself, yet the connotations of each word are also important. According to the Oxford English Dictionary, from the sixteenth century onwards, the term 'scout' has been used to refer to one who is 'sent out to obtain information' and may particularly reference a military scout who reports the position and strength of the 'enemy' to an awaiting body of soldiers. The use of 'scout' then imbues the boys' movement with a militaristic quality and inherently suggests that there is a need for a widespread network of citizens across the country that will perform a similar function to the military scout in protecting the nation from outside attack. The word 'guide' has its origins in the fourteenth century, with reference to a person who 'leads or shows the way, especially to a traveller in a strange country'. It also has an alternate definition as a person who directs the conduct of others. In contrast with the active role of the scout in protecting the waiting troops with his information, the guide has a subservient role in directing others in unfamiliar territory, or, in its other sense, a guide directs others in their actions. While there is a degree of passivity inherent in the term 'guide' in comparison with 'scout', the connection with the Gurkha regiment of Guides in India also forms an association between the Girl Guide and the imperial Other, who was often feminised. This renaming symbolised the need to transform Scouting in order for it to become a socially acceptable movement for girls. While the Guide movement, with its physical training and outdoor-adventure components, did not restrict the activities of girls to the domestic, those activities that it came to encompass were largely predicated upon caring for others, childcare, and moral responsibility and guidance.

Agnes Baden-Powell, who became the first president of the Guides, moulded the cornerstone of Scouting instruction into the Guide handbook. She did this by removing sections deemed unsuitable for girls and including appropriate tales of female bravery, inspirational poems, and instruction for good mothering and effective nursing. Just as the name of the movement for girls itself was altered to suit gender ideology that situated women as moral guides rather than active defenders of Britain, similarly the text that had served for the Scouts was not considered suitable for the Girl Guides because the express aims of each movement, and the motivations behind them, differed.

Laureen Tedesco observes variations in the skill levels required for boys and girls[4] to complete the same badges in her study of the origin of the American handbook *How Girls Can Help Their Country* (1913), as it filtered through *Scouting for Boys* and the British Girl Guide handbook. Tedesco's focus on the American Girl Scouts leads her to suggest that the militaristic tendencies of Scouting made it attractive to girls who may have otherwise been uninterested in a group whose main focus was perfecting sewing and cooking skills (1998, p. 22). Nevertheless, the American Girl Scouts did not adhere to the lines drawn between the sexes via name and uniform changes,[5] as in the British schemes, and consequently the social and cultural history of Edwardian England in the aftermath of the Second Boer War and the impact of the 'New Woman' upon the doctrine of separate spheres, particularly with relation to empire and the perceived ills of racial degeneration, is not an element of Tedesco's study.

Both Anna Davin (1978, p. 20) and Sally Ledger (1997, p. 18) argue that the New Woman was construed as a threat to the national need for women to raise a strong, virile British race. The New Woman was both a creation of popular culture, including the novel and the periodical, and a feminist ideal. She was usually presented as educated, financially independent, and not necessarily married or a mother. She championed the causes of suffrage and rational dress and was strongly associated with increased physical activity, most visibly cycling. The New Woman can be situated as the antithesis of a domestic, maternal ideal and consequently as a challenge to accepted gender boundaries. Early twentieth-century arguments for the need to ensure the health of the British 'race' continued to champion the ideal of the domestic angel and were promoted by those who had been raised in the mid-Victorian period when the imagined division between domestic and public spheres was firmly entrenched. In the popular imagination, the New Woman who sought education and employment was sometimes figured as shirking the social and moral responsibilities of motherhood (neglecting her 'queenly' domestic situation) and concomitantly veering dangerously toward masculine traits.

Julia Bush identifies the role that girls' organisations established in the late Victorian era, such as the Girls' Friendly Society (1874), the Primrose League (1883), the British Women's Emigration Association (1884), and the Victorian League (1901), played in complementing male empire-building activities such as exploration, trading, and soldiering. The unique female contribution these groups tapped into was a civilising function that would enable the carriage of British behaviour into its colonies. As Ledger suggests, the entanglement of notions of imperial destiny and racial superiority with the idea of refined English motherhood produced the concept of the English woman as a 'civilising agent' (1997, p. 67). The Guide handbook taps into the figuration of British femininity as charged with civilising potential in its portrayal of the British Empire as an 'enormous prosperous realm...with the sea for its streets' which has 'a sacred duty to carry light into all the dark places over the whole world' (p. 407).

Furthermore, social Darwinist discourses injected concerns about evolution and racial strength or quality, such as increasing the birth rate, and positing a relationship between child health and national strength, into social and political debates. Davin has shown how British mothers were charged with a form of racial responsibility as well as serving as moral guides through parenting (1978, pp. 9–14). The need to direct young girls and women to a renewed focus on domestic tasks and childcare in support of racial strength is manifest in the 1904 report of the Inter-Departmental Committee on Physical Deterioration. The Committee was convened in 1903 in response to the number of men who were rejected for service in the armed forces during the Second Boer War (1899–1902) due to physical inadequacies. Its stated intent was to determine the health of the populace, find out the causes of physical deterioration, and identify methods for the prevention of such deterioration. The report calls for girls and mothers to receive 'systematic instruction' with regard to infant-feeding in order to ensure that infant mortality rates continued to fall, and also for the promotion of organised games and 'methodical physical exercise in the open air' for schoolchildren. The desire to improve the physical strength of British children had importance for several imperial concerns: preparation for war and maintaining 'racial purity': stemming fears about the population growth of the working classes at home and miscegenation in the colonies. Two of the central aims of Guiding, namely the production of 'good mothers' and physically healthy girls, can therefore be viewed in light of wider social concerns about physical degeneration impacting upon subsequent generations (notably in the writings of Herbert Spencer)[6] and maintaining white racial superiority. We can, nevertheless, figure the moment in which Baden-Powell conceived of the Scouts and Guides as informed not only by an imperial desire for a physically and morally strong race, but also by the need to reaffirm women's suitability in the domestic sphere and for 'caring' employments such as nursing and teaching.

The provision of some form of outdoor education to exercise the body was a high priority in the minds of those who sought to 'improve' British citizens. Guiding encompassed a series of outdoor activities, including woodcraft, camping, and an extensive range of games, as well as focusing on maintaining health through cleanliness, temperance, and first aid. The drive to stall national deterioration particularly sought to combat ill health in the lower classes, who were not as likely to benefit from the burgeoning growth of physical education in more exclusive girls' schools. Agnes Baden-Powell, in her foreword to Dorothea Moore's novel *Terry the Girl-Guide* (1912), displays concern that, without participation in a scheme such as Guiding that stressed the need for physical education, girls of the lower classes were not being improved physically and morally: 'The pursuits appeal to all classes, not only the well-to-do, but also the less favoured girls who have no hockey or cricket or concerted games to lead them to a sense of honour, fair-play, and unselfishness' (p. v).

The scheme is predicated upon combating moral and physical degeneration in citizens of all classes, through training girls' bodies and characters without compromising their 'womanliness'. Accordingly, in order to maintain the strength of the Empire, it is suggested in the Guide handbook that girls must not consider those of other classes as enemies, but that girls of all classes must band together. This sentiment is enshrined in the fourth of the ten Guide 'laws', which notes that a Guide must be a 'friend to all, and a sister to every other Guide, no matter to what social class the other belongs' (Baden-Powell and Baden-Powell, 1912, p. 40).[7] The defence of Britain requires all of its citizens to form a united front: 'Remember, whether rich or poor, from castle or from slum you are all Britons in the first place, and you've got to support Britain against outside enemies' (p. 418). This construction extends to a metaphor of the nation as a brick wall: if one brick 'rots' or 'gets out of place' (representative of the moral and physical degeneration which the text seeks to counter), this places excessive strain upon the others and weakens the structure (p. 418). After noting the moral and physical decadence that is the result of girls being allowed to 'run to waste' for lack of training in good citizenship, a solution to these ills is proposed in the handbook: As the only step to counteract these evils among the women of the future, we suggest the 'Girl Guide training,' a scheme for games and badges which gives the girl something good in place of what is bad, in a form which really does appeal to them, and attracts the worst [type of girl] ... and turns them the right way (p. 447).

The Guiding scheme was partially inspired by the success of camps that Robert Baden-Powell conducted for factory girls, which were thought to quickly improve the character and discipline of the girls who attended them. Indeed, Agnes Baden-Powell suggests that the methods of Guide training are attractive to all girls, but especially so for the girls who are deemed to need it most: 'the girls of the factories and of the alleys of our great cities, who, after they leave school, get no kind of restraining influence, and who, nevertheless, may be the mothers, and should be the character trainers of the future men of our nation' (1912, p. vii). The underprivileged girl also serves as a focus of fears about inadequate mothering in Robert Baden-Powell's early conception of Guides. He states that he wants to attract, and thus 'raise the slum-girl from the gutter' (qtd in Kerr, 1932, p. 29), in order to give all girls the ability to be better mothers and Guides to the next generation. The inclusion of girls of all classes in unified pursuit of the greater national good also coalesced with an intent to counter the health issues that resulted from an urbanised lifestyle and perceived 'idleness', by encouraging activity and employment.

The handbook begins with a foreword by Agnes Baden-Powell which declares that Guides differs in detail from Scouts: 'Its aim is to get girls to learn how to be women – self-helpful, happy, prosperous, and capable of keeping good homes and of bringing up good children' (p. vii). Reproducing the idea of separate but complementary spheres, the scheme is underpinned by the belief that 'every girl can be of use' to the 'great British Empire', regardless of how unlikely it may seem that 'mere girls' could aid such a powerful entity (p. 34). The focus upon the girl and the contribution she could make to the future of the Empire is made explicit in the choice of song lyrics by Philip Trevor:

> What will you do for England,
> Dear Little English maid?
> You may be poor, weak, and obscure,
> Still you can lend your aid.
> It matters so much to England
> What you will try to do;
> You can if you will, make her greater still.
> It lies, little child, with you
> In a child's small hand lies the fate of our land.
> It is hers to mar or save;
> For a sweet child, sure, grows a woman pure,
> To make men good and brave

We English shall ne'er kiss the rod,
Come our foes on land or sea,
If our children be true to themselves and to God,
Oh! Great shall our England be.
(qtd in Baden-Powell and Baden-Powell, 1912, p. 15)

These lines directly address the girl reader, entreating her to assist the nation regardless of her social status. The location of Britain's future success in the hands of girls rests upon the construction of women as shaping, through motherhood, the men who make history: 'Britain has been made by her great men, and these great men were made great by their mothers' (p. 24). The specific role of girls is constructed as perhaps even more important than that of boys for the Empire, as girls will direct the lives of the nation's future leaders and soldiers:

> The girls of the nation have the moulding of the men of the future. This great Empire is entrusted to their care, and what it will be in the future is just what the girls try to make it. Girls have great power and influence, and can serve their country even better than men can, by forming the minds and characters of the children. (p. 411)

The section of verse by Trevor also provides a concise example of the connection between imperialism and the ideology of motherhood, with its construction of girls as the nation's future women who will nurture men brave enough to fight off potential invaders of Britain.

National degeneration

For the future prosperity of the Empire, the handbook aims to educate girls to have the skills to produce healthy and useful children – the future men of England – as well as to be suitable companions and household managers for men in the colonies. This notion of raising good citizens or 'fit and proper subjects' who will develop the Empire is presented as vital lest 'some other nation ... take it from us' (p. 408). This fear of the loss or theft of British territory throughout shows the perception of widespread physical degeneration. Both original Scout and Guide handbooks focus upon the decline of the Roman Empire and express the fear that the British Empire may suffer a similar fate if moral and physical degeneration continues to pervade society.[8] The specific reason pinpointed for the Roman Empire's weakness is the large mass of its citizens 'who became selfish and lazy and only cared for amusements' (p. 34). Roman civilisation is invoked to draw comparison with another dominant and expansive empire, but it also raises anxieties about England itself being subject to attack, potentially prompting the fall of its empire.

The physical weakness displayed by British men was a key contributor to this fear of imperial decline. In *Scouting for Boys*, Robert Baden-Powell lists a range of physical indicators that reflect poorly on the British male, from a four-inch drop in average height from 1845 to 1895, to the number of men weighing under seven stone twelve pounds rising from forty-four in every thousand in 1900 to seventy-six per thousand in 1905 (p. 184). There was a fear that poor health care was causing a rise in preventable deformities and inducing physical deterioration, which presented a threat to British military strength and to the protection of Britain itself in the event of invasion. Other statistics provided on British men who presented for service demonstrate how dramatically poor health affected Britain's ability to gather a military force: in Birmingham, out of 1900 men who presented, 1000 were not in sufficient health for the army; in Manchester, 1800 out of 2500 were not fit to be enlisted (p. 335). Further, Baden-Powell contends that half of the British casualties in the Second Boer War could have been prevented if boys had been educated about personal health care (p. 185). Without reservation, Baden-Powell attributes the primary cause of the threat to the nation from physical weakness as poor mothering and neglect: 'Much of this decadence is due to ignorance or supineness of mothers, who have never been taught themselves' (qtd in Kerr, 1932, p. 30).

While the section on 'National Deterioration' was deleted from the Scout handbook in 1911, it was included in the first Guide handbook in 1912. Yet the specific connection of work for the Empire and maintaining levels of national health through nursing and the care of children and husbands was added:

> These and many other similar reports show that much PREVENTABLE deterioration is being allowed to creep in among the rising generation, largely owing to ignorance on the part of parents and of the children themselves.[...] since most of these cases of physical decay are preventable, they open to instructors a field for doing work of national values. Girls can therefore do a great work for the country by learning the rules of health, by practising them personally, and by applying them to the care of children in their own homes, and by teaching them to others. (Baden-Powell and Baden-Powell, 1912, p. 320)

Life in the colonies or on the frontier was idealised as an opportunity for healthy and active lifestyles, attributing to nature the potential for a cure for British physical *and* moral deterioration. Urbanisation was blamed for the wholesale decay of the nation's youth – to take an example from the handbook itself, idleness that would lead to death in the wilds of the world did not necessarily spell the end of a loafer in a town.

The notion of national weakness further inflamed the fear that the heart of the Empire might be unable to withstand outside attack unless its future citizens were trained to improve their physical and moral strength and to ensure that their children learned to do so as well. The 'Notes to Instructors' section argues that the 'degeneration of character' that Guides seeks to counter is the result of both moral and physical decadence (p. 447); it is not only poor health care manifesting as physical deterioration that is at the root of Britain's woes, but also insufficient familial instruction in how to be good citizens who contribute to society. The initial pamphlet prepared by Robert Baden-Powell in 1909, 'Girl Guides: A Suggestion for Character Training for Girls', expands the suggested focus for girls on the domestic out of necessity for the Empire: 'in a Colony, a woman must know how to do many things which she finds done for her at home in civilization' (qtd in Mitchell, 1995, p. 123). The supporting function that girls performed for their male relatives in the colonies, which justifies the increased range of physical activities they may undertake, is further developed in the handbook:

> What do girls want with tying knots and tracking and camp cooking? people sometimes ask us. They are all agreed that it is useful for boys, who may go out to Africa, Canada, or Australia, and knock about and have to know how to find their way in the wilds [...] But do not girls too sometimes emigrate? and does not fate occasionally carry girls off to distant lands, where their brothers are farming or their husbands are digging for gold? (p. 94)

The final section that provides 'Hints to Instructors' cautions: 'We endeavour to show the girl that her own sphere is the best, and that her place is not as the rival to men, but as the complement or helpmate' (p. 456). Yet this place grew to encompass activities outside the domestic sphere, given the perceived needs of the Empire in light of fears of physical and moral degeneration and susceptibility to outside attack upon Britain, giving rise to civilising work within the Empire. The intent to prepare girls to support national defence motivated this increased activity, but also coalesced with the somewhat divergent ideology of maintaining 'womanliness'.

Increasing the white population in the colonies was another facet of the contribution that girls could make to empire. Both Scout and Guide handbooks suggest that while the Empire has 400 million fellow subjects, the territories are 'there, but the people [with reference to British citizens] are only coming. The white population of all these Colonies only amounts to a little over a quarter of the population of our crowded little island' (Baden-Powell and Baden-Powell, 1912, p. 274). It is stressed that Scout and Guide training aids boys and girls individually and the Empire as a whole by preparing them to succeed if they should become colonials. The Guide handbook supposes that many girls will relocate to the colonies in order to raise them into prosperous countries and that Guide training 'will come in very useful to you there' (p. 406). This expectation is made clear in the duties of a Girl Guide, which are the subject of the first of the 'Camp Fire Yarns' (which use first- and second-person narration to replicate the intimacy of a fireside chat): 'to be prepared to help your country', 'to be brave', 'to be womanly', 'to be strong', and 'to live a frontier life if necessary' (p. 16). Specific training in the skills required for subsisting in the colonies is nevertheless limited to occasional references to conditions in particular countries and is a secondary strain to general preparedness in nursing and child-rearing. Girls are instructed how to navigate via the stars in both the Northern and the Southern Hemisphere and how to familiarise themselves with natural resources for maintaining hygiene so that when 'in the wilds of the jungle' without a toothbrush, they can use a dry, frayed stick (p. 326). Girls will need to know how to be self-sufficient – how to milk a cow, cut firewood, cook the food, wash clothes, act as a nurse, 'defend yourself for your life, and many other things which you are inclined at home to leave to others' (p. 24).

The ideal of juvenile femininity presented encourages capability in support of male activities. Under the heading 'Guides of the Future', the handbook describes the way in which 'high principled women' can be of assistance to their husbands as sympathetic advisers, and as aids in carrying out their work. With sufficient preparation for that duty, girls are informed, 'in various ways women can be the guides of men' (p. 376). It is girls' duty to learn to be the aids of men to enable colonial populations of British emigrants to flourish. They can achieve this by developing an interest in men's pursuits, being able to make all of their clothes, prepare food from scratch, and teach the native 'boy' how to cook and wash the family's clothing (p. 235). A life in an unfamiliar part of the Empire that supports the actions of the nation's brave men is presented as a satisfying one as well as a service to Britain: 'To a true-hearted girl who wishes to make a man happy, there is bliss in an African hut' (p. 235).

Living in civilisation is figured as a barrier to true preparedness for colonial life or rescue work, unless extra action is taken, such as via the Guiding scheme. In a 1909 article on 'Girl as Scouts'[9] in *The Girl's Realm*, the difference in tracking skills between a colonial girl and one who has always lived in England is contrasted. The article describes a patrol whose poor tracking skills meant they were unable to find another group of girls even though the group was hiding close by:

> ...but presently the search party was joined by a young girl who had lived on a farm in South Africa, and had learnt a good deal about this branch of scouting. When she arrived she detected the tracks at once in the grass, short though it was, and hard, too, as the ground was, and she led her companions in a minute to where the patrol was in hiding. There are numbers of English girls who have never been out of their native country who become quite as proficient in tracking as the young girl in question, after a few months' training in scouting. (Roberts, 1909, p. 338)

As the first Guide handbook was intended primarily for girls living in Britain, attempts were made to formulate a relationship between civilisation and the wild such that girls could hone their skills in natural pursuits in a city or town environment: girls in London, the handbook mentions, can practice becoming adept at woodcraft through a visit to the zoological gardens and the natural history museum, while those in the country should visit a farm (p. 44). Reading the tracks of men, horses, or bicycles in a town is compared with following the foot tracks of animals in a more natural environment (p. 27). One Guide patrol in Cumberland is admired for their skill at constructing a hospital out of doors. This is discussed in the context of perhaps even having to bandage up the enemy in a real situation, lending a sense of preparation rather than play to the making up of beds in the grass. Preparation for trekking through 'uncivilised' environments is also encouraged in Britain through conducting a mock trek through 'Central Africa' during which each Guide will carry her kit and food in a bundle on her head, as the patrol constructs a bridge over a stream or paddles a raft across a lake (p. 122). These suggested activities, along with dozens of others related to observational skills, planning journeys, path-finding, signalling, drills, and simple games and exercises, worked to support two imperial tasks: to improve the strength and health of British citizens and to prepare them for life in the 'uncivilised' reaches of empire.

Separating the work of 'manliness' and 'womanliness' for the Empire

As Springhall notes in his study of boys' organisations, youth movements largely functioned to reinforce social conformity (1977, p. 16). Necessarily, efforts were made to ensure that the activities of the Guides were not perceived as breaching expectations of girlhood. While patriotism, for instance, was intended to be one of the primary motivators for girls to undertake their training, Agnes Baden-Powell attempted to distance the Guides from militarism,[10] suggesting that she was eager to ensure that the Guides were not perceived as straying into 'masculine' activities: 'I would like first of all to state that it is a feminine movement – a womanly scheme in the best sense of the word. There is no militarism in it – no idea of making girls into poor imitations of Boy Scouts. Education will be on such lines only as will make the girls better housewives, more capable in all womanly arts, from cooking, washing and sick nursing to the training and management of children' (qtd in Dyhouse, 1976, p. 111). Though imperial need could enable increased activities for girls, there were bounds to these activities, and an accompanying imperative that domestic skills be mastered simultaneously in support of the nation's prosperity.

The handbook prescribes activities from the traditionally feminine, such as cutting and sewing uniforms, to preparation for adventurous activities by making ration bags and slings for camping and nursing instruction. While most chapters and the majority of sections constitute entirely new content, there is some replication of *Scouting for Boys* with little or no alteration for girls, such as instructions on building a camp, tying knots, carrying rations, camp games, and camping lore such as observing which way the wind blows in the morning. Further, a number of the badges that girls can attain for proficiency in particular skills, such as 'first aid', 'cook', 'cyclist', 'musician', 'electrician', 'clerk', 'florist', 'musician', 'pioneer', and 'signaller', have the same requirements as outlined in the first edition of the Scout handbook (Kerr, 1932, p. 31). Some of the badges encourage competency in traditional domestic or nursing tasks and were created solely for Guides, such as 'laundress', 'matron', 'needlewoman', 'sick nurse', 'child-nurse', and 'dairymaid'. However, there are other badges, in addition to those mentioned above, that focus girls' attention outside the domestic and are physically oriented: 'flyer', 'boatswain', 'naturalist', 'pathfinder', 'rifle shot', and 'swimmer' (Baden-Powell and Baden-Powell, 1912, pp. 463–6). The primary consideration for the alteration of badges and their requirements was whether activities would compromise the instruction of 'womanliness', which was an inextricable component of the scheme.

Conversely, the aims of Scouting were to build character in boys, to encourage 'manliness and good citizenship', and to uphold the Empire; however, manliness 'can only be taught by men, and not by those who are half men, half old women' (Baden-Powell, 1908, p. 301). *Scouting for Boys* suggests that modern life was 'softening' British boys and looks to the 'uncivilised' reaches of the Empire for examples of true masculinity. Indeed, those on the frontier and in the colonies are highly idealised by Baden-Powell. Not only were these men able to look after themselves when away from the comforts of civilisation, but they were brave and strong, ready to 'fling' their lives down without hesitation in aid of their country (Baden-Powell, 1908, p. 13). The presence of girls during the instruction of 'manliness' was not acceptable for two reasons: it would contravene the aim to 'toughen' boys away from a female influence, and it was thought that character training for girls required instruction from women in caring for others and raising children. Unsurprisingly, being 'womanly' is emphasised in training for girls. The Guide handbook emphatically states that the primary difference between the schemes is that Scouting for boys 'makes for MANLINESS' whereas 'training for Guides makes for WOMANLINESS, and enables girls the better to help in the battle of life' (p. 22) [original capitalisation]. Therefore, Scouting could never be the same scheme for girls as for boys: it is not, the handbook suggests, intended to produce female soldiers who are an 'imitation' of men, but 'a girl who is sweet and tender, and who can gently soothe when wearied with pain' (p. 22). In other words, Guides would train girls to become better providers of care through mothering and nursing.

Self-sacrifice and nursing

Self-sacrifice was necessary for girls to learn, not only in the interests of better mothering, but also in order to guard the safety of others. As reflected in the third of the ten Guide laws, which specifies that girls should be helpful and of use to others, each Guide is instructed to 'do her duty before anything else, even though she gives up her own pleasure, or comfort, or safety to do it' (p. 40). This notion of girls risking their safety for the sake of others, with the overarching aim of aiding the Empire, conflicts with a perception of women as requiring assistance from men when they are in difficulty and the idea of 'women and children first' in the instance of an emergency. Indeed, the handbook argues that girls can be 'just as good as men' at enduring danger, and they are willing and ready to cheerfully sacrifice themselves for others (pp. 16–17). Girls' self-sacrificial ability not only makes them the equal of men in dealing with danger, it enables them to ensure the happiness of others and contribute to social change:

> If each girl in her measure
> Would do a sister's part
> To cast a ray of sunlight
> Into another's heart,
> How changed would be our country,
> How changed would be our poor,
> And then might 'Merry England'
> Deserve her name once more. (p. 305)

This poem refers to significant faults in the nation, with the appellation 'Merry England' no longer deemed appropriate for a country feared to be in the grip of degeneration. Again, the importance of the involvement of 'each girl' in counteracting this decline through moral guiding and improving the poor is emphasised.

The entrenchment of the concept of female self-sacrifice to the point of risking life is reflected in the hierarchy of badges awarded for saving life or 'deeds of merit'. Badges are ranked in accordance with the risk to the girl involved in the rescue, beginning with the Badge of Merit for doing her duty well without risk of harm, the Bronze Cross for saving life, and the Silver Cross for deeds involving considerable risk to the self (p. 435). The handbook encourages girls to risk their lives in the interests of saving others, particularly through the numerous, glorified, real-life examples of girls who have been involved in the rescue of children.[11] For instance, in one of the many stories of self-sacrifice in a colonial environment, a young girl of fourteen 'in the wilds of the prairie' provides a striking example of nurturing motherhood and resilience in an untamed environment: she tends unaided to her two younger siblings for six months by gathering fruit and selling pigs after her father dies (p. 32). This example follows a discussion about girls helping their parents at home and protecting their younger siblings from danger or sickness. Techniques for coping in the uncivilised reaches of the Empire are again transformed for practice and preparation in the relative safety of civilisation.

The tale of 'The Mill House on Fire' confronts opposition to girls' involvement in 'dangerous' tasks. The protagonist, Edna, is a factory worker, who upon returning home from work exhausted first ensures that she checks on her ill younger brother. Not only does Edna embody ideas about girls caring for younger family members, but she obeys the edict that Guides confront all situations with a smile; she never complains when there is no tea for her due to her family's poverty. When the mill where she is employed catches ablaze, Edna risks her life to save papers that are held in the safe, despite being told that it would be 'impossible' for a girl to complete such a dangerous job. Edna is depicted heroically as she safely throws down the papers and bravely jumps from the window: 'As she leapt from the window showers of sparks dropped on her head and shoulders, and threatened to set her clothing alight, and the crackling of flames and the sharp crashes told her the fire was increasing' (p. 187). While there is cautionary editorial against girls disregarding warnings that particular tasks may be too dangerous for them, Edna's heroic depiction serves to encourage girls to move beyond traditional expectations in the name of helping others or in the case of emergency.

Though the Girl Guide handbook contains numerous stories of girls conducting rescues at home, nursing – exemplified by the work of Florence Nightingale – is, according to the handbook, the most valorised contribution to Empire that girls can make, after mothering. It is men's work to defend the Empire 'in person'; but girls can aid their actions through important tasks such as ambulance work and nursing (p. 411). The Guides were given first-aid training along the lines of the Voluntary Aid Detachment scheme (VAD), which was inaugurated by the War Office in 1909 to provide nursing care for wounded members of the Territorial Force in the event of an invasion (Jeal, 1980, p. 470). While the men's detachments were responsible for transport and the conversion of buildings, women undertook nursing and cooking duties in hospitals and in the field (Summers, 1988, p. 944). Anne Summers suggests that the Guides provide evidence of a militaristic bent because their activities were modelled on those of women's VAD and were presented in a similar context of impending 'national peril' (1988, p. 946). The handbook conveys an urgent sense that girls and boys need to prepare for eventual invasion by 'foreigners'. If this threat eventuates, men will have to fight, but women, it is feared, will 'run away or hide or cry' without proper training in caring for the injured: 'When shooting and fighting comes, some one must look after the wounded. Would you not much rather be able to help, and band yourselves together and be ready to come at once to give them any assistance, and know how to ease their pain, mend their broken bones, and dress their wounds?' (p. 19).

The hospital course component of the programme focuses on tasks associated with cleanliness in domesticated medical settings, such as bed-making, washing, disinfecting, ensuring ventilation in the patients' rooms, dressing wounds, and purifying water; and on maintaining order, such as arranging the larder and making regular times for tasks like dusting (pp. 200–2). Nursing is specifically connected with making others comfortable rather than undertaking medical procedures: nurses are not doctors, girls are told while being encouraged to bring pleasure to invalids by learning to sing sweetly (p. 205). Further, as a source of income, the medical profession is represented as requiring years of arduous study, whereas 'Nursing is more easy, and is of the greatest advantage at the same time, for "every woman is a better wife and a better mother for having been a nurse first"' (p. 394). The ultimate convergence of womanly duties appears in the function of cooking food for the invalid, which constitutes an entire Camp Fire Yarn in itself (p. 216).

The most idealised woman in the Guide handbook is Florence Nightingale, for her service to the nation during the Crimean War. She is admired for her bravery and selflessness, particularly for the way in which she had to 'strike out a line of her own and go against public opinion, and to risk being thought unladylike and eccentric in order to do so' (p. 197). This aspect of Nightingale is representative of the way in which, in its early years, some considered the Guiding scheme to encourage boyish behaviour. An article in the *Girl's Realm* from 1909 points to the concerns that parents held about Guiding making for 'rough-and-ready' girls: 'Some parents...were rather alarmed at the idea of their children running about the country and becoming somewhat gypsy-like in their habits and ideas' (Roberts, p. 340). However, faith in the benefits of its activities for empire rendered these perceptions as secondary concerns for the movement. In Kerr's history, for instance, a Guide from this early period recounts that some mothers opposed the scheme because it allowed older girls to wear short skirts and traipse 'about the moors with bare knees like the Scouts' (1932, p. 49). While the 1912 handbook's insistence that Guide activities are about the promotion of womanliness stridently seeks to allay such concerns, at the same time it encourages girls to develop mental strength to confront physical and dangerous situations, which were integral to the scheme's primary intent to prepare girls to be 'of use' to their country and their empire.

Nightingale is presented as having given up the comforts of home in order to assist the British soldiers, fulfilling the movement's aim to prepare girls for potential departure from the civilised order of Britain for nursing work or emigration to the colonies. The repeated statement of Nightingale's courage in the face of the disapproval of her friends and the disdain of male army surgeons once again suggests that the Guides advocated the extension of activities for girls given the motivation of enthusiastic sacrifice, usually with benefit to the Empire. Yet it is still qualified that although Nightingale has become renowned, she has lived a 'womanly life' (p. 354). Within the realm of acceptable activities for women within the Empire, Nightingale is also admired for conducting a civilising or ordering function (usually within the context of indigenous populations) on the battlefield:

> She found them [soldiers] lying there uncared for in dirt and misery, covered with vermin and tormented by rats…but with energetic efforts directed wisely and with knowledge of hospital management, she soon converted the most appalling wretchedness into well-ordered, comfortable hospitals. (p. 198)

Here Nightingale has impeccable command over the abject conditions found in the war zone, as well as the mental strength to enable that command. Her work in improving hygiene in locations around the world contributes to her representation as an ideal model in a scheme that seeks to improve the moral and physical 'hygiene' of British society generally. The one quality that encompasses all of the traits that Nightingale and the other exemplary women and girls in the handbook's tales are praised for, however, is self-sacrifice – for the benefit of children, men, and the country as a whole.

Adapting adventure and physicality for girls

> 'Girls can be brave enough to shoot tigers, if they can keep cool.'
>
> (Baden-Powell and Baden-Powell, 1912, p. 284)

Significant scholarly attention has been directed to boys' adventure fiction, Scouting, and Empire,[12] yet the place of adventure in Girl Guides' outdoor activities has gone largely unstated. In the first handbook, many Guide activities intended to train girls for colonial life are imbued with a sense of mythical adventure, as demonstrated by role-plays, games, and

stories that celebrate British girls outwitting feared indigenous inhabitants. The games, designed to teach girls physical and rescue skills, draw
on conceptions of exciting and potentially dangerous real-life activities. Nursing training is incorporated into outdoor games such as 'Aid
to the Fore', in which the Guide captain calls out different 'injuries'
for which the Guide must determine treatments. To add to the sense
of real preparation, patrols are encouraged to purchase 'pomegranate
of potash' to stain the bandages red when playing the game. Drills,
including stretcher drills, are one method intended to instil discipline
in the girls. One game, 'Missionary's First Act', also draws the adventure
element into practical nursing training as girls are instructed to act as
an explorer or missionary to provide first aid. In aid of physical fitness,
a variation on Capture the Flag involves pretending to take a member
of the opposing team prisoner and bringing her safely to base, while
rescuing the team's own 'prisoner' (p. 327). The overwhelming imagery
is of practical female readiness and capability.

While there is distinct appreciation of the tracking and survival skills
of indigenous peoples of the colonies and homage to them in the naming of particular badges,[13] there is also a coexisting and contradictory
sense that Guides may need to prepare for conflict in a colonial setting.
For instance, in a play designed to teach the use of signals, girls are
instructed to adopt the roles of 'Red Indians' capturing two Guides. One
Guide is instructed to signal to the other using Morse code conducted
through blinks of her eyelids (p. 121). Boehmer argues that the 'wild' is
'transformed into the domain of the child' in *Scouting for Boys* in order
to represent imperial activity as a game and avoid the actual conflicts of
empire (2004, p. xxx). However, in the Guide handbook the perceived
risk posed by the indigenous inhabitant in the wilds of the far reaches
of the Empire is presented as a real threat in several stories. This fear
of the indigenous peoples, who would be an inescapable aspect of the
colonial experience, is overcome by the familiar trope in imperial texts
of British girls being smart enough to outwit them. This is evident in a
story to be read aloud that tells of a Canadian girl who warns her family – who are attending church – of impending attack by members of
the indigenous population, by bravely crossing a stream. Her family
and the other worshippers would have been 'massacred and taken prisoner every one but for little Ann's clever and prompt warning' (p. 90).
This example highlights the potential dangers of life in colonial locations and serves as a demonstration of how the Guides' adaptation of
military concepts such as tracking could be used by girls for their own
survival and to save lives.

Another story, 'A Brave Canadian Girl', describes conflict between the First Nations people and the white settlers. Marie Madeleine, a girl of fourteen years, dodges bullets while pursued by a 'wild warrior' (so closely that he caught her neckerchief!) (p. 288). She safely makes it to Fort Verchéres and confidently organises her little brothers and the two soldiers stationed at the fort (who had hidden in fear) to give the impression that there were several soldiers present. This ruse convinces the 'enemy' that the garrison is stronger than first thought, and it allows her to load a cannon and fire it both to injure the feared native inhabitants and to warn neighbouring farms. In the absence of a paternal figure, Marie is admired for adopting military skill to fight off the 'enemy'. Yet English girls such as those who had to 'rough it' in Western Canada are also depicted as having learnt from the 'native Indians, who were very clever with their hands' and skilled at tracking (p. 94). Indeed, obtaining skill as a Guide by qualifying for the 'Silver Fish' badge[14] – awarded for qualifying for a large number of skill badges – entitled a girl to amend the usual Guide sign or salute to reflect that of First Nation American Indians (p. 439). This reflects the uneasy and often contradictory existence of admiration for the skills of indigenous inhabitants as a component of building an adventure myth for girls – what Boehmer terms the 'hyper colonial' (2004, p. xxxvii) in *Scouting for Boys* – and criticism of their 'simple' lifestyle in order to explain why white populations needed to expand in the colonies in order for them to 'progress' and become useful parts of the British Empire.

Making strong, 'docile' bodies

The Handbook for Girl Guides; or, How Girls Can Help Build the Empire includes an illustration of Agnes Baden-Powell riding a bicycle through a hoop; she is wearing an elaborately decorated hat and a full-length gown that she is holding up slightly, leaving only one hand on the handlebars. This image, in which Baden-Powell retains balance and poise while practicing a difficult cycling manoeuvre, is representative of the place of physical activity within the Guiding scheme: although it is vital to its intent, it takes place within a larger regimen of limitations and imperatives. While the dual motivations of preparing strong girls to aid the Empire through national defence and colonial development while remaining within the nebulous bounds of 'womanliness' seem contradictory, Guiding rested upon their effective coalescence. The handbook explicitly intertwines the development of physical and outdoor skills with instilling moral self-discipline. For instance, in order to allay any fears about camp life being too 'rough', it is emphasised in 'A Note to Parents' that camping improves not only girls' health but also their morals – character training is the result of physical and practical training (p. 136). Guides encourages extended activities that range into the traditionally masculine in instances in which the Empire is at stake, but it ensures that mothering and housekeeping are also recognised as supremely important for the sake of ensuring both 'womanliness' and the nation's strength as represented by its future citizens.

In order to conduct the nursing, mothering, and colonial house-keeping work for which Guiding was intended to prepare them, girls needed to be physically and emotionally strong, and strength-building is addressed in the programme through gymnastics, drills, and dietary advice. Forms of exercise, including games, running, walking, cycling, skipping, rowing, fencing, swimming, tennis, and handball, are also encouraged. The section on 'How to Grow Strong' contends that endur-ance is not a singularly masculine quality and indeed argues, 'Some of the most fragile women have developed it by sheer determination and self-training' (p. 320). In support of this view, a programme of exercises to be performed each morning and evening – mostly reproduced from *Scouting for Boys* – is presented to make it possible for any girl, no matter how small and weak, to make herself strong and healthy (p. 328). This permission to gain strength empowers girls to dispense with ideals of feminine delicateness, such as in the recommendation of ju-jitsu as a way of acquiring physical fitness (Figure 5.1). It is promoted as a method of defence for girls, with one position that girls can attempt promoted as so painful that 'a man even can't withstand' it (p. 290). Guides must also know how to undertake exhausting physical work, such as felling small trees and branches using an axe or billhook and know how to make bridges (p. 144).

Nevertheless, the dictates of womanliness regulate the girl's body and the ways she may use it. Guides were expected to keep control of their bodies and maintain a trim appearance. This is shown in the section of the handbook that informs instructors to measure each girl and pro-vide her with standard body measurements (which were supplied by the London office of the Guides) that she should aim to meet for her chest, waist, arms, and legs. The handbook also uses techniques that mimic the ones Michel Foucault identifies as producing 'docile bodies' – those which may be 'subjected, used, transformed and improved' (1977, p. 136) – in military and education systems in the eighteenth century. Responsibility for her development is transferred to the girl, efficiently

" The Struggle,"
for strengthening the Heart.

Figure 5.1   Illustration of 'The Struggle' exercise between two girls, which is promoted as beneficial for health. Agnes Baden-Powell and Robert Baden-Powell, *The Handbook for Girl Guides*, London, Thomas Nelson and Sons, p. 321. Reproduced by kind permission of Girlguiding UK.

teaching her to assess where she 'fails to come up to the standard' (p. 326). As in Foucault's conception of panoptic permanent visibility, girls were to internalise external surveillance and discipline themselves and their bodies. Guiding's strategy of self-regulation is clearly articulated in the handbook: *'Our effort is not so much to discipline the girls as to teach them to discipline themselves'* (p. 351). Within the production of the efficient, docile body, as in the Girl Guides' physical instruction, the more useful the body becomes, the 'more obedient' it becomes (Foucault, 1977, p. 138). Therefore, while this chapter observes increased physical capacities for girls that are legitimated by imperial concerns, the power that results is turned 'into a relation of strict subjection' (Foucault, 1977, p. 138).

Guiding is similarly Foucauldian in its staged rankings, which are marked by badges that outwardly signify each girl's progress and occupation of a new position in the movement's hierarchy. Foucault describes the process of educational order in terms of students moving through a series of measures of advancement:

> [E]ach pupil, according to his age, his performance, his behaviour, occupies sometimes one rank, sometimes another' he moves constantly over a series of compartments –some of these are 'ideal' compartments, marking a hierarchy of knowledge or ability, others express the distribution of values or merits in material terms in the space of the college or classroom. It is perpetual movement in which individuals replace on another in a space marked off by aligned intervals. (1977, p. 147)

Guides similarly works in an endless progressive fashion. New Guides are awarded the Tenderfoot badge after learning the basic elements of the movement including the salute, signs, and promises, as well as the composition of the Union Jack and how to tie four different knots. The next stage in the hierarchy is the Second-Class Guide, who has to gain further knowledge and skills, including ambulance and first aid. The First-Class Guide requirements ensure Foucault's 'perpetual movement' as, in addition to a raft of competencies, she must also bring in a Tenderfoot whom she has trained (Baden-Powell and Baden-Powell, 1912, p. 434).

In addition to developing physical strength in preparation for colonial life or nursing on the battlefield, cultivating mental strength to endure such difficult situations is encouraged. In its first chapter, the handbook refers to the future possibility of foreigners attacking British towns and homes and the likelihood that its women will 'only run away or hide and cry, making themselves a burden to every one' (p. 19). To prevent such a dangerous scenario jeopardising the defence of the 'heart' of the Empire, emphasis is placed upon preparing girls to be of 'use', rather than preserving any notion of childhood innocence or refined femininity. Indeed, images of delicate women who are reliant on men are rejected in favour of psychologically strong women who can handle dangerous situations: 'Would you not much rather be able to help, and band yourselves together and be ready to come at once to give them [wounded British men] any assistance ... ?' (p. 19). Yet this is not to argue that this text is feminist, or even progressive, for there are many aims and prescriptions that contradict such a view. For instance, rather than hoping that Guides will be noted for these physical skills, patrols must keep a hairbrush for each Guide for when they go on parade, 'as

Guides are always known by their *silky* hair' (p. 458). In this way, the handbook functions similarly to a periodical such as the *Girl's Own Paper* in which girl readers must negotiate contradictory perspectives on issues throughout.

Nevertheless, as this chapter has suggested, in some places the first Girl Guide handbook challenges gender stereotypes by developing the girl's physical fitness and harnessing her mental strength to overcome expectations of feminine weakness. She is encouraged to do so precisely when the maintenance and growth of the Empire is at stake. This ideology, when extracted to the vitally important needs of empire, does create tensions with the scheme's insistence upon maintaining womanliness. The needs of Empire are elevated such that being considered 'unwomanly' in pursuit of them is not sufficient reason to avoid such activities. Nevertheless, there are concessions to perceived ideas of female delicacy, which primarily apply in peacetime within Britain: for instance, Guides are cautioned to train using a load in place of a person, for 'Girls must never try to lift heavy weights' (p. 194). Yet the very intent of the training in lifting was for girls to carry the weight of a male patient in the event of an invasion of Britain, demonstrating the perception that restrictions upon the bounds of acceptable physical activities for girls would loosen as they did when girls and women travelled to the colonies. The unique challenge of the handbook was to turn these chores into a desirable adventure at the same time as reinforcing a sense of every girl's duty to her country.

The life of *How Girls Can Help Build the Empire* as an instructive text read by girls was a short one. In 1918 a new, substantially revised Guide handbook was published, which omitted much of the imperial sentiment of its predecessor. It was the product of a post-war era in which late Victorian and Edwardian fears about the physical and moral degeneration of the British 'race' had dissipated, and attitudes about the activities of respectable women outside the domestic sphere had relaxed. During World War One, Guides were encouraged to help their country in nonmilitary ways such as via the Red Cross, St John's Ambulance, relief committees, the Soldiers and Sailors Help Society, undertaking cooking and needlework for hospitals, and caring for children while their mothers worked (Kerr, 1932, p. 118). Voeltz argues that the Guides grew rapidly after the war thanks in part to their actions serving with the Voluntary Aid Detachments, which demonstrated their abilities, and favourably swayed public opinion about the concept of the Guides (1992, p. 627). Not only had the prevailing sense of what constituted acceptable behaviour for girls altered, but the Guide movement had itself altered, with

Robert Baden-Powell resuming administrative control in 1915 from his sister and with a rapid growth in membership (from less than 40,000 in 1914 to over 160,000 in 1921) (Voeltz, 1992, p. 627). These changes shifted the Guides' raison d'être permanently, with training programs shifting closer toward those received by boys, as anxiety about what constituted suitably 'feminine' behaviour subsided, rendering this early period in Guide history a fraught and complex – and thereby highly instructive – one for the study of girlhood and empire.

6
Microcosms of Girlhood: Reworking the Robinsonade for Girls

A popular fascination in the late nineteenth century with 'female Crusoes' – women who replicated the survival feats of Robinson Crusoe, the protagonist of Daniel Defoe's 1719 novel of the same name – coincided with the emergence of independent, modern girl castaways in British fiction. These girl-Crusoe fictions from the late nineteenth and early twentieth century form the basis of this chapter and, as I shall argue, stand in marked contrast with works from earlier in the nineteenth century that depict girl Crusoes as relatively helpless members of family groups. Specifically, late Victorian and Edwardian girl castaways represent the apogee of girls as fictional adventurers and settlers, free to act on their islands without the need for any adult or male presence.

In the late nineteenth century the curious true story of Juana María, 'The Lone Woman of San Nicolas Island', captured the British public imagination. Inadvertently abandoned on California's San Nicolas Island, María survived eighteen years in isolation, but died shortly after her discovery and return to mainland America in 1853. This amazing story was propagated in magazines and newspapers for decades. In one such instance, in 1879, *Kind Words for Young People* featured an item on its 'Travel and Adventure' page about this 'Indian woman'. According to the article, when María was discovered, she was found to have entirely adapted to island life:

> She was in a small circular enclosure made of brushwood, about 5ft. high and 6 ft. in diameter, with a small opening on one side. She was clothed with a garment made of skins of the shag, a species of duck that can neither walk nor fly. This garment reached almost to her

ankles when she stood erect. She was sitting cross-legged, skinning seal-blubber with a rude knife made of a piece of hoop iron driven into a piece of wood. There was no covering on her head, except a thick matted mass of hair, of yellowish brown colour, probably owing to exposure to the sun and weather; it was short, as if the ends had rotted off. (1879, p. 300)

María's story had been printed previously in newspapers in Wales and Liverpool and the *Times*, and subsequently it appeared in *Young England* and the *Girl's Own Paper*.[1] Despite the repetitious elements of the tale as it travelled across each publication, the *GOP* added the qualification that, despite her lengthy ordeal, the woman still 'retained the virtue of female modesty' ('Another Female Crusoe', 1883, p. 646). This clarification about the wild-looking woman lends further evidence to the claim I advanced in the chapter on Bessie Marchant's novels that there was a shift in the perception of the British female settler in print culture: adapting to the demands of uncivilised environments could enable departure from certain feminine norms, so long as others were maintained. A far worse sin to avoid was idleness and helplessness. In a second article about a real-life female Crusoe, the *GOP*, with its fixation on producing useful girls, marshals this figure as an example of self-reliance and determination in the face of adversity in contrast with

the desponding helplessness which we too often witness among women, and men too, who, with every motive to industry and activity, and every encouragement to exert both, lose all self-reliance under the first shock of adversity, and pass their days in useless indolence and repining. ('A Female Crusoe', 1883, p. 439)

Similar, purportedly true, tales of female Crusoes appeared in magazines and newspapers across Britain and its colonies, including one that spread across the Empire to Australia's *Brisbane Courier*, New Zealand's *North Otago Times*, and Canada's *Ladies' Journal*. In this account, a widowed Englishwoman who endeavoured to continue her husband's business, 'Mrs Williams', captained her own ship from Singapore only to be stranded on an island of the 'Kinderoon' group. Not only does Mrs Williams competently and meticulously build a hut and eke out her supplies, but after two years on the island she shoots a 'Borneo sailor' who threatens her ('A Female Crusoe', 1891, p. 16). Mrs Williams' status as an Englishwoman mirrors a fictional shift in the female-Crusoe genre. In earlier female robinsonades, the protagonist's indigeneity could serve as an 'explanation' for her ability to survive as a castaway.[2] Stories like those of Mrs Williams, and the fictional girl Crusoes I will discuss, were able to favourably accommodate the possibility of an English female adventuring and surviving on her own. Furthermore, unlike the media legend of Juana María, with her matted hair and duck-skin coat, the girl-Crusoe delicately walks the tightrope of acceptability by maintaining a well-groomed feminine appearance. This absurd, but necessary, fiction, opposes the climate and race theory I discussed in Chapter 4 and inherently connotes the essential civility of the British 'race' in contrast with the crude barbarism of uncivilised natives living on nearby islands.

The sheer popularity of the robinsonade in the nineteenth century is evident in the periodical *Fun*, which mocked the prevalence of robinsonades at mid-century, announcing that a fictional author, 'Mr. Fussy B. Singin', 'has not half done with the subject yet, but will shortly stuff down it's (the public's) throat' narratives of 'The Australian Crusoe', 'The Pickled Crusoe', 'The Fricasseed Crusoe' and 'The Female Crusoe' (1862, p. 123). The female Crusoe, however, was not, in actuality, a fanciful subject for fiction. Jeannine Blackwell has identified a corpus of female robinsonades published between 1720 and 1880, predominantly in German, but also including four English-language novels from Britain and the United States. Moreover, C.M. Owen has recently published the first book-length study of the female robinsonade, with a particular focus on French novels of the eighteenth century that used female castaways to comment on and critique societal values (2010, p. 7). In the eighteenth century, the robinsonade was also viewed as an ideal genre for didactic instruction.[3] Out of these origins, the robinsonade developed in the nineteenth century into one of the most popular genres for child readers. Indeed, as Humphrey Carpenter and Mari Prichard note, it became 'the dominant form in fiction for children and young people' in Victorian Britain (1984, p. 458).

The previous chapters have considered the various roles formulated for British girls within the Empire, both 'at home' and overseas. The ultimate fictional test of British girlhood and girls' capacity to be actively engaged in the Empire resides in a genre that has, as of yet, merited little consideration as such, and will form the basis of this chapter. While girl-Crusoe novels and serial fiction published from 1880 to 1915 has not been addressed as a distinct group of texts in the same way as boys' robinsonades,[4] interrogation of this corpus of texts has the capacity to reveal how the genre was reshaped to support new ideologies of femininity. As Owen argues, castaway settings are 'pre-eminently suited to texts critical of society because the castaway is necessarily stranded in a kind of nowhere space, a liminal space between recognisable, opposing and equally problematic locations' (2010, p. 12). The late Victorian or Edwardian girl similarly occupies a liminal space between childhood and adulthood, making the girl-Crusoe doubly charged with the potential to evade gender hierarchies. However, these texts do not activate the critical potential of the genre to subvert the gender politics of home that Owen identifies in female-Crusoe novels. Instead, this chapter suggests that girls' robinsonades cumulatively approve of modern, capable girlhood, reinforcing the idealised femininity that is evident in a range of print culture at the end of the nineteenth and beginning of the twentieth century. More specifically, these texts show the competent girl castaway as a product of acceptable British femininity, further entrenching a broader definition of femininity that was encouraged on imperial grounds, rather than lamenting gendered restrictions in place in civilised countries such as England.

This end is achieved through the ability of heroines to domesticate their surrounds and maintain a feminine appearance, tasks which underwrite their desire for adventure and physical competencies. Andrew O'Malley has shown how robinsonades, whether male or female, are inherently about protagonists domesticating or replicating home in the places in which they are stranded (2008, p. 67). The British Empire itself, historian David Cannadine suggests, can be viewed as 'in large part about the domestication of the exotic' (2001, p. xix). Central to Cannadine's thesis about how Britain saw its Empire is the contention that Empire 'was at least as much (perhaps more?) about the replication of sameness and similarities originating from home as it was about the insistence on difference and dissimilarities originating from overseas' (2001, p. xix). While Cannadine makes reference to the reproduction of British social hierarchies, the 'sameness' evident in these girl castaways is their maintenance of the core of acceptable British femininity, even in the face of being cast away on an island. This strategy conservatively works to uphold doctrines of racial superiority in contrast with native peoples, but it also somewhat progressively affords British girls with the potential to survive independently, without any assistance, away from civilisation.

John Stephens and Robyn McCallum situate island settings as 'social microcosms in that they potentially enable the examination and reconstruction of existing social structures' (1998, p. 276). These castaway fictions utilise the microcosmic workings of isolated settings to trial modern British girlhood in its full independent capacity by removing the constraints of civilisation. They serve as an examination, not a reconstruction, of the latent potential of idealised girlhood if imperial necessity required girls to fully exercise survival skills. These girl-Crusoe texts therefore make a fitting close to this study of British girlhood and empire, marking the endpoint of a trajectory in which girls not only might be imagined sailing boats, wielding weapons, and surviving in the elements without male assistance, but also might remain unmarried and make their own fortune, or indeed their own empire. The girl Crusoe's idealised, modern femininity differs from male examples and departs substantially from mid-Victorian children's robinsonades, in which women are either helpless or restricted to non-glorified domestic tasks. Furthermore, these protagonists normalise feminine capability among middle-class girls and for middle-class girl readers, in contrast with earlier female-Crusoe novels that became popular among lower- and lower-middle-class readers.

London publisher of 'blue books' (cheap romances) Ann Lemoine produced inexpensive versions of several female-Crusoe novels, including Penelope Aubin's *The Life of Charlotta Du Pont* (1723), Marguerite Daubenton's *Zelia in the Desert; or, The Female Crusoe* (1789), and *The Life, Voyages, and Surprising Adventures of Mary Jane Meadows* (1802), in the early nineteenth century for lower- and lower-middle-class women readers accustomed to hard work (Thompson, 2008, p. 15). Due to the harsh realities of their labour, which would not have existed for middle-class women readers, the readers of Lemoine's inexpensive editions may have been undaunted by the physical competencies displayed by the castaway heroines. Nevertheless, girl-Crusoe fictions published at the end of the nineteenth and into the twentieth century not only afford their heroines an even greater range of narrative possibilities, but explicitly target the middle-class girl reader. The adaptation of the genre for girls is accompanied by a shift in perceptions of middle-class femininity, in which adventurousness and physical strength can be comfortably reconciled with an appropriately feminine concern with external appearance and maternal feelings.

The absence of women from robinsonades is somewhat transformed in the late nineteenth century when women's involvement in empire was actively sought, contributing to the creation of girl-Crusoe protagonists in contrast with the peripheral girl characters of earlier children's novels and eighteenth-century female Crusoes. Rebecca Weaver-Hightower suggests that women's absence in most castaway narratives 'show[s] women as largely incidental to the island colonization, reflecting their political invisibility in real-world imperial society' (2007, p. 55). When female Crusoes do make fictional appearances, notably at the end of the eighteenth and nineteenth centuries, their presence can be related to major challenges to and transformations of gender norms. Carl Thompson argues that fictional interest in the female Crusoe was pertinent in the 1790s because of the ferocity of feminist and anti-feminist debate. In particular, he suggests that although Charles Dibdin's *Hannah Hewit* (1792) celebrates its protagonist, the novel's 'somewhat ambivalent' portrayal of the female Crusoe perhaps verges into anti-feminist satire (2008, p. 18).[5] The use of the female Crusoe as an object of satire was more certainly expressed in *Punch*'s 'Miss Robinson Crusoe' (1847) by Douglas Jerrold, in which the castaway heroine is fixated only on her appearance and loss of her social life at home. There is no such satire or humour to be found in the girls' robinsonades, which take their subject matter and heroines seriously.

It is a familiar plot device in eighteenth-century female-Crusoe novels for the heroine to be guided or supported by men. In addition to *Hannah Hewit*, Aubin's *Life of Charlotta Du Pont*, and a translation of Daubenton's *Zelia in the Desert* from the French, the eighteenth century also saw the publication in English of Unca Eliza Winkfield's *The Female American* (1767).[6] In the early nineteenth century, there was even a mother and daughter castaway pair in Sarah Burney's *Tales of Fancy, volume 1: The Shipwreck* (1815). The latter four novels share similar tropes with respect to negotiating the gender politics of female castaways and potential racial threats posed by their movement into the Empire. In both Aubin's and Burney's novels, a male provides convenient support and protection and performs many of the tasks required for survival. Although Winkfield's and Daubenton's heroines are stranded alone, they receive initial assistance in how to survive through instructions conveniently left by male hermits. As close examination of late Victorian and Edwardian girl Crusoes will show, these heroines, in contrast, are exemplars of feminine strength and intelligence and are rendered capable of island settlement without male guidance or protection.

Nineteenth-century children's family Robinsonades

Edward Salmon's *Juvenile Literature as It Is* includes a survey from 1884 that places *Robinson Crusoe* and *The Swiss Family Robinson* first and second in favourite books among boy readers. Girls did not rate these novels as highly, but Charles Kingsley's historical adventure *Westward Ho!* is ranked first in the girls' list. (Thirty-four girls named Kingsley's novel as their favourite, while seven listed Wyss's novel, and only four preferred Defoe's novel.) Though the numbers of children surveyed are statistically small, the results imply a trend for Victorian middle-class girls to read boys' novels and periodicals. Salmon remarks that girls did so because they can get in 'boys' books what they seldom get in their own – stirring plot and lively movement' (1886, p. 524). Nevertheless, there were attempts to provide girls with adventure fiction, namely in robinsonades featuring female protagonists in the late nineteenth century. These fictions constitute the beginnings of the genre of girls' adventure stories that would become more visible and popular in the early twentieth century.

It is useful to spend a moment examining family-Crusoe narratives, the precursors to later girl-Crusoe fictions, in order to lay out the evidence for the transition that I am arguing occurs at the end of the nineteenth century in which girl protagonists crave adventure and can survive independently. Girl Crusoes who are stranded among groups or families of castaways earlier in the century play a secondary role to male protagonists or are largely unable to contribute to survival. Johann D. Wyss's didactic novel of a castaway family, *The Swiss Family Robinson*, was translated from German into English in 1814 and adapted and abridged in numerous editions for children throughout the nineteenth century. In *Swiss Family* the father is the supreme authority on all matters of survival, and he develops his four sons to manhood by cultivating their morals and physical strength by encouraging athleticism in running, riding, leaping, climbing, and swimming. The boys shoot and kill almost every one of the unlikely Noah's ark of species that inhabits the island, even causing the disturbing mass death of forty monkeys who wreaked havoc on one of the family's cottages by clubbing them to death and setting dogs on them. The mother's function is almost exclusively to cook and sew clothing.[7] Though, as O'Malley has pointed out, domesticity is essential to the process of making exotic islands home (2008, p. 67), the relegation of the most central domestic tasks that are devoid of danger and excitement to the boundaries of *The Swiss Family Robinson's* narrative privileges 'masculine' traits that as yet do not reside among the female Crusoe's capabilities.

The latter assertion nevertheless requires some qualification, as another female enters W.H.G. Kingston's popular late Victorian edition of the novel almost at its conclusion, when the children are aged between 17 and 25. The eldest boy, Fritz, sets out on his own and discovers a girl named Jenny Montrose who has survived in isolation for three years. Initially Jenny is dressed in a man's sailor suit, and it is noted that she 'should not have unable to manage all the work which ... has been necessary' (Wyss, 1812–1813, p. 304)[8] in any other costume. She poses as male when she is presented to the family, wishing to conceal her feminine identity until the Swiss mother can 'obtain for her a costume more suited to her real character' (Wyss, 1812–1813, p. 296). Jenny is an almost perfunctory plot element, inserted to enable a marriage, yet she constructs her own hut and fittings (including bows, arrows, lances, snares, and fishhooks), which according to Fritz 'evinced no ordinary skill and ingenuity' (Wyss, 1812–1813, p. 301). Her proficiency in these actions is related to her dress in male clothing, which must be removed as she marks her return to traditional femininity among the boys of the family. Unlike the twentieth-century children's novels and films that Victoria Flanagan examines in *Into the Closet: Cross-Dressing and the Gendered Body in Children's Literature*, in which 'cross-dressing' female protagonists provoke re-evaluations of gender norms through their effective performance of masculinity (2008, p. 22), *The Swiss Family Robinson* does not invite us to question whether femininity should be reconceptualised. Jenny's three years of independent survival appear as an anomaly that must be corrected through the reassertion of feminine norms in dress and behaviour, such as her engagement to Fritz at the novel's end, while the family remains on the land they have called 'New Switzerland'. Though she is an intriguing example of an early girl Crusoe who is afforded the physical and mental strength to survive in isolation, Jenny is emblematic of girlhood configured in opposition to, and separate from, boyhood. Her capacity for survival and settlement is not incorporated within her femininity, as in the examples of the adventurous, yet domesticated, girl Crusoes of late Victorian and Edwardian fiction.

By depicting four boys, Wyss avoids the problematic nature of situating a girl's education in an untamed environment. Yet there were examples of girls who were central to fictional narratives by the mid–nineteenth century.[9] Evangelical writers in English used the island setting to enact the Christian education of children in isolation from external, corrupting influences.[10] Ann Fraser Tytler's *Leila; or, The Island* (1839), for example, replicates Wyss's model of the omniscient father who imparts his wisdom to his children. In his daughter's instruction, however, Leila's father, Mr Howard, largely avoids topics that would assist in island survival or develop her physical ability to do so. Leila is primarily given lessons in keeping with religious tenets and is made to practice French verbs, despite the irrelevance of such an accomplishment in their predicament. The narrative is geared toward grooming Leila, who has been raised in India, in appropriate femininity with an eye toward eventual rescue and future marriage, rather than preparation for life in an untamed land. Nevertheless, Leila herself, with no lived experience of English culture, is enamoured of the island and expresses her desire to become a permanent settler upon it, especially after she has accumulated her own brood of domesticated animals. It is through her father's moral and cultural instruction that Leila makes the eventual decision, once a rescue ship arrives, that the family must return to England. In this highly didactic novel, Leila's recognition that civility is preferable to the happy and free life she has enjoyed on the island is depicted as part of her maturation. In contrast, the protagonist of the earlier French novel *Paul and Virginia* (1796) is tainted by her contact with civilised mores in France (the family are social rather than literal castaways) and drowns in a shipwreck on a trip to Paris because she refuses to remove her heavy clothes in order to be rescued. Owen notes that the novel was recommended for girls by Erasmus Darwin, in part because Virginia's fate served as a criticism of the restriction of girls' 'physical and moral development' (2010, p. 172). In spite of their seemingly divergent gender politics, both of these fictions show girls, in various ways, as still unsuited to permanent island settlement.

As the colonies became increasingly populated by British settlers from the mid–nineteenth century, the problem of how to maintain or revise feminine norms in a new landscape became unsolvable with a simple narrative return 'home'. The most significant girl Crusoe of the mid-century appears in Catharine Parr Traill's *Canadian Crusoes* (1852), in which the key elements of the robinsonade are set in the wilderness. This and other 'landed' Crusoe novels took on a warning function for British readers seeking to settle in colonies with untamed natural environments. The novel's preface, authored by Traill's sister, Agnes Strickland, cautions parents leaving the home comforts of England to ensure that their children are 'prepared with some knowledge of what they are to find in the adopted country; the animals, the flowers, the fruits' (p. 11). The heroine of this novel, however, is entirely unfit for survival in the wilderness. The 'Crusoes' of the title – Catharine; her brother, Hector; and their cousin, Louis – become lost in the Canadian woods, but the work of survival rests with the males. When it becomes apparent that the trio has become stranded, Catherine instructs her brothers to build a shelter 'or poor wee Katty must turn squaw and build her own wigwam' (p. 36). Catharine's racist comment gestures toward the way in which indigenous women are attributed survival capacity, much like *The Female American*'s Unca, whose native heritage enables her to straddle civility and resourcefulness and adopt characteristically masculine behaviours. Catharine is the 'wise little cook and housekeeper' (p. 126) while the boys use snares, construct dwellings, and defend the group with axes and knives. Her incapacity in the wild is literalised when she injures herself such that she can no longer walk and must be carried by the boys.

The group rescues a native girl (whom they name Indiana), who serves as an opportunity for Catharine to enact appropriate feminine colonial vocations of nursing and civilising through education: 'How did the lively intelligent Canadian girl, the offspring of a more intellectual race, long to instruct her Indian friend, to enlarge her mind by pointing out such things to her attention as she herself took interest in' (p. 181). While, ironically, Catharine does not possess the intelligence or knowledge to survive on her own, as Indiana does, the task of 'enlarg[ing] her mind' largely entails casting out any belief in the 'depraved' Indian religion, recalling Unca Eliza Winkfield's conversion of sun-worshipping island natives. Indiana significantly contributes to the welfare of the three Canadians, however, acting as a guide to the location of trees with useful properties, demonstrating ice fishing, using a tomahawk, making snowshoes, and even managing the farming of rice, a task in which she directs the two boys. Catharine does not display any of the competencies of her native counterpart; instead she is domestically oriented and maternal in her care of native children when she is taken captive. The heroism in the narrative is reserved for Indiana, who is instrumental in Catharine's rescue and fearlessly declares, 'I can suffer and die for my white sister' (p. 329).

The example of Traill's novel, then, suggests that both British fiction and nascent colonial children's literature until mid-century did not afford British girls with the capacity to become settlers without significant male assistance. Furthermore, the predicament of the castaway is generally rued or grown out of by girl protagonists, rather being welcomed with excitement for the unrestricted freedom offered by an island or wilderness. With examples like Leila and Catharine, the Crusoe form does not operate in these family novels in the way that Joseph Bristow theorises boys' novels to function: to enable heroes to 'act as the natural masters of these controllable environments' (1991, p. 94). When girls appear in fiction as lone castaways, however, as I shall discuss below, they are able to survive and prosper in their island environments without male assistance.

Late Victorian and Edwardian girl crusoes

Late Victorian girl Crusoes move beyond the categorisations of femininity in mid-nineteenth-century robinsonades. The helplessness of the *Canadian Crusoes'* Catharine, for instance, is no longer the ideal response of a civilised girl maintaining appropriate femininity in spite of her surrounds. Instead, both women and men are similarly encouraged to respond to challenges, and explicitly those posed by colonial settlement, without relying on others. The articles about real-world female Crusoes I discussed earlier in this chapter coincided with the appearance of the serial 'Robina Crusoe, And Her Lonely Island Home' (1882–3) by Elizabeth Whittaker, and indeed the illustrations of her hut match the descriptions of Juana María's brushwood 'circular enclosure'. The long-running serial elicited a degree of reader response that suggests that it was among the *GOP*'s most popular.[11] It serves as a key example of how Crusoe mythology is adapted for girl readers during a period of British imperial strength and, later, the Empire's initial movement toward dissolution. Robina is the daughter of Robinson Crusoe and displays his instincts when, in a predictable turn of events, she is placed in a sinking ship and ensures that she grabs a volume of Shakespeare, a Bible, a housewife, a knife, and a flask. She is ready to dispense with the polite norms of home as soon as necessity demands it, using a knife to slash her skirt below the knee during the shipwreck, displaying none of the impracticality of *Canadian Crusoes'* Catharine, who baulks at having a strip of cloth torn from her apron for kindling. Unlike her female robinsonade predecessors, Robina is unafraid of being stranded, wears pantaloons, and wields a knife, a staff, and bow and arrows.

Robina does not rely on a ruse like the heroine of *The Female American* (who hides in a sun idol in order to masquerade as the voice of a god) to subdue the perceived threat posed by the natives but instead loads her two pistols and takes up other weapons: 'Then arming myself with a crowbar, and placing a hammer in my belt, I presented a very formidable appearance' (p. 203). She now believes herself to be a 'match' for the natives, an observation which at once elevates her ability to defend herself and lowers the physical prowess of the natives below that of an English girl. In the late nineteenth century, several gun-toting girl-Crusoe heroines are afforded a capacity for self-defence that deflects anxiety about miscegenation. In a periodical story from the *Girl's Realm*, 'The Girl Crusoes: A Tale of the Indian Ocean' (1902) by Dr Gordon Stables, the heroine, a British consul's daughter, has become accustomed to carrying a gun on the streets of Zanzibar (p. 188). She does not hesitate to protect herself and her sister with the weapon when she becomes a castaway and is threatened by an Arab prince suitor cum slave-trader. In L.T. Meade's novel *Four on an Island* (1892), in which a family group of children become castaways, the heroine,

Isabel, wields a gun to deflect a land-crab attack on the children's dog. Intriguingly, she does so after her brother becomes incapacitated by a twisted ankle, in a gendered reversal of the disablement of *Canadian Crusoes'* Catharine.[12] The latter example prompts us to consider that these late Victorian girl Crusoes are rehearsing the possibility of colonial settlement in which male protection or assistance may not always be at hand. Indeed, as I discussed in Chapter 3, the death or disappearance of the only male in the lives of Bessie Marchant's settler heroines is a common plotline, compelling them to conduct all of the outdoor tasks required to maintain a home in an uncultivated environment and to defend themselves.

Robina Crusoe actively desires adventure – a quality shared by other late Victorian and Edwardian girl Crusoes – having 'longed for' and dreamed of the life she obtains when cast away (Figure 6.1). Much of

"I MADE A SAIL FOR THE BOAT."

Figure 6.1   Robina Crusoe at sail, 'Robina Crusoe and Her Lonely Island Home', *Girl's Own Paper*, 4, 1883, p. 289.

her adaptability is attributed to her self-education through books, in a passage that criticises limitations on girls' education:

> I cannot but wish that teachers and parents would strive to awaken a taste in their girls as well as their boys in natural science and history, as an intelligent interest in such is one means of preparing useful and common-sense wives and mothers. (p. 244)

As previous chapters have shown, similar arguments about improving motherhood through the wider education of girls were rehearsed to justify girls' engagement with nature and physical activity at the turn of the century. This serial also tempers the freedoms allowed to Robina, by ensuring that she channels her capacities into mothering. When natives visit the island to participate in 'horrible orgies', Robina rescues a mother and child who were doomed to death. After the woman dies, Robina takes on the care of the olive-skinned, dark-haired baby and educates her according to her own pedagogical theories (Figure 6.2). Robina's education of the girl, whom she names Undine, reflects the place carved out for women in the imperial project in civilising 'the natives' of British colonies, particularly by teaching girls. It is critical to distinguish that Robina is not simply acting as a Christian missionary, as Unca Eliza Winkfield does in her conversion of the natives from 'sun worship' in *The Female American*; she successfully raises Undine to fit within broader British cultural norms and to reproduce the familiar, which is evidenced by her eventual marriage to an English man. While she does not apply her maternal instincts to raise her own children, Robina channels them for imperial benefit, becoming the matriarch of a new settlement that begins with Undine and her husband. The closure of the serial nevertheless does not fixate on Robina's return to conventional femininity, as she remains unmarried. It represents a marked shift from earlier children's robinsonades, such as the popular Victorian version of *The Swiss Family Robinson*, in which union with a man ensures that the castaway girl will never need to do more in her settler's life than perform domestic tasks that are none too dissimilar from those she would have performed in civilisation.

This is not to claim that there is a universal embrace of girls as independent settlers in these fictions. In at least one example, a period of life as a 'girl Crusoe' is shown as a temporary adventure prior to marriage. Stables' heroine, Lucy, actively plans for herself and her sister to become castaways by visiting an island ten miles away, and they do not consider bringing their brother, even though his shooting, fishing, and

"I TAUGHT HER THE ALPHABET."

Figure 6.2 Robina Crusoe educating her adopted daughter, Undine, 'Robina Crusoe and Her Lonely Island Home', *Girl's Own Paper*, 4, 1883, p. 525.

tree-climbing prowess is emphasised. The sisters steer a seventeen-foot boat on their own, but stormy weather ensures that they unintentionally become 'real Crusoes'. Their first two weeks on the island are spent enjoying the delights of nature and an experience 'something like a picnic' (Stables, 1902, p. 193). When the devious Prince Sudgee, who wishes to marry Lucy, conveniently arrives at the island and endeavours to imprison them, the girls are rescued by 'British blue-jackets' and order is restored by a perfunctory double wedding. This short story situates middle-class girlhood as a period in which adventure may be safely pursued prior to marriage, not extending to the freedoms afforded to Robina Crusoe, but nevertheless embracing a state of temporary adventure in a way that is not present in earlier novels.

Deirdre David observes that female service was integral to empire-building and was firmly grounded in maternity: 'The mother country, Queen Victoria, British women: in this important political symbolization, each and all must labor to produce colonies' (1995, p. 182). The realities of colonial settlement infuse late-nineteenth-century British girl Crusoes with a capacity for survival that is not intrinsic to the protagonists of earlier children's and female robinsonades. A further point of difference is the way in which girl Crusoes draw together maternal instincts with the desire for adventure and the physical strength for survival. Robina Crusoe remains unmarried and raises another woman's child to become the matriarch of a growing settlement with plentiful natural resources, while earlier female Crusoes often marry without reference to bearing children. These tendencies can be read as further evidence of the accommodation of adventurousness within the realm of acceptable femininity from the end of the nineteenth century, with maternity no longer needing to be excluded from narratives of female adventure.

In Mrs George Corbett's *Little Miss Robinson Crusoe* (1898), the heroine, Leona, also presents an idealised model of imperial femininity in which domesticity and mothering are melded with physical labour, such as house construction and raft-building. Like Robina Crusoe, she has a love of adventure, namely sailing boats, inspired by her father's life as a sailor. She is unafraid of danger befalling her on the sea because she can 'swim with astonishing speed and endurance' (p. 7). Nevertheless, she is also exceptional in her performance of feminine tasks: 'I was really much cleverer at all kinds of feminine work than most girls of my age' (p. 29). One of the novel's plates visualises Leona without a hair out of place punting upstream on a raft immediately after fending off with an axe a wild attack by a 'sinister octopus' that attempted to drag her underwater (Figure 6.3). She maintains personal composure, feminine ideals, and the civility of home, embodying Cannadine's idea of empire as the replication of sameness, while immersed in the difference of dangerous situations and the conduct of necessary survival tasks on the island. Leona clearly represents the idealised imperial girl who is able to incorporate survival skills with domesticity.

Figure 6.3 Nell punts calmly along the water after an encounter with a giant octopus. Unknown illustrator, *Little Miss Robinson Crusoe*, John F. Shaw and Company, 1898. Every effort has been made to trace the copyright holder.

In contrast with the eighteenth-century heroine Hannah Hewit, who builds an automaton with reeds fashioned into pipes that issues sounds in the wind to fulfil her need for human companionship (Dibdin, 1792, p. 92), Leona takes a baby doll that she finds in an abandoned village as her companion and names it 'Victoria' 'after the Queen' (Corbett, 1898, p. 107). This firmly imbricates maternity with imperial settlement and positions Leona as one of the future mothers of England, highlighting the necessity of both men's and women's work to colonial settlement and expansion. When she leaves the abandoned settlement, she initially makes the choice to leave behind a cache of gemstones rather than her doll, symbolically conveying maternal priorities. She also becomes a maternal leader, in her rescue of a starving mother and daughter (who had left the village because of its perilous earthquakes). Upon their reunion with the other villagers, Leona, who has grown tall and strong, becomes the leader of the group, admired as a 'marvel of strength' and 'a heroine'. Not only does Leona make herself 'useful' by leading failed colonists to safety, but she gains great personal fulfilment that has eluded her since her father's death. The novel's closure grants her freedom from her adoptive parents and a substantial fortune, with no looming marriage prospects to neatly corral her independence.

Staving off the native within and without

Boundaries between female castaways and the native inhabitants of the islands on which they are stranded were often maintained by the physical or intellectual presence, such as through instructions left by hermits, of a male. As the examples of 'Robina Crusoe' and Stables' 'The Girl Crusoes' show, girl Crusoes' adventures were not always tied to a male presence because they were often able to defend themselves with weapons. The latest fictional example I will consider in this study, *The Girl Crusoes* (1915), permits girls to survive without male intervention but does not equip the girls with weapons.[13] Instead, it reconfigures the relationship between British males and females in their interaction with native peoples in such a way as to elevate feminine capabilities above the masculine. The novel, as I suggested of Nesbit's Psammead trilogy in Chapter 4, can be read as criticising masculine imperial conquest. The implicit critique and parody of imperialism in these texts corresponds with the close of what historian Ronald Hyam calls 'Britain's imperial century' from 1814 to 1915, with numerous setbacks from the *fin de siècle* foreshadowing the eventual dissolution of the Empire (1993, p. 311). Nevertheless, this text is still complicit with many aspects of

imperial ideology, which did not abruptly cease in Britain or its dominions, including that of racial superiority.

The Girl Crusoes was attributed to 'Mrs Herbert Strang', the pseudo-
nym of two male Oxford University Press editors, Herbert Ely and James
L'Estrange, who were best known as writers of books for boys as 'Herbert
Strang'. After a successful run penning boys' adventure fiction, the duo
compiled a number of anthologies containing 'the best girls' writers and
artists of the day', which led to their composition of an original girl-
Crusoe novel. It depicts three orphaned sisters, Elizabeth, Mary, and
Katherine (Tommy) Westmacott, who travel with their uncle, a ship's
captain, when he must complete one further voyage to the South Pacific.
The girls are determined not to marry 'for a living' and so the family farm
is set to be sold upon their return. During a storm the trio is put ashore in
a dinghy, and upon landing with no sign of their uncle or his crew, like
most girl Crusoes, they display an awareness that they 'are to be Crusoes'
(p. 76). While the girls are initially despairing, they soon take precautions
in case they should be permanently stranded, resolving that men and
boys have endured such shipwrecks on lonely islands and that there is no
reason why girls should not be able to do so. In fact, Mary suggests their
own predicament is worse than Crusoe's when they take stock of their
provisions: 'I always think Crusoe was jolly lucky' (p. 89).[14]

H. Rider Haggard's *King Solomon's Mines* (1885) is exemplary of adventure novels for boy readers that favoured adversarial approaches to native
peoples. While they are fearful of native encounters, the Westmacott girls
have, in contrast, resolved to 'make friends' (Strang, 1915, p. 82) with any
native islanders they find. Nevertheless, the sight of 'a little brown face'
(p. 121) in the bushes elicits terror in the girls and prompts a discussion
of whether the originator of the movement might have been a monkey.
Despite the girls' aspirations to friendliness, the comparison between the
native and the monkey shows lingering remnants of the rationalisation
of imperial rule. The girls' first encounter with the native people occurs
when they discover a canoe with a girl inside: 'a brown-skinned pretty
little creature, with a string of what looked like teeth around her neck'
(p. 223) (Figure 6.4). The girl, who is named Fangati, rejects clothing 'and
coil[s] herself up like a dog' (p. 229). Not only is she equated with an animal, but in a repetition of Victorian soap ads that played on the intersec-
tion of civilising, cleanliness, and whiteness, Fangati scrubs herself with
sand 'to see if she could make her brown body resemble theirs' (p. 229).
She is, however, able to show the girls fruits that they could not find,
dig for yams, and climb to reach a coconut, delineating some aspects of
survival as the preserve of native peoples. The girls' positive interaction

Figure 6.4 The girl Crusoes discover the native girl, Fangati. Illustration by Nell Marion Tenison for *The Girl Crusoes: A History of the South Seas* by Mrs Herbert Strang (Oxford University Press, 1912), reproduced by permission of Oxford University Press.

with Fangati aids in their subsistence and to some degree revises the idea of the British castaway civilising a non-white Other. In place of Robinson Crusoe teaching Friday the English language and Christianity, and even Robina Crusoe educating her adopted daughter Undine, *The Girl Crusoes* exposes gaps in Western knowledge and gestures toward the potential of native people to fill them.

Ideologies of racial superiority and male imperial conquest are further undermined when Elizabeth rescues a white male missionary. When Fangati brings her grandfather, Maku, to the girls, Tommy jests, 'Impress him with your importance, Queen Bess, monarch of all she surveys', ironically invoking the famous phrase from William Cowper's poem 'The Solitude of Alexander Selkirk' (1782) in a way that differentiates the girl Crusoe from her male antecedents (p. 241).[15] Maku's people, cannibalistic 'heathens', had been visited by a white missionary, Mr Corke, who won over the natives and caused Maku's displacement. Maku's ousting led to further degradation in the tribe's behaviour. The representation of Mr Corke's missionary attempts as folly and unnecessary intervention in the tribal structure of the natives is fully communicated when the 'savages' bring him to the island on which the girls are stranded to be sacrificed to their gods, accompanied by frenzied primal drumming and chanting. Elizabeth becomes the hero, rescuing Mr Corke from certain death. *The Girl Crusoes* shows a marked transition from eighteenth-century female Crusoes like Hannah Hewit and Unca Eliza Winkfield, who are classified as 'extraordinary' women, to the location of heroism within ordinary girls. The novel draws on familiar conceptions of girls as potential heroic rescuers, as shown in the Girl Guide handbook, to argue that any girl might become a heroine:

Heroism is a plant of strange growth. It springs up suddenly, mysteriously, in unexpected places. A simple peasant girl, tending her flocks, hears a voice; and she becomes a warrior, a leader of men, the saviour of her country. A maidservant, after a day of scrubbing floors and washing dishes, is darning stockings in the kitchen when she smells fire, rushes into the bedroom where the children are asleep, and carries them one by one through the flames into safety, at the cost of her own. Yet the capacity for heroism may be latent under many a sober coat or homely apron. The town girl who shudders at a cow, the country girl who trembles at the looming of a motor omnibus, may show under the stress of some high emotion, at the call of some great emergency, qualities that match her with Joan of Arc or Alice Ayres. (Strand, 1915, p. 275)

Elizabeth's heroism therefore affords the girl reader with the belief that she too, as a regular girl, could potentially sacrifice her life for a cause or rescue a man. The concept of heroism that lies dormant within the girl ensures that girls may return home to England to resume life as usual. Elizabeth keeps house for her uncle, Mary is learning to become a teacher, and the novel proposes that tomboy Tommy will also develop 'into a very capable housekeeper' (p. 312). Even without obligatory marriages upon their return, there is still a degree of regulation in the girls' return to civilisation, but it should nevertheless be considered in light of the girls' rescue of a male missionary, who was ill-equipped to undertake the task of civilising the native people through religious instruction. While the Westmacott girls do not fulfil the civilising function in his place, this later text, with its depiction of natives reverting to even more 'primitive' ways once their tribal structure has been dismantled, leaves room for the reader to discern that attempts at civilising should be abandoned.

To smooth the return to England, the girl Crusoe must be differentiated from native women throughout the narrative. In particular, attention to physical appearance symbolises retaining civilised norms – girls' hair can never be allowed to become the matted, rotten mess emphasised in the story of Juana María of San Nicolas Island. The Westmacott girls in *The Girl Crusoes* quickly resolve not to 'go native' like a south sea islander, weighing up whether to cut their hair short 'like a boy's' in preference (p. 109). Instead of verging into masculine appearance, however, the girls determine that they will retain their hair to protect their skin and use a makeshift comb of a fish bone and then craft a comb from wood to groom their hair. The orphaned heroine of *Little Miss Robinson Crusoe*, Leona, is brought to tears when she sees herself in a mirror, largely because of the shock of her 'mop of hair, which not a comb had touched since I was wrecked' (p. 99). She later learns how to wash her hair with 'soap leaves' in order to maintain the hygiene routines of home, and similarly the Westmacott girls devise a method for washing their clothing. These superficial concessions to feminine appearance nevertheless open up the world of independent adventure for girl protagonists.

The late Victorian and Edwardian girl-Crusoe displays an active desire for adventure, unlike her literary precursors in female robinsonades and girls in mid-Victorian children's family robinsonades. This literary figure satisfied the desire of girl readers for exciting plots featuring girl protagonists, which they had hitherto been able to obtain only in boys' books with male protagonists and which constitutes a significant element of the origins of the girls' adventure genre that was popularised in the early twentieth century. Importantly, the girls' genre appears in middle-class girls' periodicals and expensive hardcover novel editions, suggesting a target audience of middle-class readers. This likely audience implies that independent girls, within the microcosmic location of the island setting, were not perceived as transgressive. The girl Crusoe also embodies the real involvement of young women in the British imperial project and is representative of the idealisation of altered feminine norms when English women ventured beyond the safety and civility of home to settle in new lands. The majority of girl readers at home in Britain, however, might never have had the opportunity to test out their capacity for heroism. These girl-Crusoe fictions nevertheless mark the endpoint of a reconfiguration of acceptable femininity that was inextricably entangled with, and justified by, discourse about maintaining the British Empire.

Conclusion

As an eight-year-old Australian girl, I promised to do my best 'to serve the queen and my country, to help other people and to keep the Brownie Guide law'. Our Girl Guide 'hut', which had very little in common architecturally with an actual hut, what with its brick veneer, was watched over by a framed portrait of Queen Elizabeth II. The print had presumably been a fixture, along with the battered Brownie 'toadstool', since Guiding had begun in my city, the second largest in a state called 'Queensland', named for Queen Victoria. Empire still resonated in my life as a girl, a hemisphere and more than a lifetime away from the British girl readers who turned the pages of the books and magazines that form the subject of this study. With the temporal and spatial distance of my own girlhood from the height of the British Empire, the omnipresence of the Queen, whose profile graced the twenty-cent coins that my Brown Owl informed me I should always keep on hand in case I should need to make a phone call, was obscure to me. How and why would I be 'serving' the Queen? What kind of 'service' could an Australian girl offer to a monarch?

In the same way that I was oblivious to the last vestiges of imperial sentiment that informed Girl Guiding in the 1980s, so too might late Victorian and Edwardian girls have been resistant readers when confronted by exhortations to serve their empire in print culture. Nevertheless, for these girls, the presence of empire in books and magazines held a far greater importance. As I have shown throughout *Empire in British Girls' Literature and Culture*, the infiltration of imperial sentiment into girls' print culture was tied not only to ideas of feminine sacrifice in maternal and nursing roles, but also to opening up the fictional field of adventure to girls as explorers, colonists, and castaways. In these various ways, girls were constructed as integral to the British imperial project, with contributions that were equally, if not more, important than the work of boys. In this way, girls' print culture overturns conventional understandings of 'woman as the stable (and essentially passive) centre from which men could explore the exotic (and often erotic) Empire' (Hunt and Sands, 1999, p. 44). Girls were being prepared to become the future centre of the Empire, but they were also encouraged to venture beyond its circumference.

The girl reader of the period was created by a range of intersecting factors that were preoccupied with national strength and maintaining imperial rule. This unique place was predicated on the establishment of girlhood as a 'provisional free space', as Sally Mitchell defines it, between childhood and adulthood. Not confined to the nursery but not as strictly bound by the restrictions of adult femininity, the girl occupied a life stage that encompassed comparative freedom as well as training for the responsibilities of womanhood. While girls may seem doubly removed from empire because of gender and age, conversely the creation of the space of girlhood was central to their formulation as capable, and necessary, components, of the support of empire. In an imperial sense, there were three major ways formulated for girls to make a vital contribution. First, girls were identified as future mothers of the nation, who held it in their power to produce strong, healthy, and moral citizens or to permit the deterioration of the race through neglect. Second, girls were imbued with the potential to 'civilise' or improve living conditions and native peoples in colonial locations, in addition to the working classes at home. Finally, girls were portrayed as physically strong and brave in order to explore new territory, nurse in the midst of conflict, live in a colony, or even survive as a castaway. The overall picture given by these three basic variants is that girls' part in the British Empire was more important than boys' and that sometimes girls' capacities and suitability for the work it necessitated were superior to boys'.

Ensuring that womanliness was not compromised was an overarching concern in texts that draw girls into the work of empire, particularly in non-fiction examples. Both pedagogical and fictional texts attribute to girls the function of moral guide that can inspire the nation's men and shape its children. However, the preceding chapters have argued that the restrictions of womanliness were somewhat relaxed when girls were located in a colonial environment or an emergency situation. Indeed, the definition of appropriate femininity expanded to accommodate the kinds of tasks that women might need to perform in order to support the defence or white settlement of British colonies. What constituted the 'ideal girl' at home differed from expectations of what was acceptable for girls when, for example, living in an 'uncivilised' country outside England with no male assistance. Theoretically, girls at home were encouraged to physically and mentally prepare themselves for potential service to empire should there be a direct threat to Britain or should they live a colonial life in future.

The celebration of contemporary British girlhood manifests across genres of fiction, including school, adventure, fantasy, castaway, and domestic novels, periodicals, and the Girl Guide handbook. Indeed, the freedoms and education enjoyed by the late Victorian and Edwardian girl are at times held up as indicative of Britain's cultural and racial superiority that could in turn justify its civilising efforts. The process of encouraging the development of the intellect and bodies of girls was not driven by notions of equality as much as by social Darwinist thought impacting upon pedagogy that linked a girl's physical and moral health (and development) with the strength of the nation. Therefore, the reading, education, and hobbies of each girl could be understood as having imperial significance.

While girls' print culture has not been overtly connected with imperialistic sentiment in the same way as boys' texts of the late nineteenth century and early twentieth century, this study has sought to answer how girls were imbricated in the project of empire. With the sometimes conflicting imperatives of empire and fostering acceptable femininity, these texts do not provide straightforward accounts of imperialism as might be expected. The preceding chapters have interrogated and complicated the 'obviousness' of the effect of empire on children's literature and culture that I referred to in my Introduction. Instead of an obvious effect, this corpus of texts shows the complex interplay of cultural historical conditions that impacted upon the late Victorian and Edwardian girl and the texts that she read.

Notes

Introduction

1. In her reading of L.M. Montgomery's *Anne of Green Gables* in the forthcoming *Oxford Handbook of Children's Literature* (2011), Mavis Reimer makes a convincing case for reading newspapers and novels alongside each other in order to situate fiction within 'determinate political and social histories'. In her essay, Reimer draws on the idea of newspapers and novels as 'forms that produce the nation'. In my own study, I will also include magazine articles, government reports, pedagogical texts, and other non-fiction sources, considering them as forms that contribute to the production of empire.
2. Sally Mitchell establishes this point about the cultural figure of the 'new girl' versus the reality of most girls, asserting that girls were nevertheless 'consciously aware of their own culture and recognized its discord with adult expectations' (1995, p. 3).
3. Catherine Driscoll proposes that in the late nineteenth and early twentieth centuries adolescence extended to the ages of twenty-one to twenty-five (2002, p. 51). Kimberley Reynolds also situates the upper limit at twenty-five (1990, p. 25). At the younger end of the spectrum, Mitchell suggests that the fictional 'schoolgirl' is usually over the age of eleven (1994, p. 244).
4. Leigh Summers proposes that a greater number of terms could be applied to girls between infancy and their late teens ('maiden', 'young girl', 'miss', and 'young woman') because 'the lives of male children were more clearly punctuated and delineated by adolescence, increasing independence, career and marriage' (2001, p. 77).
5. Deborah Gorham similarly suggests that the ideal woman not only had 'womanly strength', but was able to remain 'permanently childlike' (1982, p. 6).
6. Spencer does not believe that noisy play for girls will induce 'unlady-like habits': 'For if the sportive activity allowed to boys does not prevent them from growing up into gentlemen; why should a like sportive activity prevent girls from growing up into ladies? [...] If now, on arriving at the due age, this feeling of masculine dignity puts so efficient a restraint on the sports of boyhood, will not the feeling of feminine modesty, gradually strengthening as maturity is approached, put an efficient restraint on the like sports of girlhood?' (1859, p. 154).
7. See the chapter 'Advice Manuals' in Kate Flint's *The Woman Reader, 1837–1914*, Oxford, Clarendon Press, 1993.
8. See K. Moruzi (2010) ' "Never Read Anything that Can at all Unsettle Your Religious Faith": Reading and Writing in *The Monthly Packet*', *Women's Writing*, 17.2, 287–303.
9. Deborah Gorham makes a similar observation regarding class difference with reference to the independence of girls. She suggests that most concern about independent behaviour was directed toward girls of the 'outcast' class who were not subject to as much 'protection' (or perhaps containment) as those in the home (1978, p. 374).

10. For instance, Richardson suggests that some New Woman writers fore-grounded the way in which women could produce a healthy middle class: 'As they saw it, the women of Britain could best serve the race, the country, and their own interest through the rational selection of a reproductive part-ner' (2003, p. 215).
11. Settling in a colony was especially encouraged for unmarried women. As Rita S. Kranidis, in her study of spinsters, suggests, unmarried women were urged to consider where they could be of most 'use' (1999, p. 20).

1 Shaping the 'Useful' Girl: The *Girl's Own Paper*, 1880–1907

1. For a consideration of contradictory attitudes to girls' work in class terms, see M. Smith and K. Moruzi (2010) ' "Learning What Real Work…Means": Ambiguous Attitudes Towards Employment in the *Girl's Own Paper*', *Victorian Periodicals Review*, 43.4, 429–45.
2. In David Reed's statistical analysis of the *GOP* articles as compared with the *BOP* in 1890, unsurprisingly, travel and adventure, science and technology, and sport are given greater coverage in the *BOP*, while history, biography, verse, music, fashion, and the domestic are more predominant in the *GOP* (1997, p. 253). Yet, less predictably, there is a slightly greater concentration of articles on foreign life in the *GOP* (2.92 per cent) than the *BOP* (1.73 per cent), and fiction is substantially less in the publication for girls (41.09 per cent, 52.44 per cent for the *BOP*).
3. The 1891 competition statistics usefully fall in the middle of the period I am concerned with. The age spans are indicative of the demographics of competition entrants prior and subsequent to this date. In early 1884, a competition in English writing attracted entrants from ages 10 to 25, with most concentrated in the 14 to 22 years age group (pp. 254–5).
4. Skelding presents the paper as an attempt to be 'a type of "universal" wom-en's magazine' (2001, p. 43) with efforts to cater to women of various classes and ages. Without discounting the existence of an audience of older women readers, including mothers of girl readers, the competition age statistics sug-gest a primary audience of girls who had not yet married.
5. Competitions occasionally suggested that the listed international prize-winners did not match the standard of the local competitors and were listed in their own section so as to distinguish them in this way. A correspondent from Australia ('Westralia') is told in an 'Answers to Correspondents' column in 1891: 'We feel a special interest in the girls of our far distant Colonies, and wish to reply to their letters with little delay' (p. 191). Nevertheless, it seems that all girls, local and international, eventually had their letters published.
6. In her essay on the figure of the New Woman in the feminist press, Michelle Elizabeth Tusan argues that the mainstream press presented a 'dys-topic vision' of society gone wrong with regard to political women (1998, p. 169).
7. See also Jenny Sharpe, *Allegories of Empire: The Figure of the Woman in the Colonial Text* (1993), for another perspective on the connection between

the establishment of racial superiority over the Indian woman and female moral agency.

8. A 'sound mind in a sound body' became the motto of the Bergman Österberg Physical Training College (renamed Dartford College in 1895) where the female school teachers of physical education were trained.

2   Developing Pedagogy and Hybridised Femininity in the Girls' School Story

1. This act complemented the Workshops Act of 1867, which prevented children under the age of 8 from working and placed restrictions on the employment of children between 8 and 13, determining that they must work no more than half time (Horn, 1989, p. 122).
2. In Brazil's *The Leader of the Lower School* (1913), the students discuss regulations at other schools including St Chad's, where all pupils are weighed upon their return to school (p. 43).
3. These points were taken from an article published in the *Journal of Scientific Physical Training* (1910) in which the pros and cons of each system are discussed.
4. The end-of-term exhibition of physical exercises in *The New Girl at St. Chad's* (1912) includes military drill and, for the first time, flag signalling. Student Lettice Talbot believes it is a skill that might prove important to have attained during catastrophe or even, inexplicably, in regular life: 'It might come in useful if there were a war…and at any rate, it will be very convenient at home' (p. 277).
5. The heroines of *The Girl's of St. Cyprian's: A Tale of School Life* (1914) follow diverse paths after their schooling. We are provided with brief updates of the girls five years after their education has been completed: one has become an entomology researcher at Cambridge, another is a kindergarten teacher and games mistress, one has a degree from Kirkton University, and yet another is engaged to a man in India and is conducting further study (p. 281).

3   Adventurous Girls of the British Empire: The Novels of Bessie Marchant

1. Rashna B. Singh suggests that Henty established the norms for imperial character that were accessible for English schoolboys (2004, p. 4).
2. *A Courageous Girl: A Story of Uruguay* (1909) includes advertisements for 'books for girls' and 'books for boys', as well as for a selection of titles authored by Henty. The advertisements in *Held at Ransom: A Story of Colonial Life* (1900) also suggest that boys may have composed a proportion of Marchant's readership, just as girls read Henty. While it is not strictly a girls' adventure (the heroine's younger brother figures in the story to the degree that he is depicted on the front cover), it is nevertheless revealing that no advertisements for girls' books are included in this edition, only for the works of Henty and 'books for boys'.
3. Terri Doughty's analysis emphasises the importance of the domestic to the femininity of Marchant's heroines. She describes them as 'domestic

goddesses, able to shoot a gun and ride a horse as well as to cook a meal or nurse an invalid, to support and protect a home as well as to make one' (2011).

4. Not all literary perspectives hold Marchant in high esteem. Donald Hettinga suggests that Marchant's readers could not have taken her novels 'seriously': 'They are at best escapist melodramas, filled with outrageous coincidences' (1996, p. 169).

5. Marchant's *The Heroine of the Ranch: A Story of Tierra del Fuego* is a rare example of a girls' adventure in which the heroine's mother is a strong figure who contains her daughter's adventures and discourages her desire to lead a pioneer life. Yet, ironically, when her mother dies, the heroine decides that she must make a home for the rest of her family and that she will derive happiness from it 'since that is woman's mission, and perhaps the excuse for her existence' (1914, p. 109).

6. Marchant married a clergyman, Reverend Jabez Ambrose Comfort, at the age of thirty-seven, which places the event chronologically close to the publication of this novel. She also assisted in training Methodist ministers and, according to her obituary, undertook 'the functions of a lay preacher' (1941, p. 569).

7. It should be noted, however, that Mitchell builds upon the work of Claudia Nelson and Kimberley Reynolds, who suggest that boys' fiction became 'more manly' at the turn of the century, to argue that fiction for girls became similarly masculine (1995, p. 137). Specifically, she argues that Marchant's later novels demonstrate this manliness.

8. There is a brief reference to a girl performing a civilising function in *The Heroine of the Ranch*. The white girl who disappears at the beginning of the novel is revealed to have been guarded – rather than 'stolen' – by the loyal native Indians Tambo and Nonook. When the girl is found at the novel's conclusion, she comments that she was looked after and fed but that she has also been able to 'teach the people' just as her father once did (1914, p. 359).

9. Her *TLS* obituary notes that Marchant was 'a traveller only on the enchanted carpet of Imagination' (1941, p. 569).

10. Chrissie Felton in *The Girl Captives* also remains unmarried. Her father marries Juliet, aged twenty-four, and Chrissie presumably lives within the family home with her stepmother.

4 Fantastic and Domestic Girls and the Idolisation of 'Improving' Others

1. *Five Children and It* was serialised in *The Strand* from April 1902, while the latter novels also appeared in serial form in *The Strand* in the year prior to their publication as complete works.

2. In Homi Bhabha's interrogation of Lord Macaulay's description of colonial governance, for instance, he teases out the contradictory coexistence of ideas such as 'the father and the oppressor' (1985, p. 74–5).

3. Amelia A. Rutledge argues that Nesbit's fantasies indicate a strategy of 'displacement and distancing with regard to feminist issues' that were concurrently emerging in adult realist fiction of the era (1999, p. 225).

4. *A Little Princess* is an expanded version of Burnett's 1888 novel, *Sara Crewe*, penned at the request of her publisher after the success of a stage play in the United States.

5. Stephen Prickett has previously noted that 'Nesbit, the socialist, is less concerned with individuals than with societies' (1979, p. 219). I shall consider Nesbit's socialism later in this chapter.

6. John Stephens suggests that their 'time out' from adults ultimately demonstrates that 'the children are unable to be effectively self-regulating and need to be shaped by adult society in order to be made fit to take their places in it' (1992, p. 132). Indeed, the children's journeys often demonstrate their naivety about the constraints of the real world. While they place themselves in perilous situations through their own errors (and as a result of the limitations on their use of magic), the children often must rely on their own abilities to escape from danger in a fantasy of agency potentially appealing to the disempowered implied child reader. More importantly, the novels use the children's time and place travels to criticise the adult society that Stephens argues that they must be socialised to fit. This analysis of Nesbit problematises the notion that the closure of each text 'asserts the values and order of the adult world' (1992, p. 127) by demonstrating the mechanisms the narratives employ to compare the realist world unfavourably with fantastic renderings of primitive past civilisations and a future utopian one.

7. Shirley Foster and Judy Simmons observe of Nesbit's novels generally that girls are frequently stronger and more insightful than their brothers 'and they tend to provide the behavioural models to which boys must aspire' (1995, p. 140).

8. I am indebted to Dr Elizabeth Parsons for this observation.

9. Stephen Prickett suggests that, particularly in a country educated with the Bible: 'To compare twentieth-century London, with all its tourist attractions, unfavourably with Babylon, not merely in terms of architecture, but even in morals and general humanity was a final calculated insult' (1979, p. 221).

10. See Monica Anderson's *Women and the Politics of Travel, 1870–1914*. She describes the debate on the subject of women as members of the Royal Geographical Society as issuing from a consensus of opinion that 'male explorers confirmed the heroism, romance, adventure, and scientific imperative of Empire, female globetrotters did not' (2006, p. 23)

11. Two other studies which make reference to Ruskin's 'Of Queens' Gardens' to contextualise gender and the garden are Anna Krugovoy Silver's 'Domesticating Brontë's Moors: Motherhood in *The Secret Garden*' (1997, p. 195) and György Tóth's 'The Children of the Empire: Anti-Imperialism in Frances Hodgson Burnett's *The Secret Garden*' (2003, p. 123).

12. Rashna B. Singh notes that Burnett, perhaps unaware of the close relationships children shared with their Ayahs, fails to include any love in Mary's relationship with her. This elision may also be a part of Burnett's deprivation of the Indian characters of any 'shape or voice other than by proxy' (2004, p. 121).

5   Be(ing) Prepared: Girl Guides, Colonial Life, and National Strength

1. The title was printed as *How Girls Can Help Build Up the Empire* on the front cover.

2. Girl Guides were aged from eleven to sixteen and were divided into patrols of eight girls, each with a patrol leader aged between fifteen and eighteen. Three or more patrols were collected into a company that was headed by a captain, a girl who was aged over twenty-one. The handbook addresses both the older Guide instructors or captains and the Girl Guides themselves in different modes. Comments intended specifically for instructors are included within each chapter of the text, where also the girls themselves could read them; they are differentiated by italicised font.

3. See, for instance, H. Brohan (1987) *Mowgli's Sons: Kipling and Baden-Powell's Scouts* (London: Jonathan Cape); and for the relationship between 'muscular Christianity' and Empire, J. E. Adams (1995) *Dandies and Desert Saints: Styles of Victorian Masculinity* (Ithaca and London: Cornell University Press).

4. Allen Warren and Richard A. Voeltz have also touched on the differences between the Girl Guides and the Boy Scouts. Their studies have, however, focused upon the history of the movement utilising Boy Scouts Association reports and the 'Girl Guides' Gazette'. While Voeltz does note that the early handbooks 'are far more useful in gaining an impression of the Girl Guides' (1988, p. 91) than are official histories and pamphlets, his references to them are scant.

5. See T. M. Proctor (2002) 'Scouts, Guides, and the Fashioning of Empire, 1919–1939' in W. Parkins (ed.) *Fashioning the Body Politic* (Oxford and New York: Berg), p. 132.

6. In an essay on physical education in *Education: Intellectual, Moral, and Physical* (1861), Herbert Spencer connects individual physical strength with racial superiority: 'Thus far we have found no reason to fear trials of strength with other races in either of these fields [war and commerce]. But there are not wanting signs that our power will be presently taxed to the uttermost... Already thousands break down under the high pressure they are subject to... Hence it is becoming of especial importance that the training of children should be carried on, as not only to fit them mentally for the struggle before them, but also to make them physically fit to bears its excessive wear and tear' (p. 132).

7. There is contradiction on this issue, however. Instructors are advised that girls should form patrols within the same class 'in order to preserve girls' manners'. They should '[l]et birds of a feather flock together' (p. 457).

8. Warren argues that the imperialist bent of the Girl Guides diminished after 1916 (1986, p. 245). Nevertheless, between 1909 (when the first unofficial 'Girl Scouts' appeared) and 1916, the imperialist overtones of the Guides outstripped those of the Scouts.

9. While the girls are referred to as scouts in the article's title, a 'scout-mistress' named Miss Fenn of the Finchley Guides is quoted extensively, and she notes that the girls are referred to as 'guides' by the 'scout-master, Mr Osborne' (Roberts, 1909, pp. 338–9).

10. Agnes-Baden Powell inserts herself into the handbook to clarify that she does not wish to suggest that girls should lead an army and that she refers to Joan of Arc only as a useful example of female patriotism: 'I only hold Joan of Arc up as an example of self-sacrifice for the sake of one's country, of wonderful obedience to duty, through immense difficulties, and of untold bravery and courage in a young girl' (p. 424).

11. Stories of rescue include saving a girl from the bottom of a well, sucking poison from a girl who was bitten by a 'mad dog', saving a child from a frozen canal, retrieving a boy who had fallen into a pond, preventing two children from being run over by a runaway cart, rescuing children from a schoolhouse after its roof has collapsed, and saving a child who was on fire and suffering a lost arm due to an exploding lamp. These tales of rescue attempt to build admiration for a combination of ideals: the protection of children and nursing care, as in the instance of a girl who saves a boy from a bull by throwing stones at it and then bathes and dresses his wounds.

12. Most notably, perhaps, Joseph Bristow's *Empire Boys: Adventures in a Man's World* (1991), and on Scouting, Robert H. MacDonald's *Sons of the Empire: The Frontier and Boy Scout Movement, 1890–1918* (1993).

13. As on many other issues, the handbook is contradictory on this issue. Elsewhere it is suggested that certain 'English' methods of survival, such as making fire from flint and steel, are superior to those used by the 'savages' in Africa and America (who rub wood to make fire) (p. 133).

14. The naming of this badge is explained as originating from a reversal of a practice in Japan, where the doll is a symbol for a girl (who will have to nurse children), and the fish a symbol of a boy (who will have to make his way through difficulties and dangers). The badge was intended for the girl who can 'battle against all troubles' (p. 371).

6   Microcosms of Girlhood: Reworking the Robinsonade for Girls

1. Further details of the life of Juana María and the techniques she used to survive in isolation can be found in T. Hudson (1981) 'Recently Discovered Accounts Concerning "The Lone Woman" of San Nicolas Island', *Journal of California and Great Basin Anthropology*, 3.2, 187–99. The story was published in the *Times* on 4 March 1879, 4. Other stories of Native American 'female Crusoes' that repeat elements of this story cropped up in the following two decades, including 'A Female Crusoe: "Alone on the Isle of Skulls"' in the *Hampshire Telegraph*, 22 October 1892, 12, and 'A Female Crusoe' in *The Manchester Times*, 17 December 1887, 6, which includes the same line about the 'desponding helplessness' of some men and women as the *Girl's Own Paper* article of 1883. Demonstrating the long delay between the events and popularisation of the story, what might be the earliest manifestation of the story in Britain was an article in *Lloyd's Weekly Newspaper*, 'A Female Crusoe', 13 November 1853, 7.

2. The most notable example of this trope is in Unca Eliza Winkfield's *The Female American* (1767), in which the heroine has Native American heritage and is described as the daughter of an 'Indian princess'.

3. Andrew O'Malley has recently discussed eighteenth-century robinsonades for children and their educative function. See A. O'Malley (2009) 'Acting out Crusoe: Pedagogy and Performance in Eighteenth-Century Children's Literature', *The Lion and the Unicorn*, 33.2, 131–45.

4. For work on boys' robinsonades, particularly Frederick Marryat's *Masterman Ready* and R.M. Ballantyne's *The Coral Island*, see J. Bristow (1991) *Empire*

Boys: Adventures in a Man's World (London: HarperCollins Academic) and S.N. Maher (1988) 'Recasting Crusoe: Frederick Marryat, R.M. Ballantyne and the Nineteenth-Century Robinsonade', *Children's Literature Association Quarterly*, 13.4, 169–75.

5. Even accounting for generic excesses, Hannah Hewit's competencies run an almost impossible, and potentially humorous, gamut from bricklayer to chemist.

6. Also see C.M. Owen's thorough discussion of female Crusoe novels in English, including Ambrose Evans' *The Lives, Adventures and Wonderful Deliverances of Mrs Martha Rattenberg and James Dubourdieu* (1719) and Penelope Aubin's other castaway narratives *The Strange Adventures of Count de Vinevil* (also entitled *The Life of Madame de Beaumont*) (1721) and *The Noble Slaves* (1722). The latter two novels, Owen argues, afford daughters who are cast away 'an unprecedented autonomy, making their own decisions, particularly in relation to marriage' (2010, p. 152).

7. This trait is common to another castaway family in Frederick Marryat's *Masterman Ready; or, The Wreck of the Pacific* (1841), in which the mother, Mrs Seagrave, and six-year-old daughter, Caroline (who barely figures in the narrative), sew, cook, and care for a baby with the fortunate assistance of servants.

8. This is the altered English-language edition based on the French adaptation by Isabelle de Montolieu (1824), edited by W.H.G. Kingston and published in 1879. This version has been used in place of the closest English translation of the original because of its popularity with readers and the contemporaneousness of this version with the girls' texts I examine. Furthermore, this edition includes the further adventures of the boys, including their discovery of Jenny Montrose.

9. Earlier French novels translated into English that feature girl castaways include Jacques Henri Bernardin de Saint Pierre's popular family castaway narrative *Paul and Virginia* (1795) and F.G. Ducray-Duminil's *Ambrose and Eleanor* (1796).

10. As Bristow argues, 'The island, from Shakespeare's *The Tempest* onwards, has provided the European imagination with an ideal scene of instruction' (1991, p. 94).

11. The regular 'Answers to Correspondents' column saw several girls inquiring about the serial during its publication run, and others wrote seeking information after its conclusion.

12. For an extended analysis of Meade's novel and its heroine's synthesis of adventure and the 'household angel', see M. Norcia (2004) 'Angel of the Island: L. T. Meade's New Girl as the Heir of a Nation-Making Robinson Crusoe', *The Lion and the Unicorn*, 28.3, 345–62.

13. As Kristine Moruzi suggested in her reading of this chapter in manuscript form, the lack of weaponry in *The Girl Crusoes* may reflect clearer differentiation of women's roles with respect to arms in response to World War I.

14. This is a more progressive view than in the earlier novel *Little Miss Robinson Crusoe*, in which the heroine compares herself unfavourably with Robinson Crusoe: 'and I could not help thinking that I was infinitely worse off than he was, for he was a strong man, and I was only a girl' (Corbett, 1898, p.

51). Though her subsequent actions go some way towards disproving this statement.

15. The famous lines from Cowper's poem from which the phrase derived are as follows: I am monarch of all I survey/ My right there is none to dispute; / From the centre all round to the sea, / I am lord of the fowl and the brute (Lines 1–4).

Bibliography

Secondary sources

J.E. Adams (1995) *Dandies and Desert Saints: Styles of Victorian Masculinity* (Ithaca and London: Cornell University Press).

R. Altick (1957) *The English Common Reader: A Social History of the Mass Reading Public 1800–1900* (Chicago, IL: University of Chicago Press).

M. Anderson (2006) *Women and the Politics of Travel, 1870–1914* (Cranbury, NJ: Associated University Presses).

D.C. Archibald (2002) *Domesticity, Imperialism, and Emigration in the Victorian Novel* (Columbia: University of Missouri Press).

P. Ariés (1962) *Centuries of Childhood: A Social History of Family Life* (1960), R. Baldick (trans.) (New York: Vintage).

P. Atkinson (1978) 'Fitness, Feminism and Schooling' in S. Delamont and L. Duffin (eds) *The Nineteenth-Century Woman: Her Cultural and Physical World* (London: Croom Helm).

S. Attridge (2003) *Nationalism, Imperialism and Identity in Late Victorian Culture: Civil and Military Worlds* (Houndmills: Palgrave Macmillan).

G. Avery (1975) *Childhood's Pattern: A Study of the Heroes and Heroines of Children's Fiction 1770–1950* (Leicester: Hodder and Stoughton).

—— (2005) 'Introduction', *Five Children and It* (New York: Penguin).

C. Banham (2007) ' "England and America Against the World": Empire and the USA in Edwin J. Brett's *Boys of England*, 1866–99', *Victorian Periodicals Review*, 40.2, 151–71.

E. Bar-Yosef (2003) 'E. Nesbit and the Fantasy of Reverse Colonization: How Many Miles to Modern Babylon?' *English Literature in Transition, 1880–1920*, 46.1, 5–28.

J. Blackwell (1985) 'An Island of Her Own: Heroines of the German Robinsonades from 1720 to 1800', *The German Quarterly*, 58.1, 5–26.

M. Beetham (1996) *A Magazine of Her Own?: Domesticity and Desire in the Women's Magazine, 1800–1914* (London and New York: Routledge).

H. Bhabha (1985) 'Sly Civility', *October*, 34, 71–80.

P. Bixler (1996) *The Secret Garden: Nature's Magic* (New York: Twayne).

E. Boehmer (2004) 'Introduction' in R. Baden-Powell (ed.) *Scouting for Boys: A Handbook for Instruction in Good Citizenship* (Oxford: Oxford University Press).

T. Boone (2005) *Youth of Darkest England: Working-Class Children and the Heart of the Victorian Empire* (New York: Routledge).

R. Bowlby (1985) *Just Looking: Consumer Culture in Dreiser, Gissing and Zola* (New York: Methuen).

K. Boyd (2003) *Manliness and the Boys' Story Paper in Britain: A Cultural History, 1855–1940* (Basingstoke and New York: Palgrave Macmillan).

C. Bradford (2001) *Reading Race: Aboriginality in Australian Children's Literature* (Melbourne: Melbourne University Press).

C. Bradford (2007) *Unsettling Narratives: Postcolonial Readings of Children's Literature* (Waterloo, ON: Wilfrid Laurier University Press).

J.S. Bratton (1981) *The Impact of Victorian Children's Fiction* (London: Croom Helm).

——(1989) 'British Imperialism and Reproduction of Femininity of Girls' Fiction, 1900–1930' in J. Richards (ed.) *Imperialism and Juvenile Literature* (Manchester: Manchester University Press).

J. Bristow (1991) *Empire Boys: Adventures in a Man's World* (Hammersmith: Harper Collins Academic).

H. Brohan (1987) *Mowgli's Sons: Kipling and Baden-Powell's Scouts* (London: Jonathan Cape).

A. Burton (1992) 'The White Women's Burden: British Feminists and "the Indian Woman", 1865–1915' in N. Chaudhuri and M. Strobel (eds) *Western Women and Imperialism: Complicity and Resistance* (Bloomington, IN: Indiana University Press).

—— (1994) *Burdens of History: British Feminists, Indian Women, and Imperial Culture, 1865–1915* (Chapel Hill and London: University of North Carolina Press).

—— (1996) 'Contesting the Zenana: The Mission to Make "Lady Doctors for India", 1874–1885', *The Journal of British Studies*, 35.3, 368–97.

J. Bush (2000) *Edwardian Ladies and Imperial Power* (London and New York: Leicester University Press).

M. Cadogan and P. Craig (1976) *You're a Brick, Angela! A New Look at Girls' Fiction from 1839 to 1975* (London: Gollancz).

D. Cannadine (2001) *Ornamentalism: How the British Saw Their Empire* (London: Penguin).

H. Carpenter (1985) *Secret Gardens: A Study of the Golden Age of Children's Literature* (London: Allen and Unwin).

H. Carpenter and M. Prichard (1984) *The Oxford Companion to Children's Literature* (Oxford and New York: Oxford University Press).

D. David (1995) *Rule Britannia: Women, Empire, and Victorian Writing* (Ithaca, NY: Cornell University Press).

L. Davidoff and C. Hall (2002 [1987]) *Family Fortunes: English Men and Women of the Middle Class, 1780–1850* (London: Routledge).

A. Davin (1978) 'Imperialism and Motherhood', *History Workshop Journal*, 5, 9–65.

T. Doughty (2004) *Selections from the Girl's Own Paper, 1880–1907* (Peterborough, ON: Broadview Press)

—— (2011) 'Domestic Goddesses on the Frontier; or, Tempting the Mothers of Empire with Adventure' in T.S. Wagner (ed.) *Victorian Settler Narratives: Emigrants, Cosmopolitans and Returnees in Nineteenth-Century Literature* (London: Pickering and Chatto), forthcoming.

C. Driscoll (2002) *Girls: Feminine Adolescence in Popular Culture and Cultural Theory* (New York: Columbia University Press).

K. Drotner (1988) *English Children and Their Magazines, 1751–1945* (New Haven, CT: Yale University Press).

C. Dyhouse (1976) 'Social Darwinistic Ideas and the Development of Women's Education in England, 1880–1920', *History of Education*, 5.1, 41–58.

C. Dyhouse (1977) 'Good Wives and Little Mothers: Social Anxieties and the Schoolgirl's Curriculum, 1890–1920', *Oxford Review of Education*, 3.1, 21–35.

V. Flanagan (2008) *Into the Closet: Cross-Dressing and the Gendered Body in Children's Literature* (New York: Routledge).

S. Fletcher (1984) *Women First: The Female Tradition in English Physical Education 1880–1980* (London: Athlone).

K. Flint (1993) *The Woman Reader, 1837–1914* (Oxford: Clarendon Press).

R. Forman (2000) 'When Britons Brave Brazil: British Imperialism and the Adventure Tale in Latin America, 1850–1918', *Victorian Studies*, 42.3, 455–87.

S. Foster and J. Simmons (1995) *What Katy Read: Feminist Re-Readings of 'Classic' Stories for Girls* (Houndmills: Macmillan).

M. Foucault (1977) *Discipline and Punish: The Birth of the Prison*, A. Sheridan (trans.) (London: Penguin).

H. Fraser, S. Green and J. Johnston (2003) *Gender and the Victorian Periodical* (Cambridge: Cambridge University Press).

G. Frith (1985) '"The Time of Your Life": The Meaning of the School Story' in Carolyn Steedman et al. (eds) *Language, Gender and Childhood* (London: Routledge and Kegan Paul).

A. Fyfe (2004) *Science and Salvation: Evangelical Popular Science Publishing in Victorian Britain* (Chicago, IL: University of Chicago Press).

R.M. George (1993–1994) 'Homes in the Empire, Empires in the Home', *Cultural Critique*, 26, 95–127.

M. Gomersall (1997) *Working-Class Girls in Nineteenth-Century England: Life, Work and Schooling* (Houndmills: Macmillan).

D. Gorham (1978) 'The "Maiden Tribute of Modern Babylon" Re-Examined: Child Prostitution and the Idea of Childhood in Late-Victorian England', *Victorian Studies*, 21.3, 353–79.

—— (1982) *The Victorian Girl and the Feminine Ideal* (London: Croom Helm).

L.M. Green (2001) *Educating Women: Cultural Conflict and Victorian Literature* (Athens: Ohio University Press).

M. Green (1979) *Dreams of Adventure, Deeds of Empire* (New York: Basic Books).

I. Grewal (1996) *Home and Harem: National, Gender, Empire, and the Cultures of Travel* (Durham and London: Duke University Press).

'Guide' (1989) def. 1a, *Oxford English Dictionary*, 2nd ed. (Oxford: Oxford University Press).

J. Hargreaves (1994) *Sporting Females: Critical Issues in the History and Sociology of Women's Sports* (London: Routledge).

D.R. Hettinga (1996) 'Bessie Marchant' in D.R. Hettinga and G.D. Schmidt (eds) *Dictionary of Literary Biography: British Children's Writers, 1914–1960* (Detroit and Washington, DC: Gale Research).

D. Hindley and G. Hindley (1972) *Advertising in Victorian England, 1837–1901* (London: Wayland).

P. Horn (1989) *The Victorian and Edwardian Schoolchild* (Gloucester: Alan Sutton).

P. Hunt and K. Sands (1999) 'The View from the Center: British Empire and Post-Empire Children's Literature' in Roderick McGillis (ed.) *Voices of the Other: Children's Literature and the Postcolonial Context* (New York and London: Garland).

R. Hyam (1993) *Britain's Imperial Century, 1815–1914: A Study of Empire and Expansion*, 2nd ed. (Lanham, MD: Barnes and Noble).

T. Jeal (1980) *Baden-Powell* (London: Hutchinson).

G.S. Jones (1971) *Outcast London: A Study in the Relationship Between Classes in Victorian Society* (Oxford: Clarendon Press).

E. Jordan (1991) 'Making Good Wives and Mothers? The Transformation of Middle-Class Girls', *History of Education Quarterly*, 31.4, 439–62.

R. Kerr (1932) *The Story of the Girl Guides* (London: The Girl Guides Association).

E.L. Keyser (1983) '"Quite Contrary": Frances Hodgson Burnett's *The Secret Garden*', *Children's Literature*, 11, 1–13.

A.M. King (2003) *Bloom: The Botanical Vernacular in the English Novel* (Oxford: Oxford University Press).

R. Kranidis (1999) *The Victorian Spinster and Colonial Emigration: Contested Subjects* (New York: St Martin's Press).

P. Krebs (1999) *Gender, Race and the Writing of Empire: Public Discourse and the Boer War* (Cambridge: Cambridge University Press).

D.M. Kutzer (2000) *Empire's Children: Empire and Imperialism in Classic British Children's Books* (New York: Garland).

S. Ledger (1997) *The New Woman: Fiction and Feminism at the* Fin de Siècle (Manchester: Manchester University Press).

P. Levine, ed. (2004) *Gender and Empire* (New York: Oxford University Press).

L.A. Loeb (1994) *Consuming Angels: Advertising and Victorian Women* (Oxford: Oxford University Press).

A. Lurie (1990) *Don't Tell the Grown-Ups: Subversive Children's Literature* (Boston, MA: Little, Brown and Company).

J. McAleer (1992) *Popular Reading and Publishing in Britain, 1914–1950* (Oxford: Clarendon Press).

R.H. MacDonald (1993) *Sons of the Empire: The Frontier and Boy Scout Movement, 1890–1918* (Toronto: University of Toronto).

J. Mackay and P. Thane (1986) 'The Englishwoman' in Robert Colls and Philip Dodd (eds) *Englishness: Politics and Culture 1880–1920* (London: Croom Helm).

A. Major (1991) 'Bessie Marchant: The Maid of Kent Whose Exciting Stories Thrilled Thousands of English Children', *This England*, Winter.

A. McClintock (1994) 'Soft-Soaping Empire: Commodity Racism and Imperial Advertising' in G. Robertson et al. (eds) *Travellers' Tales: Narratives of Home and Displacement* (London and New York: Routledge).

—— (1995) *Imperial Leather: Race, Gender and Sexuality in the Colonial Contest* (New York: Routledge).

K.E. McCrone (1984) 'Play Up! Play Up! and Play the Game! Sport at the Late Victorian Girls' Public School', *The Journal of British Studies*, 23.2, 106–33.

R. McGillis (1996) *A Little Princess: Gender and Empire* (New York: Twayne).

F. Mendlesohn (2008) *Rhetorics of Fantasy* (Middletown, CT: Wesleyan University Press).

S. Mitchell (1994) 'Girls' Culture: At Work' in C. Nelson and L. Vallone (eds) *The Girl's Own: Cultural Histories of the Anglo-American Girl, 1830–1915* (Athens: University of Georgia Press).

———. (1995) *The New Girl: Girls' Culture in England 1880–1915* (New York: Columbia University Press).

M. Mitterauer (1992) *A History of Youth* G. Dunphy (trans.) (Oxford: Blackwell).

D.L. Moore (1933) *E. Nesbit: A Biography* (London: Ernest Benn).

A. Moss (1991) 'E. Nesbit's Romantic Child in Modern Dress' in J.H. McGavran (ed.) *Romanticism and Children's Literature in Nineteenth-Century England* (Athens, GA: University of Georgia Press).

C. Nelson (1991) *Boys Will Be Girls: The Feminine Ethic and British Children's Fiction, 1857–1917* (New Brunswick: Rutgers University Press).

P. Nodelman (1992) 'The Other: Orientalism, Colonialism, and Children's Literature', *Children's Literature Association Quarterly*, 17.1, 29–35.

M. Norcia (2004) 'Angel of the Island: L.T. Meade's New Girl as the Heir of a Nation-Making Robinson Crusoe', *The Lion and the Unicorn*, 28.3, 345–62.

A. O'Malley (2008) 'Island Homemaking: Catherine Parr Traill's *Canadian Crusoes* and the Robinsonade Tradition' in M. Reimer (ed.) *Home Words: Discourses of Children's Literature in Canada* (Waterloo, ON: Wilfred Laurier University Press).

C.M. Owen (2010) *The Female Crusoe: Hybridity, Trade and the Eighteenth-Century Individual* (Amsterdam and New York: Rodopi).

L. Paul (1990) 'Enigma Variations: What Feminist Theory Knows About Children's Literature' in P. Hunt (ed.) *Children's Literature: The Development of Criticism* (London and New York: Routledge).

J.S. Pederson (1987) *The Reform of Girls' Secondary and Higher Education in Victorian England: A Study of Elites and Educational Change* (New York: Garland).

R. Phillips (1997) *Mapping Men and Empire: A Geography of Adventure* (London: Routledge).

J. Phillips (1993) 'The Mem Sahib, the Worthy, the Rajah and His Minions: Some Reflections on the Class Politics of *The Secret Garden*', *The Lion and the Unicorn*, 17.2, 168–94.

M. Poovey (1988) *Uneven Developments: The Ideological Work of Gender in Mid-Victorian England* (Chicago, IL: University of Chicago Press).

B. Porter (2004) *The Absent-Minded Imperialists* (Oxford: Oxford University Press).

S. Prickett (1979) *Victorian Fantasy* (Hassocks, Sussex: Harvester Press).

T.M. Proctor (2002) 'Scouts, Guides, and the Fashioning of Empire, 1919–1939' in Wendy Parkins (ed.) *Fashioning the Body Politic* (Oxford and New York: Berg).

T.M. Proctor (2009) *Scouting for Girls: A Century of Girl Guides and Girl Scouts* (Santa Barbara, CA: Praeger).

S. Rahn (2006) 'The Story of the Amulet and the Socialist Utopia' in R.E. Jones (ed.) *E. Nesbit's Psammead Trilogy: A Children's Classic at 100* (Lanham, MD: Scarecrow Press).

D. Reed (1997) *The Popular Magazine in Britain and the United States, 1880–1960* (London: British Library).

M. Reimer (1999) ' "These Two Irreconcilable Things: Art and Young Girls": The Case of the Girls' School Story' in B. Lyon Clark and M. R. Higgonet (eds) *Girls, Boys, Books, Toys: Gender in Children's Literature and Culture* (Baltimore: John Hopkins University Press).

—— (2005) 'Worlds of Girls: Educational Reform and Fictional Form in L.T. Meade's School Stories' in D. Ruwe (ed.) *Culturing the Child: Essays in Memory of Mitzi Myers* (Lanham, MD, Toronto, and Oxford: The Children's Literature Association and Scarecrow Press).

M. Reimer (2011) 'A Daughter of the House: Discourses of Adoption in L.M. Montgomery's Anne of Green Gables' in Julia Mickenberg and Lynne Vallone (eds) *The Oxford Handbook of Children's Literature* (Oxford: Oxford University Press), forthcoming.

K. Reynolds (1990) *Girls Only? Gender and Popular Children's Fiction in Britain, 1880–1910* (Hemel Hempstead: Harvester Wheatsheaf).

T. Richards (1990) *The Commodity Culture of Victorian England: Advertising and Spectacle, 1851–1914* (Stanford, CA: Stanford University Press).

A. Richardson (2003) *Love and Eugenics in the Late Nineteenth Century: Rational Reproduction and the New Woman* (Oxford: Oxford University Press).

J. Rose (1984) *The Case of Peter Pan; or, The Impossibility of Children's Fiction* (Houndmills: Macmillan).

M. Rosenthal (1984) *The Character Factory: Baden-Powell and the Origins of the Boy Scout Movement* (New York: Pantheon).

J. Rowbotham (1989) *Good Girls Make Good Wives: Guidance for Girls in Victorian Fiction* (Oxford: Basil Blackwell).

A.A. Rutledge (1999) 'E. Nesbit and the Woman Question' in N.D. Thompson (ed.) *Victorian Women Writers and the Woman Question* (Cambridge: University of Cambridge Press).

E. Said (1978) *Orientalism* (London: Penguin, 2003).

'Scout' (1989) def. 2a, *Oxford English Dictionary*, 2nd ed. (Oxford: Oxford University Press).

J. Sharpe (1993) *Allegories of Empire: The Figure of the Woman in the Colonial Text* (Minneapolis, MN: University of Minnesota Press).

K. Shevelow (1989) *Women and Print Culture: The Construction of Femininity in the Early Periodical* (London and New York: Routledge).

R.B. Singh (2004) *Goodly is Our Heritage: Children's Literature, Empire, and the Certitude of Character* (Lanham, MD: The Scarecrow Press).

A.K. Silver (1997) 'Domesticating Brontë's Moors: Motherhood in *The Secret Garden*', *The Lion and the Unicorn*, 21.2, 193–203.

H. Skelding (2001) 'Every Girl's Best Friend?: The *Girl's Own Paper* and its Readers' in E. Liggins and D. Duffy (eds) *Feminist Readings of Victorian Popular Texts: Divergent Femininities* (Aldershot: Ashgate).

M. Smith and K. Moruzi (2010) 'Learning What Real Work... Means: Ambiguous Attitudes Towards Employment in the *Girl's Own Paper*' *Victorian Periodicals Review*, 43.4, 429–45.

P.M. Spacks (1981) *The Adolescent Idea: Myths of Youth and the Adult Imagination* (New York: Basic Books).

J. Springhall (1977) *Youth, Empire, and Society: British Youth Movements, 1883–1940* (London: Croom Helm).

J. Stephens (1992) *Language and Ideology in Children's Fiction* (Harlow: Longman).

J. Stephens and R. McCallum (1998) *Retelling Stories, Framing Culture: Traditional Story and Metanarratives in Children's Literature* (New York: Garland).

A. Summers (1988) *Angels and Citizens: British Women as Military Nurses 1854–1914* (London: Routledge and Kegan Paul).

L. Summers (2001) *Bound to Please: A History of the Victorian Corset* (New York: Berg).

K. Swenson (2005) *Medical Women and Victorian Fiction* (Columbia: University of Missouri Press).

G.H. Swinburne (1978) *Among the First People, 1908–1936* (Sydney: Girl Guides Association of Australia).

J.B. Taylor (1998) 'Between Atavism and Altruism: The Child on the Threshold in Victorian Psychology and Edwardian Children's Fiction' in K. Lesnik-Orenstein (ed.) *Children in Culture: Approaches to Childhood* (Houndmills: Macmillan; New York: St Martin's).

L. Tedesco (1998) 'Making a Girl into a Scout: Americanizing Scouting for Girls' in S.A. Inness (ed.) *Delinquents and Debutantes: Twentieth-Century American Girls' Cultures* (New York: New York University Press).

C. Thompson (2008) 'The *Grosvenor* Shipwreck and the Figure of the Female Crusoe: *Hannah Hewit, Mary Jane Meadows*, and Romantic-Era Feminist and Anti-Feminist Debate', *English Studies in Africa*, 51.2, 9–20.

G. Tóth (2003) 'The Children of the Empire: Anti-Imperialism in Frances Hodgson Burnett's *The Secret Garden*', *The AnaChronisT*, 9, 117–47.

M.E. Tusan (1998) 'Inventing the New Woman: Print Culture and Identity Politics During the *Fin-de-Siècle*', *Victorian Periodicals Review*, 38.2, 169–82.

R.A. Voeltz (1988) 'Adam's Rib: The Girl Guides and an Imperial Race', *San Jose Studies*, 45.1, 91–9.

—— (1992) 'The Antidote to "Khaki Fever'? The Expansion of the British Girl Guides During the First World War', *Journal of Contemporary History*, 27.4, 627–38.

J. Wallace (1994) 'De-Scribing *The Water-Babies*: "The Child" in Post-colonial Theory' in C. Tiffin and A. Lawson (eds) *De-Scribing Empire: Post-Colonialism and Textuality* (London and New York: Routledge).

A. Warren (1986) 'Citizens of the Empire: Baden-Powell, Scouts and Guides and an Imperial Ideal' in J.M. Mackenzie (ed.) *Imperialism and Popular Culture* (Manchester: Manchester University Press).

—— (1990) '"Mothers for the Empire"? The Girl Guides Association in Britain, 1909–1939' in J.A. Mangan (ed.) *Making Imperial Mentalities: Socialisation and British Imperialism* (Manchester and New York: Manchester University Press).

R. Weaver-Hightower (2007) *Empire Islands: Castaways, Cannibals, and Fantasies of Conquest* (Minneapolis and London: University of Minnesota Press).

R.J.C. Young (1995) *Colonial Desire: Hybridity in Theory, Culture and Race* (London and New York: Routledge).

Primary texts

Anon. (1862) 'Important Announcement', *Fun*, 13 December, 123.

Anon. (1879) 'Travel and Adventure', *Kind Words for Young People*, 1 October, 300.

Anon. (1891) 'A Female Crusoe', *Ladies' Journal: Devoted to Literature, Fashion, Domestic Matters &c.*, 2, 16.

M. Arnold (1869) *Culture and Anarchy*, in J. Dover Wilson (ed.) (London: Cambridge, 1935).

A. Baden-Powell (1912) 'Foreword', in D. Moore (ed.), *Terry the Girl-Guide* (London, Nisbet & Co.).

A. Baden-Powell and R. Baden-Powell (1912) *The Handbook for Girl Guides; or, How Girls Can Help Build the Empire* (London: Thomas Nelson and Sons).

R. Baden-Powell (1908) *Scouting for Boys: A Handbook for Instruction in Good Citizenship,* in Elleke Boehmer (ed.) (Oxford: Oxford University Press, 2004).

D. Beale, L.H.M. Soulsby and J.F. Dove (1898) *Work and Play in Girls' Schools by Three Headmistresses* (London: Longmans, Green and Co.).

A. Brazil (1906) *The Fortunes of Philippa* (London: Blackie and Son).

——(1906) *The Nicest Girl in the School* (London: Blackie and Son).

——(1910) *The Manor House School* (London: Blackie and Sons, 1970).

—— (1912) *A Fourth Form Friendship: A School Story* (London: Blackie and Son).

——(1912) *The New Girl at St. Chad's* (London: Blackie and Son).

—— (1912) *A Pair of Schoolgirls: A Story of School Days* (London: Blackie and Son).

—— (1913) *The Leader of the Lower School: A Tale of School Life* (London: Blackie and Son).

——(1913) *The Youngest Girl in the Fifth* (London: Blackie and Son).

—— (1914) *The Girls of St. Cyprians: A Tale of School Life* (London: Blackie and Son).

——(1914) *The School by the Sea* (London: Blackie and Sons, 1936).

——(1925) *My Own Schooldays* (London: Blackie and Son).

F. Hodgson Burnett (1905) *A Little Princess, Being the Whole Story of Sara Crewe Now Told for the First Time* (London: Frederick Warne and Co., [190?]).

—— (1911) *The Secret Garden* (London: Penguin, 1994).

S.A. Burstall (1907) *English High Schools for Girls: Their Aims, Organisation, and Management* (London: Longmans, Green, and Co.).

S.A. Burstall and M.A. Douglas, ed. (1911) *Public Schools for Girls: A Series of Papers on Their History, Aims, and Schemes of Study* (London: Longmans, Green, and Co.).

Mrs G. Corbett (Elizabeth Burgoyne) (1898) *Little Miss Robinson Crusoe* (London: John F. Shaw and Company).

C. Dibdin (1792) *Hannah Hewit; or, The Female Crusoe,* 6 vols (London: Printed for C. Dibdin).

J.W. Fortescue (1893) 'The Influence of Climate on Race', *Nineteenth Century,* 33, 862–73.

J.F. Dove (1898) 'Cultivation of the Body' in D. Beale, L.H.M. Soulsby, and J. F. Dove (eds) *Work and Play in Girls' Schools by Three Headmistresses* (London: Longmans, Green and Co.).

M.A. Gilliland (1911) 'Home Arts' in S.A. Burstall and M.A. Douglas (eds) *Public Schools for Girls: A Series of Papers on Their History, Aims, and Schemes of Study* (London: Longmans, Green, and Co.).

D. Jerrold (1847) 'The Life and Adventures of Miss Robinson Crusoe', *Punch,* 11, 9–10+.

B. Kidd (1894) *Social Evolution* (London: Macmillan).

B. Marchant (1900) *The Girl Captives: A Story of the Indian Frontier* (London: Blackie and Son).

—— (1900) *In the Toils of the Tribesmen: A Story of the Indian Frontier* (London: Gail and Inglis).

——(1907) *No Ordinary Girl: A Story of Central America* (London: Blackie and Son [1913?]).

—— (1908) *Sisters of Silver Creek: A Story of Western Canada* (London: Blackie and Son).

B. Marchant (1909) *A Courageous Girl: A Story of Uruguay* (London: Blackie and Sons).

—— (1909) *Daughters of the Dominion: A Story of the Canadian Frontier* (London: Blackie and Sons).

—— (1909) *Jenny's Adventure; or, On the Trail for Klondyke* (London: JW Butcher).

—— (1910) *The Adventures of Phyllis: A Story of the Argentine* (London: Cassell and Company).

—— (1910) *The Black Cockatoo: A Story of Western Australia* (London: Religious Tract Society).

—— (1911) *Greta's Domain: A Tale of Chiloé* (London: Blackie and Son).

—— (1914) *The Heroine of the Ranch: A Story of Tierra del Fuego* (London: Blackie and Son).

—— (1914) *The Loyalty of Hester Hope: A Story of British Columbia* (London: Blackie and Son).

L.T. Meade (1898) *Four on an Island* (New York: The Mershon Company).

E. Nesbit (1908) *Ballads and Lyrics of Socialism: 1883–1908* (London: The Fabian Society).

—— (1902) *Five Children and It* (London: Penguin, 2004).

—— (1904) *The Phoenix and the Carpet* (London: Penguin, 2004).

—— (1906) *The Story of the Amulet* (London: Penguin, 1996).

F. Nightingale (1860) *Notes on Nursing: What It Is, and What It Is Not* (London: Thoemmes, 1999).

'Obituary: Bessie Marchant', (1941) *Time Literary Supplement* 15 November, 569.

C.H. Pearson (1893) *National Life and Character: A Forecast* (London: Macmillan and Co., 1913).

Report of the Inter-Departmental Committee on Physical Deterioration: Vol. 1 Report and Appendix (1904) (London: HMSO).

W.T. Roberts (1909) 'Girls as Scouts', *The Girl's Realm*, 12, 337–40.

J. Ruskin (1865) 'Of Queens' Gardens', *Sesame and Lilies: Two Lectures Delivered at Manchester in 1864* (London: Smith, Elder and Co.).

E.G. Salmon (1886) 'What Girls Read', *The Nineteenth Century*, 20. 116, 515–29.

—— (1888) *Juvenile Literature as it is* (London: Henry J. Drane).

H. Spencer (1861) 'Physical Education', *Education: Intellectual, Moral, and Physical*. (London: Williams and Norgate, 1896).

Dr G. Stables, (1902) 'The Girl Crusoes: A Tale of the Indian Ocean', *The Girls' Realm*, 4, 188–95.

Mrs H. Strang (pseud.) (1915) *The Girl Crusoes: A Story of the South Seas* (London: Humphrey Milford, 1917).

C.P. Traill (1852) *The Canadian Crusoes: A Tale of the Rice Lake Plains* (Boston, MA: Crosby and Nicholas, 1862).

A.F. Tytler (1839) *Leila; or, The Island* (London: J. Hatchard and Son).

U.E. Winkfield (pseud.) (1767) *The Female American; or, The Adventures of Unca Eliza Winkfield*, (Peterborough, OT: Broadview Press, 2001).

J.D. Wyss (1812–1813) *The Swiss Family Robinson* (Mineola, NY: Dover, 2001).

C. Yonge (1887) *What Books to Lend and What to Give* (London: National Society's Depository).

Girl's own paper articles

'A Female Crusoe' (1883) *Girl's Own Paper*, 4, 439.

'Another Female Crusoe' (1883) *Girl's Own Paper*, 4, 646.

'A Hundred Famous Women' (1884) *Girl's Own Paper*, 5, 569.

'A Hundred Famous Cities' (1891) *Girl's Own Paper*, 13, 206.

'Answers to Correspondents' (1881) *Girl's Own Paper*, 2, 400.

'Answers to Correspondents' (1883) *Girl's Own Paper*, 5, 6.

'Answers to Correspondents' (1883) *Girl's Own Paper*, 5, 192.

'Answers to Correspondents' (1884) *Girl's Own Paper*, 5, 383.

'Answers to Correspondents' (1891) *Girl's Own Paper*, 13, 16.

'Answers to Correspondents' (1891) *Girl's Own Paper*, 13, 176.

'Answers to Correspondents' (1892) *Girl's Own Paper*, 13, 623.

'Answers to Correspondents' (1898) *Girl's Own Paper*, 19, 526.

'Answers to Correspondents' (Supplement) (1898) *Girl's Own Paper*, 19, 1–4.

'Answers to Correspondents' (1901) *Girl's Own Paper*, 23, 16.

Author of 'How to be Happy Though Married' (1886) 'Between School and Marriage', *Girl's Own Paper*, 7, 769–70.

A Zenana Missionary (1885) 'Girl Life in India', *Girl's Own Paper*, 6, 492–3.

E. Brewer (1883) 'Girl Life in Germany', *Girl's Own Paper*, 5, 148.

—— (1885–6) 'The Girls of the World', *Girl's Own Paper*, 7, 94–5, 198–9, 268–9, 346–9.

—— (1892) 'The Flower Girls of London', *Girl's Own Paper*, 13, 283–5.

Bovril. Advertisement (1904) *Girl's Own Paper* Christmas Advertisement Sheet, 2–3.

E.F. Bridell-Fox (1887) 'The Arab Girls of Algiers', *Girl's Own Paper*, 8, 620–2.

Carnation (1897) 'Stay at Home Girls' First Prize Essay, *Girl's Own Paper*, 19, 102–3.

S.F.A. Caulfeild (1885) 'The Duties of Wives and Mothers', *Girl's Own Paper*, 6, 262–3.

'Competition for Professional Girls – The Five Prize Essays' (1897) *Girl's Own Paper*, 18, 412.

J. Couron (1884) 'A Lady's Journey to Texas', *Girl's Own Paper*, 5, 774–6.

D. De Blaquiére (1895) 'The Dress for Bicycling', *Girl's Own Paper*, 17, 12–14.

E. Dibdin (1901) 'Child-Wives', *Girl's Own Paper*, 21, 805.

E.B.S. (1884) 'On Emigrating as Domestic Servants to New Zealand', *Girl's Own Paper*, 6, 11.

'Education for Women at Oxford' (1885) *Girl's Own Paper*, 5, 695.

'Empire Day' (1906) *Girl's Own Paper*, 27, 491.

'Girl Volunteers for South Africa' (1902) *Girl's Own Paper*, 23, 243–4.

GOP Annual Advertisement (1904), *Girl's Own Paper*. Christmas Advertisement Supplement, 6.

E.J. Hardy (1885) 'The Importance of Women's Work', *Girl's Own Paper*, 6, 797.

F.E. Hoggan (1884) 'Medical Women for India', *Girl's Own Paper*, 5, 281–3.

A. Irvine (1896) 'My Baby', *Girl's Own Paper*, 17, 342–3.

Right Rev. Bishop Johnson (1900) 'A Girls' High School in West Africa', *Girl's Own Paper*, 22, 196–7.

A. King (1884) 'Higher Thoughts on Housekeeping', *Girl's Own Paper*, 5, 235–6.

R. Lamb (1881) 'Baby Care', *Girl's Own Paper*, 2, 474–6.

—— (1902) 'In the Twilight Side by Side', *Girl's Own Paper*, 24, 133–5.

A. Lee (1892) 'Intellectual Partnerships; or, How Men May Stimulate the Mental Life of Women', *Girl's Own Paper*, 13, 285–7.

L. Lester (1895) 'The Cinderellas of the National Household: The Match-Makers of East London. A Visit to Bryant and May's', *Girl's Own Paper*, 17, 147–9.

—— (1896) 'The Cinderellas of the National Household: Jute Girls in the East End', *Girl's Own Paper*, 17, 649–51.

'Log of Voyage to the Cape: And Diary of Army Nursing in South Africa' (1900) *Girl's Own Paper*, 21, 742–3.

'London's Future Housewives and their Teachers' (1899) *Girl's Own Paper*, 20, 737.

N. Lorimer (1898) 'The Strides of Women', *Girl's Own Paper*, 19, 570–1.

The Right Hon. Marquess of Lorne (1884) 'Miss Rye's Girls' Homes', *Girl's Own Paper*, 5, 488–90.

J. Mason (1881a) 'A Girl's Influence', *Girl's Own Paper*, 2, 425.

—— (1881b) 'About Industry and Idleness', *Girl's Own Paper*, 2, 707–8.

Medicus (1883) 'Things That Every Girl Should Learn to Do', *Girl's Own Paper*, 5, 70–1.

—— (1884a) 'Our Bodies are Our Gardens', *Girl's Own Paper*, 5, 218–19.

—— (1884b) 'Work Versus Idleness', *Girl's Own Paper*, 5, 622–3.

—— (1892) 'Health and Complexion: A Roundabout Talk', *Girl's Own Paper*, 13, 426–7.

—— (1896) 'Cycling: As a Pastime and for Health', *Girl's Own Paper*, 17, 722–3.

—— (1905) Column, *Girl's Own Paper*, 27, 11–12.

—— (1907) 'Man-Games That Murder Beauty', *Girl's Own Paper*, 27, 502–3.

'New Employment for Girls' (1892) *Girl's Own Paper*, 13, 362–3.

Mother Seigel's Curative Syrup. Advertisement (1900) *Girl's Own Paper*, August Advertisement Sheet, 2.

'My Daily Round' Third Prize Essay (1896) *Girl's Own Paper*, 18, 116–17.

Quaker Oats. Advertisement (1903) *Girl's Own Paper*, December Advertisement Sheet, 7.

B.W. Richardson (1894) 'On Recreations for Girls', *Girl's Own Paper*, 15, 545–7.

R.M.W. (1896) 'Life on a Transvaal Salt Farm', *Girl's Own Paper*, 17, 571–2.

A.T. Schofield (1895) 'The Cycling Craze', *Girl's Own Paper*, 17, 185–6.

'Seasonable Clothing and How to Make It' (1880) *Girl's Own Paper*, 2, 204–5.

L. Stratenus (1884) 'A Dutch Girl', *Girl's Own Paper*, 5, 797–8.

Sunlight Soap. Advertisement (1902) *Girl's Own Paper*, October Advertisement Supplement, 4.

'The Emigration of Girls to South Africa' (1902) *Girl's Own Paper*, Extra Christmas Part, 59.

'The Girl's Own Home' (1883) *Girl's Own Paper*, 5, 59.

'The New Girl' (1902) *Girl's Own Paper*, 24, 153–5.

Van Houten's Cocoa. Advertisement (1904) *Girl's Own Paper*, March Advertisement Supplement, 3.

L.Watson (1902) 'Athleticism for Girls', *Girl's Own Paper*, 24, 61–2.

—— (1903) 'Girls Then and Now', *Girl's Own Paper*, 24, 420–2.

E. Whittaker (1882–1883) 'Robina Crusoe, and Her Lonely Island Home', *Girl's Own Paper*, 4, 183–4+.

E. Whymper (1884) 'Famous Lady Travellers: The Adventures of Madame Godin', *Girl's Own Paper*, 6, 107.

E. Whymper (1885) 'Famous Lady Travellers: The Adventures of Lady Baker', *Girl's Own Paper*, 6, 353–6.

C.E.C. Wignall (1898) 'Down to the Sea in Ships', *Girl's Own Paper*, 19, 582–3.

A. Wilson (1891) 'Religion: An Address to Schoolgirls', *Girl's Own Paper*, 13, 76–7.

'Work for All' (1883) *Girl's Own Paper*, 5, 119–20.

Index

Page references to pictures are given in **bold**